A Game of Secrets

By S.L Wisdom and S.J Noble

Copyright Statement

This is a work of fiction. The events described in this book are fictitious; any similarities to actual events and persons, dead or alive, are entirely coincidental.

Paperback ISBN: 9798393111205
eBook ASIN: by

Cover design by Francessca Wingfield

Editing by Ria Hockey at Moon and Bloom Editing

"Tell me every terrible thing you ever did, and let me love you anyway."

Edgar Allan Poe

This is a comprehensive list of contents warnings that may have an effect on you when reading this book. Please continue at your own discretion.

Murder
Torture
Knife play
Child Abuse
Kidnapping
Domestic Abuse
Rape
Non Con
Battery
Death
MMMF

This book is intended for readers 18+.

Enjoy.

Prologue

Silas

18 years earlier

"Son!"

I hear my father shout as I finish my dinner. I know he wants me for another training session, his hold over me is the only reason I listen and obey his commands. Every day he threatens my baby brother, I know his threats are not to be taken lightly. Last time I goaded him, he showed me the depth of his cruelty by harming my mother. I knew that day I'd never lay a hand on a woman like he did. I leave my room and address him, if I don't do even this correctly I'll feel his wrath.

"Yes Father, what do you need?" I ask in an even tone.

My father replies sharply, "It's time you learned how it feels to take another's life. It will make you a man and it will ensure our legacy survives." I nod, not quite sure how to reply but knowing that refusal isn't an option. "Follow me, Son."

I follow him down to the training room, it's soundproofed for our privacy, or so he said. I know better though, it's soundproofed so he can keep his depravity a secret, whether the focus of his depravity is deserved or not.

I struggle to contain my visceral reaction to the room. I turn to one of the tables, pretending to look at the macabre array of tools on display, when in fact, I'm trying not to lose my breakfast. The memories of all the ways to kill a man play like a cinema reel in my mind. From peeling flesh to gouging eyeballs from their sockets. He has shown me how to keep a man alive at the same time as bringing him close to death both mentally and physically.

The first time he brought me here, I vomited. He slapped me so hard I fell in it and he made me watch from my puddle on the floor. Everytime I heaved or made a whimper he slapped again, harder than before. I quickly learnt how to stay silent in a room that was made to contain screams.

Once I get my reactions under control, I turn and try not to flinch as he barks, "Sit, Son." I move to sit in the chair that I always sit in, the one beside him, "No Son, you are going to sit in the executioner seat today, as you will be the one to seal the fate of this traitor."

I've avoided looking at whoever has the misfortune of being in the room with us today, my gaze glued to the floor. Slowly, bringing my eyes up to see a man, beaten and tied to a chair. I also see my fathers capo; Theo Rossi. The look in his eyes is predatory, he's as eager to watch me kill this traitor as my father.

Standing behind Theo is my best friend, Lincoln 'Linc' Rossi, my brother in all but blood and Theo's son. I hate Theo like I hate my father. What man would willingly put his child through this? But here we are and there is nothing we can do to change our fate now. I realize that's why Linc is here, if I don't do this he'll pay the price. My father will use him to make me regret not following orders.

My father sees my sudden realization and smirks as he says, "Now boy, you need to begin as I'm sure you have figured out the price you and the Rossi's will pay if you don't."

"Who is he?" I ask, needing to know that this man is someone deserving of this torture rather than an innocent man who has been caught in the wrong place at the wrong time.

"Who he is won't change his fate, boy! Are you questioning me? Shall we see how your friend feels about it?" my father says with malice in his eyes.

I look at my friend, he nods, giving me the support I need, silently telling me that when it's done, he'll be there to avenge what they have made us do. With that last thought of justice, I feel a change come over me. The weak stomached little boy who walked in here has gone. I straighten my back, lock my humanity away and turn to our traitor, the lamb that is the sacrifice in this inhuman ritual. In this man's death, I will be reborn. I read about this torture technique, it comes from Nordic legends and I know this is the moment, this was when I'd create my own legend. When I finally step out of my fathers shadow and become a man, just like he wanted.

I start to perform a masterpiece that will become my signature, the blood eagle. I block out the traitors' screams and concentrate on my work. By the time I am done, the traitor looks like a fallen angel covered in a bloody mess, his back ripped open giving a perfect view of his innards enabling me to grab his ribs and twist them to look like broken wings, it's perfect.

This is how I am now known, I didn't give him a quick death. I used my hands to feel the life drain from his body, I showed no mercy. I didn't do it because I'm a sick bastard. I did it to show my father and his men they can't break me and if they try, this is what will await them. The Merciless, Silas Salvatore.

Chapter 1

Lucille

Having mentally checklisted my son's kindergarten bag for the tenth time already this morning, I turn to go through it once more before we leave; water bottle, exercise and reading book, pencil case, a change of clothes and most importantly, Little B. How could I ever forget Little B? He refuses to leave home without that little bear. I hear his soft footfall behind me and place the bear softly inside the backpack. He's ready I assure myself.

A gentle hand pulls my t-shirt, "All finished Mommy." I turn and look down to see Teddy, my beautiful blue eyed baby boy handing his cereal bowl to me, his soft blonde waves a tangled mess atop his head. I can not help but smile. "How did you get so big, baby boy?" I ask, leaning forward and smothering him with tickles and kisses. "From eating all my cereal, Mommy," he replies between fits of giggles.
I stare in awe and agree. "Yes baby boy, from eating all your cereal. Now quickly brush your hair and let's get going. Katrina and Isabella are meeting us at the gates."

"Have a good day you two!" My bestie and I shout as we wave our babies off for the day. I'm so lucky to have a friend like Katrina, and even more lucky that she has a daughter the same age as Teddy and they get along like a house on fire, we have even joked about them getting married one day. Kat and I met when I got a job as a nurse at Summerlin Hospital and have been as thick as thieves ever since. Being single moms, working long hours and seeing the shit we do at work is hard, so we know exactly what the other is going through.

"How're you feeling about today, Doll?" Kat probes as we change into our nursing uniforms. Today is our monthly rotation at the High Desert State Prison and my turn to travel over there with one of our doctors. It's normally to help treat superficial wounds on the inmates but they do like to keep us on our toes so we never know what we're walking into. I wholeheartedly love my job but whenever this comes around, I feel sick right down to the pit of my stomach. The thought of entering the prison and the possibility of my ex being there, let alone having to treat him for some stupid prison brawl is nauseating. It's just the two of us here and I know my secrets will be safe.

"I'm shitting it to tell you the truth Kat. What if he's there? What if he's been arrested and I end up having to face him? I wouldn't know what to do. What if he escapes and tracks me down and finds out about Teddy? Oh God!" I stop, panic stricken. "What if he takes Teddy!?" The question comes out a garbled mess and suddenly with my head in my hands I start to hyperventilate, all the worst scenarios playing in my head.

Kats hands grab onto my forearms, "Look at me!" she demands. "You are going to be *fine*! He isn't there, he is over a thousand miles away, probably already locked up again anyway for some stupid shit and if he *ever* touches you or Teddy, I'll kick him so hard in the dick he'll cry for a month."

Her expression shows she is completely and utterly serious, but we both burst into laughter. God how I love this girl. I know I'm being stupid, but I would travel to the ends of the earth and back again to never let my ex find out about Teddy. I may have been stupid enough back then to let him beat me black and blue, but I will never let

9

him near my son. Kat pulls me into a tight hug. "I promise you he won't be there." *How I hope you're right,* I sigh, squeezing her back and forcing myself to get my breathing under control.

After holding onto me for what felt like a lifetime, Kat finally releases me. "You got this girl," she smiles, wiping away the mascara from my cheeks.
I nod, "I've totally got this."

"Anyway, at least you'll have Dr. Graves to keep you company," she teases, giving me the side eye as she pulls her tunic on. I shake my head and continue getting ready. "He'll take your mind off Vinny for sure, if you ask him nicely. Everybody knows he's got the hots for you," she smirks at me.

"You really think I'd have to ask nicely? He'd hump a table if it could talk." I snort and Kat throws her head back in a fit of giggles as we leave the changing room, falling into each other as we continue to howl with laughter.

After Kat reassures me once again that my ex-husband won't somehow turn up in our state prison, I make my way to the staff kitchen to grab a fresh coffee to go. I'm definitely going to need some caffeine for this journey if the only person I have to talk to has the communication skills of a teaspoon. Though the thought of spending a car ride with a teaspoon is much more appealing.

"Good morning, Lucille." An overly enthusiastic voice calls out behind me.
Here we go. I grit my teeth as I turn around. "Good morning Dr Graves," I smile politely.
He holds a hand up and grins his seedy grin as he takes a slow step towards me. "Please Lucille, how many times, call me Tom." I smile again and side step his advance.

"I'll go and make sure we have everything ready for today." I suggest, quickly skipping out of the room before he has a chance to object.
This is going to be a long day.

I gather together a few extra supplies, mainly extra sets of dressings, gauze and gloves. Most things will be available for us in the medical rooms of the prison. I pack them into a large clear container, it makes the checking in process much easier when we're being searched before entering and I set off towards the minivan that the hospital hires for these clinic rotation days. I climb in the van and plonk myself next to the window behind the driver's seat, stuffing the extra box into the seat beside me.

"I hope you're looking forward to this as much as I am Lucille. It's always such a pleasure to get to work with you one on one." Dr Graves all but sings as he hauls himself into the van after me with a grin mirroring a Cheshire cat.
My stomach churns slightly at the sight and I have to stifle down the lump rising in my throat. "Oh yeah, I can't wait." I mumble as he moves the supply box separating us onto the row behind and slides in next to me. *Great.* I can practically feel his neediness radiating from him as his knee knocks against my own while he settles himself in. Subtly, I scoot a little further over, disguising it while I cross my leg over the other in a hopeless attempt to keep as much space between us as possible.

"Right then, let's get this show on the road," the driver calls over his shoulder. As we slowly peel away from the sidewalk, a sense of what I can only describe as bitter unease nestles deep into my bones. There's definitely no turning back now. I can taste my anxiety beginning to creep in again and the thought of a 40 minute journey in such close proximity to Tom Graves literally makes my skin crawl. He's already started talking to me, something about the price of cars and a dealership down the road, but I'm drifting and I'm a million miles away, back in my shitty little run down flat in Seattle.

6 years earlier

The bruising above my right eye is already beginning to show.

"You can't keep doing this, he's going to kill you." I cry to myself in the bathroom mirror as I smash my fist into the glass, blood instantly pouring from my knuckles. I grab the first aid kit I'd been keeping in the vanity for all the times I've needed patching up and begin to bandage my wounds. I've gotten pretty good at hiding Vinny's drunken 'mistakes' over the last year and thought of some pretty good excuses for my injuries when I've let one slip. He never used to be like this, at the start he was so lovely and attentive and we really were truly, madly, deeply in love. I couldn't wait to marry him. But as soon as I did, the perfect image of the man he had deceived me with began to fade and the monster beneath began to rear its ugly head.

The beatings were light at first, only when he had been out drinking with mates. But over time, he became possessive and paranoid about where I went, what clothes I would wear and who I spoke too. I couldn't even speak to my brother without being accused of wanting to leave him. Little did he know, I'd never said a word to anybody about what had been happening behind closed doors. How could I? Especially not to my brother Max, he'd kill him in an instant and I'd be left wondering how I was ever stupid enough to fall for a man like Vinny. A man who gets off on beating his own wife half to death just because he had a bad day at work.

Flitting through my drawers desperately trying to find something Vinny would consider appropriate to wear for my shift at the local 24/7 diner, I catch his bulky frame standing in the doorway out of the corner of my eye, watching my every move. Pretending not to notice him, I slip into a pair of black skinny jeans and a white shirt then sit to pull on my Converse and head towards the door. He doesn't attempt to move and the closer I get, the more I realize he's been drinking. The darkest of eyes bore into me and my stomach drops with the knowledge of what is about to happen. As if he knows exactly what I'm thinking, a sick grin spreads slowly across his face before he lunges toward me, grabbing at my wrist as I try to side step him. Most men his size would struggle to move so quickly but he doesn't. He twists my arm and bends it at the elbow, holding it against my back then pushes me forward, cracking my head against the mirrored wall.

"Let me go!" I plead, already losing the feeling in my arm, "You're hurting me." I feel his fist ball into my hair before yanking hard to pull my face up towards his. His breath is hot against my skin, the smell of absinthe and cigarettes making me nauseous. He runs his lips against my ear and his grip around my wrist tightens. "Bitch, I've not even started," he whispers in a voice so cold I hardly even recognise it. In an instant my heart stops, my ears buzz and my vision clouds before I realize he's smashed my head into the mirror again, shattering it to pieces this time.

Bringing my free hand up towards my face, I feel wetness dripping down my cheek. Crack! Again. Crack! Again. I lose count before I'm thrown to the floor. Barely conscious, I try to crawl to the door, but I'm stopped short by a heavy weight pressing down on me from above. The air barely escapes my lungs before the weight is lifted, only to be applied again. Unable to see what is happening behind me, I still as Vinny's hands rip my jeans down my backside. My head swims as I begin to panic, scrambling

13

forward trying to put as much space between us as I can. This can not be happening! His hands grab at my ankles, ripping me back towards him. I can hear him unbuckling his belt and fiddling with his jeans.

"NO. NO. NO VINNY! PLEASE NO!" I begin to beg, sobs escaping my throat.
"Shut up BITCH, just give me what I want."

He lays down on top of me, pushing my head back into the floor. I have no fight left to give, my head feels like it might explode from the weeping gash above my brow. I lie still and silent and focus on my bloodstains painting the broken mirror, drifting off to somewhere a million miles away.

Present day

"Did you listen to anything I just said?" Dr Graves asks, cocking his eyebrow at me, instantly pulling me back to the present. I shake my head as I absentmindedly run my fingers across the scar above my brow and blink apologetically at him before turning to face the window. "Oh look, we're here." I announce, ignoring the way he's now glaring at me.

I clip my name badge onto my tunic and scrape my hair back into a bun. Driving past the huge prison gates, their presence all imposing and intimidating as they stand hard against the gray mottled walls behind. I let my imagination run wild with the crimes the men behind these walls have committed as I continue to ignore Tom's eyes burning into my skull.

The set up is standard but still a little overwhelming, there are guards everywhere. We've had our equipment searched, been frisked by security and had our background checks done all before getting into the building. The clinic room is bright, sterile and surrounded by glass windows. You can see everything going on outside, straight into some of the cells, and every prisoner and guard can see everything we're doing inside too. There is always a minimum of two guards securing the door to the clinical facility, heavily armed and ready to step in when necessary.

Dr Graves introduces himself to the prison Warden who quickly informs us of a brawl that broke out over lunch time yesterday.

"You may be seeing a lot more than you'd planned for today, I'm afraid Doc," he says dryly. "I hope you brought an extra pair of hands." Looking over at me like I'm the work experience kid, chewing on the toothpick between his teeth.

"Oh don't worry, Luci here is more than capable of attending to a few cuts and bruises. Aren't you Luci?" Dr Graves says with a smile that feels more lustful than necessary.

"Yes, Sir." I nod, turning to face the Warden, "Shouldn't be a problem." I add with the sweetest smile I can physically muster. *Prick.*

Our morning starts slowly, we share the work space but control separate sides of the room, working fluidly together to get through the long list of patients. If necessary there's a curtain pulled between the beds to allow for the smallest bit of privacy to the inmates that we're attending to. I prefer to keep it closed the majority of the time. Anything to interject the lusting eyefuck Tom has been giving me since we started. He really must be gagging for it because he usually isn't this bad.

The job itself is relatively easy, there are no instruments here other than suture ties, and even those are kept under lock and key to deter anybody that may have the brilliant idea of trying to use them as a weapon. Any major trauma is sent elsewhere, we are just here to 'lighten the load' so to speak.

We've managed to see and treat a good number of inmates off the list but as the day goes by, I get the overwhelming feeling that I'm being watched. Not just by the inmates, and not just by Mr eyefuck himself. No, this is invasive, I can feel eyes burning into me everywhere I turn. Like prey being stalked. I have to ask myself. Am I being paranoid?

The more men I see, the worse it gets. An overwhelming tense feeling that something is about to happen, that I can't seem to shake off. Chewing at the lid of my pen, I pull the patient files off the clipboard and scan quickly over the list of names we're still due to see. No Vinny Holland. I breathe a sigh of relief, though it does little to quell the nausea threatening to spew, but I continue to call the next inmate through regardless.

"Larry Hoskins," I call as I slip on a fresh set of gloves and an apron.

A weed of a man saunters through the glass doors, his face covered in acne scars and a thin black mess of stubble on the surface of his face and neck. The stench of damp and body odor lingering around him is nauseating. My stomach churns instantly as it hits my nostrils and I have to remember to keep my face in check. This really will make me barf if I don't remember to breathe through my mouth.

"What can I do for you, Mr Hoskins?" I ask politely, keeping a wide berth between us.

"My dick hurts when I piss, yano," he spits while grabbing at his crotch.

I catch Dr Graves' face scrunch up in disgust in my peripheral vision before he turns back to his station. I watch as the guard at the door raises his eyebrows and leaves the room. Where the hell is he going?

"So you gonna get on your knees and kiss it better or what?" Larry adds, stepping closer towards me, now shoving his hand down the front of his sweatpants.

The repulsion rises in my throat and I immediately step backward, bumping into the clinic trolley and knocking the tray of sterile swabs onto the floor behind me. The loud crash of the stainless steel tray smashing against the hard tiled floor perforates the air and I become acutely aware of a hundred sets of eyes watching me from every direction through the glass panes surrounding the room. I kneel quickly, fumbling to pick everything up, very conscious that Larry is slowly closing in on me, watching very closely at every move I make. I have no idea what Tom is doing or where he even is at this moment in time. Surely he can see what is happening, right?

I hear a deep groan behind me and look up to find Larry grabbing at himself now with both hands in his pants and drool spilling over his bottom lip.

"What I'd do to make you fucking scream," he says, eyes undressing every inch of me.
Tom appears beside me and places a hand on my arm, and for once I have no intention of removing it.

"I think you're done here," he states, his tone full of disgust and outrage. "GUARDS!" he shouts, grabbing the attention of the man outside the glass who unlocks the door and steps inside. "We're finished here thank you, Mr Hoskins can go back to his cell," I say in one breath.

"What!? Fuck off!" Larry begins to shout. "You haven't even done anything, you stupid slut!"

17

I move myself behind Dr Graves while two guards barrel past us, and begin to fight with a scrambling Larry to return him back to his cell. "The things I'd do to you, you bitch, you'd be screaming." Larry calls as he's dragged away back towards his block.

As soon as they're clear of the door, I slam it shut behind them and shiver. *What a fucking creep,* I think to myself. I'll definitely be taking up Kat on the offer of going for a drink tonight, I'm going to need it.

A hand on my shoulder makes me jump. "SHIT!" I gasp, jumping round to see a startled looking Tom.

"Are you okay? I didn't mean to startle you," he says with complete sincerity in his voice, his eyes roaming my face for an answer.

"Yes, yes I'm fine. Thank you Tom." I notice my use of his name makes his face change, something flickers deep within his eyes and it makes me regret it instantly. But still, I'm glad he was here to help me. I just wanted the ground to swallow me up.

Tom smiles at me. "How about we break for lunch? I think now would be as good a time as any. Don't you?" I nod in agreement and let him lead me out of the room, still a little in shock I think and allowing him to place his hand against my lower back as we walk, escorted by two new guards to the staff canteen.

Chapter 2

Here I am in High Desert State Prison. It's 6 am and like fucking clockwork every morning that damn bell goes off to remind us it's time to piss, shit and dress before being rounded up like fucking animals for breakfast. It's a schedule that is quickly learnt, I've been here just over 18 months and soon my sentence will be over. I'm just biding my time, 10 days until I walk out those doors and become the king once again where my brothers have been taking care of our kingdom. I'm looking forward to seeing them and celebrating with whores and a hella lot of alcohol. I'm not one for drugs but you can bet they will be in supply to my men that night.

I think over my time here, not a lot has really changed. I still have the final say for my crew on how we operate and transport our goods. That's the reason I had to take the fall, I'd get less time than my brother, Cole and my friend, Lincoln. They have both done their stints in this hole already. If they went down for having a firearm during a crime, they would have gotten triple the sentence for being second offenders. Me however, a first time offender, well not first time so much as first time being caught. I've probably committed far more crimes than them in our lifetimes. I got a quick stint that I was happy to do for my brothers.

"Rise and shine boys it's time for breakfast and have we got a treat for you today!" Shouts one of the guards. It sounded like Mickey or Mikey fuck knows, he's new, fresh meat to the guards, he'll learn soon how it all works in here. I hear his boots stomping around in the communal area, he should be more careful out there, the weasel is going to get shanked if he keeps shouting his mouth off like a bitch.

I finally get out of bed and go stand to have a piss in the shared urinal and then get dressed in the god forsaken clothes we all are given. I think these are the things that I'll be the most glad to see the back of. I shove my cell mate, Nicholas to wake him, dickhead has always loved his sleep but he's an alliance in this place, most of the inmates are scared of the fucker, he's massive at 6ft 6" and built like a brick shithouse. I'm not much smaller than him at 6ft 1" so the dorm is cramped. We both enjoy working out so it's not just height wise we take up space, but it's safe to say no one messes with us.

Nicholas grunts as I nudge him again. "Another day in paradise my friend," I laugh. He hate this place, he's one smart mother fucker though. If anyone found a way out of here, it would be him. He's always got his head in a book, sometimes I think it's just to avoid the reality of being in this shit hole, can't say I blame him.

Once I'm ready and Nicholas finally rolls out of his pit, Derek, the most senior guard, saunters into the pod with a few other guards, Karl, Gray and Travis. Once they are all outside our dorms, we leave 15 at a time and make our way to the showers where we have 10 minutes each to wash before the next group gets in. I've got a lot of influence in here, I go in first followed by Nicholas. The other inmates move out of our way and let us get our shit done in private. The guards tend not to make too much of a fuss about this as it's prison politics at its finest. Anyone that wants to take my spot has to challenge me and none of these fucks can take me out.

When Nicholas and I are done, the other inmates from our section take their turn.

Showers done, our group moves back to the pod for breakfast. Apparently the doctor is here today and if we're lucky, we'll be on the call list. It's a nice change to the usual routine so you can guarantee the doc is going to be busy today with STDs, time wasters, drug seekers and those suffering from yesterday's fight.

After finishing breakfast Nicholas and I make our way back to our cell. It doesn't consist of much, two single beds that aren't comfortable but it's better than having to sleep out in the communal area with the inmates that haven't made any allegiances here. At the end of the cell there's a sink and a urinal. The walls are covered in graffiti and tags from former prisoners. Not my sort of thing, my presence in this building will be enough of a reminder of me, I don't need to leave a tag, I don't intend on returning.

Sitting on my bed, I look over at Nicholas. "When do you think the next room check will be?" I ask, leaning back and looking up at the white ceiling covered in cracks and cobwebs.
"I'd say we will have one come Friday, in case any dumbass tries to pocket any contraband from the docs visit," Nicholas states, his expression showing that he's calculating his reply carefully. In the time I've spent here, I've got to know and trust Nicholas almost as much as Cole and Linc. I don't normally do this but I've given it so much thought, Nicholas is an asset here and he will have his uses on the outside too.

"I've been thinking Nick, when you get out of here you look me, Cole or Linc up. You'll always have a place in our crew, we protect our own and you've proven to me that you can be trusted. I just need you to hold on tight here, I'll get

21

my lawyers on your case to see if I can get you earlier parole as soon as I'm out of this shit hole. What do you say?"

I don't look at him, I continue to stare blankly at the ceiling so I don't see his expression but he's silent for a moment. His reply is simple, "I'd appreciate that Si. Sooner I can get out of here, sooner I can make sure my sister is safe."

I've told him time and time again I'll check in on her for him once I'm out of here but he's said he doesn't want to invade her life unless she's in danger and he never expands more than that, so I don't push it.

"Have you given much thought to who you'll bunk with when I'm free?" I ask, thinking over the other inmates, mentally doing a list of approved names that won't cause too much of a hassle for him.

He sighs and shakes his head, "Well it definitely won't be that gobshite Danny. No matter how much he thinks he's got an in with us. I'm actually thinking about the kid; Billy. He's quiet but I think he'll be loyal and can hold his own with a bit of direction."

Looking at him now I see he's sat on his bed, leaning back on his elbows, tapping his foot. Something he does when he's assessing someone or a situation. "Billy will be a good choice, but he'll have to learn to use his big boy voice in the next three weeks or you'll be having to use those fists of yours to keep the likes of Gerry and his druggies from poaching his shit."

I approve of Billy, he's a good kid. He's younger than most here but he's no fool, just a bit naïve, which I think after getting sent here has finally been knocked out of him. I just hope my friend will have enough allies here to keep him out of trouble so I can get him an early exit. I look up to the clock out in the corridor, it's 8.28am which means it's mine and Nicholas's turn with some of the other inmates to go to organize the library. Only a few of us get this job, most others have to go off site and litter pick, peel or pick vegetables but I've paid a pretty penny to ensure Nicholas, me and a few others go to the library for a few hours.

"Let's go Nicholas, it's your favorite time of the day," I say.

Nicholas smirks because it really is his favourite part of his day, he loves reading, the guy is smart as fuck, it's part of reason I want him as one of my capos. It's not just that he's loyal, he's got a brain and will use it rather than taking risks.

After two hours of mundane reading and occupying ourselves while the others do the grueling task of sorting books alphabetically, I'm glad when it's time to head outside for our hour of exercise. This happens to be my favorite time here, I get to see the sunlight away from that almost suffocating pod. I can smell the grass in the breeze. I can almost pretend I'm not here as I use the outside gym equipment.

The sweat from how hard I'm pushing myself and the blistering sun on my back is agony but I need it to get me through my days here. I look around the grounds while I pump the weights, I see several groups huddled together gossiping about this nurse that came with the doctor, apparently she's hot. I'm tempted to check for myself but I need to focus on my goal of getting free of this place, plenty of pussy will be on the outside waiting for me.

Coming in from outside, I take my seat at the top table in the canteen with Nicholas at my left and Danny at my right. Danny has come up the ranks quickly and proven himself to be an asset, keeping the rats in here in line.

"Boss there is talk of a doc's visit today, you know what that means right?" mumbles Danny.

Gripping my fork and knife and shoveling a bite of this bland pasta into my mouth, I think of all the ways this food could be improved. I swallow the mouthful, keeping my face blank, and reply, "What are you implying Danny?" I slowly place my knife and fork down and glare at him. Danny isn't always the brightest of the bunch, if he's implying that we try to get some prescription medication to sell, I'm not in. I've got 10 days until I'm on my way and out of here. That shit isn't worth the extra time so I'm going to shut it down before it's even started.

"Woah boss, I was just thinking that we don't want the rats in here to beat us to it, also last time there was that hot nurse Kat, I wouldn't mind me a piece of that!"

Fucksake, he just wants to get high on pills and get his dick sucked. But for the record, I do remember that nurse, she was hot, not my type usually but when you've not had pussy for a while most women start to look good. I'm finding it hard not to bitch slap him right now, he's testing me in front of the other inmates. I need to carefully put this conversation down before he gets any more idiot ideas. Before I have a chance to reply, Nicholas slams his hand down and snarls at Danny making him flinch. "That nurse was never going to suck your shrimp cock Danny, and about stealing the doctor's prescription meds. You are fucking mental. There is no way you will get close to that shit unless you're sucking one of the guards dicks and then that makes you the enemy. You'll be treated as a snitch whether you are one or not. So, choose now. Are you saying you're going to back stab every fucker in here or you gonna shut your own mouth so I don't have to?"

It's silent in the canteen now, normally I'm the one to remind others of their place. Nicholas doesn't always involve himself too much with this crap, but I get a feeling that nurse Kat had an effect on him, not that I'd say a word, that shit isn't my business.

"I umm, you know, I'm not gonna be on my knees for anyone. Forget I said anything, I was just throwing ideas about, sorry man." Danny stutters.
I smirk at Nicholas, he is going to be a great boss of this pod once I'm gone in a few days. I'm glad he handled that.

"So who's up first for the doctors check up?" I ask.

Billy begins to mumble from the opposite end of the table, "I think they've put a list of times up by the door, sir." I glare at him, he's an alright kid, got caught dealing some drugs but he needs to speak up not mumble shit if he's addressing me and going to bunk with Nicholas.

"You wanna say that without pissing yourself, Billy boy?" I snark at him, not breaking eye contact.
"Sorry Sir, I just….," he tries to explain, looking anywhere but directly at me, so I cut him off.
"Billy boy look, if you have some information say it, don't mumble it. Next time I won't be telling you, I'll be giving you a reminder to not make me repeat myself."

He looks like he's about to shit himself, but does manage to contain his ass falling out and shouts "Yes, Sir!" This time loud and clear.

I continue to eat my food, if you can call it that. Once I'm finished I make my way over to my cell, thinking I'll work out for a bit longer since I have no need to see the doc.

On my way to my dorm, I hear Larry the Letch gossiping with Dennis. I stop before they see me to listen to whatever they're twittering about, knowledge is power here so I lean against the wall and wait.

"So I went to get checked over just in case, my piss still stings, and man oh man I gotta tell you, that nurse she's fine! Damn I wanted to fuck her tight little ass. I'm thinking of going back there and teaching the little bitch that the guards can't always protect her. She doesn't look like she'd put up much of a fight, I like to hold them down and make them writhe around underneath me. I've never been one for consent, Dennis. She had blonde hair that you just want to wrap around your fist. I'm gonna make her scream for me, Den, fucking scream" Larry brags.

It's now that I realize the rumors about Larry are definitely true. He raped that girl he was accused of assaulting and that's why he's here. My blood is bubbling, I'm not a fan of hurting women or children, in my opinion that's as low as you can get. It's different if it's rough sex between two consenting adults, but putting your hands on a woman without wanting the outcome of it to be her pleasure, that's not something I can get on board with.

I must admit Larry has me even more intrigued, as this is the second time this nurse has been brought to my attention. How hot is this girl? I mean it's been a while since I've had some good material to beat one out to. I may need to visit this blonde beauty after all, but the only way to go to see the doctor is if you're fucking another inmate and worried about STDs or you've been in a fight. It's highly suspicious to go get checked over without a reason, which means that Larry, it's not your day! Especially now that I've learned of your perversions.

"Hey Larry," I shout. He looks like he's going to piss himself even more so than Billy earlier, fucking pussies.

"Umm, yeah Boss what's up?" he stutters.

"What's up? Well, I just overheard you talking," I smirk as his face turns ghost white and sweat beads down his forehead. Everyone in here knows I'm a zero tolerance guy when it comes to rape.

"It's not what you think, it's just kink," he stumbles back.

"Ohh Larry, it's exactly what I think. You like to force women to take your pencil dick, am I right? Actually don't answer that. Whatever you say, it's not gonna end well for you, best to just take your punishment. What do you say?" That's when I grab him by the throat and throw him on the ground. I dive onto him and punch him until my knuckle bleeds. Ohhh how I love serving justice to the scum of this place.

Once I'm satisfied, I grab his friend Dennis by the scruff of his tunic. "You didn't see anything, and If you so much as think about telling one of the guards, just remember, you'll be next. Now be a pal and clean him up. We both know that it's not your first time. It's just not his dick that you're polishing this time."

And with that, I leave to see a pretty blonde nurse to take care of my knuckles.

Chapter 3

Lucille

Today has been one disaster after another. I'm now sitting in a room opposite Tom Graves, just the two of us, while we eat our lunches together. He's still going on and on about classic cars and I just really do not care. It's almost as if that altercation with Larry simply did not happen. I roll my eyes between forkfuls of my pasta salad and nod when I think appropriate, pretending to show some interest.

"So how do you feel about a few drinks later then?" he asks.
I choke on a piece of tomato that's gone down the wrong way and my eyes begin to water. Tom eyes me suspiciously as if to consider my choking a ruse to get me out of answering him. Grabbing my water bottle from the table, I take a few good chugs. Jesus this man is going to kill me off today.
"Oh actually Tom, me and Katrina were already going to JEWEL tonight for a few drinks sor-..."
"BRILLIANT!" he beams, cutting me off. "I'll meet you both there. Say 10 o'clock? I'll get us a private booth. I know most of the staff there." Giving me a wink before getting up and exiting the room leaving me completely speechless with my mouth hanging open. Oh Kat's really gonna kill me for this.

"Not much longer to go," I chant, trying to motivate myself for the remainder of my shift. Showing my pass to the guard once again on the way into the large communal area, I head back towards the clinic room thanking my lucky stars that Dr Graves had been called into the Warden's office to offer some medical advice that apparently he would rather be kept on the down-low. Gross, it's probably some advice about him being unable to satisfy his wife or some shit. I round the corner stopping dead in my tracks. *Damn he's big,* I think as I catch sight of an inmate leaning up against the wall with his back towards me. I bet he'd know how to throw a girl around. Cursing at myself at the thought, I shake my head and carry on.

The bulk of a man turns slowly to face me and as I get closer, his eyes hold mine, burning into me like a liquid lake of molten lava, scorching it's way through to my very core. His face looked as if it was hand carved by the Italian gods with a jawline sharp enough it could cut you in two. The statutory jumper and sweatpants stretched at the seams by his bulging muscles and broad shoulders making him stand out among the others donning the same, with intricate designs of deep black ink staining his hands and arms he looked like a perfectly created red flag. I'm sure I've died and gone to heaven, or maybe I'm in hell and he's the devil that's been sent to punish me? Either way, there's no denying the dampness between my legs and the deep blush spreading across my cheeks. I have to gather myself, remembering exactly where I am and why I'm here.

"How can I help you today?" I ask, my demeanor completely faltering as soon as the guard closes the door and I'm alone with this God-like creature. Glancing down I notice his knuckles are busted and covered in blood. I rush forward and bring his hand into mine for a closer inspection. "Oh my god your hand, what happened?" I ask before realizing the seriousness and stupidness of what I'd just done. I drop his hand as quickly as I'd held it. "I'm so sorry, I didn't mean to do that." I apologize, looking everywhere but his eyes, because if I do I think I might melt. "I'll. . .I'll start bandaging you up, it won't take me too long if you keep still."

I gesture for him to take a seat on the bed and gather my equipment to clean and wrap his open wounds. Once he's sat down and I'm sure I can get close enough without inappropriately straddling the man, I get to work in complete silence. The heat from his gaze burning straight through me. I'm sure I'll set on fire soon.

"What's your name?" he asks, his voice smooth as silk, almost hypnotizing me to answer.

"Lucille Holland." I say without even thinking and my eyes go wide. Why the fuck did I just tell him my full name!? I curse myself internally. You stupid girl. I catch him looking at me with an amused grin on his face like he can somehow hear my inner self scolding me.

"Beautiful name for a beautiful woman," he replies. Damn now my cheeks really are burning. I look down and busy myself with wrapping the bandages around his hands. "I've heard some of the men in here talking about you Lucille, so I thought I'd come pay you a visit myself, see what all the fuss was about."

My whole body begins to shake as I try to bandage his left hand. He leans forward on the bed, his face now only centimeters from my own. He's so close I can feel his body heat radiating through his clothes and it's making me dizzy. "Don't worry darlin', I took care of Mr Hoskins for you. He won't be bothering you again."

Trying to compute the information he's just told me, I crease my brow in confusion. Did he basically just admit to beating that creep from earlier up for me? I look up at him quickly, hoping he won't notice and find him already watching me. My eyes hold his for what feels like an eternity, my hand subconsciously resting over his, so small against his large bear-like mitts.

He stares, a wicked grin growing across his lips. "You can thank me later," he whispers, winking at me.

My insides flutter and if I wasn't already using the bed as a support, I'd be a puddle on the floor right now. How gorgeous is this man? I take my time as I let my eyes travel over every fine detail before me. How can somebody so gorgeous be in prison? Was he arrested for his good looks? I bite my lip to stop the question blurting out. His eyes instantly flicker noticing the movement and he sucks in a breath between his teeth and shakes his head, his hand slowly reaching towards my face. I let him, entirely hypnotized by the deity that he is. His calloused thumb grazes against my lower lip before he stands, a hair's breadth between us now, and whispers, much lower this time "I'd much rather it be me biting that bottom lip," he pauses, "la mia luce."

My gasp is barely audible as I bite down harder, clenching my inner thighs as I taste the steely tinge of blood in my mouth and the waves of temptation surge through me, and just like that, without another word he leaves.

Chapter 4

Cole

All I seem to do these days is sit behind this huge mahogany desk in Silas's Strip Club, Mezzanotte. I would much rather be in my own establishment, Salvatore's Cucina but I must keep up appearances. The smell of burnt cigars linger in the air and the woven rugs do a good job of hiding the bloodstains across the floor. The room is large with windows along 2 of the walls, the dark wood floor matches the desk and the rest of the walls are covered in wainscoting. Most would think it was a style decision, however we know it was to cover the sound proofing. The left wall is covered in floor to ceiling bookcases, full of books I doubt anyone has ever read, more style of substance.

Has Silas read any of these books? I wonder as I stand from the desk and slowly drag my finger over the spines of the books. I stop when I see one that interests me. It's a graphic book in comparison to the classic novels that are wedged in here. There is a large collection of Thomas Hardy, Oscar Wilde, and even Shakespeare in there but the one I've pulled out is one that reminds me of how we used to sit and plot our revenge. The book is full of medieval torture techniques, technically it's a history book. I remember the first time I stumbled upon this at the age of 12. It was after the kidnapping, my brother Silas and Linc told me to pick any torture method I wanted and they would carry it out on the bastards who had taken me that night. The offer was a generous one but I told them that I could execute my own demons, and that's exactly what I did. I smile at the memory of their screams. Death came too quickly in my opinion but I was young and over eager. I've honed my craft over the years and learned how to keep them alive and screaming for hours. I put the book back and bring myself back to reality. Now is not the time to take a trip down memory lane, I've got too much shit to deal with in the present.

My brother needs to hurry up and get back home pronto, I've had enough of keeping things in order with his shit. I'm starting to itch with the need to let my demons play and that book has made me twitchy like an addict waiting for his next fix. I promised Silas I wouldn't go crazy with his staff if they irritated me. Sure I can be irrational sometimes, I suppose that time I threw my steak knife at a waiter because he came over before I'd finished my meal was a bit impulsive but honestly did it even look like I was finished? Lessons were taught that day, don't approach me when I'm eating. Argh, I've had enough of this damn suit too, I'm not cut out for this shit, I like to get my hands dirty not play the Don.

Sitting back down behind the desk, I let my imagination wonder. What I wouldn't give to bend Roxi over this desk and run my knife all over her pale skin. She pinks up at the slightest touch and the thought of watching her all bloody underneath me instantly has my cock throbbing. I've got meetings all day but I need a distraction. Linc is much better at all this but Silas insisted that it had to be me, something about our name…Whatever…Fuck it!

"Quinton get your ass in here!"
"Yes Boss, what do you need?" Quinton has been one of Silas's men for years. If Silas trusts him then I trust him with my life, and my schedule.
"Cancel all my meetings this afternoon, I need to release some tension."

"Err yeah, no worries Boss. Actually there's someone outside waiting to see you, might be exactly what you need." Quinton says with a smile on his face.

"Really, well you better send them in then," I say, intrigued.

I sit back and wait for whoever my guest is, my cock is still throbbing from my thoughts of Roxi. The only rule Silas has given me is not to leave any permanent marks on the girls. What Silas doesn't understand is that I'd never leave my mark on one of his whores. They're easy fucks who know the deal, I don't have to worry about them talking. Whoever walks through that door is going to get my demons today, so god help them, they better be ready.

I can't hold back my groan when Roxi walks in, hips swaying, fake tits bouncing underneath her tiny top. The skirt she's wearing barely covers her ass and she looks phenomenal. I don't like big tits normally but she plays my games so I don't care.

"Are you prepared for me Roxi?" I ask as I twirl my blade between my fingers. Her pupils dilate and her breath hitches, she nods as she comes to stand between me and the desk.

"Now, now Roxi, you know the rules. I need your words before we start."

"Yes Boss, I'm ready for you," she says as she turns and bends over my desk, Her skirt rides up and I see the buttplug I previously gave her nestled in her ass. Fuck!! That is better than anything my imagination could come up with. I give the plug a flick that has her panting, I can see the slickness between her legs growing. This is exactly what I need.

I take my blade and drag it slowly from her ankle to ass, leaving a delicious red line in its path, like seamed stockings. I sit back and palm my cock, committing the view to memory for later. I move around the desk to stand in front of her and Roxi reaches to grab my cock. Such an eager little slut.

"Did I say you could touch my cock yet!?" I yell at her, grabbing her jaw and making her arch up. I can see she's uncomfortable but she's been broken in well and loves it rough. The smirk on my face is nefarious as the thoughts of all the depraved things I want to do to her flit through my mind. I know I don't have time for everything I want to do because I never get any fucking time to myself anymore. This is going to be quick and filthy! "This is what's going to happen, you're going to stay still, no moving at all. I'm going to fuck your mouth then I'm going to fuck your pussy. I haven't decided what to fuck you with yet, that will be a suprise. You know your safe word, use it, don't use it, I don't care. I'm not going to stop until you do. Say yes if you accept."

"Yes!" she says eagerly around my grip.

"What a good slut you are, now open up for me," I say as I feed my cock past her lips. She deepthroats my cock like a pro. I'm always astonished that anyone can get their mouth around it, let alone anything more than that. I may be an asshole and a depraved fuck but I don't do anything without consent.

"Fuuuuuuuuckkk!" I moan as I pull my cock out of her mouth leaving her face all messy and covered in her own spit. What is it about a thoroughly fucked face that just makes my balls twitch with need? I stand behind Roxi and watch her panting and twitching on my desk trying not to move. The anticipation of my touch has her dripping. I take my blade and cut her just below her ass cheeks, she nearly comes right then and I love it. I run the blade over her a few more times, each time has her moaning louder and louder. Her skin is deliciously red, covered in rivulets of blood.

"You ready for me?"

"Uhhhuh!" she babbles.

I take the thick handle of my knife and I drive it into her wet pussy. It's the perfect knife for fucking. Its handle is long and thick, it allows enough space to impale my victim and not end up cutting myself. She's so far gone by this point she doesn't care, I could be fucking her with anything. I put that thought away for when I have more time. I plunge into her with the handle a few times before leaving it nestled inside of her. "Don't let this fall out now, your pussy better be tight enough to hold on or you won't like the consequences." I let go and rubber up as I watch her battle to keep the handle buried inside her. I could just let her lose and enjoy the punishment but I need a release.

I pull the handle out and grip her neck, pulling her up against me. "Ready for the real thing?" I ask. Just as I start to push my cock inside her my phone rings. "You've got to be fucking kidding me!!!" Pushing Roxi back down on the table, I grab my phone. The only people with this number are Silas and Linc. The guards in lock up turn a blind eye to Silas so he calls whenever he needs a job doing or to check his empire is still standing. This better be fucking important!

"Hello, Brother," Silas says casually through the speaker.
"Brother, you're interrupting my play time. Is this important or can I get back to bleeding and fucking this whore in peace?" I growl as I put my phone on speaker and shove into her hard.

Silas and I have shared girls in the past so this is nothing new for him. The buttplug in her ass reminds me of when we've filled other girls up with both our cocks at the same time. The noises coming from Roxi are almost feral and I laugh, I definitely pushed her to her limit today.

36

Silas chuckles too, "Remember Cole, no permanent marks. Is it Roxi today or are you testing a new girl?"

Roxi's head snaps to look at me, fuck sake she's getting clingy. Maybe I should kill the bitch after I've finished fucking her. I'd love to use this knife and slit her pretty little throat as she takes my cock.

"Brother are you still there?" Silas says, snapping me from my thoughts of how to bring her life to an end, I'd be lying if that didn't turn me on, making my dick even harder.

"Yes, fuck, yes I'm still here. Shit hold on for a minute. I need to take out the trash, this bin is full and over used. I'll find a nice new bin to dump my cum into later," I reply with an even tone. I don't want Roxi thinking I'm going to bring her back here again after that look she gave me, no way is she getting possessive on me. Bitch needs to go or I'll end her. She's gone silent and still so I know she heard every word. I push her head into the desk and bend over her with my cock still buried deep inside her. I know I'm hurting her but she needs to realize that she's nothing to me, I don't do relationships. "Go back to work, don't come back here looking for me to carve your skin up again. I've had my fill of your pussy, now leave" I say as I yank my dick out of her cunt. I'd like to say I was gentle but I'd be lying. Roxi's eyes water as she stumbles to grab her clothes to leave, she knows better than to talk back to me. Once the door is closed and the whore is gone, I sit back down in my chair. "So, how can I help you Silas? Trouble in the showers?"

Silas roars with laughter, "Good one Cole but no, no trouble there. You know I'd have too much fun beating the shit out of any motherfucker that tried to approach me. I need you to do a job for me." I wait for him to continue, what job could need doing now that can't wait until he's out of prison, it's less than 2 weeks now. Silas continues, "There's a girl, Lucille Holland, she's a nurse who works at Summerlin hospital. I need you to follow her, find out what you can, get Linc to do a background check. I want to know everything about her."

This is a strange request. Maybe he's been without pussy for too long. "Ok Brother, but what's so special about her? She suck your dick while attending to your wounds?" I joke.

Silas growls, "Watch your mouth when you speak about her Cole. You will watch her until I can do it myself. Be discreet, do what you do best, keep to the shadows and stay out of sight."

"Ok Silas, calm your tits, I'll watch the girl and get Linc to do a background check. Hey, maybe I'll like what I see..." I tease. I can't help it, he's so easy to wind up.

"Don't fucking touch her, Cole. You'll see first hand what I'm capable of, Brother!" he threatens. He just doesn't get it though, I know exactly what he can do, I'm just not bothered, but we are blood and I'd do anything he asks.

"Down boy, down. I'm only playing, I know better than to play with your toys without permission. Don't worry Brother, I'll keep her safe for you." I reassure him.

"I knew I could count you, I'll be seeing you soon," he says before hanging up.

So it looks like I've got a new project and her name is Lucille Holland. Let's see what has caught my brother's eye.

I spy, with my little eye, a little mouse ready to be caught. Let the games begin.

Chapter 5

Lincoln

The buzz of the light strip above sounds loud in my ears. I pinch the bridge of my nose and let out a sigh of utter annoyance. I can feel the frustration building in every cell in my body and I'm going to snap this mother fucker in two if he doesn't quit crying. Turning to face the two way mirror behind me, I rest my hands on my hips pulling back my suit jacket, purposefully putting my gun in full view. I see the reflection of the cheater's eyes widen in horror and I cannot help but laugh. Nobody cheats in my casino and gets away with it. I turn to look at him, my face devoid of all emotion, giving nothing away. His face is a regretful, sniveling mess.

"I've decided you've caught me on a good day today, Dean. I don't much feel like ruining this suit," I say, circling behind him and placing my hands firmly on his shoulders. "So I'm going to give you one last chance to tell me how you managed to beat my best player, at my own table, in my own club. Six times in a row! Please do not start by telling me it was just good luck." I give a warning squeeze to both shoulders before sitting down in the empty chair placed in front of him.

Dean drops his head, unable to look me in the eye and visibly shaking from head to toe. "I swear! I SWEAR, I didn't know this was your casino, Mr Rossi. Please! I'm so sorry. I'll never do it again, I swear! Please!" he chokes out. Snot and saliva mixing with his tears stream down his face.

I smile internally at his confession and lean back against my chair, tracing my finger along the stubble on my jawline, while tapping my other hand across the hilt of my gun in unison with the clock. Tick tock, tick tock. "Do you know what we do to cheaters around here Dean?" I ask, finally rising from my seat. I take my jacket off and place it over a hook on the back of the door then begin to roll the sleeves up on my shirt while slowly circling the cheater on his chair, slipping in and out of his line of vision. His sniveling is getting on my nerves now. I hate cheaters, but I hate pussies more.

I pause before a tall set of steel drawers lined up against the back wall. Choosing carefully, I pull out the second drawer on the right and a wicked grin spreads over my face at the sight of what's inside. I love it when somebody thinks they can outplay me, it means I get to outplay them. There really is no better sound than a man screaming for his life. Especially a man who has stolen from me. I trail my hand across the arrangement of tools before me, neat lines of the most perfect torture implements any man could ever need. My hand lands on the pliers without a second thought. My favorite, I grin. "When I ask you a question Dean, I expect an answer. I mean it's the least you could do after stealing from me, don't you think?"

I hear him sobbing behind me and roll my eyes. What a pussy. "I'm sor-r-ry," he stutters between gasping breaths. Eyes as wide as craters as he catches sight of the metal pliers in my hand when I return to face him. He begins to panic, "No, no, I'm sorry Sir, I won't ever do it again. I promise I won't!"

"You're right Dean, you won't and I have a sneaky feeling you're only sorry because you got caught." I lean forwards and bring my hand to his face. "Now hold still otherwise this is really going to suck for you."

Within seconds I wrap my arm around the back of his neck, grabbing hard onto his chin and pulling his head tight against my chest for support. He's wriggling and squealing like a little bitch already and I haven't even touched him. Forcefully shoving the pliers between his teeth, I grip his tongue, the pressure cutting straight through the flesh. His screams fill the entire room and I silently thank God that I let Silas soundproof the walls down here during the refurbishment, before ripping the chunk of muscle out from his mouth. The blood gurgles in his throat as he begins to choke.

"You spoke lies to me so I have taken your tongue. Now, if I EVER see you inside of my casino again, believe me, CHEATER, you will lose more than just your ability to speak." I spit into his face.

Suddenly the intercom buzzes. I whip my head around to see Cole staring at me through the mirrored glass, he's flipped the switch on the other side turning the glass transparent. He stands and stares at the scene before him with a wicked smirk turning up his mouth.

"Wrap it up big man, we've got a job to do," he says before giving me a nod. "The boss needs your computer skills."

I turn back to Dean, blood oozing beautifully from his gaping mouth. He'll live, but he'll fucking wish he didn't. Letting his flaccid tongue drop to the ground, I fist my hand into his hair, "I told you, you caught me on a good day." I say looking him dead in the face then shoving his head back and leaving the room.

Walking through the basement corridor to one of the private tech rooms, I interrupt Zack, Sully and Felix surveying the CCTV cameras that cover the entire casino floors. They turn in unison to look at me as I enter, blood still dripping from the pliers in my hand. Anger still radiating from me as I head straight for the back, toward my private office.

"We need the clean up crew in the interrogation room ASAP. Sully, throw the fucker out before I change my mind and kill him. Felix, go and get me a clean set of clothes and Zack, make yourself fucking useful and get me a whiskey, not the cheap stuff either. Go upstairs and grab a bottle, something Scottish from behind the bar." I snap my orders. "NOW!" I shout louder when they fail to move quick enough.

I slam my office door behind me and head straight for my en-suite, another good decision from Silas, it's like he knew exactly what would happen down here. I strip down and let the scalding water melt away my sins.

After washing the blood stains from my skin and changing into the suit pants and shirt Felix picked up, I exit the bathroom to find Cole already sat waiting for me. I see he has happily helped himself to my whiskey with his feet kicked up on my desk. "Boy, get your feet off my goddamn desk." I warn. I swear since Silas got arrested, this kid has let the power get to his head.

"Chill out Linc, I'm not the reason you're all pent up. I thought ripping someone's tongue out might have cheered you up a little," he says, goading me.

The image of Dean squirming beneath my hand flicks back through my mind. "Piss off, Cole. Why don't you make yourself useful and pour me a drink of my own whiskey while you're over there." I sigh and relax down into the leather couch that takes up the entire side wall. "So, what does the boss want?" I ask, intrigued as to what has him calling in a job less than two weeks before he's released. Cole laughs as he hands me a whiskey tumbler and shakes his head plonking himself beside me on the couch.

"He's fallen in love with a pretty little prison nurse."

I almost choke on my drink. "Are you being serious? He can't fucking wait ten days? He'll have all the whores he could ask for at the club when he's back. We'll be celebrating for weeks. It's been a long fucking eighteen months with him in there and now he's calling about a bloody woman?" I down the rest of my whiskey and run my fingers through my hair. Cole slaps my knee in humor,

"He wants a full background check, 24 hour surveillance and under no circumstance is anybody to touch her." I hear the tone change in his voice and note the smirk playing on his lips.

"Then that especially means you, Cole!" I say, with a warning in my voice. I know exactly what he's thinking. If she's good enough for Si, she's good enough for him too. "Hands off till the boss has his fill then she's all yours" I reiterate.

Chapter 6

Lucille

Having finally finished my rounds for the rest of the afternoon I collect my bag and pack up the few items left over from our own supplies and secure them back into the box to return to the hospital. My head is in a complete fluster from the days events, the earlier confrontation from Larry, the never ending advances from Tom that I've been dodging all day and the mind fuck from the heart-stopping, pantie-dropping criminal god that I would like nothing more than to be ravished by. It is criminal for any man to look that good. Also not to mention the anxiety I've felt all day that at some point Vinny could show up and most probably kill me.

I head for the transport van breathing a sigh of, I'm not sure what, relief maybe, and wait for Dr Graves to finish, eager to finally be getting out of this place.

With my mind still deep within the gutter, fantasizing about golden eyes, rough tattooed hands and chiseled jawlines, I sigh happily to myself just before Tom jumps into the van and pulls me from my inner pit of wanton desire.

"What a day!" he exclaims, slumping down next to me and throwing his arm over my shoulders. The initial contact makes my whole body cringe.

"Yeah you could say that. It wasn't you who was almost accosted though was it Tom," I chide, rolling my eyes and shrugging his arm from my shoulders. He tuts loudly in my ear, letting his disapproval known.

"Oh Lucille don't be silly, nothing was going to happen to you. Besides, I stepped in and the guards carried him away to his filthy little hole. He would never have stood a chance with me there. And anyway you'd think they'd at least give them soap in there, it'll take me ages to get that smell out of my clothes," he remarks, turning his nose up as the memory of Larry's stench permeates his senses. *What a pretentious asshole.*

It's definitely been a hell of a day! The drive back to the hospital is torturously slow, though I am graced by some stroke of luck that Tom is caught up in a phone call from some other doctor for most of the journey, and from the sounds of it, it's a pretty important call. I try to be nosey and listen in but to my utter shock, he moves away from me and sits down on the back row of the van to continue his conversation in private, giving me what I can only interpret as a 'mind your own business' type of look before he turns away. But anyway, at least I have some breathing space now and I can focus my thoughts on tonight instead.

Having already arranged with Kat a few days ago that my brother, Max, would be watching both the kids tonight after she drops them off from kindergarten, I rush home as soon as we get back to the hospital and i've handed over what's left from our box of supplies, absent-mindedly waving Tom off as he shouts, "I'll see you later!" across the parking lot, a grin spread devilishly across his face. Kat is going to kill me for sure!

The two minute drive back home seemed pointless considering I live so close to work but I was desperate to be alone. The face of a god and his calloused touch still lingering across my lips are all I can think about, no matter how much I try to distract myself. Pulling into the driveway, I've barely switched off the ignition before darting for the front door. And as soon as I'm inside I head straight for the

45

bathroom, slipping out of my clothes and plunging straight under the running water, letting the cool beats of water wash away the day. I shampoo and condition my hair before rinsing then slowly lather myself in body wash, and with the temptation too overwhelming I begin to tenderly stroke my fingers across the swollen bud between my thighs, with his words playing on repeat in my mind. I stroke harder, two fingers parting my already eager lips below, the image of molten eyes setting fire to my soul. I picture his rough hands in place of mine, rubbing, circling and pushing me further to my climax. Pulling my fingers back to my clit, soaked in my own juices I stroke, the pleasure building and building before it becomes too much and the delicious waves of my orgasm explode throughout my body. I shudder, knees buckling and squeeze my thighs together as I moan my release. The fuzziness in my head begins to clear, I can't believe I just did that over a man I don't even know, a fucking criminal no less! I shake my head, letting the cool water run, soothing my frazzled nerves. I really need to get laid tonight. I continue to wash my body, slathering my legs in soap before grabbing my razor and giving them the cleanest shave they've ever known and making sure to touch up my bikini line too.

Still reveling in the aftermath of my orgasm fantasizing over the inmate I can't even remember the name of. I don't even remember asking him for it actually. I collapse onto the bed and glance at the clock, it's 7pm. Kat will be here in a couple of hours. I've got enough time to pick out an outfit, eat something and put my face on before she arrives, but first I need to check in on my baby boy. Jumping up and heading to the kitchen, I crack open a bottle of wine while dialing Max.

"Hey, you alright?" Max asks, finally answering his phone.

"Yeah, I just wanted to say goodnight to Teddy before he goes to bed," I answer as I start pulling out the entire contents of my wardrobe.

Max is my older brother by six years, we are blessed with the same bitch of a mother, though I'm sure his opinion of her is much different than my own considering he was a planned for and dearly wanted child. Whereas I was the result of a one night stand, stained at birth and resented my whole life by the woman who is supposed to love and protect me, all because I supposedly ruined her figure. I'm the reason her skin is stretched and scarred, her tits are saggy and the bags under her eyes are blacker than her soul. I hear Max call Teddy, pulling me out of a spiral.

"Hi Momma!" he squeals excitedly.

"Hey baby boy, are you and Isabella being good for your Uncle Max?" I ask.

"Yes Mommy, we've had pizza and popcorn and watched a really funny movie," he replies.

"PIZZA AND POPCORN!" I exclaim. "What lucky little babies you are. Make sure you go to bed when you're told to, OK Teddy?"

"Yes Mommy, I love you, goodnight!" he sings through the line.

"Goodnight baby, I'll see you in the morning. Now hand the phone back to Uncle Max," I say, taking a huge chug of my crisp white wine. It's hard to spend the night away from him but I know I need to let my hair down and so luckily, Max agreed to have them both.

"He'll be fine Luce, you and Kat go and have a good night, I've got this handled. Don't go getting into any trouble though. I don't want to have to bail either of your asses out for a catfight over some bloke in the club." Max laughs down the phone.

Feigning shock I reply, "Would we EVER start a fight brother?" I practically hear him roll his eyes in response.

"I mean it Lucille, just be careful, please," he says, his voice now every bit serious.

"Jesus, okay Max I know, I know, we're not that stupid. I can take care of myself. I'll call you in the morning, and thanks again for watching the kids." I reply before hanging up.

He has every right to worry considering the job that he does. Being a mafia man has its pro's but it's also a life and death sentence all in one. I get it, I really do. He has made some serious enemies that could easily be out to get to him through the likes of me, or anyone he's linked to, but I didn't need him to kill my vibe this early on in the night. I haven't even left my apartment yet. I quickly polish off my glass of wine before shaking the bad vibes off. Holding two sets of outfits up, in front of the mirror. I settle on a little black silk strappy dress that criss-crosses over my back leaving hardly anything to the imagination. *Perfect!* I praise myself, pulling on a pair of hot pink peep toe heels and lining my lips to match. If I don't pull with this much skin on show tonight I swear I must have the words 'DO NOT TOUCH' imprinted on my body for every man to read.

After hopelessly trying to pin my hair back for at least fifteen minutes, I admit defeat and hope that Kat won't mind sorting it out for me because I'm about ready to throw the brush out the window.

No sooner than the thought has entered my mind, I hear her voice singing, "Girl are you ready to party?" before she saunters through the front door. Her deep brown hair is perfectly pulled back into a tight, high pony, the tail trailing down past her waist. She's wearing the shortest champagne mini dress I've ever seen, killer red heels and bright red lipstick. Kat is naturally beautiful, so when she's all dolled up like she is right now, she's absolutely drop dead. There is no doubt she'll be getting some attention tonight. Hopefully it'll be a good night for both of us, and I can forget all about prisoner number 69 or whoever he was.

Chapter 7

Cole

The night sky is lit with the bright city lights, the occasional sound of dogs barking breaks the silence of the night as I sit parked outside the woman's apartment that has enamored my brother. Only time will tell if she will have the same effect on me and Linc. I look down at my phone to the summarized profile Linc has just sent me. It's only a quick overview but it's something to go off.

Name: Lucille Holland (Preferred name Luci).
Age: 27, Date of Birth: 4th December 1994.
Occupation: Nurse currently working at Summerlin Hospital Medical Center specializing in wound care and emergency care.
Living situation: Red Rock Villas Apartments, Apartment 2.
Children: Teddy Holland, Aged 5, Date of Birth:15th October 2017. Attends kindergarten at Merryhill Elementary school.
Next of kin: Camille de la Rue (Mother)
Emergency contact: Max Costello

I have a double take of the emergency contact. What the fuck? How does that Irish scum know her and why is he important enough to be her emergency contact? I bet Linc is raging, Silas sure knows how to pick them. I pull up Linc's number and hit call, it only rings twice and he's picking up.

"Cole, if you have called to piss me off more about the girl being involved with those Irish fucks, I'll hang up now," he growls. I can hear him pacing his office in the casino. I can practically hear the floor being worn thin as he goes.

I chuckle to myself "Why would I try to piss you off? You're like my big adopted brother, an ugly big adopted brother that is, but not all of us can be blessed with my good looks." I hear him throw something that clangs in the background.

"You know full well why you're trying to piss me off! You're going to see her as a challenge now aren't you!? I told you not to go after her brother! Her being involved with the Irish doesn't change that" he rages at me.

Someone has their panties in a twist if you ask me, but he's not wrong I'm definitely more tempted than before to play with her. I wonder if she would like my games, enjoy the way my knife would feel on her skin as her blood seeps out, coating her pretty milky skin. After all, I am in need of a new fuck buddy. She might just fit the bill, but then again, Silas did give me orders not to touch his toy. I can see exactly why he was so enamored by her looking at the photographs provided. She's strikingly beautiful with her blonde hair and piercing green eyes. She can't be more than 5'4", her build is slight but with curves in all the right places.

"Chill out brother, it might not be as it seems, maybe he's the kids daddy, then if I fuck her it'll be like a slap in the face to those dirty Irish cunts." I retort, cracking my knuckles as I'm watching her house. I can see her silhouette through the window, it looks as though she's looking out at the night sky, admiring the stars that are dancing with the moon.

Linc rages some more, "That's not the answer to this and you know it Cole. Silas is going to see this as a big blow, hell those Irish fucks might have planted her in the prison to get him to lose his temper or worse psych him out to feel like he's being watched. We need to watch the girl, see what her involvement is with them, leave me to inform Silas of the situation."

I still prefer my idea, I could even leave a little permanent mark on her creamy skin so that fucker Max would see I've been in her pussy every time he fucks the bitch. I sigh, finally giving in to Linc, "Fine Linc, but if she is Costello's girl then she's fair game."

He is breathing heavily over the phone now. I think he's probably finished destroying his office. "Okay but if you do that you're on your own dealing with Silas for tapping her ass before him," he grunts in a lighter tone than before.

An old red Volvo S80 pulls up outside Lucille's apartment, music is blaring from it, sounds like 'Girls Just Wanna Have Fun,' by Cyndi Lauper. I smirk thinking it's not just girls that want to have fun. Remembering that I'm still talking to Linc I say, "Ok bro, I need to go, some brunette chick just pulled up at the apartment, I need to focus. Go get one of your whipping boys to clean up your trashed up office, speak to you soon."

Linc laughs, "Ok, I'll try to get more information on this chick and send it through soon, stay safe brother," Linc ends the call and I go back to stalking my prey.

I slowly get out of the car, I've parked far enough away so that I won't be seen. I take to the shadows and creep around the apartment building just in time to hear the brunette screech, "Girl are you ready to partyyyyy?" Lucille giggles and the door clicks closed behind the brunette as she hurries into the building.

It seems the little mouse lives facing the communal pool, number 2. I suppose it's practical with a little one. I silently and stealthily assess the position of the apartment, trying to figure out the best entrances and exits for the complex. I head around to the back window that comes from the lounge area. The window is cracked open enough to allow me to eavesdrop on their conversation easily.

"Hope you like white wine Kat, it's all I've got in." Lucille hollers from somewhere inside. I hear the clinking of glasses and someone giggles while they 'cheers'.

"Babe, you know I'm not fussy when it comes to alcohol, how did it go at the prison? Did Dr Graves behave himself?" I hear soft footsteps as she replies to her friend.

"I'm glad it's over Kat, some of those inmates made the usual crude jokes, I nearly got attacked by one inmate. I had to stop myself from gagging. He smelt so bad, it was disgusting. Oh and as for Dr Graves, he sort of invited himself tonight. I tried to tell him no, but he wasn't having any of it but the bonus is he's secured us a private booth at JEWEL tonight."

This doctor guy seems a bit pushy, maybe I'll get Linc to look into him too. Not that I'm protective of the girl, I just don't like predators preying on innocent people.

"Don't worry babe, it's a silver lining. We can always ditch him after a few drinks if he starts being a creep again!" her friend Kat reassures her. "So any hot prisoners catch your eye while you were in there? On my rotation there was this guy, he was like almost seven foot tall, always reading a book but my god I'd have climbed him like a monkey Luc!" Kat exclaimed.

I wonder if she's talking about Nicholas, Silas' roomie. Silas said he's built like a brick shit house so I wouldn't be surprised if he's caught her eye. He's smart as fuck so Silas says. He's all but given him a job when he's released too so I hope the fucker is trustworthy.

"Why Lucille Holland, are you blushing? Who took your fancy?" Kat squeals excitedly. Who indeed took your fancy little mouse? I take in a breath anticipating her answer.

"Well, no one took my fancy, but there was one inmate who was sort of hypnotizing, but I embarrassed myself in front of him. I bet he thought I was a right mess! I got so flustered, it was after Dr. Graves was being pushy about joining us tonight."

I wonder who this inmate was, Silas isn't going to like someone else moving in on his girl that's for sure.

"Don't worry about it, it's not like you're going to see him again Luci and as for Dr Creep, we can just avoid him all night after saying hi." Kat reassuringly tells Lucille.

"Ok done, your hair looks fantastic! Have you got everything? The cab should be here any minute, babe." Kat exclaims, sounding very merry by this point. How much wine have they had in such a short space of time?

"Thanks so much Kat, I love it! I'll just grab my bag from my bedroom then we can head out," Lucille replies.

Moments later I hear a horn beeping from the sidewalk, it's their cab, it's arrived to take them to the club. I hear them shut the door of the apartment, still giggling and chittering away as they make their way to the cab.

Once the cab is out of sight, I wedge the window open further and slip inside to Lucille's apartment, Silly girl not checking her windows are secure. I look around her lounge area first, it's pretty normal, photos of her and her kid clutter the surfaces. I pick up a picture in a frame, it's one of the boy, Teddy and Lucille. They are in a warm embrace. I stare at it for a moment thinking how much love this one single photo has encapsulated, he's a lucky boy to have his mother care that deeply for him. I know first hand how that is not always the case. He looks like her, not sure if I see Max in him though.

I place the frame back down. A nice gray sofa sits in the middle with a lemon throw over it. I run my fingers over the soft material as I walk past heading to the kitchen. I see the leftover wine glasses, one smeared with red lipstick, another pink. I pick one up and wonder who is wearing the pink lipstick as I smear the stain with my thumb, imagining it's Lucille's lips. I love when a woman's lipstick is smeared over her face as she takes my cock down her throat. I wonder if the pretty blonde could handle my cock.

As I walk through her kitchen I see her laundry basket, a red lace thong poking out of it, taunting me. I instinctively take them in my hand feeling the crotch area. They're wet. Bringing the thin cotton to my nose, I can smell her arousal. A sweet, vanilla aroma invades my senses. My little mouse is a dirty girl. I pocket them for later, maybe I'll give them to Silas as a welcome home present.

Lastly, I head to her bedroom, purple and gray décor throughout. A big double bed, I'm sure she barely fills this at just 5'4" with her slender frame. I lay myself down smelling her scent on her pillows, wondering if I have enough time to bang one out. I reach under my pants and stroke my already hard and thick cock, wondering if she would notice my cum over her sheets when she returns later in her drunken state. Feeling her soft bedspread, imagining all the ways she'd feel, I free myself from my pants and begin to pump my hand up and down my shaft. I grow harder at the thought of her plump pink lips wrapped around my length, taking me fully in to her delicious throat as I fuck her face. Pre-cum starts to trickle from me, and I fist myself harder. More images plague me of her, bare between me and my brothers. Taking her in every hole while she writhes and begs for her own release. Within seconds, my hot thick cum sprays from my cock over her bed spread, leaving my seed as a welcoming gift for her later return. What I'd give to see my cum spread over her milky white tits instead. I feel feral in this moment, my release awakening something much deeper, much darker, wanting to possess what Silas has already laid claim to.

Rising from the bed, I absentmindedly wonder if purple is her favorite color as I look around the room. I head out of the room and go to the front door, next to it is a small cabinet. Looking inside I find a spare key for the apartment and decide I'll take it and make a copy, she will never know as I'll replace the copy by morning. I open the front door and casually walk back to my car, making my way to JEWEL. It's time for the cat to hunt the mouse.

Chapter 8

Lucille

In the back of the cab, on the way to the club, Kat turns to me and squeezes my hand.

"So tell me more about this inmate, I want to know everything!" she squeals excitedly. I laugh and push her shoulder away playfully.

"There really isn't anything to tell Kat. I don't even know his name, he came to me with busted knuckles. He had eyes to DIE for though and he just had this sort of overpowering, I will fuck you right here kind of vibe going on. I would have happily let him do anything he wanted to me on that bed, with everybody else watching through the windows too if he told me to."

Kat laughs in delight. "Oooh somebodies got their knickers wet over a big bad convict," she teases.

I roll my eyes, almost tempted to tell her about my extracurricular activities in the shower too, but I think better of it, she'll never let me live it down. "So what about you?" I ask, topping up my lippy in the reflection of my compact mirror. "How is everything? Have you heard anything from Mason recently?" I hear a low sigh as she puffs out a frustrated breath,

"Oh, Jesus girl what you gotta bring that dickhead up for? Honestly you would think any man would WANT to get to know their own child wouldn't you?!" She reaches over to take the compact from my hand then pouts at herself. "I just don't know what to tell Bella when she keeps asking for her daddy, she's five years old. She wouldn't understand that he would rather be fucking the next barely-twenty year old that shows him the slightest bit of interest

57

than see her," she rolls her eyes and looks at me "and anyway, if he is going to be like that I don't want him anywhere near her. She needs a father figure, not a fucking ponce who drives around in his flashy fucking car with a different bitch in his bed everynight who couldn't give two shits or two cents to support his own child."

I crease my brow feeling guilty for bringing it up. "Sorry Kat, we sure know how to pick um huh?" I joke trying to lighten the spiraling mood. "What about Max? I know you eye-fuck him every time he's around and he's great with the kids obviously."

"Oh no Luce, he's your brother I couldn't!" she scoffs looking away momentarily. "I mean, I really would like to though. Your brother is so damn hot! I almost need a mop behind me when I see him." she squeals laughing.

"OH MY GOD! WE'D BE SISTERS!!" we shout in unison before falling into each other in fits of giggles.

Arriving at the club I can already feel the warm buzz of alcohol running through my system but it doesn't deter me as I head straight to the bar and order us a large pitcher of Sex on the Beach.

With the music blasting and the first sip of my cocktail going down all too easily, I slowly turn to take in my surroundings. This isn't our usual outing spot but the girls at work have been raving about it for weeks and it's girls night so it was a no brainer. I take in the decor and even through the strobe lighting, that I'm sure should come with an epilepsy warning, I can make out the industrial vibe they've gone with. The framework is exposed metal piping throughout, laying hold to bare brick walls and old industrial style light fixtures. It's quite beautiful actually. The bar area covers the back wall, allowing for a staff entrance to the far side. Thick black marble lines the top with chrome fitted taps and optics. The wall at the back is all mirror allowing the lighting to bounce and giving me the chance to check the line up of guys at the bar without them noticing. No one catches my eye just yet, but the night is young and I won't be entirely picky.

There's a dense fog about a foot thick covering the entire dance floor, seeping from the machines standing either side of the DJ booth and weeding itself through the legs of those who stand in its way. The smell instantly takes me back to our old elementary school disco's and the memory of it makes me smile. The dance floor itself is a huge area, completely swamped with people, some old, some younger, but all having a good time. Their bodies grind against each other in every direction I look. I notice a VIP section off to the right but it's a little more subdued than the rest of the room so it's hard to make out from where I stand. The toilets are on the opposite wall towards the back corner and surrounding the dance floor on the other side is a collection of tables and booths, separated by glass walls framed with black metal scaffolding, fitted with cushy velvet couches and marble top tables that match the bar. The whole club looks expensive and I think it may be my new favorite place. That thought alone brings a smile to my face. This is going to be such a good night.

"See anyone?" I shout over the thumping bass to Kat. We survey our surroundings perched by the edge of the dance floor, hoping she's narrowed down a group of good looking men for us to get friendly with and swindle free drinks for the rest of the evening. She shakes her head, sipping through one of the cocktail straws and I watch as her eyes grow wide.

"No not yet but I think somebody has spotted us," she laughs then grabs my hand and pulls me towards the VIP booth section. As soon as we stop, I realize to my horror that it had been Tom Graves and my stomach turns.

Wearing white fitted pants and a navy blue shirt with an unsightly amount of chest hair on show, his face lights up at the sight of us. That disgustingly evil grin is plastered across his face again. With his eyes practically undressing every inch of our bodies, he already appears to have had one too many drinks.

"Ladies, ladies, don't you look gorgeous out of your uniforms," he chirps, his tongue darting out over his lips. My first impulse is to turn away and somehow pretend we hadn't seen him to see if we could get away with it, but Kat is already wedging herself down between the velvety cushioned sofa and the table and pouring out three shots of vodka from the bottle collection in the middle. She eyes me impatiently and nods her head for me to follow suit and sit down too.
Three shots later and the unease has slowly begun to fade, the vodka burning my throat as it goes down.

"You're so beautiful Lucille." Tom slurs as he edges closer to me across the booth. I smile politely and look to Kat for moral support but she's too busy eyeing up some hunky blonde across the room. She's no help.
"Thanks Tom." I swallow. He shifts closer, placing his hand on my knee and stroking this thumb across my skin.
"I need a drink!" I blurt, standing up to shake him off.
"Brilliant idea," he says, standing up next to me and fumbling with his crotch to rearrange his visibly growing hard on beneath his pants. "I'll get us a bottle of champagne," he adds before quickly turning and hurrying off towards the bar. I cringe inwardly and look to find Kat wiping away tears as she snorts into her cocktail.
"Don't you dare laugh," I scold, plonking back down beside her.
"I'm sorry," she says. "It's just too funny to watch how much you turn him on, and he has no idea you'd rather eat your own eyeballs. He's like a fucking puppy wanting to

hump your leg." She's laughing again, throwing her head back and pushing into my shoulder.

"Shut up Kat, you're absolutely no help whatsoever." I say, rolling my eyes and pouring out another couple of shots before he returns.

"Oh come on doll, at least he's buying the drinks," she smirks, holding up to cheers before we down them. Sucking in air as the burn hits the back of my throat I shake my head.

"Can we please go dancing when he gets back?" I beg, Kat winks at me.

"Sure thing baby doll, but you better hurry up and get your dancing shoes on real quick cause here comes casanova."

After another round of trying to keep Tom's hand from slipping under my dress and more glasses of champagne, then we're up to dance. I weave in and out of the tangle of bodies, glad to be leaving Tom to sort his crotch out in the booth alone. I pull Kat along behind me until we hit the middle of the dance floor. The drumming pulse beating through me, the strobe lights cutting through the room, I completely lose myself, letting the alcohol and music take over. My body moves in every direction I will it to, catching eyes with Kat as we move together dancing to a remix of 'Crazy What Love Can Do' by David Guetta and Becky Hill.

As the bass drops, I feel a pair of hands slink around my waist. I look at Kat who gives me a playful wink as she taps on the guy's shoulder next to her then asks him to dance. I turn to face a dark haired man with eyes bluer than the ocean and wrap my arms around his neck, moving my hips against his in rhythm with the music. His breath heavy with rum liquor he leans down and asks for my name, his lips so close to my ear, the words send a shiver over my body.

"Luci," I say, head swaying to the music. "What's yours?"

"Franco," he replies, pulling me tighter and digging his fingers into my skin. "You're so hot," he groans, nipping my earlobe with his teeth. The she-devil inside of me does a little happy dance as I turn around grinding my ass against Franco's crotch, thoroughly enjoying the fact that I can feel him getting hard beneath his jeans. He glides his hands down my waist and places his hands over my hips before bringing his mouth round to my neck, his tongue tracing the length from my ear lobe to my shoulder.

"You wanna take this somewhere quiet Princess?" he whispers low in my ear. I turn back to face him, shaking my head with a playful smile on my face.

"I'm happy here dancing," I counter, trying to keep it light and friendly. I know I said I wanted to get laid but not with this guy. I want to stay where I can be seen, you can never be too careful with strangers. I'm not stupid and I know I'll have earned myself a pat on the back from my brother dearest for sticking to my ground. I bring my arms back round to his neck and continue to move against him hoping he gets the hint. He takes a step back then grabs my wrist.

"Come on baby, it'll be fun just the two of us." Obviously he didn't get the hint. I stop dancing, getting a little annoyed now too.

"I said no." I pull my wrist from his grasp and step back slightly. His face is a picture of utter annoyance as he pulls me back towards him.

"Don't be such a cock tease, Princess."

With my buzz quickly dwindling away, I push him hard in the chest. "Piss off, you dick, don't you know how to have fun?" I snap, leaving him waving his hand in my face in frustration as he turns and leaves muttering under his breath.

Finding Kat lip locked with the hunky blonde she eyed earlier, I let her know I'm heading to the toilets. She gives me a quick flash of a smile before sticking her tongue back down his throat. I shake my head smiling to myself, she's always lucky on a night out. I walk through the bathroom doors bumping straight into a group of women pruning themselves in the mirror. Wearing next to nothing but small pieces of cloth that barely cover their fronts and come down just past their asses. My eyes go wide and my mouth falls open in shock.

"Watch it, bitch!" one of them spits, straightening out her poor excuse for a skirt.

"Uh sorry," I mumble, trying to squeeze behind them to get into a cubicle.

"Bitch almost knocked me out, did you see that girls?" I hear from behind the door as I sit down to pee. Great, just what I need now, a fucking fight with a group of drunk slappers.

"Oh give it a rest Roxi, you're only pissed because Cole keeps blowing you off and isn't answering your phone calls." I hear one of them say.

"He just doesn't know what he's missing, that's all. He's here somewhere, I know he is. I'll show him what he's missing out on."

After I hear them leave, I finish my business and slowly exit the cubicle. I wash my hands and primp myself up in the mirror and paint on a fresh layer of lippy. *I need a drink.* I wait a minute longer, ensuring the group of girls will have moved on before walking out and heading towards the bar, hoping not to bump into Tom, Franco or those scantily clad bitches for the rest of the night.

Chapter 9

Cole

The music is pulsating around me, sipping the harsh, cheap whiskey that is served in this place, I watch from the dark shadows of a corner booth. This place is filled with people moving like puppets on strings to the music. I can smell the sweat and grime from their skin, it seeps into the air creating a stale smell of body odor. It's a low end establishment, where creatures stalk their victims. I watch my prey, my little mouse dressed as a vixen. She is a siren hypnotizing me as her hips sway, making me hunger for her, my is cock tightening in my trousers at the sight of her tantalizing body. If anything the chase has me more enticed with her, I envisage watching her, stalking her and catching her being my favorite pleasure, my favorite game. She is quickly becoming an obsession. The silk black dress clings to her curves and her hot pink heels bring her from 5'4 to at least 5'9. I study her face, her mesmerizing green eyes, flushed cheeks and perfect lips. I imagine they'd fit beautifully around my cock. I can definitely see why Silas is intrigued. I'm not sure if I'll let him keep her yet, maybe we could share her.

I watch her whisper to her friend Kat, then she makes her way to the bar. I get to my feet to make my way over to the bar to get closer to her. She's leaning over to get the bartender's attention, the low cut of her dress leaving nothing to the imagination as I can see straight down her cleavage, her tits looking perfect and perky against the tight fabric.

I slide next to her as she is ordering her drink; Bacardi and coke. "Make that two" I interrupt. She looks over to me curiously. "Don't worry topolino, I'll get these."

"What does that mean?" she asks.

"Little mouse." I smirk. "Are you having fun tonight?"

She studies me before replying, "Yeah, I love the vibe. My friend and I just needed to let our hair down. Girls night out, yano?"

I look over to her friend and see she's already dancing with some blond guy. "Well it looks like your friend has hit it off with someone." I nod over to where her friend is dancing.

Lucille sighs but turns to me and smiles. "Well that means you'll have to keep me company, Tomcat," she winks.

She surprises me, that doesn't happen often. I thought she'd have run by now, maybe Silas won't get a choice in sharing her. "It would be my pleasure, Topolino. I have a private booth over in the corner if you want to join me." I reply, sipping my drink. She smiles and nods. We make our way over as she slips in the booth and I slide in next to her. "So what do you do for a living, Topolino?" I ask even though I already know, she smiles and I catch the sparkle in her eyes as she speaks.

"I'm a nurse, I work in emergency and wound care at Summerlin. What about you?"

Well that's a loaded question, "I own a restaurant, and I'm in business with my brother and a friend. I've always enjoyed cooking so it made sense for me to open my own restaurant." I answer, keeping it short and sweet.

"Oh wow, what restaurant? Maybe I'll sample it one day," she says cheerfully. She's so honest and good, I wonder if she'll mind me tainting her.

"My restaurant is called Salvatore's Cucina, if it wasn't obvious we serve Italian food." I say, smiling at her.

"That's amazing! I love Italian! Where did you learn to cook?" she continues. I love how she's chatting so easily to me, it makes me feel calm as her eyes pierce into my soul.

"Well my Nonna taught me and my brother to cook on Sunday afternoons when we were little." I loved Nonna, unfortunately she passed away when I was 15, she was a strong and beautiful lady, and a great cook. I scold myself at how open I've been with her. "How about you? What made you become a nurse?" I try to direct the conversation onto her instead. I need to know more about her life. I'm shocked but I really want to get to know her.

"Well I suppose I always liked helping people and it comes easily to me. I love the fast pace of the emergency room, it keeps my mind occupied," she says as she maintains eye contact with me, "actually you look very familiar, have you been to the hospital recently?"

That'll be the resemblance of my brother. I laugh and shake my head, "Not that I'm aware, Topolino." Instinctively, I reach out and tuck a piece of her hair that has fallen into her face behind her ear, trying to distract her. Her breathing quickens and her eyes dart to my lips, she wants me to kiss her. I edge closer to her, taking her face in the palms of my hand. My heart is pounding and I feel like a teenager again. How is this woman having such an affect on me? Not able to wait a second longer, I pull her face to mine and finally taste her sweet lips. She tastes like blueberries and I can smell her perfume of vanilla and lilacs. Her kiss is addictive, I don't know if I can stop. Her tongue dances with mine, and I can feel the lust in the little flicks of her dominance.

Lucille is the one to pull away first, her teeth grazing my lower lip as she does. Fuck I'm getting hard, I look down and notice her dress has ridden up her sun kissed thighs, making my cock harden even more. I just want to bury my head there until she can't take it anymore. Until the only thing I hear is her screaming my name. Whimpering for a release that only I can grant her.

Interrupting my thoughts of her sweet pussy my phone starts vibrating, I inwardly grunt. Looking down at the phone, it's Roxi, I hit the reject button immediately.

"That was unexpected," I smirk, keeping eye contact.

"You tasted like peppermint and moon light," she says blushing, making me realize she didn't mean to say it out loud.

Smiling at her I feel my phone vibrate again, I look again this time it's Linc. "I'll be back in just a moment, my fratello is calling. He's not very patient so if I ignore him he will keep calling, I'll be quick though Topolino."

"That's ok, I'll be waiting for you Tomcat," she winks at me. God, I love the way that sounds.

I make my way out to the nearest private room, a small store cupboard housing brooms, mops and cleaning equipment and bringing the phone to my ear. "What the fuck to do you want?" I hiss.

"What the fuck do I want? Where the fuck are you!? You were meant to accept the shipment before following Silas' pussy and you didn't show!! You had plenty of time to do it, Dimitri had to call me and now I'm stuck here sorting out your fuck up! Why didn't you call me earlier?." Linc is always so dramatic.

I roll my eyes. "It must have slipped my mind, I'm sure you have it handled my friend." With that I hang up. It didn't slip my mind, I got bored of waiting for it. I did tell Dimitri that I'd check the shipment later though. As one of our capo's, he should be able to check it in without me. Maybe I need to remind the little bitch who I am.

I leave the store room and head back to the booth. I'm eager to continue getting to know this girl who has me captivated already. But as I near the booth, I realize Topolino isn't there… has she run from me? I survey the

67

area and notice her bag is still on the seat. She must have been in a hurry. I quickly grab her bag and head out front. Looking around the parking lot I notice a man trying to fumble his way to his car. He has someone with him who appears to be unconscious. Realization hits me, it's that sleazeball Dr Graves bundling my girl into his car.

Rage ignites me, he's taking advantage of Lucille, or planning on doing so. Before I can think anymore I move quickly, silently advancing behind Dr Graves. I bring my arm around the fuckers throat and squeeze making him struggle and gasp for air. He tries to resist, clawing at my arm but fails as I tighten my grip and I happily watch his face drain of color as he collapses. Dragging him out of sight into a dark unlit area of the parking lot. I run to check on my little mouse. The fucker must have slipped her something, she's out cold. Carefully, I pick her up and take her to my car, laying her comfortably across the back seats. I retrieve my phone and make a call.

"Linc, if you've calmed down now I need you to pick up some trash for me, keep him alive though, I'd like to execute the punishment to this fucker myself." I reel off the location of Dr Graves and his car.

"I'll meet you back at the house with him. Don't leave me waiting too long for an explanation." Linc hangs up. He's still pissed but when I explain things with Dr Graves, he'll see how I've bought him a present to say sorry.

I glance in the mirror as I'm driving back to Lucille's house, she looks so beautiful bathed in moonlight. It lights a flame of anger in me that some creep, who is in a position of trust, was going to take advantage of her. My brothers and I may be murderers, thugs and borderline psychopaths but we do not tolerate abuse of women and children in any way, shape or form.

As I pull up outside her apartment, I open the door before carrying Lucille inside. Carefully, I lay her down on the bed. I can't help smiling that it's covered in my dried seed, If only it was her covered in me and begging. She looks like an angel, I only wish she was conscious so that I could really enjoy being in her bedroom with her. I'm itching to mark her, to make her mine in more ways than one. I push the thoughts away before I find it too hard to leave her.

As I bend down, I slip her shoes from her feet and carefully peel away her dress. Fuck, seeing her lay there in her lacy black thong has me reaching under my trousers for my cock again, stroking it at the sight of her. She starts to stir and rolls on to her side, not opening her eyes. Minute's later I'm exploding over her back. Feeling smug, I wonder whether I should clean her up or leave her covered in my cum. I opt for the latter, grabbing a purple throw from the corner chair and placing it over her. She gasps something in her sleep, sounds very much like Tomcat, this makes me smile. She's dreaming of me. I stay with her for a couple more hours to make sure she really is OK. I place a glass of water by her bedside and some Tylenol I found in her medicine cabinet in the bathroom and just before I leave I write a note, I know I shouldn't but I can't resist.

I simply write; *I'll be seeing you Topolino.*

With one last glance, I leave locking the door behind me.

I drive back home to the house Silas, Linc and I share, with anger building inside of me as I remember what's awaiting me. Entering the gates, I drive and park around back. Stepping out of the car I look to the night sky and sigh "Cogliere la notte," before heading inside and down to the basement, where our playroom waits with my honored guest; Dr.Graves.

I open the door to the room housing the one way mirror that looks into our interrogation room. I glance through to see Dr Graves strapped to a chair, unconscious.

"So, are you going to explain why you had me kidnap an unconscious doctor?" Linc snaps.

"Well my dear friend, this piece of shit was just about to take advantage of il mio topolino." I say, not caring that I let slip my endearment.

"Who the fuck is your little mouse dude?" He snarls back at me.

Looking around the room I see our tools laid out ready for me. I walk over to inspect which I'll be using on the Doc, ignoring Lincs question.

"Cole, this is not the time to go psycho about some girl you don't even know!" He shouts at me.

I turn to Linc and smile, "Oh but brother I do know her, I've been watching her and I've decided, if she agrees, that we should share her. You'd like her, Linc, she's sassy, cute and beautiful."

Linc interrupts me, holding a hand up to argue. "Share her? You are out of your mind!? Silas won't agree with this. And I haven't even met her, Cole!"

I laugh because it doesn't matter what he says, I know this girl is for us, "You will see Linc, she's perfect. Her tits are phenomenal, her lips will look so good around our cocks."

Linc splutters cuss words at me both a mix of English and Italian and I can't help but laugh more, he gets so worked up over the inevitable.

When he finally calms down he looks at me dead in the eye with a finger pointed towards my face, "I don't know how the fuck you have seen her tits but *you* can explain this to Silas. I'll be staying out of it, but I'll agree that if this prick did try to take advantage of Lucille he definitely needs to pay."

Grinning back at him I reply, "Finally something we both agree on."

Returning to the arsenal of blades in front of me. I start to sing "Eenie, meenie, minie, mo. Catch a doctor by the toe. If he squeals, let him go. Eenie, meenie, minie, mo. Should we let him go Brother if he squeals?"

Linc rolls his eyes, "That would depend on how loudly and sincerely he squeals Brother."

With that in mind, I decide to use one of my favorite knives to torture our captive. He's already strapped to our iron chair but he's too unconscious for my liking. Linc looks my way and smirks as I pick up my favorite blade, the BC-41. It's beautifully made, the handle in the form of a knuckle duster made from cast iron. And I recently had the blade sharpened which excites me even more.

Linc says, "Care to make this interesting Cole? I say he pisses himself before you even make the first cut."

I laugh "Deal, if he pisses himself before I make him bleed, I'll let you be the first to have Lucille's lips around your cock."

Linc frowns then smirks, "OK, add on 10k and you have yourself a deal." He loves getting his cock sucked, so I knew he'd agree. It had nothing to do with the money, he doesn't need it and neither do I. It's just a way for him to deny being curious about my little mouse. We shake hands before we make our way through to Dr Graves.

Linc removes a syringe from his pocket and stabs Dr Graves in the neck with it, immediately waking him up with a hacking cough.

"Nice of you to join us Dr Graves." I chuckle as his eyes widen and dance around the room, I can see his little cogs turning, wondering how he got here.

"Where am I? Who are you? I think you've got the wrong person," he babbles.

71

"No we definitely have the right guy, don't we fratello?" Linc remarks, tipping his chin towards me.

"Dr Graves, it seems so formal, can I call you Tom? That's what you get your colleagues to call you, right?" I ask.

"Sure, but I don't know what you want from me. Please, if it's money I'll give it to you, just let me out of here," he begs.

My lip curls in disgust, fucking pussy is going to make me lose my bet with Linc. "We are richer than sin Tom, we don't need your fucking money." I snap causing him to flinch.

Linc looks to me and then to Tom. "So do you remember what happened before waking up in this wonderful place?" he asks, throwing his arms out, gesturing to the room.

"I don't know, I was out with some colleagues. I was giving one of the girls a lift home, she'd has too much to drink." He replies, not looking me or Linc in the eyes. What a fucking liar.

"So, Tom everytime you lie, I'm going to make you bleed. How many times have you lied so far? Hmm?"

Tom gasps at my statement but lies again. "I haven't lied, honestly. It wasn't what it looked like."

Bingo! It was exactly what it looked like you piece of shit, otherwise you wouldn't have said that. Instead of voicing the fact I move quickly towards him and slash the knife across his skin, once below his ribs and another on his bicep. He screams instantly, "Stop please!" he pleads as tears appear in his eyes and the smell of urine burns my nostrils. That didn't take long, on the plus side, I won our bet. Linc is going to be pissed but if I'm generous maybe I'll still let him be first into Lucille's pretty mouth.

I smirk up at Linc "Don't be a sore loser, Brother."

He huff's as he turns and punches Tom in the gut. "That's for making me lose, you piece of shit."

I explode with laughter, I must sound like a mad man. Tom is coughing, trying to catch his breath.

"So let's try that again. What were you planning on doing to Lucille Holland?"

Tom's eyes widen knowing that I've caught him out. "It's not how it seemed, I wasn't going to rape her," he rushes out.

Linc snaps, "So what!? You bundle her in your car and take her home after drugging her?"

Tom splutters, "No, no I didn't. I just wanted her to relax." That's it, this fucker lied again, twice. I stab him in the leg this time and then slash my blade through his ankle.

"Next time you lie, I won't miss an artery, Tom. Did you want her relaxed so you could take advantage? She wouldn't be able to stop your advances unconscious would she? Think carefully about your answer now Tom." I taunt, pointing the blade towards his neck.

Dr Graves looks from me to Linc and gulps. "Ok, I was going to try something with her but I wouldn't have done anything she didn't already want."

Linc roars at him, "How the fuck could she say she didn't want it Doc!? She was unconscious! You knew what you were going to do, didn't you!?" Linc smashes his fist into the sobbing doctor's face, splitting his lip, splashing blood onto the already bloodied floor.

Tom is hysterical now, with blood and saliva running down his chin, "Please, I didn't want to hurt her, I just wanted to feel her so badly."

Before I get the chance, Linc grabs his gun from his waist and shoots Tom in the foot.
His strangled screams perforate the air before he's begging for his life once more "I'm sorry, I'm sorry, I'll never go near her again. I'll do anything just don't kill me."

"The thing is Tom, I don't believe you and quite frankly you've already now tried to touch what didn't belong to you so what's stopping you trying this with another woman? It really doesn't sit well with us."

His words are barely audible. "Please don't kill me, please."

"Calm down Tom, I'm going to give you some options. A; You leave town and never look back but you will owe us a favor that we will call in anytime we wish and you will deliver without question. On top of that, if you so much as look at a woman in an unwanted way, we will find out and we will hunt you down and peel your skin from your flesh. Or option B; You stay and we will peel your skin from your flesh right now. So what do you say Tom?"

Dr Graves turns pale, I realize he's losing a lot of blood so he's probably on the tip of going into shock.

"Ok, ok I'll owe you and I'll leave. I promise I won't ever do this again, I'm sorry!"

"Good answer Tom, now let's get you sorted out. I think you've lost a lot of blood but I'm no doctor," I cackle then punch him with the knuckle duster part of the BC-41, knocking him out cold and probably breaking his nose at the same time.

"I'll call our guys to patch him up and make sure he leaves the city tonight." Linc adds, pulling out his phone to arrange the crew.

"Hey Linc, if you want I'll still let you have Lucille's pretty mouth but you gotta get on board with sharing." I tease. Linc just shakes his head and leaves the room ordering the clean up. I remove the BC-41 from my hand and head upstairs to get cleaned up before getting Topolino's key cut and the original returned before she realizes it's missing.

I shout to Linc who is now in the kitchen. "Oh and my friend, we need to have a chat about our capo Dimitri!" I follow him and wait for his reply.

"What do you mean?" he sighs.

"Well fratello, it seems he told you that I didn't show for the shipment but I told him that he was to sort it out and I would come by in the morning to do a final check. But instead the little bitch went running his mouth to you."

Linc looks murderous. "So he disobeyed orders and then lied to me?"

Yawning, I say, "Seems that way"

Linc nods, "We will chat with Silas about replacing him as soon as he's back on the throne, from what I hear, Silas has a friend in prison that would fit perfectly but we gotta bust him out first."

I smirk, "Well I'll leave that one to you, considering I've got enough to fill him in about with Topolinos delectable body."

Linc shakes his head. "Go shower before you scare someone with all that blood on you."

Fuck the shower, it's time to go watchout for my new playmate

.

Chapter 10

Lucille

Opening my eyes to the blinding sunlight coming through my bedroom window I groan, my throat feeling as if I've swallowed the entirety of the Sahara Desert. My head throbs instantly and I begin to feel overwhelmingly nauseous as I try to remember how I got home, undressed and into bed. "Oh God, I feel disgusting." Rubbing my eyes as I rest myself up against the headboard of my bed, waiting for the dizziness to pass. I feel sweaty and sticky, I need a damn shower. Half expecting to see some random guy lay next to me, I'm surprised when I glance around the room and realize it's only me. I notice a glass of water and some Tylenol already waiting for me on my nightstand. Without a second thought I reach over and pop the pills straight into my mouth before drinking the entire glass of water in one.

After waiting several minutes for the Tylenol to kick in, I finally muster up enough energy to get myself out of bed, catching sight of myself in the mirror as I do. Jesus I look a sight, it's a good job a guy *didn't* come back home with me last night to wake up to this. I shake my head trying to put the events of last night together. The last clear thing I remember is dancing and getting a drink at the bar, after that it all goes a little fuzzy. OH GOD, what if it was Tom that brought me back? With nausea hitting me again I stumble straight for the bathroom and throw up, my aim barely making it into the toilet bowl. Leaning back against the tiled wall and wiping the vomit from my mouth, I sit for a few minutes debating whether or not to get back into bed but hear my phone ringing from the bedroom. Dragging myself up to answer it, I croak a single "Hello?" sitting gingerly back down on the edge of the bed as my stomach threatens me again.

"Oh, so you are alive then!" Kat shouts down the receiver at me.

"Oh my God, not so loud woman." I wince. "I have the WORST head ever this morning, and what do you mean alive? Didn't you bring me home?" I ask, a little confused.

"Ummm no," she mocks, "you told me you were getting a drink. I look over to see you talking to some hottie at the bar, next thing I know you've bloody vanished and I'm having a heart attack. Bitch, I could kill you."

Leaning my head forward into my hands, I take a few deep steadying breaths. "Kat, I don't remember a fucking thing, I have no idea how I got home. I woke up in my underwear, in bed for Christ sake and I'm disgustingly sticky. God knows what the hell happened when whoever it was brought me back." I open my eyes looking down at the floor, whatever Kat is saying now is incomprehensible. My vision blurs over, then focusing again I notice a piece of paper that's sticking out from under the bed. Leaning forward I pick it up and read -*I'll be seeing you, Topolino*- handwritten in black ink across the page. Tomcat! I gasp as a vision flashes before my eyes of dark hair and soft lips.

"Luce. LUCE, LUCILLE! HELLO!? Are you still there?" I hear Kat shouting through the phone.

"Yes, yes, I'm here," I say, my voice barely above a whisper "he left a note."

"HE WHAT!? WHO?!" she shouts down my ear again.

"He left a note, the guy from last night at the bar. He left a note saying he'll see me soon." I say, re-reading it over and over as if the words would change before me.

"What a fucking creep, I'm coming over," she replies and before giving me chance to say no, she hangs up.

I flop backwards onto the bed, searching the very depths of my memory for anything else that I remember from last night but come up with nothing.

Being unable to tolerate the way I feel in myself anymore, I take the hottest shower possible and scrub my skin until it's red raw. Kat has already let herself in by the time I'm finished and is sat on my bed looking at the note when I walk back into the bedroom like it could grow legs at any minute and run away.

"I'm not sure if this is extremely hot or extremely fucking creepy," she says, shaking her head looking wide eyed at me.

"Yeah, tell me about it." I reply, pulling on a fresh pair of clothes. "It doesn't help that I don't know who it was. I don't even think he told me his name and christ how the hell did he know where I lived? I never give out my address. It's a number one rule."

She looks at me with her mouth wide open. "You don't think he... you know?" she nods to the bed, "do you?" I know exactly what she's insinuating and the thought alone makes my skin crawl.

"NO, no way. I woke up wearing my underwear and I'm pretty sure I'd know."

Kat releases an audibly loud sigh of relief. "Thank God!" she says, "How are you feeling?"

"I'm okay, he left me some Tylenol and water on the bedside table too, if he was a creep he wouldn't have done that. But still. I don't know, it's weird, I just don't understand. Anyway, what happened to you last night?" I question, hoping to distract her.

"Well," she starts, pulling her legs up and getting comfortable. "I obviously hit things off with Brendan, the blond guy I was dancing with. He ended up taking me back to mine after I couldn't find you. I let him convince me you'd let the guy you were with take you home, and well, let's just say I definitely didn't wake up with my underwear on." She squeals, kicking her legs out like an excited child and I can't help but smile at her wicked ways.

"You lucky bitch, how was it? I need to know everything and don't spare me any details. Let me live vicariously through your sexual activities." I laugh.

Kat talks me through every single detail of her raunchy escapade with Brendan leaving me feeling somewhat jealous and a little bit empty. "Sounds like you had enough fun for the both of us last night." I joke, scraping my hair back into a scrunchie.

"Oh it was something Luce, he was something," she sighs, staring out into the middle of nowhere.

I roll my eyes at her. "Come on bitch, I need a coffee and we've got to get the kids from Max's. I told him we'd take them for breakfast." With that she jumps up and skips out of the bedroom.

"Wow, if I knew you would move that quick I would have said it sooner." I laugh as she's already on her way out through the front door.

Pulling up outside Max's house, I side eye Kat as she applies a fresh coat of lipgloss and smooths down the flyaways of hair that are escaping her ponytail resting tight atop her head.

She smiles at me and shrugs, "I can't help it, I don't want Max to see me looking like a dog," she says so nonchalantly as she climbs out of the car.

"No I get it, but you and I both know you'd look hot in a fucking bin bag you cow, and even in a bin bag, given the chance he'd still. . ." I start, before being cut off by Max opening the front door.

"He would still what?" He asks with his arms crossed as he leans against the door frame, eyes bouncing between the two of us and a playful smug pulling on his lips.

"Nothing, just ignore your idiot sister." Kat snaps shoving past us both as she walks into the house.

"You dick." I chuckle as I playfully punch Max's arm before walking past him to find Teddy and Isabella sat on the sofa together watching cartoons.

"MOMMY!" they both shout when they see us, both of them clambering over each other to get to us.

"Hey baby boy!" I throw Teddy up in the air and catch him in my arms. "Have you been a good boy for your Uncle Max?" I ask, nuzzling into his neck.

"Yes Mommy," he replies, a huge toothy smile plastered across his face. I glance over at Max and he smiles and nods his head in confirmation.

"Good boy," I say, kissing the top of his head as I lower him back to his feet. "How do you two little angels fancy going for some breakfast?"

"YEAH!!" they shout in unison again making us all laugh.

"Come on then monkeys, go grab your bags and let's get going. Auntie Kat will eat her shoe if she has to wait any longer for some food," I joke.

"Or I might just eat both of you," she shouts as she grabs Isabella and Teddy, tickling them till they're screaming with laughter. I love the bond we all have. Katrina isn't related by blood but Teddy has always known her as his Auntie Kat. She treats Teddy like her own, the same way I treat Isabella as my own too. It's times like this I feel blessed to have such an amazing little family all of my own.

I look up to see Max staring at the interaction before us, his eyes giving him away, showing affection he very rarely reveals. His character is hard and serious, his physique strong and tough and it goes against everything he knows and against every set of rules he has been brought up by. I can see the kindness behind his tough exterior though. I know it isn't his fault, his father is a cruel man, a mafia boss who wanted nothing more than to turn his heir into a relentless, merciless, killing machine. Max always told me when I was younger I got a lucky escape by not being of his fathers blood.

I never understood why until I got older and walked into what can only be described as a scene from a horror movie in the dining room to our old family home. Max's father stood in the middle of the room, covered in blood with a knife in one hand and something that almost resembled a mushed up squid, which I later found out was the man's heart in the other. He had a smile I can only recount as pure evil, the devil in human form. A very dead, very mutilated body lay beneath him, bleeding into my mothers rug. She wasn't best pleased that day to say the least. But it painted that man in a whole new light for me, our relationship was never the same after that. I was much more cautious not to end up on his bad side. The image still haunts my sleep some nights, a repeated nightmare where I can never escape, the satanic beast ripping my heart out and devouring it before I die. It always ends with me waking in a fit of panic until I realize I'm not seconds from death.

Max catches my eye and stiffens, straightening up his shoulders before he turns and walks off into the kitchen. With Kat and the kids now in a giggling heap on the floor, I follow him and close the door behind me. "What are you doing?" I ask, shaking my head at him.

"What do you mean?" He responds, his back towards me with his hands resting either side of him on the kitchen counter.

"You know exactly what I mean Max." I state. "I'm not blind, I see the way you look at her when you think nobody is watching. Why do you keep her so far away?"

"You wouldn't understand Luce, you're nothing like me. You don't know the things I do. I would never be good enough for her." he sighs, then turning to face me. "It can't happen."

"Oh piss off Max, what a joke. Get off your high horse. You think I'm completely oblivious to what you do? Your drug smuggling, big man mafia bullshit. I can see your gun under your jacket from here. I leave my SON with you. Do you think I don't know what you're doing when you're in a *business meeting* for fuck sake?" I can feel the anger seething inside of me now as I start to pace the room.

"Luce, I would NEVER bring work to my door when Teddy is here. He is always safe with me, I promise and you know that. I would never jeopardize his safety."

"So what's the problem then?" I spit at him, throwing my hands up in annoyance. "Why are you so against having a relationship with Kat? Is it not the same?"

His frustration is clearly evident by this point, I can visibly see the veins fit to burst in his neck. "I'm going to say this only once Lucille so I suggest you take heed," he warns through gritted teeth, "you need to forget this romantic fantasy you have of me and Katrina because it is NEVER going to happen. Now drop it." His jaw rigid and tense, I can feel the anger rolling off of him in waves. I know my brother well enough to know when to stop pushing for now but this isn't over.

The tension is cut as Teddy hurtles through the kitchen door with Katrina and Isabella close behind him. "Mommy we're ready, can we go for breakfast now please?" he chimes, pulling on my arm.

I narrow my eyes at Max letting him know this isn't over and turn to Teddy with a smile. "Of course baby, let's go."

"Are you coming too Uncle Max?" Teddy asks, running over to him.

Max breaks eye contact with me and crouches down to ruffle the top of his hair. "Not today little man, I've got some

82

work to do, promise I'll come next time though." Teddy nods his head as he leans forward to give his uncle a hug then runs off towards the front door singing "breakfast breakfast breakfast" with Isabella by his side. I nod towards Max and turn to leave, Kat watches me suspiciously, I return her gaze with a look that lets her know not to ask, then follow Teddy out towards the car.

After listening to the kids begging for pancakes since they got into the car, we head straight to The Original Pancake House. Sliding into a booth opposite Kat, while Teddy and Isabella pick out their milkshake flavors with the waitress at the counter, she looks at me expectantly. "How much did you hear?" I ask, accepting the inevitable.

"Almost all of it," she sighs, "why did you have to say anything?"

I crease my brow, a flutter of irritation momentarily sweeping over me. "Because he's got his head up his ass and can't see what's right in front of him. He likes you Kat, I see it everytime you're around him. The way he looks at you, the way he is with Bella. I had to say something." I reach forward and grab her hands in mine. "I'm sorry if I've made anything awkward between the two of you now but I couldn't hold it in any longer."

Kat sighs and drops her head forward onto her arms outstretched towards mine. "I know you had the best intentions, but sometimes your timing is so well off." she mumbles. "You could have at least let me have a taste before you shattered my dreams. He might have been eager if he thought it would just be a good fuck," she moans lifting her head.

I cringe, feeling guilty about denying her the chance of ever sleeping with my brother and sheepishly mouth the words "I'm sorry" as Teddy and Isabella return to the table carrying two large strawberry milkshakes topped with a heap of whipped cream, sprinkles and a cherry.

"Look Mommy," Isabella says as she slides in besides Kat.

"Wow sweetheart, that looks amazing, can I try some?" she asks before dunking her finger into the cream and sucking it from the tip of her finger.

"Mommyyyyyyy!" Bella moans and pulls her milkshake away causing us all to laugh.

We spend a whole two hours at breakfast, with Kat and I chatting away like we always do, putting the world to rights and having a moan about work and how busy it seems to be lately. It's almost like people just hurt themselves for the sake of it sometimes.

"You'll never guess what happened to me on Friday morning!?" Kat says with an excited grin on her face.

"Oh God, what was it? Mr Fitzgerald didn't come back in with a sore on his backside did he?" I ask, stifling a giggle at the memory of Kat and I having to help restrain a rather large gentleman so another nurse could apply some salve and a dressing onto a Mr Fitzgerald's back passage after he claimed to have fallen onto a gardening rake.

"No, but that would have made my week if he had come back in with another excuse for shoving something up his ass!" Kat exclaimed, almost making me choke on my forkful of strawberries. "Do you remember that really hot nurse from x-ray, Ethan? Well, it turns out we were wrong, Ethan is in fact not gay, and knows exactly how to prove it," she chirps winking at me.

My mouth hangs open in complete shock. "You did not!?"

"Oh I did nothing. I let him do all the work," she smirks at me from behind her coffee.

"You lucky bitch." I whisper excitedly, making sure the kids don't overhear. "Tell me everything."

Kat giggles in response but taps her nose and winks. "You have enough to keep you busy Missy, let me have this one all to myself," she says, shaking her head and grinning from ear to ear.

"Oh you sly cow Katrina Henderson!" I chide. "Fine, if you want to play it like that. No more kiss and tell from me either." I joke as we finish our meals. She knows I'd tell her anyway so there's no point in threatening it.

After switching the conversation to something more child-friendly, we wait for Teddy and Isabella to finish off their milkshakes before leaving, making sure to tip the waitress as we go. Kat gives us a ride back home, then her and Isabella leave to go home too, much to Teddy's disappointment. He wanted Bella to stay for a playdate but Kat said they had to get home, promising another day soon.

Teddy and I spend the following day playing out in the sun, making pictures out of anything we can find around the communal pool outside of the apartment and using the flowers as makeshift paint brushes to draw patterns on the tiled floor.

"Do you want a drink Tedster? Then we can walk over to the park for a bit before dinner." I call from the double doors leading out onto the patio.

"Yes please Mommy, can I have some lemonade?" he shouts back at me, not even raising his head, still concentrating hard on placing leaves down into the shape of a giant dinosaur on the floor. I turn around and jump at the sight of Max standing in front of me.

"Jesus Christ Max!" I gasp. "You almost gave me a heart attack. What's wrong with knocking or announcing that you're here, you dick?" I say between shallow breaths.

"Just proving a point," he replies, glancing over my shoulder towards Teddy outside. "Look, I'm not here to stay, I wanted to apologize for yesterday. I want you to understand that with my job, I simply can not get involved." He runs his hand up through his hair, his decision straining

85

his face. "Katrina is worth more than just a quick fuck, okay?" He admits, "I just can't get involved like that."

I sigh in resignation. "Fine." I deflate, before pulling the lemonade out of the fridge. "Want some?" I offer as I pour out a glass for Teddy and myself, he declines and shakes his head.

The silence between us is cut short by an excited, "Uncle Max!" as Teddy wanders through the back door.

"Hey buddy," he says.

"Drink up honey then we'll get going." I cut in, grabbing my purse, keys and phone off the dining table.

"Are you coming to the park too?" Teddy asks between large gulps of his lemonade, wide eyes full of pleading as he looks up to Max who pauses for a moment, glancing over at me, unsure on how to answer.

"Sure, I'll walk with you but I can't stay long. I've got to get back to work."

Teddy beams at his uncle with happiness. "YES!" he cheers, fist pumping the air. "I'll get my airplane and we can fly it from the top of the climbing frame," he giggles excitedly as he runs towards his bedroom to retrieve the toy.

Most of the ten minute walk to Oxford Park is filled with Teddy teaching us what he's learnt at kindergarten this week. Telling us all about his new favorite book, about superheros and letting us know that he has the best lunchbox out of all of his friends because it has Iron Man on it and he is better than the HULK. I stare at him as he chats away to us both, his innocence with everything really going on in the big bad world weighing on me like a blackened rain cloud, threatening to burst at any moment. What a world it is for my brother to bury his feelings for a woman due to his job. What a world it is for me to glance over my shoulder at every turn to make sure I'm not being followed? What bigger problems there are than who has the best lunchbox?

"Are you okay Mommy?" He asks. Damn my child for being so intuitive.

"Yes baby boy, I'm fine." I answer, forcing the sincerest of smiles.

"Hey, Ted man. I bet I can beat you in a race from here to the sand at the bottom of the climbing frame!" Max goads playfully trying to distract him from asking any further questions.

Without any hesitation at all, Ted screams excitedly, "READY, STEADY, GO!" at the top of his lungs as he sprints off in the direction of the park and I can not help but laugh as I hear Max utter " you little shit" before he sprints off after him. I am grateful for the distraction as I hate pretending everything is alright. I'm now alone again with my ever intrusive thoughts as I walk slowly behind them.

The park's play area consists of a large metal climbing frame fit with a slide, foot bridge, climbing ramps, a fireman's pole and several different levels to climb across, surrounded by individual rocking seats that are fixed on top of a large metal spring, embedded into the ground. There are only two other adults here, a middle aged woman and her two kids and a man sat further out on one of the benches smoking a cigarette, dark sunglasses covering his eyes. I assume he is with the other boy who looks to be around seven, kicking a football back and forth between a post just past the edge of the sand barrier surrounding the climbing area.

"Mommy, Mommy, did you see me win? I beat Uncle Max!" Teddy runs up to me, his happy beaming face pulling away my attention.

"Yes baby, you were so fast, well done!" I smile, leaning down and kissing the top of his head. "Now go and play for a bit, I'll be right over here on this bench, okay?" I say, pointing towards the bench off to the left.

"Okay," he chirps before skipping off towards the slide. Max walks over to me, his eyes scanning the entire perimeter of the park as he does. I watch as he pauses momentarily in the direction of the lone guy sat on the bench at the back, then continues to sit down, obviously not finding what or who he was looking for.

"I want you to come to the warehouse meet on Saturday night," he says, cracking his knuckles and resting his elbows on his knees. "There's a fight night and I want you to be there."

I cock my eyebrow at him in confusion. "Why?" I question. "Are you planning on needing some first aid or something?" I add laughing to myself.

"Yeah actually," he dead-pans, looking me square in the face. "These fight nights aren't exactly on the radar, if you know what I mean. I've seen some pretty nasty shit and we could do with a good pair of hands to help patch up after. It's harder than you think trying to get a doctor on the payroll for a one off, the greedy fuckers."

I stare at him open mouthed for a minute before realizing he really isn't joking. "Oh shit, you're being serious?"

"Yes Luce, I'll pick you up. Saturday 10pm. Wear something you don't mind getting a little blood on." he instructs as he takes a stand to leave. "And for fucksake, do NOT say anything to anybody. Especially Kat." he adds, a tone of authority to his voice "I mean it."

"OK, OK." I agree, holding my hands up in defeat. "I won't say a word," and with that he turns and leaves.

Chapter 11

Silas

Today is the day I walk out of this place for good. It's 5.45am, I nudge Nicholas to wake him. "Nicholas, wake up, they'll come for me soon and I need to set some things straight with you."

Nicholas rolls over and rubs his eyes, squinting at me as he says, "If this is you about to confess your undying love for me Si, then I gotta tell you, I'm heterosexual."

Cheeky fucker "You wouldn't be able to pull a guy as pretty as me Nick so don't go getting your hopes up." We have always had great banter, I'm going to miss this. "But seriously Nicholas, you will be out in a few months and I'll have that spot in my crew for you, don't pass it up."

Nicholas simply nods "Wouldn't dream of it." The bell rings out for 6am wake up.

"This is it then Nick, I'll see you on the other side." With that, I stand and wait for the guards to come and collect me. I'm looking forward to seeing my brother and best friend but I'm also eager to find la mia luce.

Snapping me out of my thoughts, the guards shout, "Stand back inmate," at me. I step backwards thinking if they spoke to me this way outside of these walls I would have shot them through the head already. I count in my head to ten and wait for them to tell me to follow.

"This way Mr Salvatore, you'll soon be a free man again," the guard calls.

I follow them out of the pod and through into the office where my lawyer, Stephanie Lewis, awaits me. "Good to see you Mr Salvatore, we have a few things to sign and I have brought the clothes your associates gave me for you to change into," she acknowledges, dipping her head.

"Thank you Miss Lewis, I appreciate your hard work," I praise as she hands me a suit bag. I cannot wait to strip these awful clothes off and slip into my Brioni suit. I'd strip down now if I didn't think Miss Lewis would melt in a puddle and not be able to continue her job. I've only been imagining one woman I want to be completely naked with, with her lips around my cock for the last ten days, and it hasn't been my lawyer. So politely I ask for a private place to change my clothes.

Stephanie points to the room attached and says, "You'll find a washroom with a single shower through there. I took the liberty of stocking it with toiletries."

"Thanks, I'll be back." I nod at her and excuse myself to the washroom. I wash quickly and redress, this suit feels amazing. I am starting to feel like my old self already as I look in the mirror. I straighten my tie and give myself a final once over before strolling into the room and taking a seat next to Miss Lewis. She shows me where to sign and explains the conditions of my release. Of course I don't agree with them but I sign the dotted line regardless.

"I think that is everything Mr Salvatore, you are a free man. I will walk you out and then process these papers." Stephanie leads the way out of the prison and gives me a bag of belongings that I brought with me when I first arrived here.

As I walk down the steps I see a red Lamborghini waiting for me. The only person I know who would think it's a good idea to pick me up from lock up in a Lamborghini is my brother, Cole.

"Fratello," Cole sighs as we embrace for the first time in almost nineteen months.

"Good to see you, let's get out of here," I admit, eager to get as far away from here as possible.

"Here you go," Cole says, moving to the passenger side and chucking the keys to me.

"You must have missed me if you are collecting me and letting me drive your favorite car brother."

"There is nothing I wouldn't do for you brother," he states. I know it to be true as I feel the same.

"Let's get going then." I agree, sliding into the driver's seat as Cole settles into the passenger seat. The roar of the engine makes me smile. Cole hands me a pair of sunglasses and I spin the back wheels as we leave the prison in the rearview mirror.

After a ten minute drive in comfortable silence, I refuse to wait any longer, "Anything to fill me in about the business?"

"Same as last time I spoke to you. Dimitri is trying to pull the wool over our eyes, I don't trust him and I think we should watch him carefully but other than that it's all good," he answers, with no hint of emotion in his tone.

"What about Lucille Holland? Did Linc do any more digging?" I question.

"Well, fratello, you'd have to quiz Lincoln about that, you know I'm the watcher not the researcher," Cole says with an underlying note in his voice.

"As long as you're only watching brother," I warn.

"You never did like sharing your toys," Cole remarks. I glare at him knowing he's just trying to tease me but I still fight the feeling that there's something I'm missing. Finally we are on the highway and I put my foot down on the gas and feel the full speed of this beautiful car, feeling free for the first time in so long.

"Shall we get breakfast? I haven't had pancakes for such a long time," I ask Cole.

"Anything you want brother, you want a hooker to join us? I can call Cherry, she was always eager for your cock, she could suck you off while you eat." Cole says with a chuckle. The trouble is if I said yes, I know he'd make it happen, and I don't want anyone but la mia Luce.

"The pancakes will do for now Cole." Breakfast first, then I'll need to get back to business and hopefully the pleasure that is Lucille Holland.

We pull up at a place called Kim's Diner. This is where, as boys, me and Linc would take Cole for pancakes when we wanted to escape our fathers. I park the car as Cole says, "You know Kim is going to be gushing over you when we step through those doors." I smile, knowing that's exactly what she'll do. Kim is the owner of this little diner if the name didn't give it away. She's in her late fifties and is like the aunty we never had growing up, always spoiling us with extras on our plate, pinching our cheeks and never taking no for an answer.

As we step through, the bell above the door jingles and Kim pops her head from over the counter and squeals at the sight of us, "My boys!!! I've missed you! Let's get you seated and fill up your bellies. You two have some explaining to do!! Why have you left it so long?" Me and Cole laugh and do as we are told as she usher's us to a table. She calls over one of the servers as we get comfortable "Stacey, get these boys anything they want," then turns to us, "I'll be back in a second to hear all about what you've been up to." She hurries off towards the kitchen.

The waitress, Stacey, smiles and pulls out her pad and pen "What can I get y'all?" She looks barely 18, with strawberry blonde hair, a slim build and a faceful of freckles.

"Just two black coffees and two stacks of pancakes with syrup and bacon," I say without looking at the menu, Aunty Kim's pancakes are the best.

"OK they'll be out in a jiffy," Stacey remarks cheerfully and goes to put our order in the kitchen.

"So Cole, where is Linc?" I ask.

"Oh you know Linc, he's got a stick in his ass about having to go over a shipment. Plus he's taken Alessandro out for the day," Coles adds. Alessandro is Lincs son, he would be 7 now. That kid hasn't had it easy with his mother overdosing. He means the world to Linc obviously but also to me and Cole, we treat him as our own, he's family.

I nod in acknowledgement. "How's Alessandro getting on with school? Is he coping OK since his mother?"

"He's doing alright, I think he misses her a great deal, even though she wasn't the best mother to him. Linc finds that hard to understand at times but I've had chats with Alesso about it. He's a smart, level headed kid, just needs time like we did," Cole explains. When Alessandro's mother died I was in lock up, so I haven't been able to speak to the kid about it or I'd have been there for him like I wanted. I know Cole will have stepped up, he always took our mother's death harder than I did so I know he'll have helped Alesso through it too.

I nod my thanks "Thank you brother for stepping up, not just with the business but in place of me with Alesso, it means a great deal to me and Lincoln, you know this." Cole just nods as Aunty Kim comes rushing over with two cups and a pot of coffee.

"So my boys, where is my dear Lincoln?" she asks.

"He's with his boy today, Aunty K" Cole smiles.

"Oh he needs to bring him here so I can spoil him like I spoil you boys. Now tell me everything, how have you been?" Kim asks, directing the last part at me.

"First place I come from lock up is to see you Aunty K. I'm happy to be out, I just wanted somewhere familiar before I'm back to business," I tell her, knowing she would never judge, she never has.

"Oh my boys, my diner and doors are always open to you whenever you need to get away." She wraps her arms around me in an embrace, then pulls away placing her hand on my cheek. "Don't leave it too long next time! Here comes your pancakes and bacon, so I'll leave you to it. Oh and Cole, stay out of trouble!" she laughs, knowing him too well. Out of the three of us, he was the one that always found himself in a tangle.

"I'll try Aunty K, but I can't promise anything," he hollers back to her. Stacey the waitress brings our pancakes and bacon out and I demolish them in a few mouthfuls. First real food since entering prison and it's amazing. I'll be having to work out a hell of a lot if I keep enjoying food like this though.

After we settle the bill and head back to the Lamborghini, Cole taps the roof of the car "Where to next fratello?"

"Home, brother," I smile. I'm more than ready to get back to business and to find out all about la mia Luce.

Chapter 12

Lincoln

I inhale deeply, pulling at the cigarette between my lips, feeling the heaviness of the smoke seep deep into my lungs before releasing it out into the air in front of me. I really should quit smoking, but it's an easy way to keep my hands busy when I'm not at work.

Sitting quietly by myself on a bench in Oxford Park, listening to the birds singing in the trees above and the shouts of men playing at the baseball pitch behind me. I watch Alessandro kicking his football back and forth against a pole between the spring seats in the park. His wavy brown hair flopping down into his eyes, casting the perfect mirror image of his mother. I inhale another drag on my cigarette, a vivid memory flashing before my eyes. It's only been 18 months since I found her body stiff and cold from an overdose. Thank God it was me who found her and not Alesso. We may not have always gotten along, and there was no love there in the end, but I never would have wished for that to the mother of my child. Her eyes were nothing more than two deep pits in her skull. The fresh track marks still littered her skin along with the scars from all the times she'd shot up before.

The poor kid, he still doesn't understand why she left, he asks if she loved him and I know that she did, but if she did, why did she do it? An ice cold chill spreads over my body causing me to shudder and I vow to myself never to put anything of the sort into my body so long as I have Alesso to care for. That boy is my whole entire life.

A few moments later, I sit and watch as a boy a little younger than Alesso, runs straight into the park shortly followed by a man that seems oddly familiar, but I can't quite place him. Their interactions are affectionate. Maybe father and son I think to myself, pulling out another drag, when a few steps behind them is a woman, strikingly beautiful as she steps into view. Even from this distance I can see the beauty radiate from her, with long wavy blonde hair I instantly imagine being wrapped around my wrist and a tight, slim physique I'd like to undress. I don't usually feel this way about women. I don't do the dating scene, not since Alesso's mother. When I need to get my fill, I don't usually stick around to form any sort of attachment. I take a long drag of my cigarette. The fact that this stranger has aroused something deep within me, disturbs me more than I'd like to admit. Now I'm intrigued and I need to know who she is before I make my mark on her. I sit and watch as she talks to the boy before taking a seat on the bench near to the entrance of the park, leaving him to run off towards the climbing frame. I study the couple closely from behind my Ray-Bans and notice as the man stands in front of the bench and scans his surroundings, almost as if he's making sure the coast is clear before he can relax. He's obviously in the game. I follow his eyes as they sweep over Alesso and the other middle aged woman with her two children already in the park, then come to rest on me, trying to suss out whether or not I'm a threat. I search him momentarily and notice he's packing too, a gun hidden in his waistband under his shirt. He stares a little longer, the act feeling as if it's dragging on for too long. Maybe he recognises me too I wonder, and slowly I begin to slide my hand across my hip towards my holstered gun under my jacket, only halting when he then turns to sit down next to the pretty blonde and begins talking. A short sigh releases from my lips and I shake my head wondering if I'm being paranoid, or if I'm too fucking distracted thinking about getting my dick wet.

I brush it off, whatever feeling is trying to rear its ugly head and watch their entire conversation unfold before me. I'm starting to wish I was close enough to hear what they are saying as something unsettling raises the hairs on the back of my neck. The blonde's expressions flit between annoyance, shock and something else I can't quite put my finger on, while his face remains serious throughout, almost like he's ready to put his fist through a wall. It is not until the last moment when I see him stand and turn to say something before he walks off that something clicks and I finally recognise his face, my gut feeling never letting me down. "Fuck!" is the first word that comes to mind as I throw my cigarette to the ground, feeling glad in this moment that nobody else is close enough to hear me. "Fucking Irish, East Territory scum." No wonder he was fucking looking at me, I think. He's the enemy, underboss of the East Territory, Ronan Costello's only son and heir to his fucking empire; Max Costello. If he recognised me there would have been blood shed. I look over to Alesso who is now sitting under one of the trees off to the side of the climbing frame picking at the grass, then back to Max as he walks away from the blonde on the bench and out of the park, my mind is reeling.

I release the breath I've been holding and move to reach for my phone in my pocket as I hear, "TEDDY," being shouted through the park. I pause and snap my head up at the name to see the young boy running towards the blonde sitting on the park bench and suddenly a whole shower of anger pierces through me. There is NO way. Shaking my head at what is happening before me, as all of the pieces seem to suddenly fit together in an all too unfriendly way. Teddy, Max, Teddy, Max. I run my fingers through my hair, this is some sort of sick joke I think before whispering the name, "Lucille," and narrowing my vision on the woman that seems to have all the men in Vegas falling at her feet.

I feel my fingernails cutting deep into my palms as I clench my fists trying to think of my next move, weighing up my options. Do I take this opportunity to follow the Irish scum and wipe him off the face of the earth while he's out without his crew? Or do I sit and watch the woman in front of me who has my brothers in a twist, and try to get to the bottom of her relationship with Costello? I watch as Lucille ruffles the hair on top of the little boy's head before he runs back towards the climbing frame, wielding his toy airplane above his head as if to make it fly. Pulling my phone from my pocket, I tap out a message to Zack, ordering him to dig deeper into the background of Lucille and find out what her connection with Max Costello is, leaving no stones unturned. I want to know what this bitch eats for fucking breakfast. I press send and run my fingers through my hair in frustration.

A few moments pass and I'm suddenly made very aware that I have been staring at the blonde bombshell without meaning to for quite some time as Alesso shouts, "DAD!" over to me from a large Chestnut tree, bringing me right back to reality.

"Shit," I groan as I notice he is no longer alone, but stood next to the little boy who, on closer inspection, looks exactly like his mother. Both boys are staring up into the tree with their shoulders slumped down in defeat. I get up and walk towards them, noticing as I do, that Lucille is also on her way over to see what's going on.

"What's up, Son?" I ask as I reach the boys, both looking up at me.

"Teddy's plane got stuck up in the tree and we can't reach to get it down," he says, pointing toward the little toy wedged between two branches a little above my head.

"No worries," I say. "I got this." Pulling myself up on a lower branch and reaching towards the toy plane.

As I land back on the ground, plane in hand, I notice Lucille standing behind Teddy, hands resting on his shoulders protectively. Her face is a picture of bewitching beauty now that I can see her up close and I want nothing more than to ravish it.

I smile awkwardly and hold the plane out to Teddy who takes it as he smiles back. "Hey, thanks Mr!" Then he turns towards Alesso with a huge grin on his face. "Come on Lesso, let's see who can make it fly the furthest." Alessandro turns to look at me, silently asking for permission, he knows the rules. No strangers, even children can be a threat to us. I take a second to think it through before replying with a nod of approval and both boys run off towards the spring seats in the sand.

"Stay in sight," I shout behind them. I need to watch closer now than before and have my wits about me. I can not let my son get involved with the enemy, and if Costello does come back, I need to be on high alert.

I eye Lucille beside me, taking in every delicate feature of her face while her attention is still on her son, from her soft green eyes, to the dimples in her cheeks, the almost cute way her nose upturns slightly just at the tip, and the fullness of her lips parting slightly as they meet. I have to drag my eyes away before I become too enthralled, and begin my way back towards the bench I was sitting on before but I'm stopped dead in my tracks as a voice as smooth as silk cuts through the air.

"Hey, what's your name?" she asks, her voice seeping deep into my soul. I swallow dryly, knowing if I get too close, or if this goes the way that I think it might, one of us may end up regretting that we ever met, or even worse, it will end in carnage. I need to be smart here.

"Uh, Linc," I answer.

"Well, thank you Linc, for getting Teddy's plane out of the tree for him. He loves that thing so you've saved me a lot of tears this evening," she smiles at me. I wince and smile politely through gritted teeth, trying to hide the internal war that's beginning to rage inside of me, the good, the bad and the ugly all fighting for dominance. She's being so friendly, she really has no idea who I am, or what I'm capable of. I wonder if she knows exactly who her pretty little boyfriend is too and the monstrous things he does to keep food on the table.

"My pleasure," I respond monotonously.

"It's so easy to make new friends at their age isn't it?" she notes as she happily watches over our boys throwing the toy airplane back and forth to each other. I follow her gaze and watch closely at their interactions, both so carefree and innocent, an unfamiliar tug pulling deep within me.

"Yes, it's much harder to trust people as you get older and you begin to realize their true intentions." I quip, side-eyeing her to see if I could provoke a reaction, but her face stays placid, not realizing that dig was aimed at her.

"How old?" she asks. "How old is your boy?"

"He's seven," I answer, keeping it short and sweet, trying my best to sound uninterested in her conversation, "and your son? Teddy, was it?" I repeat the question back pretending I'm not already fully aware of his age, surname, which kindergarten he attends and the names of every one of his teachers.

"Five going on fifteen," she says, a small smile playing at the edge of her lips. The answer is so relatable, it catches me off guard, I can not help but stifle a laugh. "Tell me about it," I nod towards the boys. "Alessandro gives me a good run for my money these days, I'm surprised I've got him out in the open away from his computer for five minutes." Her gentle laugh threatens to pierce through my stone cold heart and I have to remind myself she is conspiring with the Irish bastards, sleeping with the enemy. She turns to face me, her eyes the most striking shade of emerald I've ever seen. Fuck, she really is breathtaking.

"You want to sit?" I ask, the voice inside me questioning my motive. I shake it off as she nods and we head over to the nearest bench together.

"It's beautiful here isn't it?" Lucille says, placing her hands into her lap and gazing out thoughtfully into the distance.

I watch her closely wondering what is going through her pretty little head. "It sure is." I whisper, not taking my eyes off of her.

"Do you live around here?" she questions, turning her head towards mine. "I don't think I've seen you around here before," her brow creasing slightly in the middle.

Ah shit, "Uh no, I'm uptown. I don't usually come to this park to be honest. I just thought it would be nice to have a change of scenery and Alessandro wanted to check out the baseball pitch so it seemed like a winner." I say nonchalantly. Shit shit shit. She studies me briefly, her eyes darting back and forth between mine, a look of something I cannot quite read flickers through them.

"Well let's hope I don't need you to rescue a plane from a tree again for me if you aren't planning to come back any time soon."

I raise my eyebrows at her in amusement. "Oh I'm sure something could tempt me back here." I glance around, "Maybe the trees?" I deadpan, noticing her biting her bottom lip trying to stop herself from giggling.

"Oh yes, the trees are lovely here," she agrees, nodding her head in exaggeration.

WHY AM I DOING THIS? I chastise myself. "I never got your name," I enquire, wondering if she will give me, a complete stranger, her real name or is she smarter than I'm giving her credit.

"Lucille," she says with the most angelic look across her face, obviously not as smart as I thought. If she is with Max Costello he obviously has no concerns for her safety, or his sons for that matter. Not enough to advise them not to use their real names anyway. I shake my head at the thought. If she were mine there would be no question as to her safety. Jesus Linc, snap out of it I think, trying to quiet the inner voice screaming inside my head to take her, make her safe, make her mine.

Laughter floats across the open park and we both turn to watch Teddy and Alessandro pretending to be what looks like pirates as they use the climbing frame as their ship. I never thought about having children until the day I found out I was going to be a father, it was never in my plan. I was always too focused on getting my hands dirty for the business and God knows, this isn't the life you want for a child, especially your own. My life changed that day, for the better no doubt. But watching him now playing with Lucille's son, it makes my heart grow weak. The thought of Alesso having a little brother to play with, grow up with, learn their way through life's lessons and mistakes with, consumes me till I feel I can barely get a breath. Instinctively, I reach for my packet of cigarettes, pulling one out between my lips and flipping open my Zippo while striking my thumb along the flint wheel in one fluid motion. I inhale deep and feel the rush throughout my body before exhaling a plume of smoke, almost forgetting that I'm not alone.

"Do you mind?" I ask.
"Not at all, go ahead," she replies, "I should probably be heading home anyway, got to get the little man fed before he starts eating the grass or something." I laugh as I take another drag of my cigarette and Lucille stands to leave as she shouts, "TEDDY!" loudly across the park, gaining the boys' attention. "We need to get going darling, say goodbye to your friend." I stand behind her, the curves of her body daring me to reach forward and touch them. Ignoring my urges before I end up in Silas' old cell for

sexual assault, I step forwards and walk towards the climbing frame with Lucille following behind me.

"Watch out Mommy, the sharks will get you!" Teddy shouts as we get closer, pretending to spear the imaginary sharks circling the climbing frame.

"Not before I get you cheeky boy," she replies, running her way towards the young boy who screams with delight as she catches him and begins tickling him mercilessly.

I look over at Alesso who watches on, a sadness in his eyes that tears at my soul. "Come here, Son," I say, holding my arm out towards him. He jumps down from the edge of the climbing frame and leans into my side as I place my arm across the back of his shoulders. What I would do for him to have a mothers love. Turning back to face Lucille, who is now carrying Teddy in a piggyback, I take one last drag on my cigarette then throw it to the floor and grind it down under my boot.

"Say goodbye to Alessandro and Linc, Teddy," she directs up at the boy who has his head perched on top of hers.

"Goodbye Lesso, Goodbye Linc," he says through a yawn.

"See you later, kid," I respond.

"Bye Ted," Alessandro chimes, then runs off to go and retrieve his football he left behind in favor of Teddy's airplane.

"Goodbye Lucille," I add, my eyes meeting hers.

"Goodbye Linc, I hope the beautiful trees bring you back here soon," she jokes before turning away, a cheeky grin across her lips making the dimples in her cheeks stand out.

"Oh I'm sure they will Love, I've no doubt about that," I reply as she walks out of earshot.

Chapter 13

Silas

Sat in my office after having an in-depth catch up with Cole and Linc on how my strip club, Mezzanotte, has been profiting and the changes that have been implemented on my behalf that I may not have been aware of. Cole's restaurant, Salvatore's Cucina is progressing with the packaging and distribution of cocaine as well as the legal profits that we are receiving from the restaurant itself. Linc has filled me in on how the casino is doing and his security measures regarding our firearm shipments and above all, i'm pleased with the way they've handled things.

My boys have also kept up our fortnightly nightclub openings at the warehouse and the monthly fight nights. The monthly fight nights are my favorite of our ventures. We invite all rival gangs to join and enter their best fighters, bets are placed and profits are made by all. We also exchange inventory and it enables us to set up deals or meetings if needed. I'm immensely proud of how they have coped, even though I know they are glad to have me back to take the reins again.

Looking at my watch it reads 18:24, it's been a long day back at the helm. I've missed it but I had hoped I'd have had time to chat more about any recent developments regarding la mia Luce. Linc filled me in with the general information about her, but what isn't sitting well with me is how she is involved with those Irish scum. Linc has been doing more digging, and Cole has been watching her. I'm not sure how I feel about Cole continuing to watch her now

I'm out, I might have to have a chat and tell him I'll take over.

A moment later both Linc and Cole come strolling into my office and take the seats opposite me. Linc is dressed in a navy suit jacket with a white shirt with matching navy tie, blue slacks and brown shoes, I can see he is concealing a gun too. Next to him Cole is wearing a black shirt open buttoned with skinny chino type trousers with black Doc Marten boots, paired with a black leather jacket, underneath he wears his gun in a holster.

"So are you going to change or do you intend on wearing the same suit you were convicted in?" Linc smirks knowing full well I intend to change into a different suit for the occasion. This isn't just a meeting with our men and associates, this is a celebration of my return to the helm of our organization.

"Actually, clever dick, Ms Lewis brought this suit for me to change into before leaving. She said one of you gave it to her. But yes I will be changing, don't worry yourself. I'll still look better than you," I snark back.

"You wound me Si, I only care for your reputation as a crime lord, you need to look the part. Maybe we should bloody our knuckles before attending to send out a message of terror. As for your suit, it didn't come from me," he comments, adjusting the strap of his holster.

"There will be enough bloodying our knuckles at the meeting. Some members need to be reined back in." I state.

"Well I must admit, I wasn't looking forward to this meeting but now I'm excited to get my hands dirty brother. Please tell me I can bring my new switchblade tonight?" Cole says cheerfully. The way he gets excited about stabbing someone is the same way a drug addict gets about taking a hit.

"Sure I'll let you have some playtime tonight, Cole," I smirk. This is going to be a fun night.

A knock at the door interrupts us. "Come in," I shout.

Marcello, my head of security, enters with a smile on his face. "Cherry dropped this off, she said you asked her to collect it." He hands me a black suit bag. Cherry offered to collect my suit along with offering her services to me as soon as I stepped through the door. Safe to say I declined her services but she got my suit anyway.

"Thanks Marcello, we will be heading out shortly to the warehouse," I tell him. He nods and leaves the room. "Right boys, best go make myself presentable," I laugh. Picking the suit up I go to the washroom connected to my office and clean up and change into a dark gray checked suit including a vest with a white shirt underneath. Like my brothers, I have a gun holster underneath my jacket with my guns attached.

Once I'm ready, I walk back to the office. Linc decides to wolf whistle me and Cole pats my shoulder, "You scrub up good Si, you will have all the hookers at the party later on their knees, mouths open and waiting." I shake my head, these fuckers always trying to tease the shit out of me.

"There is only one woman I've got on my mind, boys, and that's Lucille Holland. Once we are done with this meeting, I'm going to find out what that Irish mafia scum has over her".

"You do realize Max Costello could be her baby's father, right?" Linc asks. Cole stays silent, which is weird. I thought he'd be agreeing with Linc.

"Maybe, but maybe not, until we find out for sure, I'm choosing to be open minded," I tell them.

"Pfft why else would she be meeting him and letting him look after the kid?" Linc goes on to justify his case.

"Look, let's take a step back. Even if he is, she hasn't been stopping at his place so she's not sleeping with him anymore. She's fair game Linc." Coles jumps in. He's giving Linc a pissed off look that needs addressing but we don't have time for that right now, we're going to be late.

"Right, well I agree with Cole, but guys we need to get going. Heads need to roll and we are sat here gossiping like a bunch of girls. We will discuss this later though, you can bet your ass's on that." I add, opening the door leading the way out towards the club exit.

Some of the girls and crew will be here tonight working with regulars but the main stripper's and my trusted, closer circle of employees are already at the warehouse getting the party started. We exit the club, Cole came on his motorcycle, a Triumph Trident 660 and Linc got one of his men to drop him off.

"I'll meet you at the warehouse," Cole says, jumping on his bike and burning off before we get a chance to dispute him, something is clearly on his mind.

I turn to Linc, "Shall we go in the Porsche?" I grin, knowing he's already got the keys in his hand.

"Let's get to it Si. I want to get this meeting out of the way so we can celebrate having you home brother," Linc smiles.

Fifteen minutes later, we arrive at the warehouse. On the outside it looks like any other warehouse on the dock but inside, it's a different story. Made up of 2 floors, we have different spaces set up for different purposes. Tonight, the ground floor is set up like a nightclub. It's dark and moody, perfect for tonights party and the people attending. The warehouse houses other delights required by our line of work like our meeting room but I'm hoping I won't need to use the other rooms tonight. Cole's bike is already parked up. He must be inside already, rounding up the crew to the back room for our meeting to begin. He's unhinged tonight. I can see that from the way he sped off earlier, they'd do well to do as he asks quickly.

Linc and I make our way to the entrance, Linc nods to his men Sully and Felix who are manning the door tonight, he has left Zack running the casino.

"Watch who you let in tonight boys, Boss wants to enjoy his night not have a gang war on our doorstep," Linc instructs with a nod towards them.

"No problem, Sir," Sully replies, eyes forward at all times. He's good, he's always watching for threats. Felix opens the door letting us pass into the main room of the warehouse. I glance around taking in the sight of the party. I spot some of the girls working the pole, Roxi and Cherry. They are dressed only in thongs, their breasts are on full show, Roxi in blue and Cherry in red. I spot two more of the girls from Mezzanotte, Mercedes and Crystal dancing in the hanging cages above us. They are completely naked, pussies bare for all to see. The place is full of people dancing and drinking. I spot Enzo at the bar surrounded by girls in bikini tops and shorts, he's rushed off his feet but that's good, we will be profiting well from tonight as well as celebrating my return home. Looking around I see Quinton and make my way over to him.

"All good so far?" I ask him.

"No problems so far Boss. I'll get Dario to alert you if there are any issues but don't worry, I'm sure we won't need to. I'll handle it if I can," Quinton answers. I nod and with that, me and Linc head upstairs into the back meeting room.

Dario is waiting at the door. "Boss," he nods. I smile as he opens the door. I notice the new gray and black décor, there is a large black, round table with six high back chairs around it. One for each of us, sitting in the room waiting are our Capos; Theo Rossi, Rocco Costa and Dimitri Romano. The three remaining chairs for myself, Cole my brother and underboss and Lincoln, my consigliere.

Cole has already taken the seat to the left hand side of mine and he breaks the silence across the room "Fratello, Capo, bentornato a casa."

"Thank you brother, men, this is a warm welcome." I applaud, taking my seat with Linc taking the remaining seat to my right.

"So let's get straight down to business shall we? Who is going to tell me why the shipment of Beretta 92's received three weeks ago are still in our cargo bay?" I glare at Theo Rossi, he is in charge of shipping our firearms out to various ports for collection by various syndicates. He may be Lincs father, and like an uncle to me, but I've never truly trusted him. Anyone as close as he was to mine and Cole's father has a few skeletons and he has a cupboard full of them that he has never explained.

Theo Rossi is a tall man, slightly round around the stomach area but he still has a lot of muscle behind him and can hold his own, he also has valuable knowledge about the business. This is why I keep him at this position, but now I'm waiting for him to give me a reason not to bury him.

"I can explain, one of our syndicates from New York got searched and we haven't received their payment for this cargo, so I refused to send it." Theo begins. It's plausible but it doesn't explain why he hasn't shifted it to another syndicate and not told Cole or Linc about it in my absence.

"Interesting, but why hide it Theo? Why not make us profit elsewhere? We all know any of the syndicates would have gladly taken the cargo," I ask with an icy tone.

"I thought that I would give them 4 weeks to clean-house and then I'd charge extra for delayed payment." Theo says confidently. He's a smart man, I'll give him that but do I believe him? I'm not sure, for Lincs sake though, I'll give him the benefit of the doubt, on a few conditions.

"See to it that by the end of the week it is moved and sold for a substantial amount, Rossi. Don't test my patience on this or you will have my wrath." I snap at him. I

109

am almost certain he was hoping we wouldn't notice the money missing and he was going to make profit for himself but I have no proof, so I will let it rest for now.

Theo nods "Of course, Boss." Now that's sorted we have a bigger rat to sort out.

I clear my throat, regaining all of their attention, "Is there anything else that you all feel should be brought to my attention?" A unanimous no comes from my Capos but Linc and Cole look to each other.

Cole speaks first, "Actually brother, we've got a little surprise for our Capos," he says, smirking at Linc.

Linc stands from his chair and straightens his shoulders "Men, I think our boss needs to be made aware when a rat has infiltrated our ranks, don't you?" The three men look to one another, unsure of what Linc means as Cole walks around the table, his knife in his hand like it magically appeared.

Dimitri gulps. "Who is this rat? If he is one of my men, I'll gut him myself."

Cole is like a shark circling the water around these men, I can't help but laugh at their faces as he stops behind Dimitri.

"Cole, we shouldn't play with our food. Put them out of their misery." I bark.

"But what fun is that when they squirm so nicely?" he grins, playing with his knife.

I notice Theo is like Dimitri, both looking rather pale. Rocco is looking confident for a man who might have his neck slit in a moment, but he was trained and initiated by Cole to have this seat, so I shouldn't expect any different.

Linc laughs and says, "Theo, Father, you do not have a rat in your group." Then he turns to Rocco, "Neither do you, Rocco." Rocco nods and glares at Dimitri. Theo looks relieved, that's interesting, can he trust his men?

Dimitri gasps, "Who is it? I will clean-house myself!" Will he when we reveal the traitor? Will he be able to end his own cousin's life? I highly doubt it.

Cole brings his blade to Dimitri's throat, smiles, then whispers into his ear, "Would you really? I find that hard to believe when the rat is.."

I cut him off saying, "Cole let's not ruin the surprise for Dimitri." I nod to Linc, who steps out of the room and moments later brings in a man who is gagged, bound, beaten and bruised.

Dimitri cries out, "No cugino! What have you done!?" He goes to move from his seat as Linc throws his cousin Ricky on to the floor, but is stopped by Coles blade piercing his skin.

"I'd stay sat if I were you Dimitri," Cole spits.

Tears prickle Dimitris' eyes and I can't help but wonder if he knew it was him all along, "So now tell me Dimitri, could you clear him from your house?"

Dimitri is shaking but musters up the courage to respond, "Boss what has he done?"

I smirk, at least he's not bargaining for his cousin's life. It shows he respects our decision.

I walk over to where Ricky is on the floor and kick him, he grunts out in pain, "Wakey, wakey Ricky. Do you want to tell your cousin and the rest of us how you have betrayed us? Or shall I? Neither choice will spare your life but maybe I'll tell Cole to go easy on you when we start the whipping." I call to him, he stinks of piss and blood. Cole and Linc tracked him down earlier, and we could already see the beating he'd received which led to him admitting his transgressions.

"They promised that if I told them when and where the deal was going to be made between you and the Russians 18 months ago, that they wouldn't arrest me or my family," he cries.

"Yes, if you hadn't ratted us out to the cops, I wouldn't have been sent down. Isn't that right little Ricky?" I shout. Dimitri looks horrified, he knows exactly what punishment we will bestow his cousin now after his confession.

Dimitri looks down at his cousin, remorse etched into his features "Solo Dio può giudicarti nell'aldilà," then marks a cross over his chest before look back to me, "I understand you need to punish him for the part he has played in this but I only ask that his family are spared for his sins." I would never condemn another for the actions of one so this is no hardship to grant.

I nod in agreement "Of course, his sins are not those of his family. Now sit down Dimitri while I get my vengeance."

I turn to Cole letting him know I'm ready, "You may begin brother."

My signature death is about to take place. Cole moves to the table and pulls out a leather whip from one of the drawers built into the edge and stalks closer to Ricky and whispers, "la morte non sarà rapida," before ripping the shirt from his back and bringing the whip down hard across his skin. Ricky screams in pain but Cole continues until Ricky's back is completely torn open with blood oozing from the wounds.

I'm not actually sure when Ricky passed out from the pain but it's quiet now in the room, except for the sound of Dimitri vomiting in the bin. This torture is not for someone with a soft stomach. Linc steps in and uses a gouging chisel on Ricky's back to make an opening for me to finish our work of art and once he is done, I walk over to Ricky's limp, lifeless body, shove my hands through his back, breaking his ribs and twisting upwards and out to create wings. I pull his entrails out from the back of his chest and lay them over his displaced ribs. I step back from the masterpiece then turn to the men in the room and look at each one and say, "Let this be a lesson to you and all your men. This is what happens when you become a snitch. Cogliere la notte!"

"Cogliere la notte!" They all shout in unison.

"This meeting is over. Thank you for my warm welcome back to the helm," I say before leaving to clean myself up, with Cole and Linc following. Once we have cleaned the blood from ourselves and disposed of the bloodied clothes in exchange for clean ones, we make our way to the bar.

"Enzo, three Macallan 25 please," I shout over the bar. Enzo nods and directs one of the girls behind the bar to get our order pronto.

Once we have our whiskeys in hand Linc raises his glass, "To our Merciless leader," Cole follows suit and we all down the amber liquid feeling the smooth burn down our throats. It feels good to have the finer things in life again. A single shot of Macallan 25 costs in excess of $200.

Cole then waves over a girl and whispers something to her, she begins to lie down on the bar and Enzo places shots down her body. "You're first up brother," Cole says smugly to me, slapping me on the back. The night is just getting started and I'm enjoying every minute of it.

Chapter 14

Cole

Rihannas, 'Don't Stop the Music' is blaring around me as I watch my brother take a body shot off one of the girls behind the bar. She's thin, perky tits and I'd say 5'8". She has black hair and brown, honey eyes, a beauty for sure but when I look at her, all I see is how she is doesn't compare to the beauty of my Topolino. Once Silas has taken his shot, Linc takes the next one. When it comes to my turn, I decline saying, "Sorry boys, I've gotta stay sober tonight." They look at me suspiciously but I have my reasons. A - I want to check on Lucille and B - Roxi, who happens to be making her way over to us with Cherry in tow, both topless wearing only thongs. They look good and I'm sure they will bring in a huge profit tonight but not what I'm after. Cherry has red hair and blue eyes that are more of a dark depths of the ocean blue. She's taller than most girls, standing without heels at 5'10". She's always had a thing for Silas, not that he's ever reciprocated. He tends not to dip in his business. I'm starting to see why with how Roxi is sashaying her hips over towards me. Her bleach blonde hair is up in a tight ponytail, her brown eyes are decorated with glitter. She looks the part tonight, if my interest wasn't elsewhere I'd welcome her fascination with me.

"Hi Boss, it's so good to see you home. I hope you are enjoying your night. As a welcome home gift I've got a private dance for you, whenever you want," Cherry purrs to Silas and rests her hand on his bicep.

Silas shakes her off saying, "I don't dip in the company ink Cherry, but thank you for your offer."

He's always so polite to these whores, my temper isn't so patient. Cherry nods and then flutters her eyelashes to Linc. "Do you want to take my offer Lincoln?" Her voice is like honey, seductive and smooth.

Linc just laughs, "Not tonight darlin',"

Cherry smiles, "Oh that's disappointing, I'll just have to find some other eager client," and makes her way over to the tables putting on the charms to all who lay eyes on her. Roxi clears her throat. "Sir, can I assist you this evening?" I had forgotten she was still standing there. I glance at her and think of the politest way to tell her to get fucked.

"Roxi, I'm not interested. Go find some other dick to ride," I say in a bored tone, hoping she'll get the hint.

"But we have so much fun together," she whines.

My little patience has already gone, I turn to her and grab her throat. "Did you misunderstand our last encounter? I was being polite by saying I'm not interested but you aren't listening. Now listen carefully, I don't want to repeat myself again. I wouldn't touch your used up pussy if you paid me. Now fuck off and find some other place to rub your cunt over." I let her go, she's spluttering and holding her neck but thankfully she runs off to follow Cherry.

"Fratello, that was harsh, is she not your favourite fuck toy?" Linc questions, I'm about to tell him to mind his own business but Silas jumps in.

"Cole, I understand you have told her to back off but next time be more discreet about it would you?" I let out a breath, trying to control myself.

"There won't be a next time if she knows what's good for her. She's been calling me non-stop and keeps trying to bump into me. You know my patience isn't as strong as yours. I need to get some air and cool off, I'll catch you both later," with that I leave, making my way straight for the exit.

My obsession for seeing my topolino is growing. I've been on edge all night with the need to see her, to feel her. I need to get out of this place, it's stifling me. She's the only thing that makes me feel at peace.

I jump on my Triumph Trident 660, pushing the accelerator down, listening to the roar of the engine as I speed off towards her complex. The night sky is dancing with the lights from the city, the air feels cool around my body as I race down the highway. As I get closer to Topolino's home, I decided to park my bike a block away so that she doesn't hear the engine as I check on her. I've been sending her a single red rose since the day I met her. Just leaving it at her doorstep if she's awake. Other times I've used the spare key and left it inside for her to find, hoping it brings a smile to her face.

As I walk around the condo I hear her voice. "Teddy, how do you feel about a sleepover with Isabella on Saturday night? Aunty Kat is going to buy some popcorn and sweets for you guys. And guess what? She's got the new Minion's movie for you and Isabella to watch, how cool does that sound?"
Watching from the shadows, I peek in to see the boy looking excited, "That's great Mommy! I can't wait but can she get Reese's pieces too?"
"I tell you what buddy, why don't we buy some for you to take with you to share?" she replies, she looks so lovingly at him. How a mother should be with her child. I'm happy for the kid, and in awe of her, my mouse, my muse.
"Yesss!" he shouts.
"OK little man, now it's time to get you to bed," she tells him, leading the way to his bedroom. Ten minutes later she's returning to the lounge, she sits down and flicks through the channels, finally deciding on a Netflix series, Virgin River. I watch her, fully engrossed in what is

happening before her on the screen, until her phone flashes. She looks at the screen and smiles, "Hey Max."

The thought of her finding any joy from that piece of shit angers me, not with her but with him. This angel obviously sees the best in people, her occupation sees to that. I clench my fist and continue to listen in on their conversation, fighting back the anger.

"Yes I'll be there Saturday night, don't worry. Just make sure you don't get so hurt that I can't patch you up," she says jokingly. What the fuck? She's going to be at the fight? This is perfect for me to see her again, but I also don't want her there on their side. I want her on our team, patching our guys up. Maybe I should tell Silas, knowing he'll challenge Max. And it would be interesting to see how she reacts to seeing Silas again now he's out of prison.

"Yeah Kat will watch Teddy, don't worry he'll be fine. Drop me a message when you're on your way Saturday. I'll see you soon, love you." She hangs up and continues to watch her idyllic, shitty little program.

I am fuming! *Love you!* What? This is going to piss Silas off, and I suspect Linc too. I'm pissed off but I have a delicious plan to make her mine and not that scumbag Costello's. Deep in thought, I don't notice her moving from the sofa to the window. I quickly move to hide around the side of her building. She's looking around as though she can hear my heart beating in my chest. She opens the patio doors and says "Hello?" I feel like I'd freak her out if I stepped out from the shadows but now I'm itching to do it.

"Hello Topolino," I say, taking a step out of the shadows.

"What the hell!?" she screams before I can put my hand over her mouth to stop her.

"You don't want to wake your son or neighbors, do you?" I whisper into her ear. Her breathing is ragged, her heart is beating like mine in her chest at the thrill of this.

"Are you going to calm down and not scream if I remove my hand, Topolino?" I ask calmly. She nods, her eyes are wild. She's scared, but not of me. Who is it that she's scared of in the dark?

"What are you doing here, Tomcat? Have you been stalking me? Are you the one sending me those roses!?" She rushes out. I smirk because she's flustered by me, and my presence is making her giddy.

"Shall we go inside for a chat? Or do you prefer the moonlight? You do look beautiful in it," I say, ignoring her questions. I'm not sure she's ready for the answers.

"What? No! My son is asleep, you can't come in and I'm not talking to you out here if you won't answer my questions" she explains. I look around and spot the curtains twitching on the apartment opposite.

I sigh, "Well your neighbors are nosy and watching us. What would you prefer? Be gossiped about by Mrs Willis and her friends, or let me come in and I'll answer one question for you."

"Fine but after that you go, okay?" she says.

"Of course, if that's what you want, Topolino." She heads inside and I follow closely behind her.
I close the patio doors behind me, she turns to me and says, "Why are you here? What do you want?" Her hands are on her hips and she looks like she means business. It's very cute.

I smile, "I said one question, Topolino, which do you choose?"

She frowns at me, thinking about what to say, "Make it two and I won't call the cops." I laugh, is she really bargaining with me?

"Okay Topolino, ask away and I'll decide if I'll answer one or two questions."

"Why are you here?" she asks.

I simply reply, "I wanted to make sure you're safe and I can't seem to stop thinking about you." She looks surprised, "So no one sent you? You're the one who's been sending me these roses?"

"No one sent me, do you have enemies Topolino? Is Max Costello a threat to you? As for the roses, yes, I thought you deserved to have something to make you smile," I admit, staring into her emerald eyes. I realize I want to spend the rest of my life getting lost in them I think to myself before watching to see her reaction to me mentioning Max.

"Max? Oh god no, he's no threat." She states choosing her words carefully she continues. "Thank you for the roses, they were thoughtful. Next time maybe leave a note or you know, have a conversation with me, it's a bit creepy." She laughs like she didn't mean to say the last part, her cheeks are flushed.

I nod saying, "OK, well I've got business to get back to now that I know you're safe. I'll see you around, Topolino"

"Wait, so you don't work for Max right?" she asks.

What a strange question. Moving closer to her I whisper against her lips, "No my love, I do not. You'll see who I work for Saturday night." Her breathing has stilled and I bite her lip before kissing her tenderly before I slip away, back out of the patio doors, leaving her alone and stunned.

As I'm walking back to my bike, I think about how she didn't answer about her enemies but she did say that Max was not a threat to her. He means something to her but I'm not sure what. Linc needs to find out or I will be doing my own investigating on Saturday night. I need to know what kind of relationship she has with that trash. I'm more that willing to erase it from her memory if he's touched her more than platonically. I pull my phone from my pocket and dial Silas's number hoping he's not got his cock stuck in some pussy.

It rings twice before he answers, "Have you calmed down brother?" he asks.

I ignore his question "Max Costello is fighting at fight night Saturday…"

Before I get to finish he interrupts with a huff, "What of it brother?"

"Well I've got it on good authority that a certain blonde will be in attendance as medical stand-by for the Irish. Care to make it interesting?" I know he'll take the bait.

"How do you know this brother, where are you?" He ask, superiority leaking from him.

"I've been watching Topolino. She all but told me that she'll be there," I say casually.

"Fucksake Cole, leave her alone now. I'll be fighting that Irish cunt on Saturday and beating him for being anywhere near her. Don't you dare stand in my way or I swear it brother, you will be next in line. I've already told you she's mine!" he says aggressively.

I laugh, he doesn't get it, she'll be ours not his or mine or Lincs. She's perfect for all of us, he just needs to learn the share. "Brother, let's not argue. You don't get to decide who she picks, she does." With that I hang up on him before he tries to tell me differently. As soon as I get to my bike, I put my helmet on and speed off to Salvatore Cucina.

Pulling up in the empty space outside, I make my way into the restaurant. It's busy here tonight. I head out to the back to find Benji. "How's business tonight, Benji?" I ask once I locate him in the kitchen.

"Boss, it's going great. Crazy busy tonight." He replies, watching over the kitchen to make sure all is in order.

I nod, "And what about our extracurricular activities? How's that coming along?"

"All packed and in transit to the sellers, money has been transferred," he tells me confidently.

"Good work, Benji." I slap him on the back, "Can I get some food to go? Enough for me and my boys. I'll go have a drink in my office, come get me when it's ready," I say to the chef Giovanni. He nods.

I make my way to my office and pour myself a whiskey. As I take a sip and feel the warmth slip down my throat, I'm brought to thoughts of Lucille and how her lips melted against mine tonight. It was heaven and I can't wait to do it again. A knock at my door disturbs me from my thoughts. "Come in!" I yell.

It's Benji, "Here you go Boss, food is ready. Do you want me to lock up tonight or are we expecting another batch?" he asks.

"No batch being delivered tonight Benji, lock up as usual. I'll be back early tomorrow morning to open up," he nods and leaves. I down the rest of my whiskey and make my way out. I pack the food into the paniers of the bike and speed away feeling free as a bird as the wind whips around me.

Chapter 15

Lincoln

It's been a long fucking week since Silas returned to reclaim his rightful place on the throne. If I had to deal with Cole for much longer, I'm not sure who would have ended up with a bullet in their head first. Him or myself, and it would have been me who pulled the trigger on both. I love the boy but Jesus, is he annoying. On the other hand, to say I'm looking forward to Saturday night's fight night is a gross understatement. I haven't been able to get Lucille Holland out of my head since our interaction in the park. As much as it pains me to admit it, it proves that Cole was right, she is something special and my men have been unable to uncover any more about her past life or any information on what her relationship is with Max Costello and that vexes me profusely.

I crack my knuckles and stretch out the tension pulling at my back as I sit in my office chair, watching closely over the live stream CCTV from the casino above. My dick instantly begins to throb at the memory of Lucille walking away from me. Her curvaceous ass swaying as she went. I groan in indignation and with the frustration becoming almost palpable I slam my fists into my desk hoping that it would somehow make me feel better, but it doesn't.

A moment later, Felix swings his head around the corner from the adjoining room. "You okay Boss?" he asks, I can hear his concern laced in the question.

"I need a smoke," is all I reply as I stand up knocking the chair over behind me. "Watch the floor, I'll be back shortly," I command as I leave the room and make my way through the basement corridors leading up towards the casino's main floor.

Passing through the high-tech security door, I enter the vast space before me. It really is a grand sight, the extensive beauty it beholds leaves me breathless every time I step inside. With ginormous golden columns surrounding the perimeter, plush red carpets lining the floors, a huge marble topped bar with a designated stage for live act nights, several large olive trees potted around the room and a built in koi pond running through the center with a foot bridge and waterfall. The entire building oozes expense and I love it. Each section is decorated perfectly down to the last little detail. Slot machines, poker tables and lush velvet seating areas and finally a grand marble staircase that cuts through the trees leading up to the private members lounges on the upper floor. I suck in a deep breath and look out over my kingdom with a grin pulling at my lips. The casino itself, Casino Della Vittoria, was named after my mother, Victoria, and it means Casino of Victory. She was a beautiful woman and to see this, what I have built from the ground up, she would be so proud.

But the happy moment passes as quickly as it materialized and I now need more than just a cigarette to satisfy the aching beast within. Making my way up the staircase towards the private lounge on the upper floor, I head straight for the back room knowing full well that Mercedes, one of the regulars that works both here at the casino and at Silas' club, is on the books for tonight's private hire. I know she's already arrived as I clocked her entering about half an hour ago through the back entrance on the CCTV. I don't usually like to fuck where I put my money but tonight I'll make an exception. Not feeling it necessary to knock, I open the door to the dressing room, marked for staff only, to find her already half naked, tits on full display, curling her hair in front of the mirror. "Hey sugar," she purrs as soon as she notices me through the reflection.

"Come here," I order, flicking the latch on the door as I close it behind me. I notice her face light up almost instantly as she puts down her curling iron and skips over to me, biting at her bottom lip, her full, plump tits bouncing with each little bound.

As soon as she stands before me, I fist my hand into her hair and snap her head back so she's looking up at me. "Do not speak." I spit before spinning on my heels and slamming her back against the door behind. A playful grin shaping her lips as she reaches for my jacket. The bitch likes to be dominated and bossed around, that's why she's so popular with the punters.

"Hands," I warn her, pushing her arms away. I step back and look at her as I begin to undo my tie, raking my eyes head to toe over her body. She's hot with a pretty good rack but nothing compared to the little blonde bombshell dancing in my mind. "Touch yourself," I order as I continue to remove my shirt and trousers, slipping my belt from my waistband. I watch with hooded eyes as Mercedes slips her thong down over her slender thighs, sucks at her fingers then slowly trails them down the length of her body towards her pussy. A low moan escapes her as she pushes her fingers deep inside of her entrance. Removing her fingers, now moistened with her own juices she circles her clit, bringing her free hand up towards her breast as she tweaks her nipple between her fingertips. My erection strains at the band of my boxer shorts before I pull them down, releasing it and wrapping my hand around the length, I begin to slowly pump. Mercedes' gaze darts down towards my cock and her eyes glaze over with lust, pulling her lip between her bottom teeth she moans again and reinserts her fingers deep into her now swollen cunt.

"Here!" I order. Mercedes steps forward immediately, her tongue darting out over her lips like a hungry wolf ready to devour its dinner. "Give me your wrists," I order, my voice hard and commanding. She holds her wrists together in front of me, the excitement radiating from her naked body as I slip my tie around both wrists binding them tightly together. She looks up at me with greedy eyes and in one swift movement I turn her around and bend her over, baring her ass and pussy to me all in one. I suck in a breath as I stroke myself, my cock desperate for its release, but first I need to extinguish the frustration. Reaching for my belt, I position myself behind Mercedes before folding the leather in half and whipping it straight across her bare ass cheeks. I hear her gasp at the initial bite then bring it down again, the full force of my fury behind it. Again and again, her moans goading me on until I'm panting, and Mercedes' ass is red and raw before me. Unable to hold myself back any longer I rip open a condom kept in the side dresser and slide the latex sheath over my bulging hard on.

Without wasting any more time, I slam into her, her pussy dripping with her satisfaction, my hands hold firm on her hips as I dig my nails into her skin, making sure to leave my mark, pounding my cock mercilessly into her eagerly accepting core. Rasped screams escape her lips, and I fist my fingers through her hair once more bringing her face to meet mine in the reflection of the mirror. Her face now contorted in pleasure, pain and something else. I fuck her hard and fast, quelling the beast within, my face a greedy snarl. This is what I needed, but not with who I needed it. Her emerald eyes flash before me, her long blonde hair I'd like to have wrapped around my wrist instead. My body constricts as I reach my climax, a flourishing thought of my cock inside of her tight little pussy is my undoing. I throw my head back on my release slamming forwards one last time. "Fuck, Lucille!" I groan as I fill up the condom with my cum and collapse forward against Mercedes' back.

I glance forward, the look on Mercedes' face as I straighten myself up and pull out my still raging cock from between her legs is livid. Anger and humiliation coursing through her eyes as I throw the condom into the bin in the corner and pull on my boxers. She turns to me and holds her still bound wrists in front of me, Silently asking for her release, unable to look me in the face. I reach down and untie her before tipping her head to face me, with my finger and thumb gripping her chin firmly in place. "Don't be sour, sugar. It's nothing personal." I lean forward and place a kiss on her cheek causing her to tut loudly in disgust and pull away from me. I continue to dress myself, all the while noticing Mercedes scowling at me through the mirror while she tries to re tame her just fucked hair. I smile to myself, knowing how much I've just gotten under her skin, and although I'm now feeling partly satisfied, I need the real deal and I need it soon. I need Lucille Holland on her knees and gagging on my cock. Fuck Cole for being right.

I finish putting my clothes back on and pulling my jacket over my shoulders, I walk out of the room without another word, heading straight to the bar. "Whiskey on the rocks please Dan," I order as soon as I get there, throwing the drink back in one as soon as it's handed over. I welcome the familiar burn as it makes its way down to the pit of my stomach. "Another," I say, slamming the glass onto the marble bar top.

"Everything alright Boss?" Dan eyes me suspiciously as he pours me out another drink.

"Never better," I respond through gritted teeth as the burn hits the back of my throat once more.

He nods in acknowledgement. He's a smart man and knows that is the only answer he's getting from me and not to push it so he pours me out another drink before leaving to attend to a group of ladies waiting at the other end of the bar, all excitedly giggling to each other and eager to spend their husbands hard earned money in my casino. Now that, I won't object to.

Leaving the bar with a warm buzz now running through my veins, I pull out my phone and dial my fathers number. He's been avoiding me ever since Silas returned and snuffed out Ricky at our meeting last week for getting him locked up. I can't say I blame him, the prick had it coming and my father knows the business, he knows the consequences. He answers almost immediately. "Lincoln," his tone short and slightly hostile.

"Father," I respond with the same edge to my voice.

"What can I do for you, Son?" he questions. I walk outside into the blistering sun still peaking out on the horizon and pull my packet of cigarettes from my inside pocket, lighting one up and taking a long satisfying drag before answering.

"Have you made sure the necessary arrangements are in place for the drop off on Tuesday night? Silas is back now, your men can not afford to fuck this up again. He won't be so lenient on you a second time." I say through gritted teeth, knowing the full extent of Silas' promises when he is crossed after handing out a second chance. The man may boil my blood but he is still that, my blood, and I feel it's required of me to make sure he has a heads up, to at least give him a fighting chance. If he fucks it after my warning, then that's on him. I hear him chuckle deeply to himself down the phone line and the sound raises the hairs on the back of my neck.

"Don't worry Lincoln, he may be the big bad boss in charge right now but I have been in this business a lot longer than the both of you. All is confirmed, the shipment will be collected at ten thirty exactly and I will be there to oversee it myself."

I nod as I pull in another drag on my cigarette. "Just don't fuck it up this time." I say, the words void of any emotion. I hang up the phone and look out towards the sun slowly setting along the back of the city lights, a sudden unease seeping into my skin that I refuse to acknowledge

"Boss," Felix cuts in as he appears behind me, snapping me out of my daydream. I turn to look at him, his face serious as a heart attack. "There's something you might want to see."

Fuck sake, what now? I think to myself as I fill my lungs with air and breathe out heavily before pulling on my cigarette for the last time then stubbing it out against the wall.

"Show me." I say, blowing the smoke between my lips and straightening my suit jacket. He turns back and makes his way towards the private door at the back of the casino, weaving carefully between the throng of people now occupying the space. Straight through the door, I follow Felix down the private corridors hidden below the surface and into the surveillance room. A whole wall in front of us covered top to bottom in screens delivering a live feed straight to us from the floors above. I'm like a God down here, with an all seeing eye, nothing ever goes unseen in my world.

Felix sits at the desk in front of me, taps a few keys on the keyboard and pulls up the feed from one of the VIP booths. I watch silently as he rewinds the footage by roughly ten minutes and presses play. A scene plays out before me of a group of six men, all looking to be around the age of thirty, maybe a little younger, all gathered into a booth in the VIP section at the bar. The lights are low in the bar at this time of the evening allowing for live musicians, comedy acts and cabaret dancers to perform on stage with the spotlights trained on them. But even with the lights down and their feeble attempt at hiding it. I can see exactly

128

what they're doing as they each take cover behind the rest of the group and snort a line of cocaine discreetly from the table. Drugs are absolutely not tolerated in my casino, there are no exceptions. Fury builds in me once again.

I snap at Felix, making him jump. "Bring it back to real time," I order. He does so within seconds and the image is replaced with the group of men that have now been joined by the ladies I spotted earlier at the bar. "For fuck sake," I groan inwardly knowing this is going to be a pain to handle if the women get involved too. They're always so much more feisty than men.

"Sully, Zack, come with me," I say, turning towards the two men who are already raring to go, their faces glow with delight. "Felix, stay here and keep your eyes on them. If any of them give us the slip, I want to know exactly where they're going." Felix nods in understanding and turns back to face the screen. "Come on boys, these men obviously need their fucking heads cracking. Thinking they can bring drugs to my tables." I lead the way back up to the main casino floor, Zack and Sully tailing right behind me.

Moments later we arrive at the bar. "Gentlemen," I announce, holding my hands out in front of me as if in a welcoming gesture. Their faces pale at the sight of me before them, flanked by Zack and Sully who stand stoic besides me. "Ladies, I suggest that you leave." I say, casting my gaze over the women who had joined the group, authority laced in my voice. I don't need to ask again as they all look to one another, grab their drinks and purses immediately slipping past us as they scoot as fast as seemingly possible away from the booth. Well, that was much easier than I thought it would be. I'll make sure Dan gets them a complimentary bottle of champagne for the inconvenience, they still need to have a good night after all. As soon as I'm sure the ladies are out of ear shot I begin.

"Now gentlemen, it riles me to know that you would even THINK that you could get away with sniffing that shit in my casino." One of the group opens his mouth to protest and I hold my hand up, cutting him off. "Do not take me for an idiot, I have surveillance footage of you. So this can go one of two ways. You boys either play nice, hand over your shit and leave my casino right now or I let my men here get their knuckles bloody." A friendly smile pulls at my lips. "So what do you say?"

The biggest of the group, and the one who tried to interrupt me squares his shoulders in an attempt I find hugely comedic as he tries to make himself seem more intimidating, "Don't know what the fuck you're talking about," he stands, throwing his arms out trying to make a scene. I glance at Sully and he moves forward, grabbing him behind his head and slamming his face straight down into the table. The rest of the group gasp but choose to remain quiet.

"You broke my nose you fucking dick!" he spits as blood pours between his teeth and he pinches the top of his nose to try and stub the bleeding. I shrug my shoulders, Sully beaming from ear to ear ready and eager to cause more damage.

"Now, would anybody else like to hand it over?" I ask again. The rest of the group exchange questioning looks with each other before one of them reaches into his jacket pocket and pulls out a small bag of white powder. He hands it over, visibly shaking as he does.

"Good boy," I smirk before I turn to leave, there won't be as much of a fight as I was expecting, and honestly I think I'm a little disappointed by their lack of manhood to stand up for themselves, but whatever, they'd lose in a matter of seconds. "Search them, throw them out and make sure they don't come back." I instruct Zack and Sully who grin at each other at their given task. I smile while I walk away, having every bit of faith that my men will do whatever is necessary to get the job done and I head back down to my office to lock up.

I've just about had enough for one day and Alessandro has been nagging me for ages to watch a baseball game with him on the TV, so that's exactly what I'm going to do.

As I leave, I shout to Felix, who's still scanning over the CCTV in the surveillance room, to make sure that a round of drinks is being organized for the ladies' co-operation earlier. I tell him to give them whatever they want, on-the-house and remind him to make sure to call me if there's any trouble. If there isn't I don't want to be bothered, I need to spend time with my son. He nods his understanding and with my full trust in my men to handle whatever the night brings, I sprint up the stairs and head home for the night.

Chapter 16

Lucille

My stomach has been in knots all week about tonight. I've hardly been able to focus at work. Kat has noticed something is a little off too and has been keeping a close eye on me, constantly asking if I'm okay. I know she thinks it's Vinny, but for the moment I have to let her think it is. Max would never forgive me if I told her the truth. I've never been to one of the clubs' fight nights. I've tried my hardest to stay out of that side of Max's business for Teddy's sake and Max makes sure he keeps us out of it too. I know he wouldn't have asked unless he was desperate.

I glance at the clock, Max will be here in a couple of hours to pick me up, I need to drop Teddy off at Kat's for the night. "Are you ready, little man?" I call out to him as I make my way to his bedroom, pushing his door open.

"Almost Mommy," he replies through huffed little breaths as he tries to stuff Little B into his backpack. I cannot help but smile.

"Come here," I say as I walk over to help "there we go, all done." I say as I manage to squeeze the zipper shut and receive a celebratory round of applause from Teddy. "Are you excited for your movie night with Bella?" I ask as we make our way out the front door.

"YESS!" he shouts, flinging his arms up in the air in excitement before looking up at me "Do you think Auntie Kat will have popcorn?" he asks, his eyes full of longing.

I laugh at the seriousness of his face, "Oh I'm sure if you ask nicely she'll be able to sort something out for you.

Maybe even the kind you do on the stove and probably some extra chocolates for the top too." I say knowing full well that is exactly what Kat will have planned, she's a pro when it comes to movie night snacks. Teddy's little eyes go wide as saucers and his mouth hangs open as he moans a loud "mmmmm" sticking his tongue out of his mouth just like Homer Simpson. I roll my eyes and laugh at his response before buckling him safely into the car.

"HEY TEDSTER!" Kat bellows, a huge smile spread across her face as she opens her front door to us then ruffles his hair playfully.

"Hi Auntie Kat, Mommy said you have the popcorn we can do on the stove and extra chocolate for the top!" he says all in one breath as he flings his rucksack down and kicks off his shoes. "Oh did she now?" Kat gasps bending down so she's eye level with Teddy, "and did she also tell you that I got us some Pop Tarts for breakfast too?"

"POP TARTS!" he shouts "NO WAY!"
Kat smiles as she nods her head at him before rising to stand again, "Bella's in the front room if you want to go through little man and you two can pick out a movie to watch."

"Okay, thanks Auntie Kat." Teddy turns to me and reaches up to hug me, I reach him as I lean forwards and squeeze him tightly before kissing the top of his head.

"See you in the morning baby boy, have a goodnight. I love you."

"I love you too Mommy," he calls behind him as he's already off running towards the front room.

Kat eyes me suspiciously as I step further through the front door, "You got time for a quick drink?" she asks heading towards the kitchen. I follow behind her contemplating what I'm meant to tell her is actually happening tonight.

"Yeah sure, just a quick one though, Max is picking me up at ten."

"Oh so it's Max you're being all weird about?" her eyebrows raise as she pours us each a tumbler of whiskey. I take the glass willingly as she hands it over to me.

"You know I'd tell you if it wasn't," I say, tilting my head to the side, "anyway you have literally been breathing down my neck all week, you would know if it wasn't," I say, noting the dubious look she's now giving me. "We've just got some family shit to sort out," I finally say, knocking back the whole of my drink in one, welcoming the burn it leaves in its wake from my throat down to the pit of my stomach.

"Right okay that's fine girl, just," Kat shrugs, "you know, just remember I'm here for you," she says as she steps in front of me and places her hands on my shoulders. "If you ever need to talk, I am here."

"Jesus, it's literally just some family shit but I know, you're my best friend, I know you're there for me. Thank you." I say, pulling her into a hug. I pull back and give her a reassuring smile. "I've got to go okay? Thanks for watching Ted for me, I've got a feeling it might be a late one tonight." I head back towards the front door and peep my head around the doorway into the front room to see Teddy and Isabella huddled together under a pile of cushions and blankets, the sight warming my heart. "I'll call you in the morning," I add turning to Kat before slipping out of the door and back towards my car.

Back at my apartment I pour myself another glass of whiskey and down it in one. I have just over an hour till Max should arrive. I'm getting so nervous, I can feel my stomach doing somersaults, and I'm not even sure why. I decide to take a cold shower to freshen myself up, I need to be alert incase I am actually needed to patch anybody up tonight, that is the reason I'm going after all. Maybe I shouldn't have anything else to drink, I warn myself as the shower head rains down over my body. Having quickly scrubbed myself clean and washed and conditioned my hair, I hop out of the shower and skip to the bedroom, rushing to pull on a clean pair of black underwear, some skinny jeans and a black cami top. I'll grab a flannel shirt before I leave to pull on, but this will do for now, and Max did say to wear something I didn't mind getting blood on. The thought instantly wreaks havoc inside of my head, a mass of images all flashing before my eyes, knives, knuckle dusters, chains. I gasp at the thought, I really have no idea what I'm getting myself into in a fucking gang-war fight night. Immediately feeling the urge to down the whole bottle of whiskey in my kitchen cupboard, I try to distract myself by applying a subtle covering of make up before I start drying my hair.

I'd already received Max's warning text to let me know he was on his way and to be ready, so I was already sat waiting when he walked through the front door. Looking me over, judging my clothing choices, he sighs loudly. "Please tell me you're planning on wearing a jacket," his voice full of desperation.

The fucking cheeky prick. "Well hello to you too brother. Nice to see you, I'm fine thank you for asking. Yes I'm feeling okay about coming to your illegal mafia fight night instead of being at home with my son. And yes you prick, I'm wearing a shirt!" I huff out in one long breath.

"This isn't funny Luce, I need the men there concentrating on the fight, not on you. I don't need any fights outside of the ring. You need to cover up." The words send a threatening lump straight to my throat as if I might throw up.

"Okay, okay, I'm sorry. I'm just nervous. I don't know what to expect," I sigh, pulling on a green checked, oversized flannel shirt and buttoning it up at the front, making sure to conceal my cleavage. Max watches me and nods as I look up for approval.

"That's better, let's go," he says, already out of the door heading back to his car. I let out a huge breath and face myself in the mirror giving myself a last one over before picking up my first aid bag I'd prepacked with supplies and follow Max to his car.

Pulling up at the warehouse my nerves are really getting the better of me now as we get out of the car and make our way to the entrance. "So this is all just mafia members, right? Totally off radar?" I ask, my eyes scanning the entirety of the car park.

"Yes Luce, there's a strict entry list and security on every door. You'll be okay. Just listen to me," Max stops in his tracks and faces me. "I need you to stay alert in there, do not trust anybody, stay in sight and for fuck sake do not tell anybody anything about yourself. Do you understand?" I'm almost sure my heartbeat can be heard outside of my chest, it's hammering so hard against my ribcage I almost feel I might pass out.

A small "OK" is all I can manage to say. He watches me for a moment, a look of contemplation in his eyes. Is he questioning bringing me now? Because it feels a little too late for backsies.

"Let's go," he finally says, pulling me towards the doors.

Once we're inside it's hard to keep my face neutral. The large mass of bodies, mostly men, is completely overwhelming. The room is packed to the brim, the music so loud I can barely hear myself think. I glance around, taking in my surroundings. The ring is right in the center of the warehouse, a bar to the left and several stripper poles dotted around, each one cast in a brilliant spot light, beautifully displaying the almost naked women that are wrapped around the steel pole between their legs. Steel cages lined the back, bare naked women dancing inside of them, baring everything to the onlookers below. My eyes go wide and I see Max laughing at my reaction.

"Oh piss off," I laugh, shoving him in the shoulder, "naked dancers are not what I expected."

"Oh Luce, you really have no idea." he responds, shaking his head and chuckling to himself. "Follow me," he adds, nodding his head towards the ring. Once we make it to the front, Max introduces me to a few of the men gathered around, a few I vaguely recognise as I've seen them with Max before. I smile politely and nod my hello as I notice one of them whisper something into Max's ear, his brow creasing as a scowl forms on his face, his eyes darkening. Whatever it was he has just been told obviously isn't good. I'm distracted momentarily by a few of the men eyeing me suspiciously, their eyes roaming up and down my body until Max reappears beside me and introduces me as his sister.

"They're friendly, don't worry. Just be on the lookout for threats," Max whispers to me, sensing my reservations. Fuck what I thought earlier about no more drinking, I need a drink and I need one now.

"Hey I'm gonna go grab myself a drink. You want anything?" I shout loudly over the music.

He shakes his head and runs his fingers through his hair. I turn towards the bar but get pulled back as Max grabs at my wrist. "Luce, I've been called into the ring tonight." My eyes go wide at his words. "I didn't know it was going to happen, and any other night I'd tell them to go fuck themselves but my opponent is the West Territory Don, and if I refuse I may as well just let him kill me now as I stand. I need to do this." Oh jesus, what the fuck!? I glare at him, my eyes darting back and forth between his trying to fathom what he's feeling but his eyes are as hard as stone and black as coal. It's becoming clear that there is a side to Max that I have never seen.

"I understand," I nod, "I'll do whatever you need."

"I know," he smiles before walking off towards a door at the back of the room.

Finally elbowing my way to the front of the bar, I shout for a glass of whiskey on the rocks and a bottle of water, not entirely sure of which I need more. The bartender eyes me momentarily, maybe he realizes I look a little nervous.

"Sure thing, sugar," he says, pouring Jack Daniels into a glass. The bartender places my drinks down in front of me. "Anything else?"

"No, thank you," I shout, unsure if he can hear me over the blaring speaker system, handing him $20. I feel the hairs on the back of my neck rise, sensing somebody standing right behind me.

"Hello Topolino," his voice sends a shiver down my spine. I whip my body round to face my stalker, the man from the club, the man who has been leaving me roses, who turned up at my apartment is standing right in front of me, his face plastered with a smug grin.

"You!" is all I can muster.

"Me," he jests.

"The usual?" I hear the bartender ask from behind me. So he comes here regularly then, he's mafia. My stalker nods, "On the rocks tonight Enzo," his eyes never leaving mine. His unrelenting gaze piercing straight through me until I can bare it no longer. I take a sip of my drink to disguise my discomfort. I look back to see him grinning like a cat who got the cream at the bartender as he takes a sip of his golden toned drink.

"Are you following me?" I ask, straight to the point.

His face relaxes as he laughs to himself, "To the ends of the earth Topolino." I huff in annoyance. "Besides," he says, before sipping on his drink, "you're the one in my warehouse so I guess I could ask if it's you following me?" he raises his brows and cocks his head. Oh shit.

"You wish!" I say, resting my back against the edge of the bar unable to think of anything quick or witty to say.

"Don't I know it." I hear him respond as he leans against the bar next to me. A small smile plays on my lips. I keep running into this man, this gorgeous vessel of a man with his tanned, tattooed skin, dark hair and deep mysterious eyes I want to travel the depths of but something in the very back of my mind has my guard up and I know I should approach carefully.

"So, you're into fighting?" he asks, amusement painted across his face, completely derailing my train of thought.

"Absolutely, I love to watch half naked men get all bloodied and sweaty," I say, "don't you, Tomcat?" I flash a playful grin his way.

"I must admit I do like getting my hands dirty with the rest of them, the bloodier the better," he jokes. His answer is full of truth he doesn't even have to admit to me. The only reason he is in this place is because his whole business involves getting his hands dirty.

I gasp suddenly as I'm knocked sideways as a sway of people moves against the bar and causes me to lose my footing. A strong hand reaches out and catches me around my waist before I faceplant the floor. I glance up into my stalkers eyes, his arm tight around me now as he pulls me into him. My hands are resting on his chest, I can feel his heavy breathing beneath his shirt. His eyes are burning into me, the heat off his body almost as intoxicating as the whiskey. He grins at me, his face so devilishly handsome. "You should be more careful," he says, trailing his hand from around my waist to my hips.

"Maybe you shouldn't let such clumsy people into your warehouse," I answer, the heat from his hands leaving a scorching trail in its wake.

His lips quirk at one side, "I'll have to have a word with my security staff," he responds. I push off him shaking my head. God what is going on with all these men in my life recently I shout at myself internally then remember Max's instructions to stay alert and try to clear my head.

"So why are you here tonight Topolino? It can not be just for the half naked men," he glances around before adding "or women," and giving me a cheeky wink.

"I'm here strictly on business," I reply politely, his eyebrows rising in question.

"And what business might that be while you're under my roof?" he questions stepping closer towards me.

"Uh, I'm, uhm, here as a medic tonight, for some of the fighters," I stutter, his stance intimidating. He visibly stiffens as if my answer annoys him and I'm momentarily curious as to what's going through his mind. "And you, what are you doing here? Do you attend all the fights?" I ask, a cheshire cat-like grin spreading slowly across his lips, baring his teeth as he laughs.

"I'm here to support my brother Topolino, he's fighting tonight and I sure as hell was not going to miss it." His devilish laugh cuts through me. Something inside of me screams to get out while I can but my thoughts are cut short by the announcer calling Max to the ring. A heavy feeling hits the bottom of my stomach and I feel the urge to throw up as I watch him bounce into the ring, knocking his gloves together, pumping up the crowd. His gaze falls to mine then to my stalker standing next to me. I notice his features change almost instantly and see his jaw tighten.

Moments later the announcer bellows through the microphone again. "And challenging Max Costello, is our very own benefactor, The Merciless Salvatore!!"

"Here we go," Tomcat sings excitedly.

I watch as a large hooded figure steps into the ring, my breath is caught in my lungs as I see how muscular his back is. His broad shoulders are so toned, sharp, tanned skin and tattoos cover every inch of his upper body. Something seems familiar as he pulls down his hood and hands his robe over to a man slightly off to the side. All oxygen escapes my body and I feel as though I'm spiraling as his face comes into view. I watch as he scans the entire crowd and throws his hands high above his head. The crowd is screaming and shouting his name, then suddenly his eyes meet mine. His molten stare burns straight down to my core, igniting something deep within and the memory of me pleasuring myself, fantasizing about his touch has a flood of color rushing to my cheeks. He winks at me and grins sadistically before he turns to face Max. I suck air in almost desperate to avoid passing out. What the hell is going on? I look up to Tomcat standing beside me who is studying me closely, his devilish grin never faltering.

"He's your brother? I gasp.

"Uncanny isn't it?" he remarks. I finish the rest of my whiskey in one and rush off towards the ring leaving my stalker behind.

Chapter 17

Silas

Earlier that day

I'm sitting in my office after finishing my lunch that Cole had delivered from his restaurant. I watch the cameras displaying each room the girls are performing in. We don't normally open until later but with the fight night going on at the warehouse, we have opened for a day time stag party. In room one Cherry and Mercedes are entertaining the group of men.

Cherry is dancing around the pole, still partially clothed, she has a pair of shorts and a white see through crop top on, it showcases her perky tits and erect nipples. The men are memorized by her as she slides up and down the pole with ease. Mercedes is giving the stag a personal lap dance. In my club the rule is no touching unless the girl agrees and neither girl has given consent tonight.

Mercedes is wearing a thong and bra set that displays her lean sculpted body as she circles the stag sitting in his chair, running her hands over his arms and neck and she moves around him. As she approaches his front she straddles him, bringing both her legs over his, she never breaks eye contact and is moving her hips in a circular motion. I can already see this guy is about to blow, his dick is showing through his trousers. Her tits are pushing into his chest and her nipples are hard, I'm sure he can feel them through his shirt. Keeping one leg on the ground and raising the other to push against his crotch, Mercedes stands and brings her hands to rest on each of his thighs. She turns to face the stage where Cherry is still pole dancing with different moves, currently exhibiting a cross knee release. Mercedes then bends so she is almost sitting back in his lap and grinds into him. The stag is looking flustered but keeps his hands away from her.

As she is grinding on his dick I notice that one of the other guys in the group with blond short hair has jumped on the stage where Cherry is still dancing. As she comes down the pole after performing an aerial invert move, he thrusts his hips towards her, making her stumble and fall away from the pole. He then proceeds to grab at her ass. The guy is off his face and that is all it takes for me to alert security and make my way down to the room. Marcello is already inside with Dario by the time I arrive in the room. Dario has the fucker in head lock as the stag is trying to persuade Dario in to letting his friend go.

"Please let him go, he meant nothing by it, he's had too many beers. He'll calm down, he won't do it again" he pleads. I stride into the room, making my presence known.

"I think your time in my club has come to an end boys, the rules are simple you don't touch the girls or disrespect them, and unfortunately you broke one of my rules. I suggest you leave now or we will be forced to show you the consequences of your actions," I state clearly.

"OK, OK we are out of here, we won't cause any trouble," one of the guys says shakily. I nod to Dario to release the dumb idiot from his hold.

As he does the fucker shouts. "I was just touching what I thought I paid for. She's a whore, it's not like she didn't like it."

Well fuck me, some idiots never learn. I'm not about to let this scum talk about my girls like that. She might be a stripper and even on the odd occasion take money for sexual encounters but she deserves respect and has control over who touches her. This little shit needs a lesson in manners.

I grab the cunt by the scuff of the neck and grit my teeth, "Do you know what happens to people who don't play by my rules in my world?" He's struggling in my grip, trying to get away from me but it's no use.

"I'm sorry I just got carried away, we will leave."

I laugh at his begging and reply, "Your friends are free to go but you need to learn your lesson." I nod to Marcello as he and Dario begin to remove the other men from the room with help from my other staff. Some of his friends try to plead his case but fail. It's now just me and dick face left in the room with Cherry.

"What is your name?" I ask.

"Gavin, please, I'm sorry let me go please!" he begs again.

I roll my eyes and turn to Cherry, "Did you want this Gavin to touch you? Disrespect you tonight my dear Cherry?"

She stares at him and says, "I gave him no indication that I wanted his hands on me. Boss."

I nod, "Well now Gavin, you can see my predicament can't you. If one of my girls tells me she's been disrespected by one of our clientele, then I believe it is my duty as her boss to ensure she is safe at work. So what would you do if someone touched you and you didn't want it? Would you think a beating would be enough to deter them? Or do you think they should just be let go?"

Gavin is shaking now but responds, "It was a mistake, I'm sorry!"

"OK Gavin, here is what I'm going to do, I'm a reasonable fellow. Cherry here is going to assist me and go fetch my friend Dario and once you've given me what is owed you can go free, sounds fair right?"

He nods and I grin a big toothy smile at him.

I look at Cherry tip my chin, "Be a good girl and find Dario, I need him to assist me."

Two minutes later Dario returns.

144

"You needed me, Boss?" he asks.

"Dario my good man, I need you to hold on to Gavin here. He's accepted that once he's paid what is owed he can leave here and never show his face in my club again." Dario moves swiftly and takes a firm hold of Gavin. "Hold his hand down on the table please Dario."

He does as I request all whilst Gavin is struggling and crying, "Please what are you doing? I have money, you said what is owed, I'll pay, it was a mistake!" He's blubbering now and it's even more annoying.

"I never said anything about money Gavin, I don't need your money. I have more money than god" I tell him. I reach into my jacket and remove my switch blade and grab his hand, with a quick movement I slice his little finger from his hand, "Payment received Gavin," blood sprays from the point where his now missing finger should be and he wails in agony.

"Dario takes him to get that cleaned up, then return him to his friends." I turn to leave the room, sending Marcello back in to help Dario deal with Gavin.

Making my way back to my office, I need to collect my things then head home before getting ready for my fight tonight. As I enter my office I find Cherry sitting on my sofa, she looks up to me saying, "Boss, thank you so much for saving me, you have always been my hero." I wait for her to continue knowing that Cherry isn't finished with her thanks. "I thought maybe I could repay you after your fight tonight, release some of that tension, what do you think? It would be free, I'd serve you just the way you like." She says fluttering her lashes and pushing her tits together whilst looking up at me.

I shake my head and say "What I did for you I would have done for all you girls, I don't need your thanks or services, now go and get your things Cherry you can have the rest of the night off."

She replies "Oh OK, well if you change your mind you know where I am. Thank you again." she leaves and all I can think of is Lucille and how I wish she would give me an offer like Cherry just did, my dick is instantly hard at the thought of la mia Luce begging for my cock. I collect my things and head out to ready myself for the events ahead.

Arriving home, I head straight to my ensuite bathroom. My hungry desire for Lucille is becoming increasingly distracting, I can't get her out of my head. Turning the shower on extra hot, making the steam engulf the room, I shed my clothes and step in. Feeling the warm soothing water rain down on my back, I close my eyes, remembering the way Lucille's delicate hands touched mine. The way her breath caught at the sight of me and how the blush filled her cheeks as she gathered herself. Her luscious and hypnotic voice is cemented into my mind as are her full pouting lips. Before I can help myself my hand is on my hard length as I imagine her plump lips wrapped around my hard cock, she would take me fully into her mouth, I can almost feel how good her tongue would feel licking the tip of my erection. I pump my hand up and down, thinking of thrusting my cock down her silk like throat, her face blushing beautifully, cheeks tear stained as I fuck her pretty little mouth. Envisaging her on her knees taking me like a good girl, has me erupting over the bathroom tiles quicker than I have since I was a teenage boy. Taking a deep breath, I turn the shower to cold in a hope that will temper my desire for la mia luce. Stepping out, I can still feel this craving for her. I dress quickly, trying to put this to the back of my mind once again, I must focus on the events that will allow me to claim her.

Pulling up outside the warehouse I let out a breath I didn't realize I was holding. I need this, I tell myself. I grab my shit and head inside to let my demons out to play.

Entering the warehouse I head straight to the dressing room and start to prepare myself. This is it, this is how I will win my prize and how those Irish bastards will crumble at my feet, I will show everyone that I own this city.

Zoning out, I close my eyes focusing on my senses. The smell of bleach floods my nose, I can hear the crowd roaring and the music booming, the announcers are introducing Max Costello to the ring. I stand to face myself in the mirror, I look at my dark hair that is cut short, the tattoos that travel from my chest to my neck and down my arms. My eyes are honey brown and my facial hair is close shaven. I'm ready to take down my opponent but is la mia Luce ready for that I wonder. Only time will tell.

A knock at the door startles me from my thoughts. "They are about to announce you, Fratello," Linc tells me. I wonder where Cole has gotten to. As if reading my mind Linc says, "Cole is with the girl, he said he'll bring her to you if you win against the Irish scum, so you best win or he'll keep her to himself," he grins at me, he always likes a bet, it's no wonder he owns a successful casino.

The incentive to win Lucille has me eager to fight and claim my prize. I turn to the door that leads to the ring and pull the hood up of my black and emerald green robe. Green for her eyes that see straight through me and into my soul.

I make my way out of the changing room, as I enter the arena the announcer bellows down the microphone, "And challenging Max Costello is our very own benefactor, The Merciless Salvatore." The soundtrack I picked thunders through the speakers, 'No Easy Way Out,' by Robert Tepper.

The crowd is going wild, shouting and screaming. I try to block it all out and focus on my opponent, he's stood in his corner glaring at me as I make my way towards the ring. As I step into the ring, I pass my robe to Linc. I raise my hands to the air and look to the crowd, I find green piercing eyes looking at me with disbelief, mi Luce. Cole is looking smug standing next to her. I wink at her, then return to face my opponent.

"Costello, are you ready to see stars tonight? She's a pretty little thing at the bar next to my brother isn't she. Do you think we should make a bet? I win and I win her. You win and my brother wins her? What do you say?" I'm baiting him, I can see the veins in his head popping with anger. What he doesn't know is win or lose she's mine but I still don't intend to lose.

Max snarls at me, "You won't be touching a hair on her head, you Italian piece of shit." I laugh, not taking my eyes away from his, I step towards him as he does to me, we are nose to nose now and I can smell the blood already.

The referee steps in to separate us, "Back into your corners men," he grunts to us both. I smirk and obey as does Max. "We go for a maximum of twelve rounds, three minutes each. The one with the advantage wins the round or whoever gives the knockout blow wins the match, anything apart from weapons in this match is acceptable, are we agreed?" The ref says through the microphone but is directing the question at me and Costello. I nod, so does Max. "Are we ready?" The ref shouts to the crowd as they all cheer. "Gentlemen on the sound of the bell the fight commences," the referee explains as he steps aside and gives the nod, the bell is rang.

I hold my stance, left foot slightly forward, left arm slightly extended with my right arm held closer to my body near my chin. I'm bouncing from foot to foot, readying myself to dodge and duck Costello's jabs. My opponent comes in towards me, I throw a right hook to his face, making him stumble back and spit blood to the floor, his lip is bloody, the sight is glorious. He recovers quickly, dancing around me and making a swift jab to my left rib.

Holding my stance, I counter with a jab of my own to his stomach. He gasps as he brings his head forward as he attempts to head butt me, I dodge him. He moves quickly getting another jab to my ribs. I rapidly move to grab him around the neck, I tightened my hold on him in an attempt to cut off his air supply but the bastard winds me by elbowing me and flipping me off him. Whilst I'm down, I swing my leg and bring him to the floor. I grab him and punch him, splitting his eyebrow open, his blood splatters over me. The bell rings, three minutes is up. One round to me, another eleven to go unless I can knock the fucker out before then.

I'm sitting back in my corner, Linc is checking me over. My blood hasn't been spilt yet but I'm sure I have bruised ribs. "Listen, you need to make this a quick defeat fratello," Linc encourages. I look over to Costello, he is getting his eyebrow and lip seen to by one of his men, he grins at me with a bloody red smile. With that the second bell is rung, both of us are on our feet ready for the next round. Taking my stance again, I ready myself as Max charges at me, landing a forceful jab to my stomach. I stumble on my feet slightly but hold myself up, I counter his jab with a right hook to the side of his head making him fall to the ground. The ref dashes over and starts to count, but Costello shakes himself off. On his feet again he charges forward towards me, this time he knocks me back into the ropes, landing a blow to my face causing my nose to spray blood everywhere. As I try to regain my balance the bell rings, end of round two and we are on a draw.

Collapsing back into his corner Max looks tired. I grin and shout, "Tired already Costello?" He spits towards me. "That's not friendly," I laugh. He doesn't reply. I know I'm getting to him both mentally and physically.

As I take my seat in my corner of the ring Linc jumps in to clean the blood from my face, "Keep getting hit like that and the girl won't come near you even if you do win," he says matter of factly.

I glare at him and it's all I can do not to punch him too, "She'll enjoy every minute of the blood and sweat from my victory."

Two minutes later, the bell rings for the third time. I decide to go on the offensive and charge towards Costello, I surprise him by landing an uppercut to his face and jab to his ribs. He gasps and holds a defense stance. I take another swing towards him, and with my final hit I send the Irish bastard flying to the ground. He is out cold. The referee starts to count, one, two, three, four, five, six, seven, eight, nine and TEN.

The audience goes crazy, screaming. "And the winner is, The Merciless Salvatore!" The referee bellows down the microphone.

I grin while my brother and Linc jump into the ring to embrace me, cheering me on. I look over to Max Costello, he is staggering to his feet. I go to put my hand out as a friendly gesture. He takes it but at that moment mi Luce climbs into the ring and screams. "What have you done to him, you monster!" I drop his hand, I'm taken back by the emotion in her face and voice. She rushes to check over Costello's injuries, she's assessing him and he grins at me, looking at me like he's won the real fight.

I step forward to wipe it off his face when Cole steps in front of me and says in a low voice, "Don't rise to his bait brother, it won't make her choose you over him, it will just push her away."

He's right but fuck has it pissed me off. I turn and storm out of the ring back to the changing room with more anger than I had before. She was comforting him and she thinks of me as the monster, I didn't want her to see me that way. I look at myself in the mirror, the reflection staring back at me makes me angry, the monster she sees is looking back at me. My rage gets the best of me, I let out a roar and punch the mirror shattering the glass into a million pieces. Blood now coats my knuckles and drips onto the floor. But it's all I can do to focus on the sting to distract me from how distraught she looked.

Cole appears behind me and huff's out a breath, "Fratello, Linc has gone to persuade Topolino to come and see you. Sort your temper out otherwise I won't let you near her. Do you understand?"

I stare at him and nod. "I would never hurt her, Cole." I tell him calmly.

"You may not mean it Silas, but I won't take the risk with her if you can't promise me. She's special, so don't fuck it up for us. Be kind to her when she's here." Cole says it's like he's warning me. I don't like that but I respect him for it.

"I promise she'll never be safer than when she is with me" I say truthfully. Cole nods and leaves the room in search of whiskey to celebrate. The truth is I'd protect her and her son from anyone that means harm to them. I just need to prove it to her.

It's time for me to show this woman who I really am.

Chapter 18

Lucille

The fight only lasts 3 rounds before Max is knocked to the floor. Every prolonged second of the referee's count seemed to stab me straight through the chest. It's hard to watch as he lies limp on the floor, blood oozing from his lip and the split over his eyebrow while his opponent watches on, triumph beaming bright from his face. My anger rages louder than the crowd when the referee finally roars, "And the winner is, The Merciless Salvatore!" into the microphone and I catch Tomcat and a guy who looks vaguely familiar, hop through the ropes and bound themselves excitedly straight into his outstretched arms, celebrating his win. Their shouts of victory ignite a fire in me I never knew was possible.

Max steadies himself as he comes too, pulling himself up off the floor. Visibly concussed, he stumbles forward towards his opponent's outstretched hand. He can not be serious, he wants to shake his fucking hand!? I am full of anger and before I can stop myself I'm already climbing between the ropes and screaming in this brutes face. His beautifully demonic, bloodied face.

"What have you done to him, you monster!" I scream, unable to stop myself, while shoving at his chest. His brows furrows in the middle and his face suddenly contorts somewhere between hurt and anger. It stops me from lashing out again.

I turn to face Max and help him back onto the stool in his corner of the ring and begin dousing a cloth with warm water to soak the already dried blood painted onto his face. He smirks widely, baring bloodied teeth in his opponents direction. I scold him quietly, "Don't fucking gloat you dick, you lost!"

"But the look on his face is priceless," he chuckles, before wincing as I apply pressure to his split eyebrow.

We stay quiet for a few minutes while I debride his wound and apply a few butterfly stitches to close it. "These will hold for now but you may need some sutures if it continues to bleed. Your lip will be fine. Your ego I'm not so sure about." He scoffs at me. "Who was it you were fighting? What's his name?" I ask, trying not to sound as interested as I really am. Max's face hardens and I can tell he's deliberating his answer.

After a painfully long minute he finally spits out, "His name is Silas Salvatore. He's a piece of shit. The Italian Don. Boss of the West territory and our main rivals. They've had it out for us big time ever since one of their main guys mother got shot and they pinned it on us," he tips his chin up in the direction over to the side and I follow his gaze over to where the second man, who I now realize is Linc, who I met in the park only a few days ago, stands deeps in conversation with a group of men, all of whom are built like bloody brick shit houses.

My eyes widen and a small but audible gasp escapes my throat. "I know him," I say, eyes still focusing on Linc, now absolutely sure he is the man from the park. "I know Silas. I know them all." I say, each word getting quieter as I do.

Max's harsh grip on my arm startles me. "What do you mean you know them?" His voice more of a demand than a question.

I gape open mouthed at him, the feel on his fingers tightening around my bicep. "You're hurting me," I say.

His eyes all of a sudden soften as he apologizes. "I'm sorry, but you must listen to me. You can not get involved with these men, they're dangerous!" He pauses before repeating the question. "How do you know them?"

I swallow hard and begin to explain. "Silas was an inmate at HDSP when I did my monthly rotation there not long ago. He was waiting for treatment when I got back from my lunch break. I didn't know his name, I didn't ask." I feel the heat rise in my cheeks at the memory, hoping Max won't notice.

"Did you tell him anything about yourself?" Max asks, the answer already written on the horrified look upon my face. He lowers his head and runs his fingers through his hair.

"I only told him my name!" I blurt out. "It's not that bad is it?"

He looks up to me. "That's all he would need to know, Luce. How do you know his brother Cole, and what about Lincoln Rossi?"

I cringe debating whether or not to mention meeting Cole in JEWEL the night he looked after Teddy and Bella, and for letting him take me home after, though at the time I didn't realize it was him. He'll think I'm fucking stupid for sure at letting my guard down so easily, and I kissed him for fuck sake, I really am a lost cause. His one eyebrow cocks and I know I have to tell him. "I met him in the club, the night I went out with Kat." I say, holding my breath for his response, intentionally leaving out the few minor or maybe major details he doesn't need to know. "And Linc I met in the park with Teddy, his son was with him and he helped get Teddy's plane down when he got it stuck in the tree."

Max snaps his head immediately. "The day I was with you at the park?" His eyes now almost burn a hole into the back of Lincoln Rossi's head. I nod slowly. "I fucking knew it was him on that bench!" He roars, standing up straight. He wobbles slightly, holding onto the ropes to steady himself. "He knew who you were, Lucille. Don't you get that? They all know who you are. You're one of us and that

154

means something to them!" His voice is desperate now and his eyes are pleading with mine. "You need to stay away from them, they're dangerous."

I blink at him, unable to respond straight away. He grabs onto my elbow and attempts to leave the ring. "Get off me Max," I say as I snatch my arm away. "How bad can they be, really? You brought me here, you knew whose club this was. If you didn't want me involved then you shouldn't have fucking asked me! Don't mind putting me at risk when it helps you, do you?"

Max looks at me like I've just stabbed him in the chest. "Luce, I…"

"Don't bother!" I say, holding my hands up as I start to retreat backwards. "I'll find my own way home." I turn quickly on my heel and climb through the ropes back into the crowd of people still singing Silas' victory.

I'm almost at the exit and unsure how the hell I'm going to get home. I can't call Kat, it's way too late and the kids are probably sleeping, when a sharp tug on my wrist stops me from going any further. "For fuck sake Max, I said…," I start as I turn to face him, but the rest of my words fail me as I come face to face with Lincoln Rossi. I gasp in shock, he looks like a different version of himself than when I met him in the park, more serious, more threatening. I look at him properly this time, my eyes looking for any indication that he'll hurt me, but there are none and I'd be blind if I didn't recognise how beautiful he is. Just like the other two, with tanned skin and dark features, a light shadowing of stubble across his jawline and the edging of tattoos, creeping up from his collar, that I imagine line all the way across the dips of his muscles beneath his shirt. I breathe in trying to remain calm.

"We need your help," he says, matter of factly. I blink, mouth agape in utter astonishment, who are they and what the hell do they need MY help with.

155

Glancing quickly at the exit, trying to judge how long it would take me to get there if I pushed him and ran. He immediately senses my hesitation and releases my wrist, holding his hands up as if to let me know he comes in peace. "I won't hurt you Lucille, please trust me."

The little voice in my head is screaming loudly at me to run. Surely only people who are about to hurt you tell you they won't hurt you, and the people who tell you to trust them, you really shouldn't. I take a slow step backward edging closer to the door. "Did you follow me and my son to the park last week?" I ask nervously, unsure if I want to know the answer.

I notice his jaw tighten and his muscles flex beneath his shirt. "No Lucille, I did not. I was already there with my son and I didn't recognise Max either till he was leaving. If that was your next question." I think hard about his answer, so many questions springing to mind, but before I can ask any of them he starts again. "I won't lie to you Lucille. I knew who you were as soon as I figured out it was you on that park bench. I could explain it all, but you're going to want to hear this from the boss, and right now he needs a medic. So please, will you help us?"

"Boss? As in Silas?" I ask, my mouth drying at the mention of his name. Linc nods and holds his hand out for me to take. I glance down at it, and raging a war against all of my instincts to turn away, I place my hand in his and nod. I need some god damn answers and if this is how I get them, then so be it.

Linc leads me back through the crowd, the music blaring louder now and the lights turned down low, the excitement from the fight still buzzing through the air. We head towards the changing rooms at the back of the warehouse and come to a stop outside of a room marked PRIVATE where he drops my hand and turns to face me. "He's through there," he points, his chin towards the door. "He's expecting you."

I tut and rolled my eyes in disbelief, so they knew I'd just accept their cries for help then. I reach forward and grab hold of the door handle, my palms already slick with sweat. I'm so nervous it's seeping out of my skin.

Linc leans forward and gently places his hand on my arm. "He won't hurt you Lucille. If he does, I'll kill him myself," he says, his face deadly serious before leaving me alone at the door, his words reeling through my head. That was kind of hot in a fucked up sort of way, and if I wasn't about to come face to face with the devil it may just have turned me on. I swallow hard, *it's now or never* I say to myself, trying to hype myself up, unsure of what to expect when I open the door. I lift one hand to the solid wood and knock three times so he knows I'm here, and taking a deep breath, I slowly tilt the handle and push the door open as I step inside the dressing room.

Silas is sitting on a long wooden bench in between two lines of lockers running the length of the walls as I step through the threshold, slowly closing the door behind me until I hear it click into place. To the left of me there's a punching bag hanging from chains attached to a bracket from the ceiling, a running machine and a weight rack set up to my right, and a little further across, rests a huge full length mirror that's been shattered into a thousand tiny pieces. A mixture of blood and glass covers the floor like little sparkles of confetti. I gasp, my mouth instantly drying at the sight of the carnage in the room and the bare chested beast before me, plastered in blood and sweat.

Some of which is his, some of which is my brothers.

I have to avert my eyes towards the floor to be able to speak, otherwise I'm sure to implode under his penetrating gaze, "I will only help you if you promise to give me some answers," I start, squirming uncomfortably, hoping my voice sounds more confident than I'm feeling inside. I hear what sounds like a chuckle escaping his lips and dare to glance up at him. I'm caught off guard by his rugged good looks, even with his busted nose. My bravado disintegrates and I know in this moment that he knows it too, he intimidates the shit out of me. I stand as still as a statue with my back flush against the door, as he stands too, and begins slowly creeping towards me, like a predator stalking down its prey. Each agonizing step causes my heart to pound hard against my chest, threatening to escape, and I'm sure he can hear it.

He stands before me, his entire body almost double my own. I can feel his breath hot against my skin and the smell of musk, whiskey and blood, all tingling through my nose. "You'll do well not to blackmail me, la mia Luce," he whispers, his lips now inches away from mine. My breathing hitches as I remember the warning that Max had given me about how dangerous these men are. Silas takes a step back, a smugness coating his face as he looks down at me and raises a blood soaked hand towards me, turning it over to reveal a shard of glass wedged deep into a laceration across his knuckle. "I'll answer whatever you ask, bella." I try my best to regain my composure as I reach out for his hand and take it in mine. I lead him back to the bench in the middle of the room, silently instructing him to sit down. He obliges immediately and takes his seat. "There's a first aid kit in the bathroom," he says, nodding his head in the direction of a single door at the back of the room.
"If you had a first aid kit, you could have just done this yourself." I jeer at him before walking to retrieve it.
"Ah," he smiles on my return. "It is much more fun to inflict pain on others than it is to do it to myself." The smugness on his face beginning to irritate me.
"Is that why you're doing this?" I ask, a fire igniting in my belly. "You think it's funny to hurt people?"

His face drops as soon as I've said it. "Mia luce, I would never hurt you," he says, pulling me in between his knees with a firm grip on my hips.

I push him away, "I can not help you if you do that," I scold, leaving him smiling again.

Pulling his hand back to mine, I sit on the bench next to him, placing his hand on my knee for support. I feel him tense at the contact but try to ignore it and carefully begin to prize the glass shard from his knuckle. "Why are you having me followed?" I ask, narrowing my eyes at the intricate task in front of me.

"From the first moment I saw you in that prison, I haven't been able to get you out of my mind. You have consumed my every thought and encapsulated my soul, la mia luce. I needed to make sure you were safe. I trust my men, I knew they would watch over you until I was able to get to you myself."

I furrow my brow thinking his reply posed even more questions than answers. "Why wouldn't I be safe? I have never felt in more danger than I do now. Now that you've implanted yourself into my life, now that you're having me watched."

His free hand grips the edge of my chin and he tips my head up to look at him. "You will never be in danger with me Lucille," he says, his eyes full of intent, "you have my word."

I tsk my teeth loudly, his promises nothing but whispers in the wind. Pulling my chin from his grasp I look back down to wrap a tight bandage around his injured hand now I'm satisfied that all of the glass fragments have been removed. I pull firmly on the fabric and tie a knot, ensuring it's secure, causing him to wince slightly.

"Done." I say, looking back at his face. "Just don't punch anything else for a while and it should heal quickly," I remark.

He cocks his lips on one side and smiles, "Deal!" he says, his face full of boyish charm.

Noticing his eyes roaming down over my body, I suddenly remember he is only half dressed in front of me, his shorts leaving very little to the imagination as they stretch out over his bulky thighs, his bare torso hard and lean, his muscles straining against his tattooed skin. Desire floods my body and I can already feel the dampness in my panties, picturing all the things this beast of a man could do to me. I run my tongue across my bottom lip, resisting my inner urge to mount him right here right now.

Silas watches me, eyes hooded, his want and need practically dripping from his body. "I can't do this," I whisper, standing and turning towards the exit door, I need to get out of here.

"Where are you going?" he barks. "Back to that Irish scum?" His words pierce through me and I turn to face him.

"What did you just say?" I ask, the fire inside now doubling in size, ready to explode. Desire now replaced by fury. This man really knows how to get under my skin.

"Costello," he spits venomously. "I saw you pawing yourself all over him, that Irish prick all smug in the ring after I fucking beat him."

"DON'T YOU DARE!" I scream, running forwards to where he's now standing. I fling my arms like a wild animal aiming for his face, chest, arms, anything within my reach. In one swift swoop his hands grasp tightly around my wrists, holding me in place. My eyes widen in shock, then narrow at him. "DON'T YOU DARE CALL HIM THAT YOU PIECE OF SHIT!" I rage in his face, his angry yet beautiful, bloodied face. "Is that all I am to you?" I rasp. "Just a piece of fucking meat in your little game of secrets." I can not hide the hurt in my voice now. "Just a fucking pissing contest!"

Silas is still for a moment before his pupils constrict into narrow slits, completely transforming his face into something demonic. "So you won't trust me, but instead have the Irish eating out the palm of your hand?" his grip on me tightens. "Silly little girl, I would watch what you're saying. I've already told you I would never hurt you so don't test me. But him, he will bury you and never look back," he snarls.

"Fuck you, Silas!" I shout, trying to free myself from his hold so I can take my own shot at his face. Suddenly a loud growl erupts from his throat as he slams me backwards into the lockers, smacking my head hard against the metal. Now with one hand restraining both of my arms above my head and the other at my throat, he renders me completely defenseless.

"What does he have over you that you would choose him over me? What does he have that I cannot give to you!?" He seethes, through gritted teeth. I can see the anger pulsating in his temples and rippling through his biceps as he holds me firm against the lockers. I have to stay focused because the angrier he gets, the wetter I become. I shouldn't like this but I do, my body is betraying me and right now I want him to hurt me, to bend me to his will, to make me scream his name.

"He's my fucking brother you prick," I spit in to his face.

Instantly his grip around my throat loosens and he pulls back his head to look me dead in the eyes. I freeze beneath his gaze, my chest rising and falling rapidly as the adrenaline courses through my body and I try desperately to regain my own breath.

All of a sudden the world seems to spin on its axis with Silas and I dead in the center. With a flash of movement he fists his hand into my hair at the back of my head and crushes his lips to mine. I fight it at first, the overwhelming concoction of emotions still raging through me so out of tune with each other. I try my hardest to resist, but my struggles are nothing compared to his overbearing weight

161

pressed against me. I give in and part my lips to his, giving him a green light and as his tongue begins to explore my mouth, my own fights his back with just as much vigor. A deep feral growl escapes his throat as we wrestle for dominance in each other's mouths.

Silas pulls back from me panting loudly, "I need you now," he rasps, before releasing my hands from above my head and claiming my lips again with his hands holding either side of my face. A treacherous moan slips between my lips and it only adds fuel to his fire. He pulls back again, and with his eyes black as coal and an animalistic snarl pinned on his face, he looks terrifying. Terrifying but beautiful. I gasp as he slips his hands down my chest and hungrily rips open my shirt, scattering the buttons across the room.

"I can't," I struggle to protest but am cut off by his lips once more as he devours my mouth and pushes my shirt off my shoulders. My mind is reeling at what's happening, I know I shouldn't be doing this, I shouldn't be enjoying it but I am and I need to feel him inside of me right now, I need the real thing this time not my imagination.

With primal desire taking over me, I push hard against his chest pushing him a few steps backwards. He looks startled at first but stands and stares at me as I pull my tank top over my head and drop it to the floor. As I unbutton my jeans, he realizes what I'm doing and his eyes become wild with desire. I begin to shimmy my jeans down my legs, keeping my eyes locked on his the whole time. Am I trying to be sexy? Who knows, sure as hell not me. I watch as his gaze roam over my body only covered by my underwear, feeling smug that I decided to wear a matching lace set today. At this moment, Silas makes me feel like the sexiest woman in the world. Within seconds he's on me again, his mouth hot and heavy, suffocating me with his tongue. "Enough," he growls, lifting me and slamming me back into the lockers, placing his hands on the back side of my thighs, keeping me in place. I wrap my legs tight against his waist and link my arms around his neck. "Beg me," he whispers, his voice sending shivers straight down to my core. I move against him, trying to feel the friction between my legs. "BEG ME!" he orders again, his voice hard and impatient this time.

"Please Silas," I moan against his lips. As soon as the words escape my mouth he frees one hand and adjusts his shorts. I feel his fingers trace their way between my legs and pull my panties to the side. My stomach instantly flips at the feel of him and the anticipation of what's to come. His fingers gently graze the edge of my pussy lips before he pushes them inside and a sigh of approval leaves his throat. Christ that was hot.

"So wet for me Lucille," he praises, biting a trail from my earlobe down to my collar bone and with a quick dip of his hips he lines the tip of his rock hard cock to my entrance and thrusts deep inside of me. I gasp loudly, almost breathless at how full he makes me. Never have I felt this full from a man's cock before. His girth stretches me wide enough that it edges on the side of painful. But when he moves his hips again pulling back, he leaves me empty and wanting more.

"Beg me, Lucille," he pants, grinding his hips into me slowly and painfully teasing me until I can take it no longer, and I need to find my release.

"Silas. Please, I need this" I groan, the frustration building. He answers my pleas immediately and thrusts his hips forwards, hitting my sweet spot deep inside. He fucks me hard and fast against the lockers, pounding into my desperate pussy with his nails biting at the bare flesh on my ass, that I'm sure will leave some questionable marks, as he holds me exactly where he wants me. I fist my fingers through his hair and pull harshly, dragging an orgasm inducing groan from within him. He fucks me like an animal, wild and dirty, all the while I can feel my climax burning bright toward the point of explosion. His cock stretches me to fit him each time he enters me. Each of his hip thrusts hitting the top of my clit as he grinds against me, building and building until I can feel the pressure ready to blow. I clench my legs around his waist as he tips me straight over the edge, eyes rolling back into my head as a feral scream breaks free from my lungs and a deep sated grunt from his as he plunges deeper inside of me once more. I feel his length judder inside of me as my muscles clench around him, and I milk him of everything he's got as he reaches his climax inside me. My head lolls forwards against his shoulder as he comes down from his high, my vision glazing over.

Silas kisses me one last time, his lips a delicious mixture between soft and hard before he gently lowers me back to the floor on trembling legs. I feel him slip out of me, his cock still standing proud in front, as his release seeps slowly from my core. The instant empty feeling from where he was just belly deep inside me, is now a gaping hollow, like the black abyss. Like some sinister part of me has been ripped out at the seams. Why do I feel so empty? With my senses suddenly heightened I can feel every hair on my arms stand to attention. I need to get the hell out of here. I should not have done that, I shouldn't have been so stupid. Still feeling the sticky residue clinging to my thighs I hastily pull on my jeans and T-shirt, all the while feeling Silas' burning gaze on the back of my head. "We shouldn't have done that," I whisper. "I have to go."

Silas grabs my wrist as I try to leave. "I don't regret anything Lucille and neither should you," he says, the lines edged in his face are stern but I see the concern in his eyes.
I shake my head, pulling my arm from his hold.
"I'm sorry," I cry as I'm unable to hold them back any longer.
I turn and run, leaving the beast behind me.

164

Chapter 19

Cole

Music is blasting as I grab the bottle of whiskey from behind the bar, the beat is pulsating in the air. People are celebrating Silas's win and the Costellos have swiftly left the warehouse.

Intoxicated bodies are swaying in the dance area as I make my way back to the locker room where I left Silas to calm down before Topolino joined him. I'm hoping they have reconciled and he's charmed his way into explaining things to her. Silas can be an alphahole and sometimes struggles to let people see his softer side.

As I'm making my way down the corridor leading back, the door flies open and Topolino runs out. Tears are running down her blush filled face, her hair is tussled, her lips more pouty than usual. Then it clicks, she looks freshly fucked. As she goes to pass me in a hurry, I grab her elbow softly, and pass her my keys, leaning into her ear to whisper, "Wait for me by my bike, I will have a word with my brother and ensure you get home safely." Her big watery green eyes look up to me and she nods then races past me towards the exit.

I glare over to my brother. He has his hands in his hair watching her run away from him, then looks over to me once she is out of sight. "She freaked out, we argued, then she told me who Max Costello is to her." He pushes his hand through his hair again, tilting his head back looking to the ceiling, taking a deep breath he says, "He's her brother, I couldn't help myself and I made the first move, she consented but the aftershock had her running." I nod and understand emotions are running high between them.

"It's OK brother, I will make sure she's safe, but you need to make this right with her once she is calm and not in a frenzy from your dick," I laugh out.

He looks at me and shakes his head. "You always know how to lighten the situation Cole. Watch out for her. I don't think I could handle anything happening to her." I can see the genuine concern running through his features.

"Don't worry, she has the three of us watching over her now, you'll see." I tell him, before going after Lucille.

As I leave the warehouse building, I see her standing next to my bike. Also standing next to her is Roxi. Oh shit. I take in a deep breath before strolling over to them. I ignore Roxi standing there and pull Topolino into my arms and whisper to her, "If you have questions about me, Silas or Linc come to us and we will always tell you the truth. But first, let's get you home." I release her and pass her a helmet to my bike. Turning to Roxi I ask, "Is there something you need, Roxanne?"

Roxi flutters her eyelashes and looks at me. "I just saw she was upset and came over to see if she's OK. If she's a friend of yours I'll look out for her." By looking out for her she means she wants to mark her territory like a bitch in heat, but she doesn't get that I'm all Lucille's now.

"Lucille is none of your concern Roxanne. The only concern you should have is why you are outside not doing your job inside with good paying customers?"

She looks from me to Lucille and smirks, "I was on my break, and was about to find you to assist you on my knees." I count to ten in my head, my patience with her is on thin ice. I'm tempted to pull my gun out and shoot her between the eyes for trying to come between me and Topolino.

"Roxi, like I've told you over and over again. I won't ever need your services again and I haven't needed them for a long while. Especially since you've got yourself acquainted with Lincs father, you know I see all Roxi." Her face burns red with anger and she storms off back inside. Maybe I should have mentioned that one earlier.

I turn to Lucille, "Let's get out of here. I've had enough of this place tonight."
Securing Lucille's helmet and my own, I jump on the bike, waiting for Lucille to get on behind me. She hesitates for a second but climbs on. I can feel her breasts pressing at my back as her arms delicately find their way around me, her hands settling on my toned stomach. I smile at how right this feels to have her holding on to me. "Topolino, hold on tight and get ready to feel free." I tell her before putting my foot down and racing through the city. As we hit the highway I finally feel her relax behind me, ten minutes later we were pulling outside her house.

I bring the bike on to her driveway, and Lucille dismounts the bike, taking a few steps towards her front door. As I begin to follow her she suddenly turns to face me before opening her door and says, "Look, thank you for bringing me home. You don't need to make excuses for your brother or even yourself. I get you are a rival gang to my brothers and I was just collateral damage. Just a pawn in your games to see who could win some dick measuring contest but you know what? Fuck you, fuck you all! I deserve more." I see the rage in her eyes but I also see the fire and the hurt at thinking she wasn't enough and that we only wanted her for some gang warfare. I move closer towards her, she steps back so her back is now pressed up against her door and my hands are caging her head on either side.
"Well, as you've made your mind up about me and my brother and probably even Linc, I'll have to work extra hard

to show you just how much you have come to mean to me, and them. Topolino, do you understand why I call you that? Little mouse?" Her eyes are wide as she shakes her head. I continue, "Because from the first moment I saw you, I knew I'd never stop chasing you. I'd never tire of you and most importantly, you are mine and I am yours. I will not have anyone hurt you, that includes my brother and Linc. Even myself, do you understand?" I am so close to her now my lips are less than a centimeter away from hers. I step back and wait for her to respond. She just looks at me chewing her lip, her chest is rising and falling with her panting breaths as she tries to think of what to say.

"If that's true, why did you let Linc come and fetch me and throw me to the biggest wolf of them all?" she finally says.

I look at her and smirk, "Because you were in no danger with Silas. What he took from you tonight was something that was given freely by you. You just need to accept that he is yours as I am and as Linc will be too. Do you wish to continue this conversation on the doorstep where Mr. Walker is peeking out of his window?" I ask.

She looks over to her neighbors house and sees the curtain twitch, then huff's, "Fine, come in but this time you will answer all of my questions Tomcat! First being your real name!"

She unlocks the door and storms off into her house. I step inside, taking my shoes off before entering her lounge area where she has already grabbed a bottle of vodka, taking a large swig out of it before handing it to me. I take the bottle looking at it and say, "Let's make this interesting, every question one of us asks we answer. But if it's something we can't or don't wish to share, we take a drink of this." Waving the vodka bottle at her.

"That's just like playing, 'Never have I ever'," she says, rolling her eyes.

"Well it's better than just drinking ourselves into oblivion without finding out some truths, don't you think, Topolino?" I grin at her.

"Fine, you answer first. What's your real name?" She asks seriously.

"Cole Valentine Salvatore. Not many people know my middle name, it's after my mother." I answer truthfully and she nods.

"Do you regret tonight?" I ask.

She sucks in a breath, surprised by my question then shakes her head, "I don't regret it, but I wish it would have happened differently." I understand that, probably in an ideal world she would have met Silas under different circumstances.

"I understand that but know that Silas, however his actions might have come across, he cares about you. He would never mean you harm. He's not good with his words, he sometimes doesn't think before he speaks or acts especially when he's emotional. Do you wish I'd never approached you in that bar?" I ask.

She looks at me, really looks at me, and shakes her head again. "No I'm glad you did, you made sure I got home safe, didn't you? I don't remember much from that night but you made me feel happy and safe. I suppose this is the second time you've made sure I'm safe, plus you've given me my first motorcycle ride. I've never felt freer, I think you might have me addicted."

I smile, I don't mind her being addicted as long as she only rides with me. Smiling at her I say, "Like I said Topolino, I'll never let you get hurt. So, if that means ensuring you get home safely, or watching out from afar if you don't want anything more to do with me after tonight, then that is what I'll do. I wasn't lying when I said I wouldn't let anyone, not even my brother, Linc or myself harm you. That goes for Teddy too, I will protect him too with my life if needed."

Lucille shifts, and moves closer towards me. "Thank you Cole, your brother and your friend are lucky to have you fighting in their corner. Do you not care that your brother fucked me tonight? Does that not make you want to run a mile?"

I take her hand in mine and look at her. "Lucille, I've never been normal. I'm a bit unhinged if you haven't already noticed. Things like that don't bother me, what bothers me is if you're happy and as long as you are, I will do as you wish." She squeezes my hand, I then ask, "Who is Teddy's father?" She freezes and picks up the bottle and downs at least a quarter. I frown, maybe that's too personal of me to ask, but it makes me wonder if we should look into who it is, if they are a danger.

"Have you slept with Roxi? Is she your girlfriend? Or ex?" She asks quickly to change the subject or maybe the alcohol has given her courage to ask this question.

"She's none of those things, she's just someone to get my dick wet with. One I've unfortunately used a couple of times." I reply leaving it at that, she's not ready to hear about my kinks tonight.

She nods and says, "Do you have any more questions for me? I'm going to get changed out of this if you don't mind." She stands waiting for me to respond.

"Are you hungry? I can make you some food if you like while you shower and change?" I ask her.

Her stomach grumbles at the mention of food and I smile as she replies, "That would be great, I don't have much in though. Do you really like cooking? Was that what you told me when we met or did I imagine that?"

I like that she remembers our conversation. "Yes I enjoy it, go get cleaned up and I'll whip something up."

She turns and saunters off to her bedroom. I make my way to her kitchen and look in her fridge. She has eggs, milk and butter and some other items. I look in her cupboards to see if she has some flour and syrup, she does. I decide to make her pancakes because who doesn't love pancakes. I hear the shower turn off as I'm dishing up, I put the syrup on the table and some cut up strawberries in a bowl next to the pancakes. I turn to see her appear at the doorway. She looks magnificent with her hair towel dried and still damp but tied up in a bun, her face fresh from makeup. She's in a cute pajama short set, the shorts are purple and white checks, the top is a light purple color.

"You look beautiful." I say before I can think.

She frowns at me, "Sure I do, are those pancakes I can smell? I love them!" and she walks past me taking a seat. I sit next to her and watch her eat. I occasionally have a strawberry or two but I'm not all that hungry and when she asks I tell her so. "These are the best pancakes I've ever had! How did you learn how to make these?" She asks between mouthfuls.

"Aunty Kim taught me. She has her own diner. I'll have to take you and Teddy there one day, she'll love you both plus she has some dirt on me, Linc and Silas that I'm sure will be of interest to you," I jokingly say.

After she finishes I take the dishes to the sink. "Leave those, let's go back to the lounge." she insists and I do as she says, following her. She grabs the blanket and sits, waiting for me to join her. I make my way over to her and she puts on some movie I haven't heard of before called 'The Best of Me', it reminded me of The Notebook type of film.

I look over to her and ask, "Is there anything else you want to ask me?"

She continues to watch the movie and says, "Will you stay with me tonight? We don't have to do anything, I just don't want to be alone." She's still looking at the TV, I'm not even sure she's even paying attention to it.

"Of course I will, anything you want Lucille."

She snaps around to me and says, "You always call me Topolino!" She looks hurt.

I move closer to her, taking her by the waist, pulling her on to my lap and saying, "If you prefer for me to call you Topolino, I will. I mean nothing by it by not calling you that." She nods and fidgets on my lap, I hold her in place and smirk. "If there is anything I can help you with, it would be my pleasure Topolino."

She blushes but moves closer to my face and bites down on my lip before kissing me wildly. I move my hand over her thighs and up towards her shorts and play with the hem before picking her up and taking her to her bedroom. Her legs wrap around me as we hungrily kiss, feeling my tongue against hers. She tastes sweet from the syrup. I place her on the bed before removing my shirt.

"Topolino, this is all about you tonight. You understand, I have no expectations of you. I'll help you relax then we can sleep." She nods, biting her lip, staring at my toned stomach. I work out a lot, not as much as Silas but enough to show my abs and definition. I move closer to her and slowly remove her shorts, pulling them down her tanned legs, she's bare underneath and the sight has my mouth watering. "Topolino birichino," I groan and trail my fingers down to her sweet pussy. As I massage her clit, she gasps, "It's so sexy when you talk Italian." My little mouse is wriggling, I insert two fingers inside her as I'm kissing her neck and whisper, "Mi divertirò a leccare questa dolce figa tutta la notte, Topolino."

I move down her body kissing her, her cunt is squeezing my fingers and she pants, "More Cole." Her pussy is getting so wet, I'm imagining all the ways she'll come on my cock one day, not today though, she's not ready for my type of play yet. My dick is hard at the thought of her pretty red blood, trickling out of her whilst she orgasm's around me.

I get to her thigh and trail my tongue up towards her pussy and then lick and suck her clit as she continues to ride my fingers. She is writhing beneath me, moaning my name. Her hands come down to my head and she grips her fingers into my hair. I remove my fingers and replace them with my tongue and massage her clit with my thumb. I feast on her as she explodes over my tongue, tasting her sweet watermelon tang with a hint of saltiness left behind by my brother. Her screams echo around the room. As she's climaxing, I bite down on her thigh, sucking and leaving a mark on her creamy skin, claiming her as mine.

I move away as she's panting looking at me through hooded eyes. "I hope you enjoyed that as much as I did Topolino." She's in ecstasy, unable to verbalize her thanks, she just smiles and nods. I help get her cleaned up and into bed. I tell her, "I'll go get some sleep on your sofa, then head out once I've got a couple of hours in. I'll try not to wake you as I leave."

I kiss her on the forehead as I go to leave but she grabs my hand and whispers, "Stay and wake me up with your tongue anytime." Her eyes are closed but she's grinning at me. I do as she says and climb in behind her, holding her close to my body, listening to her breaths as she falls into a deep sleep. I find myself wishing I could stay with her in this moment forever, then I suddenly realize I've never felt this happy before and it's fucking terrifying.

Chapter 20

Lucille

Vivid scenes of Silas thrusting me into the lockers at the warehouse and Cole lashing his tongue across my clit in my bed last night flash wildly through my dreams. A small moan escapes my lips as I roll over, my pussy throbbing beneath the sheets and already soaked with my arousal. I reach my arm over beside me and realize the bed is empty. A sudden wave of disappointment rushes through me but I try to ignore it. I shouldn't feel this way, it's not like I'm in a relationship with any of them. I wonder idly what that would be like. Three hot boyfriends to lie in bed with and have their wicked ways with me whenever they pleased.

I smile at the thought and replay the events through my mind once more, trailing my hand down under the waistband of my pajama shorts and straight to my aching clit, spreading my juices over the sweet bud of nerves. Almost instantly I'm ready to explode, my climax building fiercely in my belly, one last swirl of my finger and I'm done. "Fuck!!" I shout as I clench my thighs together, squeezing my fingers against my throbbing pussy, dragging out every last drop of my orgasm. I lay still regaining my breath for a short while before finally deciding I do need to get up today.

Ripping back the sheets and jumping out of bed a flash of red catches my eye. On my dressing table lies a single rose atop a piece of paper. I walk over and pick up the rose, holding it to my nose, it smells so sweet and beautiful. On the paper is a short note that reads, -*"I'll be seeing you soon, little mouse."*- The words make my stomach flutter and I can not keep the grin from spreading across my face. "What the hell is happening to me?" I say out loud to nobody but myself, exasperated at the thought of these men forcing their way into my life and now into my bed. I need to talk to Kat!

After I've finished dressing and getting myself ready for the day, I grab a quick piece of toast and lather it with Nutella, stuffing it into my mouth as I fetch my keys from the bowl by the front door and leave, making sure to lock up behind me.

Pulling up outside Kat's apartment my phone starts buzzing in my pocket, retrieving it I see Max's name flashing on the screen. I roll my eyes, I'm still pissed at him for last night. I'll let him stew a little bit longer I think, so I cancel the call and switch my phone off, sliding it back into my pocket. I walk straight through Kats front door calling out, "Hello!" to announce my arrival.

Teddy comes barrelling at me from the kitchen before I've even managed to shut the door. "Mommy!" He shouts, running towards me with his arms in the air, excitement beaming from his face.

"Hey baby," I coo, bending to pick him up. I playfully throw him in the air before catching him again and smothering him with kisses.

"Mom," he groans, pushing me away playfully as he giggles "get off".

"Oh but I love you so much baby boy, I could just eat you." I laugh, pretending to chomp on him. Teddy screams loudly in fits of giggles as I carry him back Into the kitchen to join Kat and Isabella who are sat next to each other at the dining table making farm animals out of Playdoh,

"Hey, here's my two favorite ladies," I chirp, as Teddy

wriggles out of my arms and pulls his chair back up to the table.

"Hey Auntie Luce," Bella sings, holding up a red and purple creature, "look at my chicken!" she says, face full of pride.

"And look what I've made Mommy," Teddy calls, pointing to a selection of shapes on the table. I sit in the chair between Teddy and Isabella and respond to each one of their creations with a "wow," "ooo," or "that's amazing," as both kids take turns to show me their collection of rainbow coloured cows, chickens, pigs and horses.

"These are amazing guys, well done!" I praise.

"Coffee?" Kat asks as she stands from the table, heading over to the coffee machine.

"Please Love," I nod, getting up to follow her. "Carry on guys, see if you can make us a big tractor next to carry all these animals," I say to the kids.

"OK," they reply in unison, not looking up from the table, concentrating hard on building their sculptures.

Kat narrows her eyes at me as I lean against the counter top and bite the skin around my thumbnail nervously. I had planned exactly what I was going to say in the car over here but now I'm here I'm chickening out. "What!?" I finally snap, unable to take her eyes much longer.

"You got laid didn't you?" She responds matter of factly.

I gasp in astonishment. "What the hell Kat!" I say turning my back towards the kids sitting at the table. "SShhhh!" I hiss through my teeth.

"Oh behave, they can't hear us. But come on, spill the beans," she responds, handing me a steaming mug of black coffee with a smirk pulling at her lips. "I want to know everything."

"I don't know what you're talking about," I object, looking up to the ceiling feigning all knowledge of what she's implying.

I hear her tut before saying, "Girl it's written all over your face, now spit it out."

I roll my eyes and sigh a long draw out, "Fineeeee, but this is mad okay so keep up," I warn her.

An overly exaggerated giggle coming from her mouth as she skips up and down excitedly clapping her hands together. "I knew it!" she exclaims, unable to stop the Cheshire cat like grin she has on her face. "Come on we'll sit outside," she says, leading me towards the rear porch door that's connected to the kitchen, opening straight onto a small private seating area in her apartment grounds.

Taking a long sip on my steaming hot coffee, I relish the way it burns at my insides. Kat's eyes are still on me, eager with anticipation.

I suck in a deep breath and begin. "So it turns out that the hot guy from the prison is no longer in prison anymore, his name is Silas Salvatore and he just so happens to be Max's number one enemy. He called him into a fight last night because he thought me and Max were a thing!" I scoff at the thought and Kat's brow creases in confusion but she stays quiet while I ramble on. "Remember the guy I met at the club?" I ask and Kat nods. "Well that was his brother Cole, who he had follow me until he got out! He was at the fight too." I blush, looking at the floor. "Things got real heated after the fight between Max and I and he warned me to stay away from them, said they were bad people, dangerous even. I got pissed and stormed off but Lincoln, their friend who I'd also already met in the park last week with his son, got to me before I could leave and said Silas needed my help. I was so pissed and I had questions I wanted answers to, so I went to confront him." I take a breath and another sip of coffee then carry on still unable to look Kat in the face. "He said he basically couldn't stop thinking about me and sent his brother and friend to watch out for me until he could have me himself. We argued, and let me tell you now, you wouldn't have been able to resist either. Before you judge me just picture fucking Hercules or something and try saying no when he picks you up and fucks you, hard!" I laugh shakily, trying to make it seem like it's not so bad. "Anyway, I left after that and for some stupid fucking reason that I will never know, I then let his brother take me home and ended up coming on his fucking face last night in my bed!" I gasp. "And what's worse is that I enjoyed it all. They were the hardest, hottest orgasms I've ever had." I squirm uncomfortably in my seat and bite my lip waiting for an onslaught of abuse from my friend, but it does not come. I look up sheepishly to see Kat staring at me open mouthed and in shock. "Please say something, anything. I'm freaking out here and I have no idea what to do."

Kat begins to laugh, quietly at first, but then contagiously and I can not stop myself from laughing too. At myself, at my situation, at my absolute lack of self restraint with hot men. I laugh until hot fast tears begin to paint my face. "I don't know what to do." I gasp between the sobs choking my throat.

Kat reaches over and grabs onto my hands. "Stop that right now," she scolds. "You don't want your son to see you like this."

I nod and swipe at the tears pooling in my eyes. "You're right, I'm sorry. I just don't have a clue what's going on right now. I'm confused and I just fucked a convict and then let his brother stick his tongue between my legs." I exclaim. "It sounds fucking ridiculous."

A laugh escapes Kats throat again. "No babe, it sounds fucking HOT!" She smiles at me. "So why did Max tell you these men are dangerous again?" she asks, sitting back in her chair. I pause for a moment, I need to be honest, if she's going to give me sound advice she needs to know it all.

"They're mafia," I say, cringing as the words leave my lips. "Silas is the fucking mafia Don. His brother Cole and Linc both work under him, they practically run half the city." Kats mouth gapes once more and a long drawn out "Oh shit" is all she can respond. I nod, sipping on my coffee, only now really realizing what the information means and the severity of my situation.

The ringer on Kat's mobile breaks our silence and a quizzical expression breaks over her face as she picks it up to answer. "Umm hi Max," she says into the receiver. "Everything okay?" Kat's eyes snap to mine. "Yeah she's here," she says. Fuck, I groan, forgetting I'd switched off my phone before I got here. "Yeah sure," I hear Kat say before she holds the phone out towards me looking a little sheepish. "He wants to talk to you," she says, mouthing the words "I'm sorry" as I place the phone to my ear.

"Can I help you?" I ask, my tone harsh and to the point.

"Where the fuck have you been!?" Max shouts into my ear. "I have been trying to get hold of you all morning. Do you have any idea what you have put me through these last couple of hours? I've had my…"

"What I've put you through!?" I cut him off. "What about what you put me through you selfish piece of shit! You knew last night that it was a risk taking me to that place but you didn't give a shit, and then you have the audacity to lecture me about my safety. How fucking dare you!" I spit down the phone.

I hear an exasperated breath down the line. "For fuck sake Lucille, I said I was sorry, but I've been worried sick. I couldn't find you after you stormed off last night and when you didn't answer your phone, I thought the worst. I could have started world war fucking three just now had you not been with Katrina." I scoff audibly showing my irritation.

"Are you okay?" He asks now with a calmer tone to his voice.

"Yes I'm fine Max, please I just need some space. Some time to think."

The end of the line falls silent for a few moments before he agrees. "Okay, but Lucille, you keep your phone on you at all times."

"Fine," I sigh, not having the energy to continue the argument any longer. I end the call and hand the phone back over to Kat who's watching me with eyes as wide as frisbee's. Her eyebrows are so high they're almost joining her hairline.

"Jesus, what the fuck?" she says. "Does he know what happened between you and the brothers?"

I splutter my coffee as she asks the question. "God no!" I exclaim. "There's no way, and if he knew I'm pretty sure he'd be out for their blood not mine. He can never know!" I warn, narrowing my eyes at her.

"I hear ya girl," she yields, throwing her hands up in surrender.

I lean my elbows against the table and hold my head in my hands and groan. "What the hell am I supposed to do Kat?" I ask in desperation.

"Are you still on the pill?" My breathing hitches, I hadn't even thought of that, thankfully I am but what a fucking thing to overlook. How stupid am I?

"Yes, I'm still on the pill."

"Okay good, that's one less thing to worry about," she says.

I look up to her, scowling my face. "You know if this is meant to make me feel better, it really isn't," I snap.

"I'm just trying to be practical but seriously now that you've been," she raises her hands and makes a quotation mark sign with her fingers, "marked by the mafia, I think you can say goodbye to your sex life because no other man is going to want to touch you now," her voice full of pity.

"Great, I'm going to be a fucking spinster for the rest of my life." Kat chuckles and in an attempt to cheer me up offers to marry me herself.

After spending the rest of the morning at Kats with her never ending assault of questions about Silas, Cole and Lincoln and her trying to pry out of me which one I think is hotter, I thank her for watching Teddy for me and promise to keep her up to date on any further advancements on the tragic mafia romance I now seem to be stuck in the middle of and drive us back home.
I almost hope that maybe this is just some sort of competition between them and my brother to see who wins, some sort of ego trip, because that seems a lot more easy to comprehend than them actually liking me the way they say they do. I don't trust them, not knowing who they are now and my previous experience with the wrong kind of men. I need to keep my wits about me and not get sucked in by their nice words, hot bodies and the fact that they know how to please a woman. Well, two out of three at least.

My stomach flutters at the memory and I do well to keep myself in check as I pull up outside the house. Teddy runs straight to his room as soon as we get home, an excited little giggle echoing down the hallway. He disappears for a few minutes before returning clutching the pillows from his bed in his arms and dragging his duvet along behind him. I smile knowing what his intentions are as he climbs onto the sofa, spreads out his pillows and bundles himself under the duvet until only his head is on show. "Can we watch a movie please Mommy?" He calls from his pit. How can I refuse?

Chapter 21

Silas

Stepping out of my Porsche, I take in the surroundings of our home. The building itself is a traditional villa style house with its beautiful stone walls and high arched windows. We have a long driveway and a garage that has enough space for Cole's bike and Lamborghini, Lincs Ferrari and my Porsche and has extra space should we decide to add more to our collections. Inside, the main house is divided into separate living spaces for each of us. The east side of the building is where Linc resides with Alessandro. The west wing is Cole's play area. And the top floor is my residence. The majority is sound proofed so we don't hear what each other is up to. Down stairs is a shared kitchen and living area as well as a meeting room and office. In the basement we have various torture chambers and storage along with a panic room. We also have a pool area that can be accessed from the patio that the lounge area leads onto. We have plenty of land around us so we aren't overlooked and no neighbors close enough to hear what goes on here.

As I step inside, I hear raised voices coming from the kitchen. Taking my jacket off, I hang it over one of the dining chairs as I pass, on my way to see what all the commotion is about. I roll up the sleeves of my shirt and rub my hands over my arms. I need to get these tattoos finished, I think to myself.

Pushing the door open to our open plan kitchen area, I see Cole and Linc in eachothers faces standing next to the island in the middle of the workspace. "That's not the point, you don't know who she is or how far involved she is with the Costellos, Cole. You can't be so drunk on her pussy that you forget who she was there to aid at the fight!?" Linc spits venomously at Cole.

Cole sees me behind Linc, always watching his surroundings, he smirks, then nods in my direction. "If anyone is pussy drunk it would be Silas. He's the one that filled her tight little cunt after he won the fight against her brother. I'd say that would make her partial to our side, wouldn't you?"

Linc sputters and turns to face me. "You did what!? She's Irish blood!?"

I glare at Linc and tell him, "Yes, Max Costello is Lucille's brother. She has no part in the Irish gang apart from a sisterly concern to her brother."

Linc growls, "I don't care, you can't trust her!"

I see red at his words, rushing forwards and grabbing him by the throat in a rage "You do not tell me who I can and can not trust, fratello!"

Linc headbutt's me in the face, causing me to step back, releasing him in shock. I take a swing, clocking him in the jaw, making him stumble into the island.

Cole chuckles from the side lines.

"I don't know why you are looking so smug Cole. You didn't come home and sleep here after the fight night. You didn't spend all night at the restaurant either. Do tell dear Silas whose bed you kept warm that night!" Linc spits, full of animosity.

I turn to Cole. I knew he took her home and was intrigued and protective of her but I didn't think he was foolish enough to cross this line with me. "Tell me the truth Brother. Tell me you didn't put a mark on her, you didn't betray me!" I snarl at him taking a step forward. He doesn't even flinch, he's probably the most insane of us all, it's what worries me the most. If he's crossed that line with her and becomes obsessed, I don't know if either of them would survive it. Cole would claim her as his own and she would have no say in the matter.

"I'll give her time to adjust to you both before I fully make her as ours. However, I did taste her that night and I'll admit, she is exquisite. I'd be happy to enjoy her for every meal." He says, casually checking his nails as though this is a normal fucking thing to say. I go to punch him but he swiftly dodges my advance. "Brother, calm down. You have had her first and she's perfect for all of us. I don't understand why we can't agree to share," he explains.

This time I land my punch to his ribs, knocking him back and stealing his breath. "Cole, she's not yours and we've talked about this. Your tastes aren't what everyone likes, she's not for you. Don't obsess over her!" I warn, throwing another punch his way but he evades contact.

"Maybe you should be telling Linc here not to get obsessed, Silas. From what Mercedes has been telling some of the other girls, Linc can't seem to get her out of his head. He even called Mercedes by her name whilst fucking the whore. Now that sounds to me like he's got a growing infatuation himself. Maybe that's why he's so wound up." Cole reveals throwing his arms out.

"I do not have an infatuation with her!" Linc bellows in response.

Cole throws his head back and laughs, "But you are obsessed with her and she's in your head, right? I mean she's in mine, I'm not afraid to admit it. She's definitely in Silas's. I still propose we share her. We aren't normal men, we would never be able to give a woman everything she needed separately, but between us we could give her the damn world."

Linc is silent, I know he's considering it, and for once I'm thinking Cole is being the most level headed of us all. It's a crazy fucking idea, I don't like the thought of anyone else with la mia Luce but if it had to be anyone, it would be the two men standing before me.

I turn to Linc, "You might not trust her, but I see in your eyes that you like something about her. If what Cole says is true, and I know he wouldn't lie to me, then can you agree to put our differences aside and share her, if she agrees?" Cole is grinning like a kid at christmas.

Linc nods, "I'm not sure I'll want her the same way you both do, but I'll try. But I still think there are more secrets to unravel with her, I think she's hiding something."

I slap him on the back and turn to Cole. "So you got what you wanted, how does it feel to be the one that talks sense into us two for once?" I joke with him.

Cole's looks at both of us, his eyes are devoid of emotion. "I made her a promise. I will not let anyone hurt her or her boy, that includes you both. So this is your first and only warning: if she accepts one of us or all of us, you treat her well or I'll let my demons out in her honor."

I look at him, Cole really is the most psychotic of us all. His unhinged need to protect her will drive him to do whatever it takes. I respect that in him because I wholeheartedly agree. "Message received Brother but I won't hurt and neither will Linc." I reassure him.

He nods and turns to the fridge as if nothing happened and says, "So are you hungry? I can cook some pasta if you are."

I smile, he's at home and at ease when he's in the kitchen. "Sure that would be nice."

Linc laughs, "Yeah I'm starving, after all the whiskey I've been knocking back I need something to soak it up, it's the only reason you landed that punch Si."

I laugh at him. "Sure it is Linc, whatever you say."

Chapter 22

Lincoln

It's been several days since the revelation between Lucille and Max Costello came to light. Silas and Cole are over the moon now that she's been labeled as 'fair game' and their plan to share her seems to be all they speak of, but I still have my reservations about her. Don't get me wrong, I can't seem to get the woman out of my head and would love to see her take my cock in between those perky pink lips of hers, but there's still something niggling at the back of my mind telling me she is not to be trusted, something I will get to the bottom of.

I glance towards the clock on my bedside table. It's 02:05 and I can not sleep for the life of me. I palm the heel of my hands into my eye sockets and rub my eyes until I feel like they might burst. "Fuck it!" I sigh, ripping back the satin sheets and swinging my legs over the side of the bed. I need to get to the bottom of this before it fucking eats me alive.

Heading towards the ensuite connected to my bedroom, I stretch out my upper torso pulling at the muscles across my back. Fuck I need a massage, I think to myself, feeling the knots tightens as I strip off my shorts and jump straight into a freezing cold shower, letting the icy downfall pierce my skin, quelling the unsavoury feeling beginning to brew in the pit of my stomach. After thoroughly drying myself and fixing my hair which doesn't consist of much. I was blessed with my mothers goodluck for it always looking so effortlessly perfect as it falls into place, I pull on a pair of loosefitting grey sweatpants and matching sweatshirt because like fuck am I donning a three piece suit at this time in the morning. I tuck my gun securely into the waistband at the back of my pants and pull the sweatshirt down to conceal it. Grabbing my phone, keys and pack of smokes on the way out. If anybody questions me, I'll shoot them. It's that simple, and it might even make me feel a little better.

As I make my way to the front door of the house, I pull up short outside of Alesso's bedroom and as quietly as I can, I open the door. The sight of his chest rising and falling as he sleeps so soundly fills my entire being with warmth and I can not help but smile. There isn't anything I wouldn't do for my son. The reason I do what I do is for him, God I can only hope he doesn't end up like me though. I watch contentedly for a little while longer before pulling the door gently until I hear the latch click into place and continue my way out the front of the house onto the large gravel driveway. Praising myself for not bothering to park inside the garage when I got back last night, I slide into the drivers seat of my Ferrari and reach for my phone, quickly typing out a message to Silas and Cole who are still in the house.

Gone to the office. I'll be back to take Alesso to school.

After sending the message, I release the handbrake and allow the car to creep slowly down the mile long driveway, the slight down slope making it easier. I don't want to start the engine near the house in case I end up waking Alesso. As I approach, the wrought iron gates open automatically, recognising my car. Sufficiently far enough away from the house I start my baby, she roars to life like a demon. I put my foot down and floor it.

Arriving outside of the casino a few miles down the road, I pull into the reserved space marked outside the back of the building. Usually I would throw the keys over to the parking valet but if they took any longer than a minute to open my door tonight I might break their fucking hand off. Needing to bite back the urge to put my fist through something or someone I light up a cigarette before stepping outside of the car and pull the smoke deep into my lungs, throwing the packet onto the driver's seat as I shut the door. The sudden rush of nicotine through my system sends an exhilarating shudder throughout my body and I have to shake myself to relieve the intensity of it.

As I lean against my car finishing off the last drags of my smoke I feel my phone start to vibrate in my pocket. Knowing it can only be a rare handful of people at this time I take a glance to see Silas' name flashing across the screen.

"Everything OK fratello?" he asks, his voice high on alert, definitely not just interrupted from his slumber. No doubt he was wide awake going through numbers and reviewing the recent shipment orders to make sure everything is up to standard, his standard that is.

"All is good Brother. I just need to get to the bottom of something." I say as I release another cloud of smoke into the air, and get to the bottom of it I will, I add on silently to myself.

I hear what almost sounds like a hint of relief in his voice as he replies, "Call if you need us. I will watch out for Alessandro."

I nod my head and although I know he can not see, he knows I would call if I needed to. I end the call and slide my phone back into my pocket and throw my cigarette butt to the floor before grinding it with the heel of my shoe.

I enter the building through the side entrance only ever used by the staff and I'm pleasantly surprised by how busy the place is. I glance at my watch and note that it's almost 03:00 and the floor is still heaving with patrons as I make my way through the heavily packed bar area and back towards the private door leading down to the maze of corridors. I give a subtle nod to Dan as I pass by who's elbows deep in a large group of visibly drunk women on a hen do, shouting their cocktail orders over the bar at him. I receive an exaggerated eye roll in return causing me to laugh, poor bloke, he looks like he's about one cocktail away from a breakdown. I chuckle to myself and begin down the darkened stairwell towards the surveillance room housing my office.

Walking through the heavy metal door, Felix swivels in his chair towards me, a look of concern marring his usually somewhat charming face. "Everything alright Boss?" he asks. "Saw you pull up a few minutes ago and thought you looked a bit pissed."

I chuff at the remark. "Is my face that miserable?" I joke, pulling a bottle of beer from the fridge stacked in the corner of the room.

Felix grins at me. "Well not all of the time," he jokes, turning back to face the screens of CCTV footage.

"I've come in to do some more digging on the Holland girl."

"Jesus! Again Boss? You've looked through everything ten times over!"

"Well then I'll look an eleventh time," I quip, knocking the top off my beer and taking a long gulp, it's 5 o'clock somewhere right? "Any trouble this evening?" I ask, hovering behind Felix and scanning my eyes over the live footage in front of me, still smirking at the sight of Dan losing his shit with the hen party at the bar.

"No Boss, it's been a busy but uneventful one. Zack and Sully are up on the top floor making sure the girls finish their sets without any problems but they're regulars up there anyway so there shouldn't be any trouble." I nod, pleased at the thought that even without me I know my kingdom will run smoothly with my purposefully hand-picked men at the helm. I slap Felix on the back letting him know he's doing a good job.

"I'll be in the office if you need me," I call, walking through to the adjoining room and closing the door behind me. Walking over to my desk, I crack my knuckles and roll my neck releasing the tension radiating through me. Right, even if this takes me all fucking night, I will uncover what our little love is hiding. Pulling up the file I've already accumulated on Lucille, I look through every document twice over just to be sure nothing has been overlooked. Discovering nothing we didn't already know, I open up the police database and search for her name, no previous misdemeanors or felonies. *There's a shock,* I think running my fingers through my hair in annoyance. Next I search through city records, again without success.

Okay change of plan. I'm looking at this from the wrong direction so I load up the copy of Teddy's birth certificate and maximize it to full screen. I browse the document narrowing my eyes as I notice a slight pigmentation in the space of the birth fathers name. I look closer, hovering the magnifying tool across the area and almost choke on my beer as I realize the document has been edited.

"FUCK!" I shout, punching the air with my fist. "I fucking knew it!" The small glitch in the paperwork is completely unrecognizable to the untrained eye, that's why we haven't noticed it sooner. I note the fact that I need to submit the guys for explicit training in spotting fraudulent documents for later and excitedly with fumbling fingers, I open up a separate app used to turn edited photos and documents back to their original forms and load the copy of the certificate into the system. Waiting with bated breath, I take another chug of my beer working to quell the anticipation spiking through my nerves. Slowly but surely, right before my eyes, the copy of the birth certificate reverts back to its original form and the spaces that were made to look blank now hold new information.

Full name of child's Father: Vincent James Holland
Fathers Occupation: Unknown
Fathers age at time of birth: 27

I double fist pump the air this time as I read and reread the information letting it sink in as I then slowly begin to realize that this has been covered for a reason. By who? I don't know; maybe Max? He would definitely have the know-how to be able to do this, but why? That is what is really bugging me. I type Vincent's name into the police database and press search. A list of previous convictions line the screen. Jesus! The guy's a fucking mess. He's been arrested for drunk driving, possession of drugs, assault, theft and has a restraining order against him from none other than, holy shit, Lucille Holland. Applied for and granted on 3rd January 2017. Shit, that would mean that, if I'm thinking about this correctly, he has absolutely no idea about Teddy being born, and I bet my fucking life on it that Lucille doesn't want him to find out either. I mull over my findings becoming more and more frustrated at the thought of this fucking sad excuse of a man giving Lucille a reason to run. I have to bite back the overwhelming urge to put my fist through the screen as I open his mug shot attached to his police file. Standing at 5'10" with dark hair, dark brown eyes and a scar running from his ear to his jaw he's not a bad looking bloke over all. A hard face and arms full of ink he looks capable of murder and I bet he doesn't like being told no. I snap at the thought and fly my beer bottle across the room sending the glass shattering across the floor.

Within a split second Felix flies through the door glancing between me and the broken bottle and eyeing me up very carefully. "Boss?" he asks, tiptoeing his way into the room and taking a glance over my shoulder towards Vincent's face. "Someone we should worry about?" he asks, tipping his chin towards the screen.

"Not for the minute," I say, through gritted teeth. "He should be very worried about me though," I add, barely above a whisper, balling my hands into fists and cracking my knuckles.

Felix stands quiet for a moment then turns to leave. "I'll call Andrea down to clean the mess," he says, then closes the door.

I'm sucked so deep in concentration flicking through files upon files of Vincent's past police records that I barely notice Andrea, a short, plump lady who always wears her thick brunette hair in the shape of a donut on the top of her head, tiptoe her way into the room to start sweeping up the broken glass behind me. Andrea is one of the only maids we let down into this section of the building, she poses no threat and we pay her handsomely for her indifference. I glance up and nod thanking her then turn my attention back to the screen having to do a double take when I notice that Lucille Holland is written down as spouse on more than one of them. What the fuck? I stand bolt upright and fist my fingers through my hair. WHAT THE FUCK!? I calm my breathing and go back to Lucille's file. Absolutely nowhere can I see any mention of Vinny or a marriage certificate for that matter. This chick has some serious explaining to do. I can't say this is going to please Silas, knowing she's already taken somebody else's last name before, but if he is truly as infatuated with her as he says he is, maybe it just won't matter at all. I save all of the information I've gathered and email it over to myself knowing the boys back home will need to see it. Glancing down at my watch, I realize just how long I've been here, it's almost 07:00 and I need to get back to take Alessandro to school. Shutting down my computer and rubbing my eyes that are now beginning to burn from lack of sleep, I groan as I begin to stretch, kicking out my legs willing them to wake up after sitting for so long. I notice Felix asleep with his head on the desk when I walk back through the surveillance room and smile. Fucker never likes to leave. I decide not to wake him before I go, he works like a dog. The least I can do is let him get a couple of hours rest before he starts over again. I lightly tread past him as quietly as I can, and sprint back up the stairs to the now empty casino. The only people occupying the space now are the cleaning staff who I acknowledge with a polite smile as I exit, making sure to thank Andrea once more as I whisk past her on my way out.

As I pull back into the driveway, I notice the garage door is up and Silas' Porsche is missing. He must have left for the club already, it's been nonstop business for him since he returned. The fight night has been his only night off and he was still causing trouble even then, but the fucker enjoyed himself and got laid so who's complaining.

Before I've even opened the front door the smell of bacon in the pan hits my nostrils causing my stomach to growl at me with the reminder that I cannot live off cigarettes and beer alone. I enter the kitchen to find Cole cooking at the hob. The boy has two true happy places that I know of, the kitchen and in between a woman's legs. But right now, I've never seen him happier, Lucille really is changing him.

"Fratello!" he sings when he spots me pulling up a bar stool, flailing his arms out in a welcoming gesture.

"Cole you are far too fucking happy for this time of a morning," I joke, grinning at him as I lean over to steal a piece of bacon from a plate on the bar top.

"What can I say?" he smirks, tossing a pancake up in the air and catching it again in the frying pan. "Pancakes put me in a good mood."

I roll my eyes and laugh, "Okay brother, whatever you say. Has Silas left already? There's something I need to show you both but I think it's better if I do it when we're together."

Cole looks over at me. "Can it wait?" he asks, wanting to know the severity of what it is I have to say.

"For now," I respond, nodding my head nonchalantly as I lean forward to pick up another piece of bacon from the plate. "But it will need to be today." Cole nods and turns his attention back to the stove top, pouring more pancake batter onto the pan. "Come with me to drop Alessandro at school and we'll head to the club together." I say, wanting this off my chest as quickly as possible.

"Sure thing fratello. Heads up!" he calls as he slings a pancake into the air aiming for the plate next to me. It lands perfectly, earning a smug look from Cole.

"WOW!" I hear behind me. I turn to see Alessandro standing in the kitchen archway with his mouth wide open and eyes bugging out of his head.

"Heads up, here comes another for you big man," Cole calls, slinging another pancake up through the air.

"Thanks, Uncle Cole," he beams, climbing up onto the stool next to mine and aiming straight for the bacon. That's my boy, I smile to myself.

"Hey Son, are you ready for school?" I ask as I watch him stuff a forkful of pancake smothered in syrup into his mouth, catching him off guard.

"Yes," he muffles between sloppy mouthfuls of food and an over exaggerated nod of his head.

"Good lad, eat up we'll have to leave soon," I tell him, patting him gently on his shoulder and standing from my chair. "I'll put your bag in the car."

After dropping Alesso off at school, I drive Cole and I to Mezzanotte to meet Silas. When we arrive the club is almost empty with it still being so early. There are a few dancers on the poles at the back doing their warm up routines for later tonight when the show will be in full swing. I clock Roxi and Cherry leaning against the stage whispering to each other as we walk in. Roxi immediately straightens her back and sticks her tits out as soon as she locks her eyes onto Cole. He must notice too as I hear him curse under his breath as we walk through to the back room.

I can't help but laugh. "Just let her suck you off man, she might leave you alone then."

"Ha, I doubt it. She's insufferable, like a fucking dog on heat. I thought I was bad but Jesus the bitch has issues," he says only loud enough so that I can hear.

Like clockwork Roxi appears snaking her arms around his waist, "Hey gorgeous," she purrs. "Anything I can help you with?"

Cole looks at me with an '*I told you so*' expression plastered across his face, leaving me desperately trying to stifle my laugh. Part of me wants to leave him to suffer but another knows I need to get the information painfully burning a hole through my chest out into the open so I don't have to suffer in the knowledge alone. "Roxi love, be a doll and fuck off for a minute would you. We've got business." I warn in a deep monotonal voice letting her know there will be consequences if she refuses.

Her arms instantly drop from Cole's side and with venom in her eyes she spits, "Fine. I've got work to do anyway." She spins on her heel, flicking Cole in the face with her ponytail, causing his eyebrows to raise up into his hairline.

"Now shit, if I'd of said that she'd think it was a fucking invitation," he gawps at me, completely taken back by Roxi's lack of resistance.

"You clearly don't have the right tone in your voice," I mock and punch him playfully in the shoulder. "Come on, I've waited long enough. I need to show you both something." I nod towards Silas's office.

Cole grabs my shoulder and looks me dead in the eyes before saying, "Brother, I hope you're not getting your dick out again, I feel sorry enough for you as it is," he laughs then skips his way towards the door. Well I walked myself straight into that one, fucking asshole.

Entering through the frosted glass door to Silas' office, I suck in a deep breath knowing this information, no matter how I relay it, is not going to sit well with him, or Cole. God knows he's fucked in the head, he might be out for blood after he finds out our little love has been keeping a secret from not just us, but her estranged piece of shit husband too.

Silas turns to face us as we enter, his face softening slightly at the edges as he listens to the business call he's currently taking. He nods a welcome to us and knowing we'll need it, if not something stronger, I pour three glasses of scotch from the decanter on his desk. Silas's questioning gaze meets my eyes but he accepts the glass from my hands and takes a long sip of the fiery liquid.

Cole has already made himself comfortable and is lounging across the leather sofa along the back wall with his boots resting on top of the glass coffee table in front. I roll my eyes at his impertinence and slap his feet down handing him his drink. "Sit up boy!" I snap, before dropping down next to him causing him to huff out loudly and stick his middle finger up at me. "Very mature," I groan, punching his shoulder.

"I don't fucking care how it gets done, just fucking do it!" Silas snaps down the phone before hanging up and slamming his fists into his desk, causing his knuckles to blanch white across his skin. After a quiet moment he regains himself and straightens up running his fingers through his hair as he finishes off his scotch in one mouthful. I stand almost instantly as he places the empty glass on top of the counter and pour him another to which he declines. "It's early Linc, just the one for now."

I turn to face him and hand him the drink I'd already poured. "Trust me brother, you'll need it." I say and although his eyes are dubious, he takes the glass from my hand without another word and sits back into the leather chair behind his desk and unbuttons his suit jacket. Holding his hands forwards he gives me permission to say what it is I need.

"The floor is yours Fratello."

I steady myself for a long minute, sipping on the amber liquid and feeling the burn travel down my throat before I begin. "As you both know, I couldn't sleep last night so I ended up going to the casino to do some more digging on the girl."

Cole sits up now as I've gained his full attention at the mention of Lucille. "For fuck sake Linc, let it go, she's perfect for us. There's nothing else to it. Yeah Max Costello may be her brother but I'm willing to look past that once she's screaming my name," he snaps, locking his eyes on mine a savage grin pulled up at his lips.

"She's married," I say, my voice calm and lacking any emotion.

Silas' face goes hard, his jaw visibly tensing beneath his skin and his eyes grow dark. "What the fuck do you mean she's married!?" he demands, standing in full form and stepping towards me.

"She is married. His name is Vincent Holland, lives in Seattle, 32 years old, he's an absolute piece of shit with an extensive record." I take a breath studying my brother's faces before me, Silas visibly full of rage while Cole still appears calm and collected but I know him better than he knows himself, I can read his tells, and under the surface I can see the violence burning in his eyes.

"He's the boy's father. The birth certificate was doctored, that's why we hadn't noticed it before. Must have been Max's doing. There is no record I can find of a marriage certificate but she is marked as spouse on more than one of his previous police records. They wouldn't accept it if there wasn't proof."

"SO WHERE IS THE PROOF!?" Silas shouts, slamming his fists into his desk.

"The marriage certificate is nowhere to be found brother, probably Max's doing again if he was the one to falsify Teddy's birth certificate, but she has his last name, there is no denying it."

I pause for a second and swallow the anger rising inside of me. "He has no idea about the boy," I say, ignoring Cole who is now pacing the room flicking his knife back and forth between his fingers, anger rolling off him in waves. I throw back the rest of my drink and suck through my teeth as the burn hits my throat.

"I think she ran," I say, not wanting to admit what I know would have been the likely cause for her leaving. "Actually, if his past record is anything to go by, I know that's what she did. She would never want him to find out about her being pregnant with his child and got scared he would after she'd put him on the birth certificate, and I bet that's why she got her brother to amend the document."

"IF HE HAS LAID A FUCKING HAND ON HER I WILL KILL HIM!" Silas roars, his eyes black with hatred and the venom in his voice sharp enough to cut glass.

"He will burn," Cole adds, gripping the blade of his knife so tight that I can see the blood seeping through his fingers.

"I'll send his file to you both, everything I can find."

"Good." Silas cuts in then turning to Cole says, "Don't get blood on my fucking carpet Cole!" he seethes. "Go, both of you, I need to fucking think."

Looking at Cole I tilt my chin towards the door and swing my arm out in front of me. "Come on, I'll get you a fucking bandage from behind the bar."

Cole doesn't say a word as we turn to leave. We are stopped in our tracks as Silas calls behind us. "Not a word to anybody, Luci is not to know we know," he says, face stern and full of execution. We both nod at our instructions then leave as he pounds his fists into his desk again and swipes the entirety of his desk across the room causing me to cringe. I know this is going to eat him up inside.

I drag Cole out of the room and leave him on a stool as I go round the bar and grab the first aid kit. It's there incase of emergencies or if any of the girls sustain any superficial injuries during their sets. I glance around, praying Roxi doesn't try to push her luck again because I'm pretty sure Cole might put her head through the bar if she does but thankfully she is nowhere to be seen. Feeling a little relieved at that, I reach for Cole's hand and apply pressure to the self-inflicted laceration across the palm of his hand, cussing him for being such a reckless idiot.

After subduing the bleeding, I wrap a bandage tightly around the rest of his hand causing him to grunt.

"Fucking wish it was Topolino wrapping me up instead of you, you ugly fuck."

I huff out a low laugh and throw a punch at his stomach. "Yeah well shut up and put up you fucking idiot cause I'm the best you've got for now."

Cole stills for a moment before grabbing the sleeve of my sweatshirt. "Do you think she loves him, Brother?" he asks, looking up at me, his face full of sorrow and desperation making him look much younger than his years. Fuck, the poor kid, he's got it bad.

"No Brother, otherwise she wouldn't have ran."

His hand grips tighter onto my sleeve as his brows furrow. "She might have run for the boy, doesn't mean she doesn't love him."

I pull away and shake my head. "All this talk of love boy, I'm starting to think you've gone soft."

He jerks at this and pushes me hard in the chest, wincing at his injured hand. "Fuck off!" he seethes, standing up from his stool. "It doesn't matter anyway, I'll fucking kill him regardless." He turns and walks towards the front door and I start to follow. Not before I kill him first, Brother.

Chapter 23

Roxi

Spinning and twirling around the pole for hours on end is tiring. I'm ready to clock off for the night, so I make my way to the boss's office to let him know I'm done. As I approach, I hear talking on the other side. I lean in close to listen to what's being said to see if there's any juicy gossip I can take advantage of.

"Look, Max is her brother, that's the only secret she's hiding. Try not to let this consume you, OK? I'll see you later, I've gotta run through these numbers before I finish for the night."

I move away from the door quickly before someone catches me and make my way back to the changing room lost in thought. I know that name but I can't think where….Max? As in Max Costello? No, surely not! Oh this is juicy and I know exactly who will have a field day with this information, Theo Rossi.

Theo absolutely hates the Irish gang. He has had a personal feud with them for years. He could take Max out and maybe I can convince him to get rid of that blonde bitch too. Ever since Lucille showed up, Cole won't even look at me, he's obsessed with his *topolino*, yuck! He never gave me a nickname. I always felt powerful knowing I was his favorite girl and now I'm nothing to him.

Shit, I was too busy protecting my ass that I forgot to speak to Silas. Fuck it, I'll call him.

"What?" he growls down the line.

"Hi Boss, sorry to bother you, just wanted to let you know that I've finished for the night. Do you need me for anything else?" I say, hoping he's up for some company before I have to go home.

"No, go home Roxi," he says and ends the call.

Fine, if Silas doesn't want to spend some time with me, I know someone who definitely will. Daddy Theo pays me well and I know this bit of information is going to make him extra generous. I shoot him a text asking him to meet me.

Roxi - Hey Daddy, wanna play a game?
Theo - Daddy is busy right now.
Roxi - Trust me Daddy, you want to play my game. I have a secret and you definitely want to hear it. Play with me Daddy, I'll make it worth your while.

I gag at the thought of his flaccid cock.

Theo - I'm in a meeting for the rest of the night baby. Meet me tomorrow night at my place, 11pm. I'll send you some money, get yourself cleaned up for me and I'll play your little game then. It better be good though baby, otherwise I'll have to spank you.
Roxi - can't wait

My phone dings as his money hits my account. I open my app and see that it's more than usual. Daddy is feeling generous tonight. I sit in my car and make an appointment with my beautician and hairdresser for tomorrow morning. I want to look extra hot for Theo while I rock his world and get him to remove that bitch from our lives for good.

The following morning after getting plucked and primped for hours, I head to the club for my shift. I look fucking amazing and the leering looks I'm getting from the guys in the club confirms it. I'm practicing my set with

Cherry and a few other girls, the music is pulsing as I dance. I move my body up and down the pole without any effort. It takes a lot of training and skill to be as good as me. I see movement near the entrance and flick my gaze over to see my darling Cole and Linc arrive. I pull out some of my extra special moves in the hope of catching Cole's eye.

Unfortunately I have no luck so I whisper to Cherry, "I'm just going to see if Cole needs anything then I'm going to use the restroom, I'll be back later," I say, winking at her.

I straighten my back and push my tits out so you can't miss them, or so Cole won't. I sashay over to where Cole and Linc are standing and snake my arms around Cole's waist. I feel him stiffen slightly, he's always so tense. I know exactly what he needs so I purr to him in my sexiest voice. "Hey Gorgeous, anything I can help you with?"

Cole looks to Linc and as he's just about to reply to me Linc interrupts "Roxi, be a doll and fuck off for a minute would you. We've got business to deal with." He turns his back on me, dismissing me.

Not letting him have the final word, I quickly reply, "Fine, I've got work to do anyway." I turn, flicking my hair so that it catches Cole in the face.

I plaster a smile on my face and hold my head high as I walk over to the restroom to freshen up. I'm not going to let any of them ruin my buzz tonight. After finishing up in the toilet, I wash my hands and check myself over in the mirror, then it clicks. They are all here tonight, this must be important. I can't miss this opportunity to gather more information for Theo. I quickly give myself another once over and I use the back stairs to Silas' office. I make sure no one is watching me or following me as I creep up to the door.

I can hear raised voices. Suddenly the sound of a fist hitting a table startles me enough to make me step back from the door slightly, but I keep listening, trying to decipher what is being said between these three powerful men. I only seem to catch snippets of the conversation, something about her being married to Vincent James Holland. Who the fuck is that? And then something about a birth certificate. Deciding that I have heard enough, along with not wanting to get caught, I lock his name away in case it's important, it could be more ammunition to use convincing Theo to help me take Lucille out.

Quickly returning to the main room, I see Cherry and some of the other girls standing near the stage. I join them, they're chattering away but I can't seem to focus on their conversation. All I can think about is how I'm going to get Cole back, all to myself and how glorious that will be.

Someone nudges me. "Are you even listening to us, Rox?" Cherry glares at me.
I roll my eyes, it's not like these girls have so much to say that I haven't heard it all before, but I play along, knowing I need to meet with Theo soon.
"Sorry girls, I think I must have eaten something bad, I'm really not feeling great." Cherry and the other girls are all looking at me with concerned faces. I put on a show, bowing over, holding my stomach and telling them, "I keep getting stomach cramps, I'm so sorry girls I don't think I'm going to be able to perform tonight."
"Oh no Rox! Maybe you should go home, rest up so you can work tomorrow. I'll call Crystal. I'm sure she'll swap shifts with you!" Mercedes screeches in her annoying high pitch voice.
I reply in the most sincere voice I can muster. "Oh, you'd do that for me? You are the best Mercy!" putting my actressing skills to good use, I pretend to double over again.

"Of course Roxi, go home." Mercedes says rubbing my back.

I collect my things as quickly as I can, trying not to rush too much and give it away. I head out the door and rush to my car, ready for my meeting with Mr Rossi.

I park up outside Theo's house and adjust my dress as I step out of my car. I make sure my cleavage is on show. I didn't wear any panties, I'm not ruining a pair as I know how the night will end with his pencil dick shoved inside me. I knock on the door and when it opens he looks surprised to see me. He smiles and says, "Couldn't stay away from me eh? So come on, tell Daddy all about this game of yours."

He grabs my ass and I want to gag but I don't. "Come on Daddy, you know how a game works. We play and the winner gets the prize." I flutter my eyelashes at him as he walks me through his home. I've never been here before but I've heard enough horror stories from the other girls to know that I need to keep my wits about me. Theo may seem like a harmless old guy but he has a ruthless, vicious side that has left more than one girl scarred for life.

"A prize you say, well then, you better make this worth my while. He slurs, and I get a whiff of whiskey, great he's been drinking. He takes me through to the lounge area and drags me down to sit on his lap. "Get on with it then, I haven't got all night."

"OK Daddy, this is a game of secrets. I have a secret and you have to guess what it is." I'm praying he plays along because I need him.

"A secret? You can't keep a secret from Daddy. Maybe I should just spank it out of you." He says, as he grabs hold of my throat.

"While that sounds like fun Daddy, I'd much rather you fill me up with your huge cock!" God I deserve an Oscar for this performance.

"Hmmm now you're talking baby! Tell me again how big my cock is, I bet you can feel it digging in your ass. It's so fucking hard for you, baby."

I try really hard not to laugh, there's nothing digging in my ass, apart from his boney knee. How the fuck did I end up with pencil dick after an adonis like Cole. Fuck this, I can't play this stupid game anymore. I need Theo to take the bitch out so I can get back to my man.

"How about I tell you a bit of the secret and you can see if you can guess the rest?" I offer, he nods for me to continue. "There's a new little bird that has caught the brothers' eyes. She isn't who she seems……who am I talking about?" I ask.

"How the fuck should I know who they're interested in. Wait, I do know the answer, it's that girl from the fight. I saw Silas fucking her in the changing room and Cole took her home. Is my baby feeling left out now because the brothers have a shiny new toy? Don't worry baby, I'll look after you."

"She isn't a shiny new toy Theo! She's dirty Irish scum!" Oh shit! Did I say that out loud? Theo stands, making me fall to the floor.

"What did you say?" He roars, grabbing me by the throat again raising me up to the tip of my toes. "Irish scum? You better start talking now because it would be a shame to ruin such a pretty face." This hasn't gone at all like I planned it too.

"Lucille! The girl Silas was fucking, she's Max Costellos sister!" I gasp, Theo looks down at me, his grip loosens slightly as he processes the new information. I reach up and hold on to his hand, using it to help me stand.

"Does Silas know who she is?" he asks. I can see a plan forming in his head. I ignore his question, I need to make sure he does my bidding in whatever plot he's formulating.

"That's not all Daddy, that blonde bitch is married too! Can you believe it? She's a rat, has to be!" I say, hoping he will take the bait.

He stares at me, eyes deep in thought and then laughs. "This is great, maybe you should befriend her, see if we can get her to spill any information about those Irish bastards," he tells me.

"Seriously? Do I have to? Can't we just get rid of her?" I whine at him. I'm losing my grip on the situation. Trust him to turn this into something else. I need him angry and out for blood.

"Look, I know you don't like her pawing at Cole but we need to get the information first then we can sell her off. I have some clients that would pay a pretty penny for a girl that looks like her. Do you know the name of her husband? Maybe we can sell her to him," he explains. Oh that's a good idea. Why hadn't I thought of that?

"His name is Vincent James Holland but I want a cut of the price you sell her for Theo." I demand.

"Of course baby. We can come to some agreement. You did good bringing this to me. Let Daddy treat you for being such a good girl. Get on your knees and I'll let you suck my cock," he says, forcing me down. Hardly feels like a reward but I'll do anything if it means Lucille disappears.

I open my mouth and let him prod my tongue with his little cock. It's like giving a straw a blowjob. I try not to laugh at the thought and let my memory drift to the last time Cole fucked my face in his office, well before he kicked me out.

Spurts of warm cum hit my face, bringing me out of my daydream. Nice. I look up at Theo through the cum hanging from my eyelashes and try not to gag. He pats me on the head and falls back on the sofa with a satisfied huff. "You can let yourself out," he says before swiftly falling asleep.

"Charming," I whisper to myself as I stand up to find a bathroom. I find one by the front door and clean up. Thankfully none of his cum got in my eye. I don't need a dose of pink eye to top off this week.

I grab my purse and a bottle of vodka from Theo's bar, a well deserved treat if you ask me. He's fast asleep now, curled up like a little baby in the fetal position across his couch, murmuring about Irish scum and retribution. I smile as I close the door behind me and head to my car. While tonight might not have gone exactly to plan, I do have Theo on my side. It's only a matter of time before that blonde bitch gets what she deserves. This is going to be so much fun!

My

Chapter 24

Silas

I'm seething. How could this have only just come to light? She's married and not only that, all signs point to it being an abusive relationship. I've wanted to protect her since the moment I laid eyes on her. Now I find out that some creep who vowed to have and to hold her, from that day forward, for better for worse, for richer, for poorer, in sickness and in health, to love and cherish has likely beat her black and blue. Those vows meant shit to this Vincent James Holland. If I had made those vows she'd have been treated like a princess, worshiped night and day.

I slam my fist against the table in a rage, I want to smash someone's face in but I won't do that until I have answers. I'm not sure if I'm angry that she married someone who isn't me or that her judgment is lacking. I mean obviously I'm fuming at her being abused and having to run away from her life with her baby, but part of me is glad she's away from the fucker and now in our sights. My jealousy that she loved someone else enough to marry them almost matches my anger at her being hurt. I feel an itching need to see her, to hold her and make sure she is safe. I decide then and there that I can't sit here for a minute longer. I need to hear from her sweet angel voice what that prick has done to her. I can't take the what ifs, but mark my words, if he's hurt her in any way, he's going to wish he was a dead man because what I'll have in store for him will be a God damn crucifixion.

I stand and make my way towards the door, grabbing my jacket and shrugging it on in a hurry. I head out the back to avoid Cole and Linc seeing me leave the building. I don't want Linc to talk me out of this and I certainly don't want Cole to try to join me in this endeavor. I do however type out a quick text to Quinton to let him know I've left the club to deal with personal business if anyone should need me.

I jump into my Porsche, I check my watch it's 15:15, from the intel that has been fed to me from the surveillance team I have on Lucille, she should be picking up Teddy from Kindergarten. I put my foot down and burn through the city. I make my way towards Teddy's school, as I arrive I notice her car. She's bent over buckling Teddy in so she doesn't notice me parked up across the street, the curve of her ass has my trousers tightening on sight. She moves to the driver's seat and pulls away into traffic. I follow her in my car from a distance. I expect her to drive straight home but instead she stops off at a grocery store. I park my car at the other end of the parking lot and I watch as she gets her son out of the car and walks hand in hand into the store.

Teddy is chatting away to his mom, you can see the boy adores her. She is smiling at him and playfully chatting away. I decide to make my move, I need to speak with her. Getting out of my car, I make my way into the store and grab a cart. Some of the staff and public look my way. I'm a big guy, kind of hard to miss, plus my tattoos don't make me look like the average guy that comes into a nice grocery store like this. I look around the aisles, I grab a few items so I blend in, milk, bread, cheese, apples. Then I see her at the other end of the aisle, she's radiant, beautiful. I'm captivated by her. Her blonde hair is tied up in to a ponytail, I imagine holding it whilst fucking her from behind, pulling my hand through my hair to snap myself out of my fantasy. I make my way towards her, knowing this is my moment to bump my cart into hers. "Oh my goddess, I'm so sorry!" she exclaims before her eyes meet mine and a look of horror plasters her face.

"It's alright la mia luce, I'm happy to have run into you," I say, smiling at her.

She brings her fingers across her lips, as if she's remembering our heated kisses after the fight night. "You, how are you here?"

"Well I needed groceries," I shrug.

Just then a little voice pops up. "Mom, who is that giant man?"

I laugh waiting to see how she introduces me. "Oh this is... um...Silas, he's a friend sweetie," she says nervously, glaring at me.

"That's right buddy, I'm a friend of your mommy's, I've not seen her in a while. I've been wondering how she is."

She scowls at me and replies, "I'm fine, we need to get the rest of our groceries now so I'm sorry I can't stay and chat, Teddy's been saying he's starving so I need to get him some dinner."

I nod, "Well how about I take you both out for dinner? Who likes Chuck E Cheese? It'll be my treat." I say hoping that I'm convincing enough or at least Teddy can be bribed.

Before Lucille gets a chance to answer Teddy jumps in. "That's my favorite!!! Please Mommy, let's go, you can talk with your friend then, please!!!"

Lucille looks down to her son and smiles but then looks back at me and frowns. "Fine, but it's just as friends and you're paying," she points at me.

I laugh, "Sure la mi luce. I hear Chuck E Cheese has the best ice-cream too."

"They do! They have rainbow coloured ice-cream, have you tried it before?" Teddy asks excitedly.

"I can't say I have buddy, we'll definitely order dessert, if that's okay with your Mom," I tell him.

"Pleaseeee!" he squeals at Lucille.

She's smiling and giggles. "Only if you eat some veggies first Teddy."

Teddy pulls a face but sighs saying, "OK, can I have chocolate sauce too giant man?"

I laugh because this kid is too cute. "I'm sure we can arrange that Buddy."

"I think you should be my friend as well as my moms. I like friends who buy me ice-cream with chocolate sauce," he tells me in a whisper.

I smile and tell him, "I'd be honored to be your friend buddy."

I look at Lucille who is looking unsure, I smile and say, "How about I follow you home so you can drop off all this stuff then I'll drive us?" motioning to her cart of groceries.

Lucille looks at me and says, "Only if you don't drive a motorcycle like your brother."

I chuckle thinking it's typical of Cole to show her a dangerous ride. "No, my car has a lot more room and is a far nicer ride than Cole's."

By the time we have checked out at the grocery store and made it back to Lucille's apartment, it's just after 16:00. I decide it's better for me to hang back on this occasion and wait for them to finish putting away the groceries as I stand outside, leaning against my Porsche. My phone buzzes while I'm waiting, pulling me from a nice little daydream about living a happily little suburban life. "What do you want, Linc?" I snap, feeling annoyed that he feels the need to check on me, and that he's so abruptly put a stop to my unrealistic fantasy. Deep down I know it's only because he cares. Unlike me and my brother, Lincoln has a more reasonable head on his shoulders and is able to keep us both in line when things get a bit out of hand. I guess it's just the shit hand he's been dealt, it makes him assess his situations differently to the rest of us.

"Cole just informed me you're at Lucille's. What are you doing?"

I shake my head, my brother knows no bounds to his stalking. At least I know he's watching over her whether I'm here or not. "I'm getting to know her and her boy. You can tell Cole there isn't any need to be watching while I'm with her, he can fuck off now. If he's that bored he can go check the shipment is being packed and distributed effectively on the slip road."

I hear Cole grunt in the background. "I was on my way to do that anyway, make sure you keep them safe brother." I hear the roar of his motorcycle.

"He wasn't actually watching you guys, as soon as he saw you pull up with Lucille he left his post and came back here, you should know he trusts you." Linc explains.

Reading between the lines I feel Linc is trying to tell me not to fuck it up, not that he'd actually admit this, stubborn bastard. "I know that Fratello. Enjoy your night, make sure you win big at the casino tonight," and I end the call.

Pocketing my phone, I notice Teddy running over towards me. "Wow giant man, this is cool! I can't wait to tell Bella about this!" He tells me excitedly looking at my car.

"Teddy, hold on a minute, I need to grab your car seat." Lucille shouts to him.

"No problem la mia Luce, me and Teddy will grab it. Won't we buddy?" He beams up at me and I can't help the smile that takes over my face. I make my way over to Lucille's car, Teddy shows me his car seat and how it's attached. We grab the seat out and he helps me to secure it in the back seat of my car. Teddy jumps in and Lucille buckles him in. I hold the door open for her to sit in the front seat, she hesitates but walks around getting in, she's wearing light jeans and a light blue shirt with white converse trainers. She looks casual and effortlessly gorgeous, her hair is still in a ponytail and I have to force myself not to fantasize about the things I'm aching to do to her again.

After a pleasant twenty minute drive, we arrive at the restaurant and are seated quickly. We order a double pepperoni with extra cheese to share and some veggie sticks on the side. True to his word, Teddy actually eats some vegetables. It shows what a great job Lucille has done bringing him up, he respects her. "So I've eaten some veggies. Can I get some ice cream now please Mom?" Teddy eagerly asks.

"Sure thing, but do you want to go play in the play area for a bit? I'll order it once me and Silas have finished eating," she tells him.

"Okay!" He shouts, running off to the soft play area that isn't too far from our table.

"You've done an amazing job raising him, you are a great mother Lucille, he's a lucky kid." I say to her.

Lucille blushes slightly. "Well he's an easy kid to raise, I'm the lucky one." I nod, debating on whether I should question who his father is but before I get a chance Lucille takes a deep breath and says, "His dad isn't involved, I've raised him on my own through my own choice. Vinny isn't a great guy. I feel I should be honest about that with you."

I notice her hands are trembling, instinctively I grab them and squeeze. "He won't hurt you Sunshine, I won't let anyone hurt you or Teddy. Don't feel pressured into talking about him but know I'm here when you do want to tell me everything."

Lucille has tears in her eyes but nods, "I can't talk about him more than that, I'll try to tell you more in time, I promise." A lone tear rolls down her cheek and bringing my hand to her face, I edge closer and kiss her tear away. She gasps, staring at me as I lean back, still holding her one hand in mine and the other on her cheek. I notice she's not

214

trembling anymore but her green eyes are full of fire and lust.

"La mia Luce don't look at me like that, I can't act on my fantasies here."

She giggles and shakes her head. "Always trying to get in my pants, Big Guy. I better order that ice cream for Teddy, he'll be back any minute for it." She waves a waitress down and orders his rainbow ice-cream with chocolate sauce. "Thank you for this, Teddy really has taken to you. I have a feeling Cole and Linc will be no different. I just ask that if you guys are serious about me, that you understand I'm a package deal with my son," she tells me seriously.

I nod, "We understand, and we will love him like our own. We won't just protect you but him too, from any threat whether you choose us or not la mia luce."

She looks at me quizzically but before she is able to say what's on her mind, Teddy comes running up to us yelling, "Mommy!!! Look who is here!"

Lucille turns and spots a young, brown haired girl hand in hand with Teddy. She looks to be his age, behind them follows who I can only assume is the little girl's mother. She looks similar to the little girl, brown shoulder length hair and large brown eyes like her daughter. Lucille stands and rushes over and embraces the brown haired women in a tight hug.

"Kat! Bella! How are you guys?" Lucille asks happily.

"Hey girl, we are just here to collect our order and my favorite man spotted us. Are you going to introduce us to your friend?" Kat says, eyeing me up from across the table raising her brows at Lucille.

Then it clicks, this is her colleague and best friend. I smile at them and put my hand out. "I'm Silas, a friend of Lucille's."

Kat smirks but shakes my hand firmly "I'm Kat, I'm Luci's best friend so know, that if you hurt her I'll be coming after you no matter how massive you are buddy. Oh and this angel is my daughter, Bella." I can't help but smile. This chick is crazy to threaten me but I'll let it go as it's coming from a good place and anyone that Lucille cares for isn't in any danger from me, even her brother.

"No plans on hurting her, ever."

They shout out Kat's order. "That's our pizza Bella, we gotta get going. I'll see you at work tomorrow, love you girl, love you Tedster," she tells Lucille as she ruffles Teddy's hair and then gives Lucille a hug, she whispers something in Lucille's ear that makes her smile.

"Nice meeting you Silas," she nods in my direction then leaves with her daughter to collect their food.

Turning to the table, Teddy noticed his ice cream had been served while we were distracted. "Yessss ice-cream!" Teddy shouts, rushing over to the table and diving into the multicolored sweet treat.

Once Teddy has finished his dessert, I settle the bill and we head back out to my car. Teddy has been talking nonstop about his school, Bella and how he wants to meet up with his friend Alesso soon. When we pull up to their home, I walk around the car to open Lucille's door.

"Thank you for this evening Silas, we really enjoyed ourselves," she tells me jumping from the car.

Teddy runs at me and wraps his arms around me and says, "Thanks Giant Man, I had such a great time. Mommy has the best friends."

I'm shocked at the outburst, but I put my arm around him and reply, "Any time buddy."

Lucille is unlocking the door to her home as she turns to Teddy to say, "Go on in, take your shoes off, wash your hands and brush your teeth Teddy. I'll be in in a few minutes." He rushes off inside waving at me as he passes, leaving me and Lucille at the door. I step closer to her and she looks up to me. I bend down and press my lips to hers, but I'm hungry for more than just a kiss, my tongue slips inside her mouth and hers delicately but assertively dances around mine. My hands wander to the curve of her ass and then she pulls back breathlessly pushing at my chest, "Goodnight, Silas," she pants before moving inside and closing the door behind her. I stand there gaping like a love sick fool. The trouble is I'm starting to realize I am a love sick fool when it comes to this woman.

Leaving Lucille's complex, I call Cole to see how the shipment change went. It goes straight to voicemail making me suspicious with what he's occupying himself with. He only turns his phone off if he's murdering or fucking, he best not be fucking around on Lucille.

I call Linc next, this time I get an answer. "Linc, where is Cole? Did he sort the snow shipment out?" I ask as he picks up.
"He did. I've just arrived at the casino to check some footage. Alesso is asleep, Sully is standing guard in my quarters. Cole is playing with some wanker that ran his mouth off about us. He's currently in the chamber having some fun." Linc chuckles as though it's a normal thing. I mean for Cole it is but most people don't torture for fun.
"Right okay, I'm heading home. I'll check he's not getting too carried away."
"You know this has more to do with him feeling helpless for Lucille, right fratello? He needs to exercise his demons" Linc sighs at me. This right here is the reason he's my right hand man. Always offering the words of wisdom and making me see through the fog, enabling me to see the full picture.
"Thanks Linc, I'll be in touch if I need back up, if not I'll see you later."

Once I've parked the Porsche I head in and get changed into a white t-shirt and gray jogging bottoms. I don't want to get blood on one of my favorite suits. I head down to the torture rooms and look through the one-sided glass to see Cole standing over a guy who is currently strapped to a rack torture table. Cole can't see me so I take a seat, watching him carefully prepare his various items on a stainless steel table. The man on the rack looks to be in his mid forties, black hair that is thinning on top. He looks to be of average height and build, not too muscly but not skinny either. He is unconscious so I can't tell his eye color but he has a long pointed nose and looks as though he works at the haulage yard with grease and oil on his hands, even embedded into his finger nails. I notice Cole sharpening a knife and glaring at the man. I also notice the mans hands begin to twitch. Cole lets out a low cackle "That's it Paul, it's time to start coming back to the land of the living," his tone even and cold.

Paul, the captive, starts to stir, his eyelids flickering open and he tries to move his hands, then realizing that they are bound on to the rack. He immediately tries to budge his legs, registering they are also bound to the rack he is laying on.

Cole grunts and shakes his head. "Paul look, I did warn you not to go spouting gossip around the haulage yard two months ago when I last ran into you. Now you need to be taught a lesson in respect. Now stop moving or those bindings on your ankles and wrists will only get tighter the more you struggle. I for one am hoping to make this last for a couple of hours at least before you pass out from lack of blood, or breath."

I smirk behind the glass, Cole loves a long game. I'm watching as Paul freezes in horror, "Look Mr. Salvatore, I didn't mean anything by it. I just heard some things and thought it was common knowledge, I'm sorry!" He's crying now. I feel almost sorry for Cole, this guy is not going to last too long if he keeps sniveling, meaning he won't get to play with his knives for as long as he wishes.

"Common knowledge? Umm well if that was common knowledge, then surely it's common knowledge that your wife has been fucking my brother's men everytime you come to deliver our company's goods?" Cole quizzes.

"What? My wife isn't fucking around on me!" Paul exclaims angrily.

Cole's laughs psychotically blurting out, "Oops, maybe it's not common knowledge after all, but it's certainly true."

I continue to watch as Cole brings his knife to Paul's chest and using one hand to keep him steady, he slowly and methodically slices off his right nipple. Paul's chest spurts with blood onto the white marble floor while his screams echo throughout the room. "Ahh look, your blood looks like pretty paint on my floor, do you think I can make you my new canvas, Paul?" Cole chirps in a light and airy tone, almost skipping around the bound man. It's like he gets high on the violence. I sit patiently, waiting for Cole's next move.

"Please, I didn't mean what I said!" Paul is begging now.

Cole moves quickly and slices his left nipple off causing another earth shaking scream from his hostage. "Now Paul, what was it you said? Now I quote this, 'The Salvatore brothers and that limp dick Rossi are all pussy whipped by some nurse'. That's what I overheard right?" Cole seethes at him making quotation marks with his hands. "You need to understand that the private life of me and my brothers is not to pass through your filthy fucking lips. I know all of your dirty secrets and those of your wife's, but I do not gossip around like a little fucking cunt. That is respect and unfortunately for you, you have now lost that from me. So, my dear fellow, this is going to be a long and messy ride. I hope you're ready."

Rage consumes me at the fact this fucker has the audacity to speak of Lucille. I stand and roar into the intercom. "STOP!! I need a word before you continue."

Cole looks at the glass, he can't see me but he looks straight to where I'm standing. "Oh look Paul, we have a guest, it's the big bad Silas Salvatore, let's invite him to play shall we?" Cole smirks at me. I push my way through the door, walking towards Cole, my bare feet splashing through the already pooling blood. I embrace my brother and whisper into his ear, "Let me turn his pale skin blue before you finish your punishment."

He nods and turns to Paul. "My brother here wants a couple of rounds and who am I not to oblige his request Paul. Tap me in when it's my turn, won't you?" Cole slaps me on the shoulder as he fetches a stool and places it in the corner of the room, his elbows are on his knees as he perches forward watching like it's a movie, only missing some popcorn.
I shake my head at the crazy fucker.

"So Paul, what is this I hear about you speaking of things that don't concern you?" I ask.

"Sir, I didn't mean anything by it. It was a mistake, please, please..." he cries.

I tut. "Paul, I'd brace yourself. Oh wait, you're all tied up." I laugh and deliver a blow to his stomach then to his face. Blood explodes from his nose over my white t-shirt. Paul is shouting and begging for me to stop as I land more hits to his body, causing his skin to redden and split open. More blood coats the floor, I barely feel the sticky liquid under my feet as I continue to punch him, his chest, his face, his stomach.

Lost in rage, I only stop when I feel a tap on my shoulder. "Is it my turn yet Brother? I did hope he'd be conscious so I could hear him scream when I deliver my punishment." Cole all but pouts. I can't help but snigger at him. I step back from Paul and his beaten body, his face is puffy and his eyes are swollen shut. His almost inaudible whimpers are all he can manage "please stop."

I turn to Cole. "Your turn, brother."

Cole jumps up and down eagerly, staring down at Paul. He stands at the table of instruments and picks up a flamethrower gun, and smirks at me. "You might want to hold your nose for this one Silas. I hope you like BBQ Paul!" Within seconds, Cole is setting Paul's body a light, burning his flesh from his skin and laughing maniacally while he torches him to death.

Once Cole is done and Paul's screams have long since faded, we are left with the remains of his body yet I can still see the flames that are still dancing in my brother's eyes. I press the sprinkler system button to extinguish the last of the blaze. Cole drops the weapon and looks up to the ceiling, letting the water rinse off the filth. "Let's go brother, I'll get a crew to deal with this." I nudge him towards the door. He grunts and moves out of the room. I feel lighter now that I have released some of the pent up frustration from earlier. Me, Cole and Linc are all alike in that way. We have to get the anger out some way, either by fucking a tight hole, or torturing a poor bastard to the end of his life. I only hope Lucille will forgive us for our sins and accept the broken edges of our souls.

Chapter 25

Cole

Staring down at the stove smelling the delicious aromas of the pan fried chicken with garlic and lemon that I am cooking, all I can think of is how I left Lucille in bed a week ago and I haven't touched her since. The revelation about her ex is still fresh in my mind too. Torturing Paul didn't do much to quell the burning rage. I'd say that I haven't seen her but I have been outside her house every night to check they are safe. I'm relieved that Silas and Linc have finally agreed to share her, it was inevitable that they would come around to my way of thinking but I wish they wouldn't have been so stubborn in the first place. I take a long breath and remove a saucepan filled with fresh, homemade spaghetti, taking it over to the sink to drain. . I add the pasta to the sauce and pile it onto a plate and top with some chopped fresh parsley. Realizing I'm not that hungry for food, I whistle Benji over and push the plate towards him. "Have at it Benji, my appetite is elsewhere this afternoon." I tell him.

"Thanks Boss, I appreciate it." Benji replies.

He takes the plate to the dining area to eat it, just before he gets to the door I say, "I'm heading out, I'll be back late this evening."

Benji nods, "Me and Enzo will hold the fort." With that I grab my jacket and head off on my bike to the place that has been occupying my thoughts for the last week.

As I pull up outside of Lucille's apartment, I decide to conceal my bike around the back of her property in case her nosey neighbors get any ideas of calling the police. I mean, you would think they had better things to do at 13:20 in the afternoon but you can't be too sure.

Opening the door to her home and walking straight in, I'm flooded with her scent, it lingers in the air and ensnares my senses. I can smell her vanilla perfume that she must have used before leaving for work this morning. Looking at my watch to check the time, it's almost 13:30, she'll be on her way home now as her shift just finished. I look around her kitchen to see if she has anything that I can cook her in case she hasn't eaten yet. She has some bread, cheese, ham and various salad items, so I could make her a sandwich if she so wishes. I notice she has some breakfast dishes left in the sink so, completely out of character, I decide to help her out and wash them for her, hoping that will give me more time to be around her if she has less jobs to do before picking up Teddy. Once I've finished doing the dishes I make my way to the lounge and take a seat, just as I'm about to turn the TV on, I hear a key in the door, knowing it's her. I smile and wait for her reaction to me being here. As she comes into the lounge she shrieks, "Jesus Cole! What the hell are you doing here!? You can't just let yourself into people's homes, you psycho!"

I can't help myself, I get up and walk over to her and pick her up with the biggest smile on my face, she's stiff at first but I feel her relax in my embrace after a few seconds. "Topolino, quanto ti sono mancato?" I say into her ear, pulling back to take her all in.

She frowns at me, "I don't know what you said but you can't sweet talk me Cole. How did you get in here?"

I smirk at her, she's still in my arms and hasn't tried to move away, must be a good thing right? "I used my key, Topolino." She looks back at me as if she's shocked I'd do such a thing but I ignore her and continue, "So have you had lunch? I could make you a sandwich or something? From what you have in your fridge I think that's about all you have, or did you plan on going shopping again? I didn't check your freezer, maybe you have more food in there."

Lucille suddenly snaps out of her shocked state and she gals at me "You've been through my kitchen? And what did you mean shopping again? How did you know I've already been? Have you been watching me?"

I laugh, "Oh il mio topolino, of course, I make it my job to know what you have been up to. If I can't be with you then I should at least know what you're doing."

She shakes her head and laughs sort of bewildered. "You are actually crazy, do you know that? And what does that say about me to attract such a crazy person?"

I take her hands and lead her to the sofa. "So how about that sandwich? Let me take care of you."

She smiles politely but refuses to sit down, "Look Cole, I think you mean well but you do know that you can't just let yourself into my house. What would happen if I had Teddy with me? He would freak out, he doesn't know you. Also as lovely as a sandwich sounds, I actually have already eaten. I need to get showered and changed before picking my son up. So as you can see, I'm fine but I think you need to leave."

I frown at her, not understanding why she wants me to go, I've only just seen her. "How about I help you shower, then I'll come with you to pick up Teddy? Then he won't be shocked if he ever sees me."

She laughs as if she thinks I'm joking. "As much fun as I'm sure a shower with you would be, I'm not sure if that's such a good idea. Obviously you are not going to leave, so I tell you what, you can come with me to get Teddy but you're a friend, nothing more if he asks OK?"

I nod agreeing. "If that's what it takes to spend time with you and your son I'll take it, Topolino and you're right, if I help you shower, we wouldn't have time for what I have planned anyway. Your pussy might have to wait a bit longer for me to feast on it again. I've craved it for the last week, I'm sure I can hold on some more." I wink at her. She gapes at me until I slap her ass. "Well go on, we don't want to be late for Teddy now do we?"

She shakes her head hiding back a smile as she scurries her way to the ensuite, making sure to give me a quick glance before heading in for her shower. With the door left slightly ajar, like I know she's done it on purpose, I can't help myself as I sneak inside after her.

I move to the door, the room is full of steam but I can see her silhouette behind the glass panel of the shower. She looks magnificent, her curves make me want to jump in there with her but instead, I watch her as she lathers the soap over her body, caressing herself as she does. My hand is in my pants before I can think, pulling my dick out and pumping myself as she continues to lather the soap over herself, her hands are moving down her body nearing her sweet pussy and I can't help releasing a moan. Her head snaps towards me, her eyes on mine, she shifts her body to face me. She's on full display to me now, I can see her nipples are hard and her tits look fucking perfect. She has a determination burning in her eyes as she steadies her leg on the side of the bath spreading herself open for me to see, her hands slowly move down to stroke her juicy swollen clit, her eyes on mine the whole time, she's egging me on. I move my hand faster over my cock, her eyes dart to see my movement and she lets out a moan as she sees me working my own hard length at the sight of her. She slips her fingers inside herself matching my speed. "Topolino, will you come when I tell you to?" I grunt.
She replies in a moan. "Yes Cole, I haven't stopped thinking about your mouth on my pussy, pleasuring me, feasting on me." She moves her fingers faster, bringing herself closer to an orgasm.

"Do you like seeing my cock, Topolino?" I ask, quickening my hand as she takes another look at my length.

She pants. "Yes, it's so big. I need to feel you inside me Tomcat!"

I smirk at her want for me. "Not yet Lucille, we have much to discuss before I fill you with my cock. I plan to devour you and take my time exploring every inch of your body with my hands and then my mouth, before stretching you out on my cock. For now this will do. Keep moving those fingers in that pretty pussy for me. Make yourself come thinking about how good it will feel to have my cock inside you soon, filling you up." I order her, my eyes glazing over.

I pump myself more vigorously, then she floors me when she asks, "Can I come now, Cole?"
I grunt out, "Yes Topolino. Come for me"

She screams as she comes, clenching her thighs together and at the same time I spill my seed over my hand, coming completely undone at the sight of her. Cupping my cum between my fingers, I move across the room to Lucille. She's still trembling from her orgasm as I open the shower screen door with my clean hand then reach over to insert my dripping fingers into her swollen cunt, pushing my release deep inside her. She lolls her head forwards and moans as I continue to drive my fingers in and out of her, using my thumb to circle her clit. Her breathing becomes hitched and she scrunches up her face letting me know another orgasm is cresting. She's fucking magnificent when she comes. I lean forward and whisper a single command low into her ear "Let me feel you come, little mouse." Instantly she lets out a cry and leans her head into my shoulder as she comes for a second time. Her body convulsing as her muscles clench my fingers tight inside her pussy. I thrust my hand again stroking her sweet spot, draining her of every last drop before removing my fingers and sucking them clean. "I'll let you finish up. I'll wait for you outside." I lift her chin up and kiss her tenderly kiss her trembling lips before turning to leave.

About 20 minutes later, Lucille joins me outside. She's wearing light blue jeans and a plain navy t-shirt with white Converse trainers. She looks over to me and says, "Come on, let's go in my car. I'm not letting my son see that you have a motorcycle. He's definitely too young to be riding one." I nod, she's so sexy as a protective mama bear. I follow her to her car and jump in the passenger seat.

"I really should buy you a better car." I say, looking around the interior.
"What!? You cannot buy me a car Cole! We hardly know each other!" she huffs at me.
"Well I just had you coming on my fingers so I beg to differ. But anyway, that doesn't matter, I want you and Teddy safe, and this doesn't feel safe enough for either of you." I tell her.
She looks at me angrily, "No Cole, you're not buying me a car. This is not up for discussion."

Well if she won't let me buy her a car, maybe Linc or Silas will do it. She didn't say they couldn't. I reach into my pocket and text them both in our group chat to tell them. Lucille is side-eyeing me but I just smile at her sweetly.

Lucille parks up outside of Teddy's kindergarten and just as I'm about to get out of the car, I feel her hand on my bicep "Remember Cole, we are just friends, okay?"
I nod "I get it Topolino, let's go get him. I'm excited to meet him, kids love me."

She laughs as we get out of the car and make our way to the classroom. "I really don't see how kids love you, you're kinda scary."

227

I reach for her hand and give it a squeeze. "You'll see il mio topolino."

I let go of her hand reluctantly as she pulls away, only because she said she wants Teddy to think we are friends. I follow her through the gates and to Teddy's classroom and wait for the teacher to let him out. The teacher opens the door and one by one the children are let out as the parents are recognised. Teddy comes rushing out with his backpack on and a big piece of paper in his hands. He looks happy to see his mom. He runs into her arms forgetting his hands are full and crumples the paper. "Oh no Mommy! I almost crushed my painting. Look, it's me and you, we are at the beach!" He explains happily beaming up at Lucille.

"Wow Teddy bear, that's amazing! We will have to take a trip there soon, we could build a sandcastle like in your picture," she tells him.

Just then Teddy notices me and frowns. "Who are you?" he asks, furrowing his brow.

I smile and look at Lucille, she looks nervous. "I'm a friend of your mommy's. My name's Cole. I hope it's OK that I came to collect you with her today."

Teddy looks from me to his mom, and she smiles at him. "That's okay, right baby boy?"

"Mommy, I'm not a baby boy anymore. Of course it's OK for you to have a friend, as long as he can be my friend too!" he tells her.

"I'd be honored to be your friend Teddy. But I do have a question for you and it's a big one. Which is your favorite dinosaur?"

He looks at me thinking hard about it but replies with a smile, "I think a Tyrannosaurus Rex because he's the biggest and meanest of them all! Roarrr!"

"That's just the answer I was hoping for, he's my favorite too." I pull out a small three inch dinosaur figure from my pocket, which happens to a Tyrannosaurus Rex.

"So this here was mine when I was a little boy, I used to take him everywhere. Could you look after him for me?" I ask him.

Teddy's eyes light up. "Yes! I'll take good care of him! Is that OK Mommy?" he turns to Lucille.

She smiles at us both, her eyes glazing over. "Of course, Teddy. If that's what Cole wants."

I nod and Teddy squeals, "Thank you Cole! Can we go get ice cream?"

I look to Topolino because that sounds like a great idea to me.

"Well let's go for dinner and if you eat it you can have some ice cream after, ok?" Lucille tells him as we walk back to her car.

"Yes, I love ice-cream! Cole, are you coming too?" Teddy asks.

"Sure, if that's OK with your mommy?" I say looking hopefully at Lucille.

"Sure it is, do you have anywhere you'd recommend as you own a restaurant, you must know the best places to eat in this city," she asks.

"Well we could go to my restaurant. I'll message ahead and tell them to expect us and to get our food ordered. Any preferences?"

"PIZZA! Extra cheese and pepperoni please!" Teddy shouts as he is being buckled into his car seat.

"OK what about you, Topolino?" I ask, laughing at his boldness.

Lucille blushes, I'm not sure why but then says, "That's fine with me too."

I walk around and open the passenger door for her, she looks at me strangely. "I'll drive us there, that way you can chat with Teddy about his day." She pauses for a moment before she nods and gets in. I message Enzo and Benji to let them know to get a table ready and to prepare our food, also telling them to prepare a little surprise for Teddy before pulling off driving us to Salvatore Cucina.

As we arrive, Teddy is bouncing with excitement. "Wow this is yours? And you sure they have pizzas and ice cream here?" He exclaims, holding Lucille's hand tightly in one hand and his little dinosaur in the other.

I laugh, "Yes buddy, it's the best in town. We even have chocolate ice-cream and chocolate sauce but we don't call it ice-cream, we call it gelato."

Teddy looks at me like he's trying the word out. "If it's chocolate I'll try it, it better be as good as ice cream, why do you call it gelato? That's a funny word."

"Well I'm Italian, so that's what ice cream is for me," I tell him.

He nods, "My friend Lesso is Italian too, we met him at the park."

I smirk, "Well I've got a little surprise for you when we get inside." I wink at Lucille and take her other hand, leading us through the doors.

Enzo greets us as we enter. "Boss, table's this way."

He leads us to a corner booth. As we round the corner I notice Teddy's surprise is already sitting in the booth waiting for us. Teddy squeals, "Lesso! How are you here? This is the best day ever!"

Alesso looks at me and gets up to give me a hug. I may not be his father but we have a close bond, he helps me out in the kitchen sometimes after school when Linc has business to deal with that isn't child friendly.

"Hey Teddy, this is my Uncle, Cole. I was so excited when he told me we were going to have pizza with you and your mom!"

I look at Lucille, she's got a teary look in her eyes as I step closer giving her hand a reassuring squeeze. "Is everything ok Topolino?"

She nods at me and sighs gently, "Yes everything is fine. Let's sit down, I'm sure you boys are hungry!" Alesso sits first with Teddy by his side then Lucille sits and I slide in last next to her resting my hand on her thigh.

Alesso and Teddy chatter away animatedly about dinosaurs and ice-cream flavours while Lucille looks on and smiles.

"He's like a nephew to me, I'd do anything to make him happy. As I would you and Teddy," I whisper to Lucille. She moves her hand under the table and places it on my leg mirroring my own on hers. My cock twitches as she rubs small circles with her fingers. I put my hand on hers to stop her. "Best you stop that unless you want me to take you to the restroom and have a different meal than what we have ordered."

She blushes a deep shade of crimson and removes her hand. "Thank you for this Cole, it means a lot to us. It means a lot to me to see Teddy happy."

Before I get a chance to reply, our pizzas arrive. The boys fill their faces as Alesso tells us all about his favorite Pokémon and Teddy tells us his too. Once we've finished our pizza's, my waiting staff clear the table and bring chocolate gelato out for both boys. They even make a treat out of it with a sparkling candle in each dish. The boys are beyond excited. "So, did you like the chocolate gelato, Teddy?" I ask.

He grins at me with a chocolate mustache, "It was the best! Mommy can we come again?"

Lucille smiles and turns to me, "If that's ok with Cole?"

"You are always welcome here." I tell them. I look at my phone as it vibrates in my pocket. "Alesso, your dad is here. I'll walk you out to him. Why don't you say goodbye to Teddy and his mom before you go."

Alesso stands, "It was so much fun seeing you Teddy. Luci, can you ask my dad if we can have another park play day again?" This kid is hard to resist with his big eyes boring into Lucille.

"Definitely, we would love that!"

I move to kiss Topolino on the cheek "I'll be back in a moment then we can go."

Alessandro grabs my hand and we walk out the back where Linc is waiting. "Hi Fratello, all okay?" I ask taking him into an embrace. He nods but looks tired.

Alesso grabs his dad, giving him the biggest hug. Linc smiles, "I've missed you today, Son. I hope you've been good for Uncle Cole." I'd normally offer to take Alesso back for him so he can rest but I have to see Lucille and Teddy back first.

"Alessandro has been brilliant, I'll see you at home later okay my man?" I fist bump him and then give him a quick hug before he leaves with Linc.

I head back into the restaurant area, Teddy and Lucille are putting their coats on. "You ready to go?" I ask.

"Yeah I need to get Teddy to bed, it's getting late." Topolino says, glancing towards the clock.

"Of course, is it ok for me to accompany you home? Then I'll get my bike and go. I don't expect to come in." Lucille frowns and contemplates my words but nods as we leave the restaurant.

On the drive back to Lucille's, I glance in the back and see Teddy has fallen asleep. I smile and look at Topolino, she's looking out to the sky. "I love the stars. We don't always see them because of the city lights. Where I grew up, you could always see them every night. I miss that sometimes." She sounds sad, I don't like that.

"I'll take you stargazing one night, just me and you if you like," I offer, hoping it will cheer her up.

She looks at me excitedly, "I'd love that Cole!. Tonight has been great. You really are great with kids. Teddy is quite taken with you, so is Alesso."

I nod and then pull up to her driveway. "I told you. Would you like me to carry Teddy in?" I ask.

"No it's ok, I've got this," she tells me as she opens the car door to get out. I walk round to her front door and open it as she is lifting Teddy from the car. Once he's out, I lock the car for her and wait for her to get safely inside. I hang her keys up and lock the door with my own key before going to grab my bike. I don't expect a goodbye. She's probably tired and focused on getting Teddy sorted and I don't want her to feel pressured into having to give me a goodbye if she's busy, so it shocks me when she comes back to the door and shouts, "Cole, aren't you going to say goodbye to me?"

I turn to her and stalk toward her, taking her face in my hands. "I didn't want to put any pressure on you to feel you had to come back out to me."

She just smiles. "You Cole, are full of surprises." She kisses me softly then steps back into the house "You best send me your number so we can go find the stars together." Then closes the door, locking it.

I quickly retrieve her number from the background check from Linc and text her straight away.

Buonanotte il mio topolino, sognami.

I jump back on my bike and drive away before I go back and climb through her window and never let her go.

Chapter 26

Lucille

"Goodnight sweetheart," I whisper gently, planting a kiss on Teddy's forehead as I tuck him into bed. He smiles sleepily and rolls onto his side, tucking little B under his chin and falls quickly into dreamland murmuring, "I love you Mommy," as he drifts off.

I tiptoe my way back out of the room leaving the door slightly ajar letting the light from the hallway seep through the crack in case he wakes up through the night and quietly head to my bedroom to change into my comfies. I scrape the hair back from my face and retie it into a loose ponytail on the top of my head before rinsing my face off with a warm flannel and cleanser to remove all of my make-up. What a day, I sigh at my reflection. Work has been such a drag these last couple of days, and the full intensity of both Silas and Cole taking us out for dinner for the last two nights has been somewhat overwhelming. Both mentally and physically. It's an unbelievably hard task to try not to be so sexually attracted to men who are so damn hot! What makes it worse is the fact that Teddy absolutely adores them both, all of them really, Alesso too. I hope this works out, whatever it is, between these men. I don't think I could handle my own heartache let alone Teddy's. Ugh men, three huge, sexy, infuriating men. I wonder if they realize what they're actually doing. Toying with a young boy's feelings. If this doesn't work out with a relatively happy and civil ending. I swear, I don't care how big they are, I'll kill them all.

As I walk back through the hallway, I head straight for the kitchen pouring myself a large glass of red wine and pull out a bag of share size potato chips. Share size, I don't think so. I flop myself down onto the sofa and bring my knees up to my chest as I pull the blanket resting across the back over my legs, and flick on the TV. I scour the channels trying to find something to watch until defeatedly I open Netflix and settle for the horror film, IT. I snuggle deeper into the sofa cushions and take a large gulp of my wine. I hate clowns but I love horrors so there's no way I'm not watching it and there's definitely no way I'm getting through it without alcohol.

I can already feel the adrenaline spiking through my system as the film gets creepier until I'm well and truly on edge and the loud PING from my mobile almost has me spilling my wine into my bag of potato chips. "Fuck," I laugh at myself for getting so jumpy. I reach forward and grab my phone from the coffee table.

Buona sera luce mia, I enjoyed our time together yesterday but it's not enough. I can't get you out of my mind. Have dinner with me tomorrow evening?

My stomach flips as I reread the message several times, it's Silas I know it is, he always calls me his light but how did he get my number? I bet Cole gave it to him, the ass that he is. I'll have to have a word with him about giving my number out to people. I take a long sip of my wine and without thinking, i'm already typing out a reply.

Like a date?

I throw my phone down beside me on the sofa and try to concentrate on the film but Silas's words are swimming through my head. It's not enough, I can't get you out of my mind. I bite at my nails anxiously waiting for my phone to ping again. Why does this make me so nervous? I'm like a high schooler when her crush is texting her. Should I even be entertaining the idea of going to dinner with him? God I don't know, I've already fucked the man so I suppose we're already a little past dinner dates. One date wouldn't hurt would it? PING. My stomach flips again as I pull up Silas' reply.

Yes Lucille, a date. Meet me at Mezzanotte at 8pm. I'll take you to dinner and drive you home after. I know this may all seem sudden but give me a chance and I promise you, you won't regret it.

I swallow roughly, my tongue licking out over my lips to stop them from drying out as I try to come up with some sort of excuse as to why I shouldn't do this. But I can't. Some insane part of me deep down wants to jump at this chance to dance with danger and go for dinner with a blood thirsty Mafia boss. Call me crazy but the thought of it sets my soul on fire. The memory of his thick muscular arms pinning me against the lockers as he fucked me into oblivion races through my mind straight to my already throbbing core. There's no way I'm getting out of this I admit and unashamedly I accept his invitation then down the rest of my wine and shove a fistful of crisps into my mouth.

One chance, big guy. See you at 8.

Throwing my phone back on the coffee table I distract myself and watch the end of the film then make my way to bed, eventually falling into a fitful sleep of vivid dreams full of strong men and deep piercing eyes.

When I wake up the next morning with the sunlight streaming through the curtains, I sigh heavily. The bottle of wine I finished off last night resting heavily on my head this morning and leaving a dull ache behind my eyes. I glance at the clock that reads 06:40. I haven't got long till Teddy wakes up and starts scouring the cupboards for food. The child is like a human garbage disposal, he never stops eating. I reluctantly peel myself out of bed and head straight for the shower in my en-suite, letting the cold water wash away my hangover. After drying myself off and pulling on a pair of navy jeans, black T-shirt and cardigan, I slip on my shoes and head to Teddy's room.

Unsurprisingly, he's already out of bed and stood in front of his wardrobe picking out his clothes for the day. "Morning sweetheart," I call from the doorway.

"Morning Mom," he replies, tugging his joggers up over his legs.

"PB and J or Pop Tarts this morning?" Fridays are our treat day so he always gets an exciting breakfast and dinner when we're at home, or me and Kat have the kids for sleepovers for alternate weekends.

I watch his little eyes light up as he throws his arms up over his head and shouts, "POP TARTS!" at his reflection in the mirror. I laugh at his excitement and head off to the kitchen to make us some breakfast. Teddy saunters into the kitchen when he's ready and pulls himself up into the barstool and patiently waits for his breakfast of Pop Tarts and a side of fruit. My own breakfast consists of strong caffeine and a banana. I'll make sure to grab something for lunch at work. I'm not sure I can stomach anything else at the moment.

After greedily munching down his breakfast and watching a few cartoons before we leave, I help Teddy to pack his bag ready for his day at kindergarten and strap him safely into the car.

"Are you looking forward to tonight little man? You've spent a lot of time at Kats recently haven't you? I promise next week Bella can stay at ours for the weekend. How does that sound?" I ask, watching for his reaction through my rear view mirror as I pull out onto the main road from our gated apartment complex.

Teddy smiles widely at me, his mouth forming the shape of a perfect circle. "Yes please, Mommy, that would be so cool. We could go in the pool and to the park and build a fort in the living room and stay up and eat chocolate all night!" He squeals excitedly, reeling off another hundred things that we could do over the weekend.

"Okay I'll have a word with Auntie Kat and see what she thinks. Remember she will pick you up from kindergarten today, okay? I will come and get you in the morning." Teddy beams at me again, no sign of sadness that he is spending the night away from me again though I still feel the guilt heavy in my chest at leaving him so much recently. Should I really be going on this date tonight? I shake my head, he's happy and he loves spending time with Kat and Isabella so stop over thinking I scold myself. He's fine, it's okay.

A little further down the road I pull up in the drop off zone outside of Teddy's kindergarten and help him out of the car making sure he's got his bag ready and his lunchbox tucked under his arm. I crouch down and plant a kiss on his cheek. "See you in the morning sweetheart, have a good day. I will call you later, okay?"

Teddy wraps his arms around my neck and smiles. "See you tomorrow Mommy, love you," he calls as she skips off towards his teacher that's waiting at the door.

"Katrina Henderson will be picking Teddy up today." I call to his teacher. She nods and writes it down on her clipboard. The security at this place makes me feel so much more at ease knowing that the only people who would ever be able to collect Teddy other than myself are Max and Kat. Now I just have to get my head into work mode when all I really want to do is curl back up in bed. No rest for the wicked.

It's 13:45 and I'm only just sitting down to have my lunch after a hectic morning in the clinic. One of my patients decided to have a meltdown in the waiting area and ripped out their stitches which subsequently ended up in a massive blood spill and them fainting so my work list ran late.

I sigh heavily as Kat enters the coffee room and takes the seat opposite me. "You okay sugar? I heard what happened with Mr Crane."

I laugh and shake my head. "Oh yeah, all in a day's work isn't it." I joke, rolling my eyes as I do. Kat laughs with me as I take a bite out of the sandwich I picked up from the hospital canteen and wash it down with a mouthful of Dr Pepper. "So I'm going on a date tonight." I blurt out before taking another bite of my lunch.

"OH MY GOD, where, what time and with who?" She squeals in delight, her face lit up with genuine excitement for me.

I swallow nervously before meeting my eyes with hers. "Umm Silas. I'm meeting him at his club then he's taking me for dinner." I say quietly so that Chris and Lisa sitting on the other side of the coffee room don't overhear. I watch as Kat's eyes widen in response and brace myself for a grilling, but it doesn't come. Instead she leans forward and brings both of her hands to mine and holds them tightly.

"This is it, isn't it?" she remarks

"What do you mean?" I question, genuinely confused.

"You're hooked on mafia dick aren't you?" She asks with a straight face.

"KAT!" I scold, rolling my head back and laughing with her. "Bitch!" I say as we sit back on our chairs in fits of laughter. "It's not like that," I say, "I don't know exactly what it is like, but it's not that. Even if it is all I can think about." I add on in a hushed voice.

Kat raises her one eyebrow at me suspiciously, "Girl just admit it, you want to fuck him again."

"Kat! Shut up!" I scold again, looking over her shoulder to see if anybody heard her, and taking a deep breath when nobody seems to be paying us any attention.

"You'll fill me in on all the juicy details right?" She asks winking at me with a cheeky grin pulling at her lips.

"I promise," I say, rolling my eyes as I cross my finger over my heart in the shape of an X.

"Good, now I'll leave you alone. Call me later. I want to know how it goes!" she says before standing up and leaving me back with my thoughts while I finish off my lunch break.

I make it home by 17:30, completely exhausted and ready to crawl into bed. I just about make it through my front door, I've already kicked off my shoes, thrown my cardigan over the back of the sofa and pulled my t-shirt off over my head on the way to my bedroom and as soon as I see my large double bed I collapse onto it, wrapping myself up in the duvet and close my eyes.

A loud PING of my phone jolts me awake and I'm still half asleep with blurred vision as I reach for it out of the back pocket of my jeans. It's Kat asking what I'm planning on wearing for my date tonight. SHIT. I sit up and bolt to the bathroom, I fucking fell asleep and now it's 19:00. God dammit Lucille, I curse at myself as I fling my clothes around the room and quickly jump under the shower. There's no way I'm meeting up with Silas with the stench of work lingering on me from today. I quickly shave my legs, bikini line and underarms then shampoo and condition my hair. Jumping out, I wrap a towel around my body and head for the bedroom standing in front of the full length mirror to dry my hair and quickly go over it with my curling wand leaving it in a loose wave that falls down over my shoulders. I run back to the bathroom and apply a little bit of makeup, lining my lids with my black pencil and coating my lashes in mascara. Less is more right? I run back into the bedroom, nerves eating away at my insides as I start tearing out clothes from my wardrobe and throwing them on the bed when they don't feel right. I finally settle on a low cut black skater dress that accentuates my waist and flows out over my hips. I slip on some red heels and run a layer of red lipstick on to match. This will do. I quickly snap a picture of myself in my bedroom mirror and send it to Kat for approval who quickly responds with a heart eye emoji and a flame emoji. I grin and with her moral support give myself another once over before I grab my keys and a small red clutch bag and drive over to Mezzanotte. I fight down the waves of nausea, excitement and sexual tension that are all battling to see which comes out on top.

I pull into the dimly lit parking lot outside the club and swallow down my nerves as I cut off the engine and make my way to the entrance. I'm greeted at the door by a tall man, dark hair, clean shaved and shoulders as wide as a goal posts. My eyes widen at the sight of him and I know he notices it as a smile pulls up the corner of his lips. I watch his eyes take me in from head to toe and feel a chill run up my spine. "Alright darlin'? What can I do for you?" he asks, his voice smooth with a hint of deadly.

"I'm here to meet Silas, my name's Lucille." I say, hoping my voice doesn't give away my jumbling nerves inside.

At the mention of our names, any flirting disappears. The man's face hardens and his body visibly stiffens. "Follow me Miss, my name is Dario," he grunts, tipping his chin towards the door before walking me inside.

I gasp at the interior of the club, the whole room is dark, brooding and flush with velvet furnishings. A large stage runs along the back wall, fitted with poles and half naked women dancing around them to 'Black Velvet' by Alannah Myles. Through the spotlights I can make out a large crowd of men sitting around the front of the stage, wooing a large breasted woman who has her legs spread open leaving absolutely nothing to the imagination. A large fair haired man with a thick mustache and food stains down his shirt

241

eagerly slips some dollar bills into the strap of her thong and she winks at him as she saunters off towards her pole. Women are working their way through the group of men, sliding their arms strategically around their necks to give them a good view of the goods they have to offer while others are carrying drinks to and from the bar. I turn my attention back towards the brunette on the pole, almost finding myself mesmerized by the way she's moving, her hips swaying perfectly in time to the music. "This way, Lucille," Dario calls to me from the bar, pulling back my attention. "I'll take you up to the office, the boss is just finishing a call," he says, leading me towards a metal set of stairs leading up to the second level.

"That's okay, I don't mind waiting here if he's busy," I say, stepping closer to the bar. I'd hate to get in between his business and I think I need a bit of liquid courage anyway because this is absolutely wild.

Dario watches me with a hint of uncertainty pulling at his brows. I'm pretty sure he's questioning whether he should go against his boss's orders by leaving me here or go against my wishes by escorting me upstairs. I give him a friendly smile and nod my head. "Dario, I am fine here. I will have a drink while I'm waiting." I slip on to a bar stool and take a glance at the time on my phone, it's 19:58. "Tell Silas he has two minutes," I add, giving him a cheeky wink and sending him on his way.

He shakes his head and chuckles. "Quinton, get Miss Holland anything she wants, on the house," he calls over to the guy behind the bar before he turns and heads towards the stairs. I gape after him at the fact he knows my last name. Obviously I've been a topic of conversation around here already.

"What can I get for you darlin'?" Quinton calls over the bar as I swivel myself back around on the stool to watch the performance on the stage. "I'll have a whiskey, on the rocks please," I say over my shoulder, unable to take my eyes away from the same brunette snaking her arms around a petite blonde wearing nothing but a G-string. I take my drink from Quinton and take a long slow sip, letting the burn trail its way down my throat. A few moments later the room seems to get darker, the only lights are now trained onto the stage. The dancers are changing over, and making their way to the center stage is a bleach blonde with legs like a runway model and a redhead who has a small tattoo of a cherry on the inside of her hip. The music drops and 'Girls Girls Girls' by Motley Crue starts blasting through the speakers. Instantly the two women, wearing nothing but lace knickers, move around each other with ease. Their hands caressing each other, teasing their male audience. I feel a large presence behind me and with a rush of excitement I bring my drink to my lips and throw it back in one knowing exactly who it is.

"Like what you see la mia luce?" a deep velvet voice whispers into my ear, sending a shiver straight down my spine. I feel Silas' fingers graze around the back of my neck as he shifts my hair to one side and traces his lips gently across my skin. I suck in a breath of air and watch as the blonde on stage runs her tongue down the valley of the redheads chest and carries on down all the way to her red lace thong. This is fucking insane I think to myself closing my eyes and leaning back against Silas' chest. "You look sexy as sin tonight in that little dress Lucille," Silas growls low into my ear, taking a sharp bite of the lobe. "You'd look even better out of it though, standing on my stage, dancing for me and my brothers," he adds, sinking his teeth into the flesh on my neck and sucking hard on my skin. I wince slightly at the initial sharpness but his words and the feel of his hands and lips on my body melt away everything else, eliciting a painfully delicious throb between my legs. A deep moan escapes my lips and I feel his body stiffen at the sound. "We will never make it to dinner if you make noises like that." Silas coos, releasing his hold on me, leaving me wanting more, so much more.

His large hands spin the stool to face him, he's dressed all in black, trousers, jacket and shirt with the first few buttons open revealing his beautifully tattooed chest. I drink in his appearance as he does the same with me, his hooded eyes roaming over me not missing a single inch. The look of lust is pure molten, burning me on the spot. If I was completely sober I'd be cringing at myself, so I'm grateful for the boost of confidence the little bit of alcohol is giving me. "Are you ready to go?" Silas asks, not taking his eyes away from mine.

I bite my lip having to break away from his intense stare. "I need to freshen up first," I say because if I don't compose myself before I get into a car with this man I am absolutely going to lose all sense of self resistance and straddle him before we've even left the parking lot.

Silas grins as if he can read my thoughts, "Of course, la mia Luce. This way," he smirks, holding out his hand for me to take before leading me over to the ladies restroom.

"I just need a moment," I say before dipping in through the door marked with a motif of a stripper, how fitting.

The door opens behind me a few moments later, just as I'm touching up my lipstick in the mirror and Roxi saunters in, the girl who came up to ask me if I was okay after the fight night, wearing a red lace bralette and a pair of silver hot pants and a smug grin on her face. "Hey babe, didn't think you'd ever step foot in this place," she says standing next to me and combing her fingers through her bushy mane of hair.

I huff a small laugh, "Yeah it's not exactly somewhere I thought I'd come to either."

Roxi turns to face me and leans her hip against the counter unit housing the sinks. "You know I'm not the bitch everybody says I am, we could be friends." She gazes down at my outfit making me feel a little uneasy, like she's picking me apart piece by piece. "I could even take you shopping. I know what kind of things Silas and Cole like." She smirks looking down at my dress again before adding, "and what they don't," under her breath just loud enough for me to hear.

"Thanks, but I think I'll be okay, I like to keep my men guessing, not just lay it all on the table," I reply, pushing up my own hair. I watch Roxi's face turn sour in the reflection and try to keep my face straight at the reaction, that'll teach you, bitch. I straighten my dress and smile at Roxi as I leave. "See you later," I say with a saccharine sweet voice. I almost swear I heard her mutter something that sounded like 'not if I have anything to do with it' under her breath, but I can't be too sure.

I walk out of the bathroom to find Linc leaning against the bar opposite with Silas a little further behind talking animatedly over the phone. Linc's smile falters as Roxi walks out of the bathroom closely behind me and he instantly steps forward. "What has she been saying?" He snaps, narrowing his eyes at Roxi who tuts loudly by my side

"Now, now, Lincy poo, don't be like that. We're all friends here, right Louise?"

I raise my eyebrows at her blatant attempt to rile me and turn to face her, two can play this game. "Yeah sure Rosie, we're all friends here," I smile, winking at Linc who is trying to keep his face straight.

"Boss won't be long, he's just had to take a quick work call," Linc states, tipping his chin towards Silas.

"Roxi you should get back to work, there's a stag-do in booth two that needs their pockets emptying."

Roxi's face hardens for a moment. "I could always empty your pockets," she sings, fluttering her fake eyelashes as she slides up to Linc's chest.

He instantly stops her, placing both hands onto her biceps, his knuckles visibly whitening at how hard he's digging his fingers into her skin. "Not interested Rox. Never have been, never will be. Now get back to work," he snaps, pushing her backwards, leaving her even more frustrated as she flicks her hair and walks away.

Linc turns to me after he's watched Roxi straddle herself over one of the men in the VIP booth and shakes his head. "Nasty piece of work she is."

I smile and laugh at his seemingly true remark. "I've had worse. She seems quite hung up on you guys though." I say, searching his eyes for any hint of emotion towards the scatty bitch.

Linc holds my eye contact as a smirk pulls up the one side of his mouth. "Trust me love, she is nothing but business to us. The punters love her, that's the only reason we keep her around. You've nothing to worry about," he says while bringing his hand to my face and tucking a loose strand of hair behind my ear. I close my eyes at the brief contact and sigh inwardly, these guys really are getting to me in every which way. I feel like an army of butterflies has just been released inside of my stomach. I can feel the heat rise in my cheeks as I blush. How can such a big hard scary looking mafia guy have such a gentle way? Or is it all just a show? Silas steps into view and Linc lowers his hand. "Enjoy your night, Lucille," he whispers before turning to Silas. "Brother," he nods, then makes his way towards the metal staircase taking the steps two at a time before he enters a glass-fronted office.

"Sorry la mia luce, I had to take that call. Are you ready to go?" Silas asks, pulling my attention back to him.

I smile and nod. "Yes please. Where are we going?" I question, letting him lead me out the door, past Dario and over towards a black Porsche. He opens the passenger side door for me to slip in before closing it and getting in next to me and starts up the engine. He looks over at me with a delicious grin on his lips. "I was thinking Thai. I know a lovely little place, nice and quiet. I have a private booth so we won't be interrupted."

"Sounds lovely. I've only tried a little bit of Thai food so you'll have to tell me what's good on the menu."

Silas laughs, concentrating on the road ahead as he drives. "Oh la mia luce, the tastiest thing in that restaurant won't be something you can find on the menu." I blush instantly, his words sending a wave of excitement straight between my legs. I clench my thighs together and subconsciously start to pick at my fingernails, praying the darkness of night filling the car is concealing the effect he has on me.

A little while later, after a journey full of comfortable small talk, Silas pulls the car up outside a quaint little restaurant called Thai Orchid. The outside is lit up with hundreds of fairy lights wrapped around a small but cozy outdoor seating area, making it look like something out of a movie. "It looks beautiful," I gasp.

Getting out and walking around the car to open my door for me, Silas takes my hand and leads me inside to the restaurant host greeting customers as they walk in.

"Ah, Mr Salvatore, good evening," he calls, greeting Silas with a familiar handshake. "The usual table?" he asks, grabbing two menus from behind his stand.

Silas nods and smiles at the small but happy man, "Please Nam, thank you."

"Right this way," Nam says, gesturing us forwards towards the back end of the restaurant.

As we make our way through the dining customers, I take in the beautifully decorated interior. The walls are painted white and red with golden scroll details throughout. There are giant Buddah statues placed in every corner with incense sticks, candles and flowers placed at their feet.

Bamboo screens separate off different sections of the floorplan, while large ceramic pots of tall grass plants separate the rest of the tables and multiple candles around the room give off a beautiful mood lighting.

Nam leads us to a secluded corner of the restaurant, hidden by a wall of foliage and fairy lights and ushers us into a booth. "For you, beautiful lady," he sings, handing me a menu. I giggle and thank him politely but notice as Silas scowls at him as he lays a cotton napkin over my lap. "And for the gentleman," Nam adds, turning to Silas offering out his menu. "What can I get you for drinks?" Without a beat, Silas orders a bottle of white wine and a jug of fresh iced water for the table.

When Nam arrives back at the table with our drinks, I let Silas order food for us both as he knows what the best options are and Nam skips happily away again to the kitchen to pass our order to the chef.

Silas relaxes beside me and places his hand onto my thigh, just below the cut of my dress.

"Thank you for agreeing to have dinner with me tonight. I know this is all very sudden, me and my brothers coming into your life like this but we have the best intentions when it comes to you and your boy. You just have to give us a chance to show you." Silas says, gently squeezing my leg in reassurance. I shift a little under his hand, unsure whether I need him to remove it completely or move it further towards my already throbbing clit.

I take a sip of my wine. "Why me?" I ask through barley a whisper.

Silas looks at me with a rare smile. "The first moment I saw you in that prison, I knew I had to have you. You are the first person I think of when I wake up and the last person I think of before I fall asleep. You are more than special, la mia luce. You are my light in all of my darkness and you will come to accept that. I will do everything in my power to let you know just how much you mean to me," he

248

says, leaning in close enough for me to taste his breath against my lips. I try to think of anything other than how close his lips are to mine, the smell of his cologne mixed with the taste of whiskey on his breath sending my head spinning. I lean back slightly and gaze up into his eyes. Eyes that look like they're on fire, eyes that bore straight into my soul.

"How can I trust you?" I sigh. "I know who you are now. I know what you do." I look away briefly and turn my head away but Silas brings his hand up to my face and brings my chin back towards him firmly slamming his lips to mine. I resist at first but soon my mouth is opening, allowing entry to his eager tongue. I melt forwards and bring my hands to his chest feeling his drumming pulse beneath my fingers. I feel his hand run slowly up my leg and beneath the hem of my dress while the other snakes around the back of my neck, holding me against his mouth. I couldn't say no even if I wanted to, I guess it's a good thing that I don't. Silas is hardly touching me and I'm already aching and needy. His hand trails further up my dress and lands over the lace material of my thong. I involuntarily shift my position to give him better access and I feel the smile pull at his lips as he continues his assault on my mouth. He knows exactly what he's doing, and I can't help but let him. His hand strokes gently across my clit, the friction from my underwear feels delicious against me, eliciting a small moan between our mouths.

Silas bites down on my lower lip before sucking it between his own. "Do you want me to stop, baby?" he asks. I pause for a moment then shake my head, opening my thighs further for him, gaining a satisfied grunt of approval. "Good girl. Now keep quiet, we wouldn't want to draw any attention to your dripping pussy would we?" he growls low into my ear. I gasp, suddenly remembering where we are but the possibility of being caught with this man's fingers deep inside of me, right here in this restaurant turns me on even more and I clench my inner muscles in desire.

Silas slips my thong to the side and with a swift move his fingers are inside me, gently teasing the inside of my channel.

"Fuck," I gasp through gritted teeth as he expertly circles his thumb across my clit while gently pumping his hand back and forth. I dig my nails into the fabric of the seat either side of my thighs and throw my head back while I close my eyes, his assault all too adequately delivered.

"You look incredible with my fingers so deep inside you." Silas moans against my neck as he trails kisses from my collarbone to my earlobe. I can feel the familiar ache pooling inside of me, building delicious waves of ecstasy. Silas curls his finger stroking against my sweet spot, the sensation almost tipping me over the edge already. I move my hips to meet the thrusts of his hand and have to bite down on my lip as a whimper escapes my throat.

"Be quiet baby, I want this all for myself," he whispers against me before pulling my face back to his and plunging his tongue into my mouth. I can feel myself letting go, my thighs are shaking beneath me and my chest is flush with heat. Silas pulls away from my lips, his fingers thrusting deeper and faster inside me. "You can trust me, Lucille. No other man will make you feel like I can, like my brothers can. Nobody else will ever make you feel as good. Let go baby, trust me, come for me."

His words are my undoing, I jerk my hips forwards and try to stifle my cry. With another deep thrust of his fingers, I come hard and heavy over Silas' hand. My walls clench his fingers as I arch my back, pushing forward to ride out the waves of pleasure. Silas leaves his fingers inside of me until my body relaxes and my aftershocks have passed before he slides out of me and brings his fingers to his lips, slick and glistening with my release he dips his fingers into his mouth and sucks them clean. It's one of the hottest things I've ever seen and instantly has my pussy aching again. Silas watches me with hooded eyes before leaning in and planting a gentle kiss on my neck, just below my ear as he whispers, "The only thing sexier than watching you come on my fingers, would be watching you come on my cock," he purrs. Fuck, that is the sexiest thing anybody has ever said to me. This man will have me committed for insanity.

I turn to face him. "This is just a lot," I admit, straightening myself back out and flattening the bottom of my dress across my legs, because really it is, all of a sudden I've gone from a happy single mom to the main attraction of three dangerous mafia dogs. I shake my head, "I just don't know what to say." Thanks for some of the best orgasms of my life but please let me think about being in a relationship with you? It even sounds crazy in my head!

Silas dips his chin slightly and his face relaxes as he smiles at me. "You don't have to say anything right now, there is no pressure here, Lucille. The decision rests entirely with you, and whatever you do decide we will honor it. For now let's enjoy our evening." I nod in agreement, I have a lot to think about but he's right, I don't have to decide right now so I'm going to enjoy myself before I end up making any rash and possibly stupid decisions. Silas sits back and rests his arm along the top of the seat behind my shoulders just as Nam arrives pushing a trolley laden with plates and bowls of delicious looking food.

"This all looks and smells incredible," I gasp as Silas takes one of everything and loads them onto a plate for me. My mouth is already watering, I can't wait to dig in.

"You have to try these dumplings," he says with a smile while placing two onto my plate.

We enjoy our meal with comfortable and easy conversation. He asks me about Teddy and how he's getting on with kindergarten and in turn tells me all about him and Cole and what they were like when they were growing up. If I didn't already know it, I would never guess that this man was a mobster. I had almost forgotten the warning Max had previously given me until Silas shifts and I notice his gun tucked into the back of his waistband. But it doesn't deter me, if anything it just makes him a hell of a lot more sexy, if that is even possible.

Silas settles the bill once we've finished and opens the door for me once we get to his car. "I'll take you home, I don't want you driving back after you've been drinking," he says, pulling out onto the main road.

I blush slightly and twiddle my thumbs in my lap. "What about my car?" I ask, concerned at how I'd be able to pick Teddy up from Kat's.

Silas squeezes my thigh gently with one hand still on the steering wheel. "I'll get Dario to drop it off in the morning before you've even woken up, don't worry la mia luce, you will be on time to pick up Teddy," he replies as if he read my mind.

I smile a sigh of relief. "Thank you Silas. Thank you for tonight, it really has been lovely." I say resting my hand on top of his. His genuine smile as I do has my defenses slowly crumbling just that little bit more.

I leave my hand resting with his the entire drive home, even keeping it in place when he switches gears. When we pull up outside of my apartment, Silas opens the Porsche door once more to let me out then walks me up the driveway. I open the door then turn to face him, unsure whether or not to let him inside, because if I do, I know he will end up in my bed. He takes a step towards me, placing both hands on either side of my face and crushes his lips to mine, deepening the kiss as he slides his tongue against my bottom lip before I do the same in return.

"I won't come in," he says, breaking us apart his

breathing rapid, "because if I do, I'm afraid I won't ever leave." I swear this man is inside my head. He kisses me again, softly this time with his lips molding to mine like they were made to fit together. I bring my hands around the back of his neck and pull him in closer before he pulls away for the last time and grits his teeth as if it is the hardest thing in the world for him to leave. "Goodnight Lucille, make sure you lock up before you go to bed," he orders, running his hand through his hair as if debating what his next move should be. Then he turns and walks back down the driveway and gets into his car.

"Goodnight Silas," I whisper, walking through my front door and locking it securely behind me.

Chapter 27

Vinny

I watch as she parks her car outside of this fancied up whore house. Lucille Holland. As she opens the door to her beat up car, I see her lean tanned legs step out, she's wearing some red fuck me heels that make her body look even more delicious than I remember. Her black dress clings in all the right places. I wonder if she still has the scars I left on her? She always did look pretty when my fists had blackened her skin. Wetting my lips at the thought of her being mine again, this time she won't get away. The call I received telling me where my property was hiding wanted a hefty sum of money for the information, luckily we had managed to come to a mutual agreement.

Lucille turns and locks her crappy car, then walks over to the entrance where she is greeted by a dark haired man that's built like a house. She talks with him for a moment and follows him in. I fight the urge to follow her inside, wanting to know what she's doing every second of every minute. But I wait, biding my time in my blacked out car until I see a shadow appear beside my car window. I roll it down. It's a portly man, with little to no hair.

"Wondered when you'd turn up for that little bitch. She's about to go on a date with our boss, perhaps you can grab her after that?" he slurs, he's obviously been drinking but he's the contact that told me about Lucille's hiding place so I say nothing to show my disgust.

"Theo, I assume?" He nods. "I need to have the element of surprise, watch her daily activities and that of my son's, then I'll strike." I explain.

He grunts. "Fine but don't take too long to get the bitch out of our way." With that he leaves to enter the club.

A few minutes later, Lucille leaves the building accompanied by a large Italian looking guy, with dark hair and dark features. It must be their boss, Silas. I can tell from here he's well built by the way his suit jacket pulls across his shoulders. She's grinning at him as he opens the car door for her to climb on in and it makes me want to wipe the smile off her pretty little face. She shouldn't be smiling at another man. She shouldn't be getting into his car, silly little whore. She'll get what's coming to her. I wait for them to start driving before I turn my engine on to follow them. Just as I'm about to pull off, some broad decides to stand in front of my car. This bitch must work at the whore house as she's dressed in next to nothing. Probably a good fuck with the size of her tits but her cunt is likely to be swarming with disease. I roll my window down, "Get the fuck out my way." I bark.

She smirks at me, looking a little crazy. "I know where they are off to if you want directions." she chirps.

Realizing I've lost sight of them I nod and reluctantly unlock the door, gesturing for her to get her ass in. "You can show me the way and suck my cock once I'm there for making me loose sight of them in the first place." I snarl at her as she closes the car door.

She giggles, "Alright sugar, it'll be the best blow job you'll ever get, name's Roxi."

The whore, Roxi, directs me to my target like she said she would. As I pull up outside of the restaurant that Lucille and that motherfucker Silas are at, I click my fingers at Roxi, and like a good little slut she leans over and starts to get to work on my dick. Her mouth is wet and she knows what to do with her tongue that's for sure. As her head is bobbing up and down giving me a well earned release, I blow into her mouth. I push her head down on to my cock to ensure she swallows every single drop. Fucking whore needs a good meal and that's what she's got. I hear her gag slightly before letting her up. Her face is flushed and wet from the tear tracks that are running down her face. "Right, now fuck off will you?" She looks shocked at me for a second, as if a blow job could make me forget the woman who has escaped me for the last time, and I will have my revenge on her.

"I thought you might want some company," she finally says, hopeful that i'll change my mind.

"The only company I wanted was your mouth on my dick, I got that, so again, fuck off before I slap some sense into you." That makes her move. She exits the car quickly and slinks off down the side alley of the restaurant away from my car.

I wait until Lucille and her boyfriend leave, again I follow them and eventually they lead me to her home. I watch and wait for Silas to leave. I will bide my time, once I gather enough of her normal routine, the bitch and brat are mine and I'll make sure I make her pay for daring to leave me. She thinks these men can save her. She's wrong. I'll ruin her and they will never even touch or look at what is mine again. She thinks she can run and hide my own child from me? I don't care much for the boy but he will come in handy to keep her in line I'm sure.

I'm coming for you Lucille Holland. My lawfully wedded wife.

Chapter 28

Max

It's been too long since I last saw Lucille at the club fight night. It's almost time for the next fight night and the stubborn little shit has ignored every one of my texts and calls. I know she's angry but I'm trying to protect her, that's what big brothers do.

"What's up Boss?" Jax asks as he slides through the door to my office and slings himself onto the chair opposite my desk. Jax is my newest recruit but he's been showing his enthusiasm and commitment to the business so I hold plenty of hope for him even though it's still early. His broad shoulders and sharp features make it hard for people to say no to, which is exactly what I need. He is exactly what the club needs.

"Any movement?" I ask, pursing my lips as I subconsciously run my eyes over tonight's collection details.

"Nothing new Boss, all seems above board," he comments, shifting uncomfortably in his seat.

"Anything else Jax?" I ask, not looking up from the paperwork.

"Why do you have me tailing your dad again?"

I look up to see him watching me, curiosity etched deep into his young and inexperienced face. "I just want to make sure the old man stays out of trouble," I reply, keeping my tone level, not wanting to let on it's actually because I don't trust the man, not since he started sneaking around and causing trouble on a few of his recent job runs. I've had Jax trailing him for a couple of weeks now and other than the fact that he has a sickening need to get his cock sucked by hookers, nothing new has come to light. Not yet at least. I know there's something though, this gut feeling I have never usually lets me down. "You can leave," I add, focusing back on the numbers in front of me.

Jax leaves without another word, another reason to keep him on, he's smart and learning the rules quickly. My phone buzzes in my pocket and I reach to answer it. It's Trigger, my second in command. I'd be lost without him, I owe the man my life. We've been caught too many times on the battlefield but we're yet to be snuffed. "Trig," I smile into the mouthpiece.

"Boss, you're going to want to see this," he breathes down the phone. For fucksake what now? "I'm sending you a photo." My phone buzzes as the image comes through, I zone in on the image of that piece of shit Salvatore holding onto Lucille at her front door. My anger bubbles and I can feel it sitting heavy in the pit of my stomach, a horrible volcano of acid, ready to erupt.

"When was this?" I snap, almost crushing the phone in my grasp.

"About 10 minutes ago, he left and she went in alone, Boss. Nobody else has been around since."

I grind my teeth in frustration knowing it's time to cut this bullshit stubbornness and go and talk to my sister. "I'll stick around tonight Max, don't worry." Trigger adds, and that's why he is my second, he will look out for her with his life and do whatever necessary to keep her safe, I don't have to ask.

"Thanks Trig, I'll relieve you in the morning. Eyes up brother."

"Eyes up," he responds and I hang up, throwing my phone across the room. Too distracted to finish adding up numbers now with the intrusive thoughts of the enemy touching my sister when I have repeatedly asked her to stay the fuck away makes me see red. I call it a night and head home.

After a long and sleepless night of thinking how best to approach the situation with Lucille, I find myself outside her apartment just as dawn cracks. I've given Trigger the nod to leave and taken up his watch post but my patience is wearing thin and I couldn't care how early it is or whether she's awake or not. I tap my knuckles against the door and surprisingly hear shuffling from the other side. A moment later Lucille, still dressing in mismatched pajamas, like she used to when we were younger, opens the door and frowns when she notices it's me. "Expecting somebody else?" I ask, stepping past her into the kitchen-living area, not bothering to wait for her to invite me in.

Lucille eyes me up and makes her way to the fridge. "I was just making a coffee, do you want one?" She asks nonchalantly.

"No thanks, I'm sure you'll be kicking me out soon after I say what I have too anyway." I pull up onto a bar stool and take a deep breath, here we go. "Lucille, the Salvatore brothers are bad news." I watch as she carries on pouring her coffee with little to no emotion showing on her face. "I don't want you getting involved, for Teddy's sake. I love you both so much but I'd never forgive myself if Teddy got hurt over something I can prevent."

That does it. She snaps her head up and narrows her eyes at me. "Fuck you Max, don't you dare!" she half spits. half shouts at me. "You have no fucking right to tell me who I can and can't get involved with and don't you DARE bring my son into this. You didn't seem to care when you asked me to help at that fight night, so don't you dare change your tune now!"

"Luci, you know I wouldn't have asked if I had anybody else. These men are dangerous, ruthless, and they will stop at nothing to get what they want."

"What, you mean like you?" she snaps back at me flaring her nostrils as she slams the milk container onto the counter top. "I know what they are, who they are, but you dear brother I have no fucking idea who you are anymore." Her words hurt more than they should, everything I've ever done I've always tried to keep Lucille in the dark, especially with her past and her previous life, more so now she has Teddy. I love that boy like he's my own, maybe that's where I went wrong and now I'm paying the price.

"These men will hurt you." I say, trying to get her to see reason.

Lucille's face hardens. "Then it's a good job I know how to patch myself up isn't it," she spits. "I know what it's like to be hurt Max, in case you had forgotten."

I stand up off of the stool and hold my hands up like I'm taming a wild animal. How could I forget that? That day, almost six years ago, when Lucille turned up out of the blue on my doorstep, battered and bruised half to death because her shit of a husband had too much to drink, will go with me to the grave. "This is different, Lucille. Vinny left you barely alive, these men will finish the job," I say through gritted teeth, my hands shaking at my sides.

Lucille watches me and I can see the anger burning behind her eyes as tears threaten their escape as she all but croaks "Thank you Max, but I am fine. You do not need to concern yourself with my safety anymore."

"I swear to God Lucille, if they so much as hurt one hair on yours or Teddy's head, I'll bring hell down on their entire empire and they'll be sorry they ever messed with a Costello." I grab hold of Lucille by her shoulders and make her look me dead in the eyes. "Take this as a warning, little sister. If they put so much as one foot wrong, I will burn them all to the ground one by one and dance on their remains." I growl before I leave, slamming the door behind me.

Chapter 29

Silas

"Can we go get pancakes this morning for breakfast Uncle Cole?" Alesso asks as he's making his way into the kitchen where myself and Cole are having our morning caffeine fix. Linc is behind him on the phone.

"Make sure it's sealed and sent with the shipment tonight, Father. I don't want to hear anymore about it unless you want to be put on the chopping block for Cole to play with." Linc snaps, looking pissed but pockets his phone and grabs a coffee smiling at his son.

"Sure dude, we can go to Aunty Kim's diner. She's been banging on about seeing you," Cole answers Alesso with a big smile.

"Yessss! Can we all go or do you and Uncle Silas have to work Dad?" Alessandro questions, jumping up and down with excitement.

"I'm free as a bird this morning kiddo," I tell him.

Linc takes a gulp of his coffee, "As soon as I've finished this we can get going Son," gesturing to his coffee.

Alesso has the biggest smile on his face, he loves being with us all. He's told Cole time and time again how he wants to be one of us when he's older. We don't pressure him on joining the company but if he wants to, the door is always open. In some ways I wish he wouldn't, so he can have the life we all wanted and were denied.

I finish my coffee and grab my jacket as the others do the same. We opt to travel together in the black matte Range Rover that we keep for family occasions. The windows are blacked out too. Cole is tapping away on his phone grinning like an idiot. I'd say he's talking to our woman but with Cole he could be watching torture videos for all I know. He moves to take the driver's seat as I take the front passenger seat, leaving Linc and Alessandro to slip into the back. As Cole drives us to Aunty Kim's, I hear his phone vibrate in his pocket. "You're popular today Brother. Is it our Lucille blowing up your phone?" I ask.

He grunts at me but has a slight smile on his face. "All will be revealed in good time Silas, be patient, God knows I have been with you and that dumbass in the back. Alesso is the only one that doesn't test my patience in this car." Alesso looks up and smiles as Cole winks at him in the rear view mirror.

As we pull up in the parking lot we see Aunty Kim cleaning some tables outside. When we get out, we hear her screech and run over toward us. This plump little woman wraps her arms around Alessandro. "My boy! How wonderful it is to see you. You look like you need some of Aunty Kim's pancakes in you! Come, come all of you. Cole said you were on your way so I've cleared the best seats for you all," she says, patting Alesso on the cheek as she winks at Cole. As we make our way into the diner I see exactly what Cole meant by patience. There at our favorite table, is a little boy with the biggest smile and the most beautiful creature I have ever seen. Her eyes light up as she sees us coming over.

"Alesso!!! I've been so excited since Mommy told me we were seeing you today! Are the pancakes really as good as Cole told Mommy?" Teddy squeals with excitement. He's full of energy and Alesso is waving his arms as a 'hello' as he runs over to the table to greet them both.

Cole steps in-between me and Linc, draping his arms over our shoulders and whispers to both of us, "Do you like my surprise brothers? I mean she'd look better sitting on my cock with one of your cocks in her mouth but we have to have that chat with her first, and what better time than after pancakes. Aunty Kim has agreed to distract the boys for us."

I scoff at him, and I'm pretty sure my mouth is hanging open in shock, but also in pure amusement. "Always planning, always scheming Cole."

As we make our way over to the table, I look Lucille up and down, her hair is loose and straight, she's wearing a black skirt with some slip-on pumps, and a gray cami top. She looks stunning, I can't take my eyes away from her until Cole clears his throat behind me and pushes past.

"You spend all your time staring brother, you're always gonna lose at getting the spot next to her." He takes the seat next to Lucille as Alesso takes the seat next to Teddy on her other side and Linc sits opposite Alesso. Leaving me to sit opposite Lucille.

"I hope you don't mind me and Teddy joining you guys? Cole text me this morning telling me he'd finally show me where he learnt his pancake making skills from," Lucille explains, nudging Cole with her elbow. Cole playfully pretends he's wounded making Lucille roll her eyes but I notice the way she smiles at him, adoringly. It takes me a second to register how easy going Cole is around her. Linc jumps in when I'm too speechless to say anything. "Cole failed to mention anything to us but we are happy to share our secret of the best pancakes in the city with you."

"I knew they were gonna be here, me and Cole planned this," Alessandro is quick to confess, looking smug.

"It was on a need to know basis, me and Alesso were the only ones who needed to know, and dude you ratted me out." Coles says jokingly with Alessandro causing him to chuckle and stick his tongue out.

263

Alesso and Teddy continue to chat between themselves, as Lucille turns back to Cole, "So how did you guys find this place?"

"We've been coming here since we were young, Aunty Kim kept us fed and out of as much trouble as she could."I say, finally finding my voice.

I notice Cole has slyly placed his arm around Lucille's shoulders but before she can speak up, Aunty Kim comes over with endless stacks of pancakes, bacon, eggs and lots of syrup. As she placing them down onto the table she looks to us all one by one, "So boys how have you been?"

"Great thanks Aunty K. Business is booming but we've missed your home cooked food. Alesso has been begging to bring his friend Teddy here for a while," Linc replies.

"Well I'm glad you have finally brought your friend Alesso, and I'm glad your dad and uncles have brought a friend too," she says, giving Lucille a friendly smile. "You best look after them both, she looks far too beautiful for you rowdy men." she adds on with a stern look at me.

"Of course Aunty, I always look after my treasure," Cole says, looking at Lucille as she blushes.

"Right, enjoy the pancakes, I gotta get back to the kitchen. It's the morning rush and I've got lots of mouths to fill. I'll be back out when you're done and the young ones can come help me with some baking." Kim turns and goes back to the kitchen.

"Momma! These pancakes are the best!" Teddy says with a mouthful of food.

"Teddy, don't talk with your mouth full, but you're right, they are pretty delicious."

I lean my head back and look to the ceiling. This woman doesn't make it easy on me, all I can think of is filling her mouth full of my cock. Damn I hope she agrees to this arrangement, she's too fucking perfect to let go.

I look over and she's frowning at me. "Are you OK, Silas?" she asks, concern sweeping across her face.

"Yeah la mia luce, I'm all good. How has your morning been?"

"A bit rushed trying to get my uniform and Teddy's school stuff sorted for tomorrow. I'm working a double shift Monday so I've had to arrange for Max to pick Teddy up from kindergarten." Lucille explains.

Linc leans forward. "If you ever need any help with picking him up you should give us a shout, one of us always collects Alesso, so it wouldn't be any trouble to have Teddy too." I smile at him, he's trying and that's all I can ask for. He's a sucker for a woman that cares for her child. It's what Alessandro has never had and I know he wishes that were different.

Lucille looks at him and his facial features soften under her gaze. "That's very kind of you. I'm sorted for Monday but I'll keep it in mind for the future. I'm sure Teddy would love to hang out with Alesso one afternoon."

"Mommy, can we go help Aunty Kim in the kitchen now?" Teddy asks, shoveling the last piece of pancake into his mouth.

Cole moves his arm from behind Lucille and stands. "I'll go take the boys to the kitchen and help Aunty K get sorted. I'll be back as there are some things we'd like to discuss, Topolino." He bends and kisses her cheek and she blushes at the gesture looking away for a second. The boys get up from their seats and accompany Cole to find Aunty Kim, leaving me and Linc with Lucille.

Linc stands, moving to sit where Teddy had been seated next to Lucille. He takes her hand in his and caresses the knuckles of her fingers. "I know you don't know me as well as the others, but I'd like to get to know you more, Love. And I hope that once Cole is back, you will hear what we have to say and agree to what we have to offer." Lucille looks unsure and I'm sure a little pissed off, but before she has a chance to say anything back Cole rejoins the table and slips back in taking her other side. She is now boxed in between my brother and friend as I sit opposite them, watching her mind ticking over.

"Il mio luce, we have a proposal for you. You have completely captivated us. You've changed everything we thought we knew we needed in life and have given us hope. Of a better future, a better life for our family. A hope for redemption. We are completely under your spell. And we know it's an unorthodox relationship we are asking for, but we feel that it would work for us and you. So instead of one of us, we are proposing all of us. Would you be open to that?"

Lucille looks down at her hands, anxiously picking her thumbnail. "I'm having a hard time believing I'd be enough for all three of you. I have to say though, I don't think I'd ever be able to choose between any of you. Each of you has caught my attention in your own way" I watch her facial features as she thinks, ranging from absolutely mortified to deeply curious and as she pouts her lips and looks to meet my gaze she smiles. "How will it work?"

"Easy, we spend time with you individually and together. There is no allocated time. We will go with the flow and respect each other's time with you. You are in charge here, Topolino. It's all on your say so, and we will endeavor to make you happy." Cole interjects before I get the chance.

"What happens when you get bored of me?" she blurts out, voicing her true concerns.

"I highly doubt you will ever bore us, Love. You are something special." Linc comforts her sliding closer along the booth.

Lucille finally looks at us all. She looks us each in the eye contemplating her final decision before nodding her head, "Okay, I'd like to try. I don't know how to explain this to Teddy but I'm sure that will work itself out. He likes all of you and it has been amazing to see the time and effort you're all putting in to get to know him, as well as me."

"One more thing Lucille, we don't share outside this table, understood? You are ours and we are yours." I warn her. She blushes and nods again, letting out a little squeak as Cole slips his hand beneath her skirt.

"Cole" she whimpers, turning to face him, opening her legs a little further. Linc brings his hands around her from behind and gently pulls her against his chest, providing Cole a better angle and tipping her face up as he kisses her, slipping his tongue between her lips. I can hear her moans from my seat and I have to readjust the solid hard on in my trousers and she continues to ride my brother's fingers. She's panting and rocking her hips to meet every thrust of his hand, her cheeks are flush and her eyes are already glazing over. I've never seen anything so fucking hot in my life. She looks like a goddess, whimpering as Cole picks up the pace as he watches his own fingers penetrating her dripping pussy. Linc whispers something I can't hear into her ear before sinking his teeth into the lobe and bringing his hand over her mouth. Lucille's eyes instantly flash open and lock straight onto mine as she climaxes, Linc's hand stifling her cries as her body shudders and her legs become rigid. I can't be sure but I swear Cole almost came at the same time, and with a savage look across his face I can't help but feel a little jealous as he sucks her cum from his fingers.

"You look so beautiful when you come, la mia Luce, especially between my brothers" I praise her.

She's flushed and trying desperately to straighten out her skirt again. "I can't believe we just did that" she says, shaking her head, "The boys could have seen!" she exclaims, bringing her hands up to hide her face.

"Get used to it Topolino, we plan to let everyone know who you belong to. Oh, and brother, if you would have moved quicker to sit down next to her, you could have had her juices dripping from your fingers instead," Cole laughs, smirking at me. I roll my eyes at his teasing and lock eyes with Lucille again. He doesn't need to know that I did the exact same thing at the Thai restaurant, but I had her all to myself. I bring my fingers to my lips at the memory of her honey covering my fingers.

Her embarrassment suddenly forgotten Lucille holds out her hands to Linc and Cole "Don't forget if this is going to work, then you belong to me too, so you best tell those stripper's to keep their hands off."

"Don't worry they will know. I like the jealous side of you, Love. It's sexy" Linc chuckles into her ear. Cole brings his fingers to his mouth and licks them again like a man starved, making Lucille blush even more.

Once the boys have rejoined us at the table. I take my opportunity as we are walking Teddy and Lucille to their car to speak with Teddy and Alesso.

"Hey boys, how would you feel about having a sleepover next weekend?"

Teddy shouts, "That would be so cool! Could we order pizza? And watch the new Sonic movie?"

Alesso smiles, "I'd love that, would that be okay with you Luci?" He acts older than he is but he's so polite.

"Well yeah, that would be okay with me if your dad doesn't mind," Lucille asks, glancing over at Linc.

"We'd love to have Teddy over, but I was thinking of a group sleepover, you'd be invited to" I explain.

Lucille looks between us all, the realization slowly creeping in at what my intentions are. "Oh yeah, that sounds… fun." she squeaks nervously.

"Yes! Mommy I can't wait!" Teddy exclaims.

I smirk as I whisper into Lucille's ear. "What's that saying? There's no rest for the wicked? Well baby, we're pure fucking evil. You'll be begging us to stop" I kiss her on the cheek and move away leaving her speechless with her mouth open staring after me.

Linc pulls her into his chest, embracing her tight and kissing her head before Cole steps forward and looks straight into her eyes and speaks Italian to her. "My little mouse, I will dream tonight of the taste of your lips and the feel of you on my skin. I will hear your sweet whimpers and remember the way it feels when you come under my touch. Until we meet again," he kisses her passionately, leaving her breathless as she gets in the car and drives away.

I have to stop myself from chasing after her and starting my promise of hourly orgasms from this moment on. As we get into our own car and start driving, Alesso is hooked on his tablet. "She took it well, didn't she?" Linc comments.

Cole nods, focusing on the traffic ahead. "She took it better than I thought. The sleepover date lands on our fight night though, so we might have to deal with that before making our way back to the house. I'd love nothing more than to parade Lucille around, show the rats who she really belongs to. The boys can stop with the nanny and a security team until we get back. Do you think she'll come with us?" I ask, not really caring for their objections.

Cole sniggers, "Brother let's not give her the chance to object, she's our queen and we are the kings, the peasants need to be reminded of that. I'll sort Aunty K to come over instead. Lucille will feel more comfortable with that."

"Sounds like Cole has it all planned out fratello, don't worry." Linc reassures me.

When we arrive back home, Linc takes Alesso out the back to play some basketball while me and Cole head in to deal with business in the office upstairs. Sitting at the computer, I scan the documents of the received shipments and Cole is on the phone to one of our distributors.

"I expect to see the amount you owe transferred or deposited in our account by midnight tomorrow. I have been very lenient with you so far Dwayne. Don't make me have to pay you or your whores a visit. They didn't seem so thrilled the last time I strolled through your neck of the woods. Next time I'll take body parts as payment if you are late. They won't be calling you Big Daddy any longer, I can assure you." Cole hangs up and throws himself down on the sofa. "Why are these people always so exhausting to deal with? Meet the fucking dead line or I'll cut your dicks off, cunts. It's that fucking simple"

I shake my head and wonder how this guy went from whispering sweet nothings to our girl to casually threatening to cut off genitals. Just another day in the Salvatore organization.

Chapter 30

Lincoln

The memory of Cole finger fucking our blonde beauty as she leant panting against me at breakfast has been tormenting me for the last 48 hours. So much so that my cock feels like it's about to burst through the zipper on my trousers and the ache in my balls is so heavy they feel like they might combust at any second. I swipe my hand over my face and try to shake away the feeling but all I want is to bury my own fingers, tongue and cock into every hole Lucille Holland has to offer and have her screaming my name while she comes. There is no point denying it any longer, even if I won't admit it out loud just yet, she has me as hooked as she does my brothers and I am ready to fall head fucking first.

I get up from my office chair and shake out my legs, jumping up and down on the spot to try and use some of my pent up energy. It's fucking useless but I have to do something or I'm going to jack off over my desk right here and now. A moment later my phone pings loud throughout the room bringing me back to reality. It's Sully.

Boys are looking good for fight night, Boss. Little Zip is a fast fucker, they won't see him coming

I can feel the grin spread across my face, excellent, I chuckle to myself. I've had Sully whipping the shit into a few of the new boys who seemed like they had a lot of potential in the ring for our club fight nights over at the warehouse, and it seems like it's finally paying off. Pedro or 'Little Zip' as we call him, is a tiny little fucker but full of muscle and ridiculously fast on his feet, hence the name Zip cause he zips around the place like a bloody fly. I caught him running from the feds not long back and couldn't believe the speed of him so instantly took him under my wing, offered the clubs protection and now he'll be returning the favor in the ring for me. I type out a reply and chuck my phone back down onto the desk.

Excellent! Keep them focused, strictly no booze or pussy before the fight. I don't want any distractions and I don't want sloppy punches. I have a lot of money on this match. If anybody has a problem with that, send them to me.

Feeling slightly less frustrated, and almost grateful that my cock isn't fighting to break out from my trousers anymore. I walk to the adjoining room and pull up a seat next to Zack who is watching over the casino floor like a hawk. I catch his sharp eye honing in on camera screens seven and eight, the two that cover the very front of the bar on the main floor. I narrow my eyes wondering what it is that's caught his attention when I notice a movement so slight and precise that no normal eye would even notice. I grab for the walkie-talkie perched on the side of the desk and call out for Felix. He replies almost instantly letting me know he's ready to do whatever I need. "There's a code white at the main bar. Blue shirt, prey is a blonde woman wearing a green dress." I pause for a moment. "Bring him downstairs." I add on before flexing my fingers and cracking my knuckles as I stand.

"On it, Boss," Felix replies and I watch through the live stream as he makes his way towards the guy we've just watched slip something into the green dress lady's drink while she momentarily dropped her guard. I stare at her face while Felix escorts the unwilling man away as confusion and a fleeting sigh of relief passes over her face.

Suddenly my thoughts are back to my own blonde and the anger in me begins to bubble up at the thought of somebody spiking her drink, her piece of shit ex-husband and that piece of shit doctor that would have done God knows what if Cole hadn't stepped in. I leave the room in silence and head straight for the interrogation room.

I enter the shockingly sterile room with stainless steel cabinets lining the back wall opposite a large two-way mirror and the strip light blaring down onto a struggling middle aged man who squirms helplessly beneath Felix's steel grip. "Get the fuck off me you wanker," he seethes, trying to free his arms. Felix squeezes him tighter and shoves him into the single chair waiting in the middle of the room then makes quick work of securing his hands behind his back, keeping him in place.

I dip my head to Felix as he stands letting him know he will not be needed in here and he swiftly exits the room leaving just me and the piece of shit in front of me. "I don't know who the fuck you think you are doing this to me!" He shouts, spitting towards my feet.

I shrug off my suit jacket and hang it over the hook on the back of the door, something I seem to do religiously when I'm in this room. A ritual before I'm about to inflict pain and make somebody bleed. "Oi, you fucking wanker, answer me!"

Before I can stop myself, I've rounded on him and slammed my fist into his jaw causing a well of blood to pool into his mouth which begins to dribble slowly down his chin. I grab hold of his chin and dig my nails into his stubbled skin. "I suggest you shut your fucking mouth unless you want me to shut it for you." I seethe into his face before shoving his head away and walking towards the cabinets at the back of the wall. "There are many things I tolerate in life, but sleazeball men who think they can take advantage of women are not one of them." I begin to say, picking up a knuckle duster from the top

273

drawer and slipping it onto my fingers. I round back on the man and study him carefully, his brown eyes watching my every move as I pace before him.

"I don't know what the fuck you're talking about you stupid cunt," he roars straining against his restraints.

The pinprick scars at the creases in his arms below his rolled up sleeves turn my stomach as vivid flashes of Alesso's mothers cold, dead body intrude their way into my mind. I shake my head and swallow down the disgust rising in my throat, and like it has a complete mind of its own, my fist connects with his jaw again and a spray of blood covers the floor from his already bleeding mouth. I hear him grunt loudly in pain but pull my fist back again and crack it hard into his stomach.

He whines loudly as I double him over and sink my fist into him once more, feeling the crack of his ribs underneath my heavy metal cased fist.

"What makes you think you can take advantage of a woman and get away with it? You piece of shit!" I shout between more throws of my fist. The man slumps forward in the chair, pulling on the binds that are keeping his hands behind his back and a wet gurgle escapes his lips as blood trickles out of a large split in his lower lip. A malicious smile encases my face and I instantly see red, a large veil coming into place over my eyes, my fists are working on their own as I pummel into him, his face, his chest, his stomach, anywhere I can land a hit. "What. Gives. You. The. Right!?" I grunt between each hit. Fighting against images of a stone dead Cassidy morphing into Lucille burning beneath my retina's until I feel myself physically being pulled away.

I throw my hands in the air and turn to face Felix with his hands up in surrender letting me know he poses no threat, his eyes take in my bloodied appearance and his lips straighten into a grim line. "That's enough, Boss," he says, nodding towards the chair, not taking his eyes off me.   "He's done." I breathe in deeply, filling my lungs with the scent of blood and despair and turn towards the limp body hanging from the chair. "Have nothing to say now do you. You fucking junkie!" I bark, spitting his blood from my mouth at his feet. I turn quickly, catching a glimpse of my reflection in the two-way mirror, my face and shirt covered in blood. I run my fingers absentmindedly through my hair only to realize those too are covered in the fuckers blood. "FUCK!" I scream at the top of my lungs flying my fist at the wall. The frustration I now feel at my lack of restraint. "Clean this up," I snap at Felix as I throw the knuckle duster across the room and grab my jacket from the back of the door and start making my way towards the only place I can think of, to the woman I can't get out of my mind.

I speed through the streets utterly desperate to lay my hands on Lucille's body. My brothers have had their fun, now it's my turn. I just hope she doesn't mind a little blood because I didn't give myself time to change.

I pull up outside of her apartment complex and almost swing my car door off its hinges, I'm in such a rush to get to the front door. I knock desperately but as soft as I can make it, knowing Teddy will already be in bed as it's just turned 23:00. I glance down at myself and suddenly feel a twinge of guilt at showing up looking like this. I turn my back on the door almost toying with the idea of leaving but stop suddenly as the light from her front room bleeds through the crack and Lucille slowly peeps her head around the door to see who I am.

I turn slowly, so as not to shock her too much at my bloodied state, but my need and want for her is too much and as soon as she gasps my name when she takes in my appearance, my restraint completely snaps and I've pushed my way through her front door and held her hostage against my lips.

I brace myself for a fight but she molds into my body, instantly parting her soft lips to mine and allowing access for my tongue to entwine itself with hers. A feral growl escapes my throat and it's all I can to do not fuck her right here and now in the doorway. My hands have a mind of their own as they greedily caress her body. I take her plump breasts into each hand and squeeze, gaining a pleasurable whine from her mouth against mine. Trailing my hands around her back and down to her ass, I dig my fingers into her soft cotton pajamas and lift her effortlessly to straddle my waist as I carry her over to the couch.

"Linc," is all she can gasp as I grab a fist full of hair at the back of her head and pull, tilting her chin up to allow my kisses to trail down her neck. I can already feel her arousal warm against my thighs as she dry humps my lap. Lucille brings her hands to my chest and runs them down along the buttons of my bloodied shirt, pausing before she rips it straight open, flying the buttons across the room and pushing my jacket and shirt off my shoulders in one. She gasps again at the bloodstains splattered across my chest then strokes her fingers idly across the red spatter leading up to my face.
Once her eyes catch mine, I see the flare behind them, she needs this as much as I do and who am I to deny a woman of such a thing. "Linc, please!" she mewls again as I brush my finger across her bottom lip, not breaking eye contact.

"Fuck, Love. The sound of my name on your lips is going to be my undoing," I groan, lifting her up from the couch with her legs still wrapped around my waist. I carry her to the ensuite attached to her bedroom and lower her down so she's stood before me. "Take off your clothes," I order as I lean in and switch on the shower then proceed to fully undress myself as Lucille does the same. I almost gasp at the sight of her fully naked before me. The way her hair rolls down around her shoulders. The way her nipples harden against my touch and her thighs squeeze together has my cock throbbing for its release. "Fuck Lucille, you're gorgeous," I whisper as I stroke my fingers from her neck all the way down to her pussy. I swipe my index finger across her clit that makes her whimper. "Did you like that, love?" I ask, swiping my finger once more.

"Yes," she chokes, holding herself steady against my arms. As I bring two fingers together and slowly stroke them between her folds, her arousal is already coating her slick center and dripping down her thighs. I close my eyes and grin, the thought of my cock sliding in and out of her has precum beading at my tip.

"Fuck Love, you are so wet for me," I whisper into her ear before pulling her into the shower with me and slamming her back up against the tiled wall. A sharp intake of air fills the small space as Lucille takes in the sight of my solid cock jutting out between us and without me having to ask she reaches her hand out wrapping her slender fingers around my thick girth and begins to pump me slowly. I grin, baring my teeth then wrap my fingers through the wet strands of her hair and bring her lips to mine, shoving my tongue into her mouth without permission.

With a single move I turn Lucille around to face the wall and place her hands shoulder width apart, kicking her feet out to the same width. I gaze down at her perfect ass and slap my hand across her creamy skin causing her to yelp. "You're so fucking perfect, Lucille," I tell her, hoping she can here the truth of my words as I grab the base of my cock and line it up to her glistening opening and slowly push it through her folds that clench oh so deliciously around me. An exquisite whine escapes her lips that has my cock twitching inside of her as I thrust my hips forwards, the tightness of her wet cunt threatening to defeat me already. I still for a moment so that she gets used to me being inside of her, stretching her wide on my girth, but as soon as I hear her eager pleading of my name again and she looks back at me over her shoulder with those pretty fuck me eyes, I let loose, letting all of my restraints fall to the floor. I hold onto the base of her neck with one hand while the other digs into her hip, helping to pull her back to meet my thrusts as I fuck her hard and deep with the shower water running red with the blood being rinsed from my body. The sight has my balls tightening as they slap against her clit. "Fuck Lucille, you have no idea how fucking good you look like this, bent over with my cock inside of you." I grunt as I pound her into the tiled wall. "I want you to come for me love, scream my name as you come all over my cock."

I feel her pussy tightening at my words as I reach my hand round between her legs and begin circling my fingers across her clit. "Come for me baby," I whisper, leaning myself down to her ear and hammering my cock straight to her sweet spot.

"Fuck, Linc!" is all I hear. She's done, I can feel it before it happens, her pussy tightens like a vice around me and her sultry moans become a strangled cry as she calls my name once more. The gush of warmth I feel over my cock deep inside her has me weak and as she comes down from her high I feel myself letting go. My release almost cripples me as fill up her tight hole and I have to bring my hands to the wall to keep myself upright.

"Fucking hell!" I groan as my cock twitches with aftershocks, I can feel Lucille still shuddering against my chest.

I wait a minute for Lucille's breathing to come back down to a steady rhythm before I slip my cock from between her swollen lips and watch as my cum leaks out and dribbles down her thigh and although it's the sexiest thing I've ever seen, I need to clean her up and get her into bed. "Let me clean you up," I whisper, before grabbing a washcloth from the shelf along the wall and covering it with her vanilla scented body wash. I gently caress her body, taking extra care between her thighs. As I stroke the cloth over her pussy she flinches and my cock almost stands to attention straight away, ready for round two. I watch her watching me as I leave a trail of kisses behind where I drag the cloth and notice the desire still burning behind her eyes. "I had every intention of taking you on a date tonight Love, but fuck this was a much better idea." I admit.

A smile plays on her lips as she bats her eyelashes at me. "I think this was a brilliant idea," she purrs, leaning forwards and planting her lips onto mine as she delivers a soft but sensual kiss. "It's my turn to clean you now," Lucille whispers, surprising me as she's already taking the cloth from my hands and applying more body wash before she scrubs the remaining blood from my skin. "What happened?" she asks quietly as she trails her hands up behind my neck, keeping her gaze away from my own.

I sigh deeply, not wanting to fully admit that I lost my shit at the thought of her being taken advantage of and took it a step too far, trying to teach somebody a lesson. I lower my forehead to rest against hers and wrap my hands around her back pulling her closer to my chest. "Just business Love. Nothing you need to worry about," I say, planting a kiss on the top of her head. "Come on, let's get you into bed," I add, switching off the shower and wrapping her body up in a bath towel. It may not be the answer she wanted but I don't want to burden her with my own demons, not when she has her own.

As we enter her bedroom Lucille slips off quickly to check in on Teddy and as she steps back into the room with a shy smile on her face. I instantly melt at the sight of her standing in front of me with her little short shorts and tank top. Jesus this woman is incredible, freshly showered and freshly fucked. My eyes lower and I know she senses it too as she glances over to the bed. "Fuck Lucille, if you look at me like that much longer, I'll have you in that bed and your screams will have the neighbours knocking on the door to check you're still alive."

A red heat instantly floods her cheeks as she bites her bottom lip and takes slow steady steps towards me then sinks to her knees and pulls down the front of my boxer shorts letting my already painfully hard erection spring free. This woman will be the death of me. I suck in my breath and watch as she expertly caresses her hands around the base of my cock and kneads my balls gently with the other while trailing her tongue back and forth across the length of my hard on. Her eyes are locked on mine as soon as she takes my cock to the back of her mouth and begins to suck, hollowing out her cheeks as she effortlessly swirls her tongue around the head each time she pulls back. "Fuck baby," I groan, running my fingers through her hair as I pin it back from her face. "That's it, fuck my cock with your pretty little mouth." I'm already beginning to feel the build of my second orgasm ready for it's release. The sight of this goddess on her knees for me is something else entirely. I tilt my hips and thrust forwards, pushing further into her throat, the little gag that escapes her lips as a trail of saliva and precum drips down her chin is my undoing, and I grunt loudly thrusting forward as my cock jolts and I can feel my release filling up her mouth before she swallows around me, sucking me dry with each gulp.

"Fuck," I say again, unable to comprehend anything else at this moment in time and slipping my spent cock back behind my briefs. I lift Lucille and grasp her face in my hands, slamming my lips to hers and dominating her tongue with my own, not giving a shit about tasting my own cum against her tongue. "You are fucking incredible," I breathe as I push her away and onto the bed.

"I know," she grins playfully at me, "and you have a magnificent cock" she adds, trailing her fingers across my six pack.

"I know Love, I know," I laugh and flash her a cheeky wink before pulling her down onto my chest.

We lie together in comfortable silence for how long I'm not completely sure. A feeling of complete contentment washing over me, something I haven't felt in a long while, with her fingers trailing across my chest and mirroring the outlines of my tattoos before she breaks the silence. "How did you meet Silas and Cole?" I smile at the question and run my hand down her back absentmindedly resting it over her ass and reveling in the way it fits perfectly in my palm.

"I'm surprised you haven't already asked, Love. I've known them ever since I can remember. We're brothers through more than blood. Their father Matteo, was a piece of fucking work, well he was Don until he got sick years back and Silas stepped up in his place. My father was his second while they were still in command and I guess that's where it started. We did everything together. Silas and I are six years older than Cole, and those six years taught us more than we would ever like to admit." I pause slightly. taking a deep breath as the memory of Silas' initiation night comes flooding back. The way his father used me as leverage to get him to commit his first kill is all I can think about. What a fucking thing to threaten your own son with, his bestfriends life, the son of your own best friend too! A shudder racks my body but as Lucille's hand rests gently against my face I shake off my reverie and continue. "Anyway, after my mother was killed it brought us all closer. The need for revenge pulled us all together. We've bonded over life and death on more than one occasion. I've witnessed them draw their first drops of blood and I will be there to see them draw their last." I pull my gaze up to Lucille's face to see her already intently searching my own. "I trust those men with my life, as they do me and until you Love, nothing has ever come between us."

Lucille gasps slightly, parting her lips, just loud enough for me to hear and I smile sincerely, tracing my thumb across her bottom lip. "Don't worry, we like to share," I wink.

Her brows furrow slightly and she sits herself up. "I don't want to come between the three of you. I don't want to be the one reŝponsible for breaking up a bond like that," she admits, turning away from me.

I sit up and pull her face back to mine. "We have all agreed, including you, that we are going to do this, you are going to be ours, Lucille. Not Silas' or Coles' or even mine, but ours. Together."

"But what if one of you gets jealous?" she asks, her eyes flicking up to mine.

I smile at her innocent question and bring my lips to hers placing a gentle kiss onto them before whispering into her ear "Baby, there is nothing to be jealous of when we all get to fuck you like you're the last woman on earth." I graze my teeth gently across the lobe of her ear. "And if you're a good girl, we'll all fuck you at the same time." I sink my teeth into her ear lobe again, harder this time and elicit the most erotic groan deep within her throat that I have ever heard. "Fuck baby, do you like the thought of that? The thought of us all fucking you into submission and filling each of your holes with our cocks?" I whisper, trailing my hand up her thigh towards the heat between her legs, noticing when I stop above her pussy that she is already soaked through her thin pajama shorts and I have to bite back the urge to stick my tongue between her slick folds. "I'll be more than happy to relay the message to my brothers at how wet you are at the mention of the three of us fucking you raw baby." I coo into her ear. She blushes again, trying to steady her breathing and I have to look away and remove my hand before I'm tempted to never leave her bed again, only fucking her till I have nothing left to give.

"I don't understand," her small whisper snaps me back to reality.

"What don't you understand, Love?" I ask tucking a loose strand of hair behind her ear.

Her eyes flick down to her hands in her lap while she picks at her thumbnails, a nervous habit I've noticed she has. "I was in love once, you know." She starts and the words instantly have me wanting to put my fist through a fucking wall but I let her finish what it is she has to say. "At least I thought I was at first but it wasn't love, it was a lie. I tried so hard for that relationship to work but it broke... Me... That relationship broke me." Her words are barely a whisper and my sudden anger turns to heartbreak as I spot the tears threatening to spill down her cheeks. I know how hard this is for her. "One man who vowed to love me, but could not and now I have three of you promising to share me, to protect me and my son and want for what in return? Nothing?" She finds my eyes once more, and I note the pleading and sorrow deep within her irises before she shakes her head. "I just don't understand Linc."

I frown but pull her closer into my lap once more, making sure she feels secure in my arms. "You do not need to understand Love. We are asking for nothing, we only want you in any way that you willing give yourself to us. We are not your husband, we would never," I notice Lucille flinch slightly in my arms at the word husband and sigh, "we would never hurt you." I finish, leaning my forehead against hers. She says nothing, but her silence is deafening in this moment but the fact that she is not denying or refusing us is all that I can ask, given her complete lack of trust in men and that really she hardly knows us at all. A few weeks ago we were all complete strangers getting on with our lives and now we've selfishly imbedded ourselves into her life and expected her to accept it. "I should go," I say, slipping from beneath her and standing to slip my bloodied clothes back on.

"Wait, Linc, can't you stay?" Lucille leans up and grabs my arm as I pull on my jacket, the horrified expression on her face almost has me on my knees.

"I can't Love, trust me I would but I have to be back to take Alesso to school in the morning."

She sighs deeply and nods her head. "I understand."

Jesus, what the fuck am I doing?

I watch her fake a smile, like she's trying to cover the fact that she is disappointed I'm leaving but I ignore it and pull her forwards. "I'll call you in the morning," I say before planting a kiss against her hair. "Have a good night's sleep, Love. Lock up behind me and dream of me, won't you?"

"Always," she whispers just low enough for me to hear. Damn this woman has me more than she realizes.

I leave her room as quietly as I can, tiptoeing past Teddy's bedroom door with Lucille following behind me. As I leave the front door, I instantly scan the surrounding buildings and exterior, as my training has taught me, for anything out of the ordinary. Feeling satisfied, I watch and listen out for the sound of the lock as Lucille closes her front door and flicks off the light to the front room of her apartment. Walking out of there was one of the hardest things I think I've ever done. The look on her face almost killed me when I said I had to leave. And even though I could have stayed and made sure I was back in time to take my son to school, I know it's the right thing to do, she needs some space, some time to think. So as difficult as it is, I get in my car and drive back home.

It's a little after 02:00 and the roads are empty so I make it home in record time, strip off my bloodstained clothes and slide straight beneath the cold silk sheets of my bed and with the vanilla scent of Lucille's body wash still lingering on my skin. I drift off and dream of the three of us fucking Lucille in every possible way until she's spent and sore.

Chapter 31

Lucille

After locking the door behind Lincoln I check in on Teddy once more before heading straight to bed. I'm in a euphoric state of exhaustion and it takes seconds for sleep to overwhelm me, pulling me into lucid dreams of Lincoln, Silas and Cole as young boys running through the park and playing hide and seek with one another. The dreams turn dark and flash as the young boys transform into grown men with blood dripping from their hands as a disfigured body lies at their feet. I move closer and it's almost like I'm floating, my feet don't seem to be touching the ground but as soon as I notice the face, the dream swirls to black. His eyes snap open and a stream of deep red blood rushes out of the sockets covering his face before he calls my name, choking on his blood as it drowns him. I jolt awake suddenly gasping for air, a layer of sweat sticks to my body and I have to swallow the bile rising in my throat. The sunlight is just starting to pierce through the window and although I know I'm alone in my room, a sense of unease rests heavy on my chest. I instinctively get out of bed and head straight to Teddy's room, he's still fast asleep so I leave him be for a while longer while I jump into a cold shower to rinse the tension from my body.

Showered, dressed and halfway through making breakfast, Teddy strolls into the kitchen.
"Morning, Mommy," he yawns, pulling himself up onto a barstool.
"Morning, sweetheart," I call, spreading raspberry jelly onto a stack of toast before placing two pieces onto a plate

and sliding them over to him as I eat one of my own and start making a packed lunch for him to take to kindergarten. "Do you have your bag ready for today baby boy?" I ask as I pour myself a coffee.

"Yes Mommy, all ready," Teddy replies, shoving the last half of his toast into his mouth and laughing at himself getting jelly over his face. I giggle to myself as I watch him try to chew with too much in his mouth then playfully scold him for being so greedy. "But it tastes so good," he groans through exaggerated chews.

"Well I'm sure it would taste better if you ate it properly," I chide, ruffling up his hair in a light-hearted way. "Make sure you wash your face before we leave, or you'll be going into class with jelly on your chin," I call over my shoulder as I make my way to my bedroom to pull out a jacket and some trainers to slip on to go to work in. I finish my coffee as Teddy gets himself dressed but I have to escort him back to the bathroom to make sure he scrubs his breakfast from his face before we're finally ready to leave. "Come on then mucky-pup, let's get you to kindy," I smile as we leave the house and I help him buckle up.

"Mommy, when can we see Alesso again and your friends?" Teddy asks from the back seat.

I glance at him through the rearview mirror and smile. "Soon baby, I promise. Do you like my friends, Teddy?" I question, flicking my eyes between the road and his beaming face.

"Yes Mommy, they are so cool. Silas is huge like a superhero and Cole says he will take me to Auntie Kim's for more pancakes whenever I want and Linc is so cool cause he's Alesso's dad and he helped get my plane from the tree. Do you remember?" he exclaims, all in one long breath with his arms and legs flailing excitedly from his car seat. I laugh at his reasoning behind each one and smile at him through the mirror.

"Well in that case then we'll see them very soon and you and Alesso can have a sleepover, if that is okay with

286

his dad too." I tell him, and although I'm completely over the moon that he has accepted these three strangers so well, I can not help but think how heartbroken and confused he would be if things didn't work out and I asked never to see them again; because if that truly is what I wanted, that's what they said they would do. Leave and never bother us again.

"Mommy, where are we going?" Teddy calls, snapping me out of my heart broken daydream. I'd switched to auto pilot and almost driven past the kindergarten drop off point.

"Shit!" I blurt before I can stop myself.

"Oooooh you said a bad word," Teddy jests from his seat. "That's naughty."

I feign a sorry look and shake my head tutting to myself. "I know baby, I'm sorry. Mommy shouldn't have said that word. Don't tell your teachers, OK?" I whisper, pulling into a free space.

"Okay Mom, I won't but only if you call Alesso's dad and ask for a sleepover." I roll my eyes at the cheek of my own son trying to barter with me as I help him out of the car.

"You cheeky monkey. Get into class. I will ask Lincoln soon." I say, kissing his forehead before he slips off with a massive grin on his face, waving behind him as he goes. I don't move from my spot for a few moments and just simply stare after him, even long after he's vanished from my view inside the building. I'm not sure what it is, maybe my nightmare is just unsettling me but a feeling deep down within my body has me surveying the street before getting back into my car and driving to work.

"Hey doll, you okay? You look like you have the weight of the world on your shoulders right now," Kat asks as she studies me closely while we're setting up our clinic area. This girl knows me too well.

"Is it that obvious?" I sigh, stacking a pile of bandages onto my desk.

Kat drops her hip and cocks her eyebrow, throwing all her sass my way. "Girl, you know I can read you like a damn book. What's going on?" I shake my head and laugh, she's right, absolutely right. Even if I think I'm hiding it well, Kat always knows when there is something on my mind. I furrow my brow unsure where to even begin.

"I don't know, you know? I'm just so caught up in these guys all of a sudden. I'm having the most mind blowing sex of my life but my mind is still plagued with him." I admit, perching myself onto a chair. I notice how Kats jaw tenses and her brows pull together before a veil of sympathy masks her face. I look away, not wanting her to feel sorry for me but continue anyway. "These three men want to *share* me." I hold my hands up before Kat can interject. "It's crazy, I know, but I might be even crazier for agreeing to it. They've met Teddy, and he loves them. He even asked when we could see them again on the way to kindergarten this morning. That got me thinking maybe it was too soon, that I shouldn't have introduced them. One man would be enough, but three?" I shake my head and absentmindedly begin to pick at my nails. "I don't know what the fuck I'm doing Kat."

The room is silent while we both process what I just confessed and although I know she would never judge me, I'm too nervous to look up to meet her eyes.

"Babe." she whispers, kneeling in front of me and taking my hands in her own. "First of all, this is a lot for anybody to deal with and with your past you're bound to have some reservations," she squeezes my hand gently in a reassuring gesture and I finally look up to her face. Her smile is serene as she continues and her eyes hold nothing back. "You are the most courageous, selfless woman I know. You do everything for anybody when they ask and with what you have overcome, I am in awe of you. So who cares if you want to fuck three men at the same time?! Who fucking wouldn't! Hell see if they've got any friends for me would you?!" I laugh at her bluntness and she smiles back at me. "There we go, there's that smile. Girl you deserve to be happy. Teddy will be fine, he's too young to know anything anyway at the moment. To him they're just friends, it's not like they're asking him to call them Dad, and when they do, if they do, then you need to reassess the situation but until then girl I say just enjoy it."

I bite my lip and cringe at her words before I'm unable to hold back my laughter any longer. "Fucking hell Katrina!" I choke, falling back into my chair, the laughter racking my body and bringing tears to my eyes.

"What!?" She shouts, her face letting me know she's offended by my outburst.

"Have you ever considered being a shrink?" I gasp, holding my stomach as I try to regain my composure.

Kat grins immediately and pushes at my shoulder playfully. "Bitch!" she jests, joining me in fits of laughter.

After we've composed ourselves and wiped the tears from our eyes, Kat stands and places the rest of the bandages onto the desk along with some sterile scissors, saline and dressing tape. "Come on girl, pull yourself together, we've got a heavy list to get through. You can moan all you like about having three guys who want to fuck your brains out to me over lunch," she says, winking at me.

"You're an amazing friend, do you know that?"

"Yeah, yeah, you've told me before. Now make me a coffee bitch or I'll make your morning hell on earth cause I was in such a rush to get Bella to kindy this morning, I left my thermal at home," she shrieks, waving me out the door and making a broken hearted sign with her hands.

"Extra sugar for you coming right up then," I chuckle, making my way to the staff coffee room to make us both a drink.

"Hey Lucille, there's a guy asking for you out by reception." A voice calls from the doorway as I'm pouring hot water into two mugs and my stomach does a sudden flip. I swallow dryly as I turn to see who the owner of the voice is.

"Oh, hey James, thank you. Do you know who it is? Is it one of the regulars?" I ask, curious as to who else would ever ask for me by name, especially at work.

James, one of the male staff nurses, shrugs his shoulders at me and shakes his head. "Sorry Luci, I've no idea. Never seen him before but I told him you would just be a minute. He's sat in front of the reception desk."

"OK, thanks James, I'll be there in a second." I smile politely and finish off making mine and Kat's coffees. The little voice inside of my head is screaming at me as I walk out into the waiting area and I have to do everything in my power to push it down and bury it as I head to greet the stranger waiting for me.

I stand in front of the reception desk but nobody is waiting there. I glance around and look towards the patient toilets but the only people I can see are the staff. What the hell? The hairs rise at the back of my neck causing me to shudder. I pop my head around the door to the closest room and find James sat at his desk. "James, where did you say they were waiting?" I ask in case I somehow misheard what he said.

"They're right there, in front of reception," he says, walking over to point at the row of chairs in the waiting area, but when he gets there and sees that they are empty he stops short. "Oh, well I guess they couldn't wait. Don't worry about it. If it was important, I'm sure they'll come back."

I cough out a short laugh, trying to cover up my anxiety. "Did they say why they were here at least?" I ask as he sits back down in his chair.

"No, sorry Luci. I just assumed it was a patient waiting for you this morning or something."

"Thanks James," I whisper, as a tightness pulls at my chest. I walk back into the coffee room and brace my hands onto the counter top, close my eyes and breathe in through my nose and out through my mouth slowly while counting to ten. *Just a patient, just a patient, just a patient.* I repeat to myself. A few sets of deep breathing later and I'm more collected, panic over. Hopefully enough that Kat doesn't interrogate me again because if I had to say that somebody asking for me at work has freaked me out she'll tell me I need my head examined.

I take our drinks and walk back to join Kat in the room we've set up for our bandage clinic and place her coffee on the desk. "You ready for this?" She asks, spinning on her chair to face me with a beaming smile as she holds her cup out to me. Our bandage clinics are always super busy, that's why we like to double up and work through it together.

"Ready as I'll ever be," I reply, bringing my cup to meet hers in a cheers. "Let's do this!"

Our morning ran smoothly until an elderly gentleman with a gushing wound on his forehead decided to collapse as he was walking into the room. The calm of the morning is soon forgotten as it's all systems go and we push the emergency alarm. The room floods with nurses and doctors within minutes, all of them clawing to help as the gentleman loses consciousness and his open wound pulses blood onto the floor. We work hard and fast between us and manage to stop the bleeding while attaching IV fluids and propping his feet up on a chair to elevate his blood pressure. He slowly regains consciousness but is confused and becomes visibly agitated at his debilitated condition. I catch eyes with Kat as the man starts shouting for us to get off him as he doesn't know who we are and she cringes, knowing this won't end well. "Somebody call the porters, we need to get him fully assessed and admitted." I shout over my shoulder before turning back to try and calm the gentleman down.

Before we know it, it's already 14:00 and our stomachs are growling for attention having missed our chance for a break due to all the commotion.

"What a bloody show," Kat groans, flopping into a chair in the coffee room and kicking off her crocs.

"Oh God, don't. Something always goes wrong when it's going so well." I sigh, opening up a packet of BBQ flavor chips and a large bar of chocolate.

"Healthy lunch there," Kat calls, dipping her chin towards my snack.

I smile. "Something has to get me through the day," I grin, offering her the bag, "Want some?"

She stares at the bag as if just by looking at it, it will make her put on 5lbs then chews her lip. "Oh fuck it, go on then," she gives in, reaching her hand into the bag and pulling out a large handful of chips and munches on them happily. "So tell me," she crunches, "who has the biggest dick?"

I almost choke on the piece of chocolate in my mouth. "You're so brazen!" I laugh, "But I haven't seen them all yet so I couldn't possibly say." I wink at her.

"Christ girl, you're so lucky. I wish I had one dick to fuck let alone three! I'm definitely putting my name forward for the next prison day. Hopefully that good looking guy is still there from my last visit and he sends his friends after me."

I tut loudly and roll my eyes. "Look at you, fantasizing over a criminal."

"You're one to talk," she retorts playfully.

"Yeah from one criminal to the next." I mutter under my breath referring to my ex-convict ex-husband.

"Hey, don't think like that. Vinny was a piece of work. He manipulated you and treated you like shit. If you hadn't run when you did God knows what would have happened."

She leans forward and squeezes my hand and I smile in thanks.

"I know, I know." I sigh in defeat knowing exactly what she really means. He would have killed me if I hadn't left. I scoff the rest of my chocolate and share the bag of chips with Kat as she fires question after question at me about Silas, Cole and Lincoln and I'm left feeling more drained than ever. It's an exhausting thing reliving your sexual activities with your bestie and by the end of our half hour lunch break, I'm glad to be getting back to work.

As we make our way back to the waiting area I feel my phone vibrating in my pocket. I quickly skip ahead of Kat and into the room to see who is calling me and my stomach drops as I see the contact profile for Teddy's kindergarten flashing across the screen. I click to answer and bring the phone to my ear.

"Hello?"

"Hello Miss Holland, this is Merryhill Elementary here.."

"Is everything alright? Is Teddy OK?" I cut her off.

"He is fine, I am just calling to clarify the authorisation of a Mr Holland who has arrived and tried to collect Teddy today. The only contacts we have on our green list are Katrina Henderson and Max Costello," she continues speaking but I no longer hear her words, my heart thrums loud in my ears and drains out everything else.

He found me, he found us. How did he find us? I can't even comprehend the thoughts that are fighting to consume me right now and when the door opens and Kat walks in, I break. My phone slips through my fingers and I bring my hands to my throat clutching the skin as I struggle to breathe. Kat rushes to me and holds my arms. "What's wrong? What happened?" She asks, the concern desperate in her voice.

"He found us!" is all I manage to choke out before she picks up the phone and answers the lady still shouting "hello" repeatedly down the phone.

"No, he doesn't have authorisation," she says calmly then hangs up.

Thank God she's keeping it together because I surely am not, then suddenly something clicks. The unease, the feeling of being watched when I dropped Teddy off this morning, the guy in the waiting area. My eyes practically bulge from my head as I gasp. "I knew it!" I gasp, the realization washing over me.

"Knew what Luci, what is it?" Kat pries gently.

"He was here, he's been watching me. There was a man this morning asking for me but when I went to him, he had gone." I snap my eyes to hers. "Kat, he watched me drop Teddy off this morning. I didn't see him but I felt him, I *know* it was him." I screech, becoming hysterical once more. I need them, I need my men.

"Give me my phone," I say, holding my hand out. The first person I can think of is Cole. I know he'll come. I press his number and it begins to ring as soon as he answers I break again, the sobs wracking my entire body as they bring me to my knees. "Cole, I need you. I need you now, he's tried to get to him. He found us. He can't ever take him from me."

Chapter 32

Cole

Water rains down on my body, washing away all traces of blood and dirt from my skin, the water is stained red. Remembering the way it felt to extract every organ from our enemy's minion's body. I felt every scream and every second his life drained from his body and I was greeted with a sense of retribution. After all, the thug tried to shoot at my men and had been abusing his son. If he'd have just been acting on orders to shoot at us, I may not have hunted him but the abuse his son had been receiving was not just physical, it was sexual and emotional, which tipped me over the edge. Memories of my past were triggered making the sick son of a bitch my prey. The fucker didn't know I had been watching him for months, waiting for my chance to pounce. His son is now free of the bastard. I'd made sure to arrange with some associates that he be placed in a safe house and helped get some support before going to a family that would keep him safe.

I feel myself relax under the soothing warmth of the shower and just as I close my eyes, I hear Avicii - Addicted To You, echoing through the room. My eyes immediately snap open and I rush out of the shower to answer the phone, the water dripping down my still naked body.

"Il mio topolino, what a pleasant surprise." I purr down the phone to her. Her breathing is labored, making me panic instantly. "Topolino, is everything OK?" I ask quickly.

"Cole, I need you, I need you now, he's tried to get to him. He found us. He can't ever take him from me." Her words are hysterical and I can hear her tears through the phone.

"Slow down, tell me where you are, I will come to you," I instruct her, praying this is a misunderstanding.

"Cole, I have to get Teddy, he's at kindergarten. Can you meet me there? I'm already on my way. I'm freaking out Cole." She rushes out. It sounds like she's running. Fuck this is insane.

"Topolino, I'll meet you there. Please be safe, wait for me once you're there." I order her, unsure she'll listen.

"I just have to get to him, Cole, please hurry," she begs and the call ends.

Before I know it, I've thrown some dark denim jeans on and a white plain t-shirt, slipping on my Doc's. I'm rushing out the door grabbing the Range Rover keys. I call Silas and Linc as soon as my phone connects to the car.

"I'm heading to Teddy's kindergarten. Lucille is in a panic, I'm not really sure what's happened. I'll call you both once I know what's going on." I tell them.

"Does she need us too? I'll drop this meeting now if she needs me, Cole" Silas advises me.

"No brother, continue the meeting but keep your phone on you in case the situation changes." I reply.

"I'll be going to get Alesso shortly but if she needs me in any way, do not hesitate. I will not have her safety at risk." Linc states.

"Don't worry, she and Teddy will be in safe hands."

I hang up and put my foot down. I'm at the kindergarten in record time, I pull up outside and park. Jumping out of the car I see Lucille hugging Teddy at the gate, I rush over. As I get closer to them both, I notice Lucille's bloodshot eyes from her crying and it pangs deep in my chest.

"Ciao piccolo uomo, ciao Topolino, fancy seeing you both here." I say, trying to sound cheerful, like running into them was an honest coincidence, I'm just relieved to see them both in one piece.

"Silly Cole, this is my kindergarten. What are you doing here? Mommy looks like she's been crying. Are you here to make her laugh?" Teddy explains hugging Lucille a little tighter.

I swallow down the lump that fills my throat. "Well, I'd be happy to try. I came here to check how you are doing and wondering if maybe I could join you guys for dinner tonight?" I look to Lucille for some kind of reassurance that she is okay.

"Of course, sweetie. I invited Cole to have dinner with us and asked him to pick us up as Mommy didn't bring her car today," Lucille explains to Teddy. She gives me a warm smile and a short nod. My heart races knowing that my presence is comforting her, this is a new concept for me. Being the source of someone else's comfort.

"Let's go, I'm parked just over here, do you have everything?" I ask, not taking my eyes off Lucille.

"Exactly how many cars do you have?" Lucille questions raising her brows in disbelief.

"This is so cool!" Teddy shouts jumping into the back seat. Lucille is close behind, strapping him into the car.

"Many cars. I'll give you one if you want? It would make me feel more at ease with you driving one of our cars rather than the death trap you call a car." I tell her.

She giggles, shaking her head. "When are you going to give up on that?"

"Whenever you give in and let me buy you a car. I'll give you the world, Topolino, if only you'd let me" I tell her truthfully. She blushes and walks past me getting into the passenger seat.

I glance over to Lucille but she doesn't make eye contact with me. I'm a bit confused. Did I say too much?

Just as I am about to question her, Lucille whispers, "I was so scared that Vinny had taken him, Cole. I didn't know what to do. I promise I'll explain everything later, once Teddy is asleep. Can you just not ask until I have him settled at home?" I nod, noticing her hands are clasped together to stop herself from shaking. I grip the steering wheel hard, whitening my knuckles, I'm not angry at her. I'm pissed that some dickhead has scared her so much.

Once we pull up at her apartment we hop out and make our way inside. Teddy is chatting away about his day at school to us. When faces us and ask, "So are you like my mom's boyfriend?" shocking me and Lucille as he stands and stares at me, waiting for an answer.

"Well I guess you could say that little man, would that be okay with you?"

He looks thoughtfully and replies. "Yeah but I think you have some competition with that giant guy and Alesso's dad. I mean as long as you make her happy, I don't mind." I can't help but laugh. This kid is perceptive.

"We all want to make you and your mom happy, Teddy. Listen, if anyone you don't know approaches you and your mom isn't there or can't get to you, you ask for the Salvatore's okay? Me, my brother Silas, the giant guy, and Linc will always help you."

He stares at me wide eyed. "Do you like Lego, Cole?"

"Sure do, you got some?" I ask him, a little taken aback.

"Yeah, let's go play while Mom cooks us some dinner."
He grabs my hand and drags me to his room. I look round to see Lucille with tears in her eyes again, God I hate seeing her cry. She puts her thumb up to show she's fine but it does little to ease my worrying.

After a while of building Lego, we've built an airplane, a ship and attempted to build a castle. Lucille shouts us as dinner is ready, it smells great. "Teddy, let's go wash our hands then help your mom set the table." I say to him,

"Okay, I've had fun building with you Cole. Can we do it again sometime?" He asks as we make our way to the bathroom to wash up.

"Sure, anytime you want, little man" I tell him ruffling his hair and he rewards me with a big smile.

Once we are back in the kitchen, Teddy shows me where all the cutlery is kept. Lucille has cooked homemade macaroni cheese and chicken tenders. It looks amazing. "Wow, a woman who is beautiful and can cook, we have lucked out." I grin at her.

"Well you're not the only one that can cook, we will have to share the kitchen sometime," she calls.

"I'd like nothing more, I love to share." I wink at her, earning a deep blush that creeps up her neck.

Once we have finished dinner, I offer to clear up while Lucille helps Teddy get ready for bed. She scoops him up into her arms clinging onto him tightly "Let's go get your favorite pajamas on and you can pick whatever book you want me to read." She really is perfect in every way. I've never felt so possessive of anything in my life, that goes for them both. Playing house isn't my thing, but I could get used to this. After cleaning up the kitchen, I wait in the lounge for her to come back. Sitting on the couch, thinking how perfect this day had been minus the whole Kindergarten situation. I got to unleash my demons this morning and now I've spent some time alone with this amazing kid and his beautiful mom. I don't think it could get any better, but then it does, as my angel walks back into the room.

"He's out for the night. Cole I'm sorry I called you so panicked. I owe you an explanation for it all, but thank you for coming to me and thank you for how kind you have been to Teddy. I honestly don't know if I would have kept it together without you today," she blurts fighting back tears.

I stand and gently grab her hands, bringing her to sit next to me on the sofa. Keeping hold of her and staring into her hypnotic emerald eyes I say, "Listen to me, you call I'll come running, don't ever forget that. You give me only what you want to give me, you hear me? And I'd always be kind to you and Teddy. You are mine to protect, mine to cherish and mine to love."

She whimpers at my words, wiping the tears from her eyes "I just was so scared. I'm going to tell you now, about him. You deserve to know. All I ask is that before you say anything, you let me finish, Okay?"

I nod giving her hand a reassuring squeeze, urging her to continue "I won't interrupt but I will also ask that after you're done, that you listen and give me the same when I tell you mine." She nods and taking a deep breath in, she begins her story.

"It was a normal night, waitressing in a goddamn diner. It was not my dream job. I only had nine more months to go until I qualified as a registered nurse and then I could walk away from the place and never look back. Some of the customers were less than desirable but I could handle it knowing it wasn't forever. It was a late night cafe for drunks to come in to fill their stomachs to sober up. I remember the first time I met Vinny. I thought he was my knight in shining armor, how wrong I was. I was stupid and naive to believe him.

It was like any late shift, full of drunks looking to sober up before heading home. This particular night I had a couple of guys who were particularly handsy and crude. I brushed it off and I remember wishing my final hour would fly by so I could head home. Studying and working was hard but it was the only income I had. One of the guys decided he wanted me for dessert and grabbed my arm, pulling me onto his lap. I screamed and tried to move away when this shadow appeared over me and I remember looking up into the bluest eyes I've ever seen. They weren't looking back at me though, they were focused on the jackass who grabbed me. The guy helped me up and then he dragged the two guys out of the diner. I stood there completely mesmerized. I'd never had a guy stand up for me before. Most of the diner customers kept their heads down and ignored what was going on around them.

When he came back in, I realized that he was someone I'd spoken to a couple of times during my shifts. I thanked him and got him a coffee and slice of pie to say thanks. I called him my knight in shining armor. God I was so gullible. He told me his name was Vincent but his friends called him Vinny. He stayed with me while I locked up and walked me home. He came into the diner every night after that and eventually he asked me out on a date. I was so in love with him by that point I nearly jumped him there and then. That was how enamored I was. I couldn't see through his act. Looking back now I feel like a fool for falling for him so easily. I was desperate to be loved and he was like a character out of my books, my knight, my hero.

I persuaded him to move in with me after a month and even though he protested and made out that he didn't want to rush or encroach on my space, he quickly changed his mind. I couldn't bear to be away from him. My studies slipped, I fell behind because he occupied my every waking thought. Even my dreams were filled with him. Two months into our relationship, he proposed. I said yes immediately, I couldn't imagine not spending the rest of my life with this man. My first indication that something wasn't right should've been when he convinced me to get married without any of my family there. He made it sound romantic, just us there confessing our love for eachother. We didn't need anyone else.

Once we were married that's when cracks started to appear. At first the beatings were light, only when he had been out drinking with mates. I later found out that his mates were in fact the same guys that he threw out the diner that night. He had planned everything to make him look like a good guy. When I confronted him about it, that was the first time he beat me enough to knock me out. I woke up the next morning not sure what to do, he acted so sorry and was back to what I thought was his normal self. I forgave him instantly because he'd say things like he was drunk and he didn't mean to do it and that he wouldn't do it again. He manipulated me, he made me feel like I was wrong for questioning his actions.

Over time he became possessive and paranoid about where I went, what clothes I would wear and who I spoke too. I couldn't even speak to my brother without being accused of wanting to leave him. He'd ask for sex and sometimes I wouldn't want to, especially after a long shift at the diner, but I'd say yes because I couldn't bear to let him down. That's how much he had manipulated and gaslit me into believing everything I did was resolved around how he felt and what he would do if it wasn't what he wanted. I was genuinely scared for my life but he would tell me that no one would believe me. That I had no friends, that I didn't bother with my family so they wouldn't help me. He made out that it was my decision not to involve them in the wedding. I felt well and truly alone. Things just went from bad to worse. Then one night as I was getting ready for work, it was my final week at the 24/7 diner. My pin for my registration for nursing had come through and I'd had a successful job offer at the local hospital. I was over the moon, even though Vinny kept nagging at me saying he still wanted his dinner on the table and expected me to keep the house clean. Luckily the job was night shifts so I'd be out of the house while he was drinking and back in time to sort everything he wanted out. It's crazy how I thought that was normal. That night, I was desperately trying to find something Vinny would consider appropriate to wear for my shift. I caught his bulky frame standing in the doorway out the corner of my eye, watching my every move. Before I knew what was happening, he's grabbing my wrist as I tried to side step him. He twisted my arm and bent it behind my back then pushed me forward, cracking my head against a mirrored wall. I pleaded with him to let me go, shouting that he was hurting me but that just spurred him on. Just when I thought things couldn't get any worse, he beat me badly. I was trying to escape but he grabbed me and held me down. I could hear him behind me, unbuckling his belt and fiddling with his jeans. He laid down on top of me, pushing my head into the floor. At that point I had no fight left to give. I lay there still and silent focusing on my bloodstains on the bedroom wall until I blacked out.

At some point I must have gotten up or Vinny had moved me. I can't remember, all I know is one minute I was on the floor and then I was lying in bed and Vinny was gone. When I eventually came to, his car was missing from the driveway.

I knew then that that was the last time he'd ever do that to me. I grabbed a few items of clothing and my bank card and passport. I left everything else behind. I shoved it all in a rucksack, took one last look at this hell I'd called home and left it behind me. First I went to an ATM and withdrew as much as I could before destroying the bank card. I then made my way to the local bus station and got on the first one out of town. I headed straight to Vegas. I turned up on Max's doorstep half dead and about a month later I discovered I was pregnant. I had nowhere else to hide and I couldn't risk Vinny finding Teddy. It wasn't about me anymore, it was about my baby and keeping him safe."

Lucille stayed silent for a while after she'd finished before she looked at me with tears forming in her eyes, her hands were shaking, fuck her whole body was shaking and it broke my fucking stone cold heart. The shit she went through, I can't even imagine. It makes my blood boil hearing all the shit he put her through. I swear I'll kill him.

I bring my hands to her face making her look me in the eye before gently kissing her soft lips "Topolino, I'm so sorry that happened to you, but know that he will never get to lay another hand on you or get close to Teddy while I'm around. I will lay down my life for you both." Tears begin to fall down her face and I swipe them away with my thumb. She inches forward and kisses me again, harder this time as if she needs it to take away her pain. It's heaven and I'll easily lose myself in her spell if I let her continue, but I have to move back. I have to tell her my fucked up past. "I need to tell you my story, Topolino. It's not a happy one, it doesn't start happy and doesn't end happily either. It only ends with my vengeance and I hope to God it doesn't frighten you away from me." Her eyes widen in response but she stays silent allowing me my time.

16 years ago

"Coming home from school never felt like a relief for me. Most kids run home and look forward to chilling out and spending time with friends and family. It definitely wasn't like that for me. My father ruled with an iron fist and being a child wasn't an excuse as far as he was concerned. After our mother died, it was like she took the soul of our home with her. There were so many secrets held within the walls, secrets I wished I didn't know. Silas and Linc always tried to shield me from the violence but there's only so much they could do.

Most days, Silas or Linc would meet me when I got home from school to check in and make sure I got something to eat. On this particular day, there was no one waiting for me. I shrugged it off, figuring our father had them on a job. I walked into the kitchen to grab a snack before I made a start on my homework, when I heard the front door open. I figured it was Silas or some of fathers men so I carried on until I realized that it was eerily quiet. One thing about our house was that there was always noise somewhere. I looked up and saw three men standing in the doorway dressed all in black with balaclavas covering their faces. How fucked up is it that I didn't even flinch. I didn't even scream. It wasn't until they walked into the kitchen that I realized something was wrong. I tried to run but they grabbed me and tied my wrists and feet before stuffing a rag in my mouth. All I remember thinking is that they weren't there for me, I was just being secured so that they could get their job done. I went limp and complied, thinking they would move on and leave me alone. How fucking naive! A needle pierced my neck and the room swayed. The last thing I remember is the three guys laughing at me as it all went black.

When I came to, I had no idea where I was. It was dark and cold and wet. It smelled like death. I remember thinking that it smelled like the basement at home. I wasn't allowed in there, Silas and Linc always told me that I was better off not knowing what went on in there.

It felt like days before I saw someone, they chucked a bottle of water at me and forced pills down my throat. I didn't care what the pills were by that point. My arm was broken and I just wanted a break from the fear and pain. This routine continued for a few days before one of them finally spoke to me. They told me that I had been taken to make my father get in line, to know his place. I just remember thinking that I'd never get out because there was no way my father would do what they wanted. My only hope was Silas and Linc, I just had to hold on for them to find me.

By that point I was well and truly hooked on the pills they were feeding me, I craved the silence and peace they gave me. My dreams were an escape.

One time I woke up feeling more sore than usual, memories of mens hands touching me, whispers in my ears of depraved things, things I couldn't understand. My asshole was on fire and I couldn't sit properly without pain. My mind wouldn't allow me to comprehend what was happening. It was like I didn't have access to that part of my brain or my memories. I didn't care, I just wanted to go back to sleep.

My next round of pills were delivered and I greedily guzzled them down with my water. I laid down, waiting for oblivion to take me away but it didn't come. I looked around the dank room and watched a group of men filing in. They stood around my mattress on the floor watching me, grabbing at their crotches. I tried to call out but realized that I couldn't move or talk. Whatever pills they'd given me this time were different to the usual ones. I panicked and their smiles grew. It was like they were enjoying it.

I'll spare you the details of what happened next because I don't think either of us are strong enough for that." I look up at Lucille to make sure she's OK. Her face is soaked in tears that fall freely down her face. She hasn't moved a muscle since I began, and doesn't try to comfort me as I continue, which I'm secretly grateful for.

"After they finished with me, they filed back out of the room laughing and patting each other on the back, like they'd achieved some great feat. Sensation had returned to my arms and legs hours before but fear had held me prisoner. I was so scared that if I moved, they would get more imaginative. Once the door closed and I heard the lock engage, I let it all out. I cried and cried until no sound came out at all. I crawled into a ball and dragged a dirty blanket over myself, desperate for sleep to carry me away.

I woke up to the sound of an explosion rocking the building. Dust and debris fell on me but I stayed as still as possible, desperately trying to hear what was happening. I remember hearing Silas' voice between the bursts of gunfire. It was like a ray of light in the darkness but as soon as the feeling of happiness hit me, it was overshadowed by shame. I didn't want my brother to see me this way. I didn't want him to know that I was broken." I take a breath, battling with the familiar tendrils of anxiety flowing through my body. I need to finish this now, I wouldn't do this for anyone other than my Topolino, bearing my soul to only her, she is my everything. She needs to understand why I am the way I am.

"I managed to grab a few scraps of clothing that were left on the ground. The thought of putting on my uniform again was weird. It was one of the reasons I never returned to school. Linc found me first. It was like he knew I'd been through hell. He didn't ask questions, didn't even ask if I was OK, he knew I wasn't. He gave me his shirt and I followed him out of the basement. The sight that greeted me is ingrained in my mind forever. Silas stood over the bodies of my captors covered in blood, chest heaving as the adrenaline of the kills ebbed and flowed through him. He looked like Satan himself. He turned to see me standing in the doorway, nodded and we walked out. I don't remember what happened next. My next conscious memory is being in a facility. They helped me detox from the drugs and helped me heal physically. Mentally we all know that I'll never be normal but I hope that helps you understand why I am the way that I am. My scars run deep"

Lucille still hasn't moved, she's still sitting next to me, tears pouring down her face. I lean over and take her face in my hands again brushing my thumb over her lips. "Topolino, please say something. I understand if it's too much to handle. I understand if this changes how you see me" She takes a deep shaky breath but never breaks eye contact with me.

"We are not our pasts. Would you ever hold my past over me Cole?" she asks, searching deep within my soul.

"Never, Topolino."

"Cole, I called you today because as crazy as it sounds. I trust you. I trust you with my heart, but most of all, I trust you with my son. I know deep down that you would protect us with every fiber of your being. Our souls call to each other, yours the dark and mine the light. Together we complete each other and wherever we are, in whatever lifetime, we will always find each other. I know that now."

I smile at her, it's a genuine smile and I have to blink back my own tears as they threaten my eyes. She sees me, she understands me, she accepts me.

As if a band snaps, we dive at each other. Our lips collide and I want nothing more than to drown in her. I trace my hands down her body while her hands explore mine in return.

Her curves are irresistible, my hand finds the waistband of her pants and I slip my hand inside and beneath her damp underwear. She's wet for me, she wants me so badly but I need to show restraint, I want to be selfish with her. I stroke her clit and move my fingers between her folds, as she gasps into each kiss. I push a finger slowly into her sweet pussy and she moans as I begin to move my fingers in and out of her, so agonizingly slow. Her mewls let me know she's hungry for more and she rolls her hips against my hand. "Your greedy pussy likes that, Topolino." I whisper into her ear as her hot mouth sucks on my neck.

I increase the movement and insert a second finger into her tight opening causing her to cry out, "More! Cole, I need your cock." Fuck I deserve a medal for the amount of restraint i'm showing. I continue to thrust my fingers and rub my thumb on her clit quickly pushing her to her climax as she gushes over my hand, panting and shivering from her high. She rests her head on my shoulder as I remove my hand to lick her juices from my fingers.

"So sweet," I mumble, sucking them clean. She looks at me, hurt and confusion taking over her face. Oh Fuck. I can't stand the way she's looking at me like that. I close my eyes and sigh. I have to tell her the truth. She will definitely run from me after this. I take a deep breath and prepare myself for the aftermath of my revelation, "Topolino, it's not that I don't want to, you have to know that I want nothing more than to sink my cock into every one of your tight holes over and over until you all but beg me to stop. But I can't, not yet. You have to know that my tastes are different from normal. I need control and restraint. I prefer to work in a playroom. I have a lust for knives and blood and dominance. I know it's not everyone's taste and I don't want to pressure you into anything you're not comfortable with. I can still be with you like this and satisfy you but if you're open to it, I'd like very much to show you. Sex is different for me, it's transactional in nature because of my past. That doesn't mean that it isn't mind blowing and I can assure you, I will push you to your limits but we can discover those together. You need to be sure first, think about it, really think about it, Topolino. I have never wanted to share any of this with anyone before you. Not even my brothers know the true extent of what happened to me in that basement. How fucked up I really am. It's the hardest thing in the world for me to not plough you into oblivion, but I won't without your full understanding, your full consent." I stand to leave afraid that she'll kick me out anyway if I don't.

Lucille looks shocked as I move, I can see her taking in everything I just laid bare. I move away as she stops me, "Thank you for sharing everything with me Cole. Telling you about my past and knowing that you understand means everything to me... I'll think about what you said. I'm intrigued but I need to sit with it for a while. But please know that It doesn't change how I feel about you."
I smile at her, this beautiful fucking woman isn't scared. She isn't angry. She isn't disgusted. She accepts me for me and that's more than what I could have asked for. I'll marry her one day, I swear it.
"Buonanotte, il mio topolino."

As I get into the car to leave her house I make a final phone call. "Enzo, I have some business I need to take care of but Lucille needs some security. I want you over here now to stay outside her apartment while I'm gone."
"I'll be there in ten, boss" He answers.
"This will be your top priority from now on. I'll wait here until you arrive."

As soon as Enzo parks up around the corner, I nod to him and leave. I'll arrange for one of Silas' men to take the day shift watching her tomorrow. My little mouse will come to no harm unless it's from me, which I expect she'll enjoy every minute of it. I now need to hunt that cunt of a husband of hers.

Chapter 33

Lucille

Cole leaves without another word and I feel like I've just been blindsided. I knew when I woke up this morning that something seemed off but to end the day like this is not what I had in mind.

I make my way to the kitchen, automatically stopping to lock the front door as I pass it, then pull out a bottle of wine, forfeiting the glass as I take a large gulp straight from the bottle. I have to suppress the thoughts of Cole as a child being beaten and abused plaguing my mind and the horrific thoughts of what could have happened today if Vinny had managed to get his hands on Teddy. I feel the weight of today heavy on my chest but my soul feels freer than it has in years now that Cole understands my past. My throat feels like it's constricting as I gasp for breath. The tears come hot and heavy from my eyes and I collapse to the floor, dragging my back down the kitchen cabinet, bringing the bottle of wine to rest beside me. Everything comes rushing to the surface and I no longer hold it all in, I kept myself strong for Teddy when I ran to him at kindergarten, and when I knew he was safe with Cole and myself. I kept myself together when I retold my story of Vinny and I nearly kept myself together when Cole laid his past bare to me, but now with nobody to see me, I fall apart. I sob for what feels like hours, until I have no tears left to cry and I have finished my bottle of wine. My eyes burn raw but the flash of headlights across the windows shock me into a hyper-state of panic, imagining it to be Vinny. I scramble to my knees and while crouching I try to peer through the window by the front door. A few moments later and I haven't been able to see anybody outside but my nerves are still shot and a wave of goosebumps covers my body. Suddenly the loud ping of my mobile makes me shriek as it sounds and I realize I've been holding my breath the entire time. "Jesus Christ!" I curse out loud to myself, fumbling for my phone in my pocket. Releasing a sigh of relief as I see Cole's name ping up on my screen.

I've got surveillance on your house through the night, don't worry little mouse, I won't let anything happen to you while I'm not there. I'll see you soon. If you need me just ring me.

I swallow the knot that's formed in my throat and although I am thankful for the fact that he has somebody watching over me and Teddy, I would have rather it been himself or Silas or Linc that was here with me right now. I walk over to the window and peer out at the black SUV parked at the bottom of the drive. I can't see from my standing point who the driver is but I know they'll do whatever their boss asks of them, it's the way of the club. I pull the curtain back over the window and steadily make my way to the bedroom, my head is already beginning to thump and I'm regretting finishing that bottle of wine. I pull on a fresh pair of pajamas but instead of getting into my own bed, I make my way into Teddy's room and squeeze myself right next to him in his bed and rest my hand gently over his. I need to be extra close to him tonight. I soon let a deep and dreamless sleep consume me.

The following morning I wake early with a hard to swallow lump in my throat and when I open my eyes, the room spins on its axis. That'll teach me to finish an entire bottle of wine by myself. I peer over to my left to find Teddy still fast asleep, the light fluttering of his eyelashes against his cheeks letting me know he's deep in dreamland. I smile as I watch his face twitch under his subconscious dream state then as slowly as I can manage without waking him, I trudge my way to the bathroom and get straight into a cold shower, hoping it will shock the hangover out of my system.

Feeling a little better and dressing into some comfy joggers and a sweater set, I walk to the front of the apartment and peer out the window in the same spot as last night. The sun is casting a beautiful orange hue across the sky and easily allows me to assess the driver of the surveillance car that Cole sent to watch the house last night. I recognise him, I've seen his face at the fight night and around at Silas' club but I can't remember his name. I hope he hasn't been too bored or cold out there all night just sitting in his car. Maybe I should take him some coffee. That's it, that's exactly what I'll do. I make two cups of coffee, strong and black, one for myself and one for my watcher then slip my feet into some slippers and head out with a coffee in each hand. I walk gingerly down the driveway towards the car and instantly the man's head snaps in my direction. I hold out the coffee letting him know my intentions and his face visibly relaxes as he rolls down the window to his car.

"Thought you could do with something to warm your bones," I say, offering over one of the steaming mugs.

"Thank you Miss Holland," he says politely, dipping his head.

"Oh please, call me Lucille," I insist, wrapping my free hand around my own and shivering slightly as the early morning wind wraps around me. "Thank you for spending your evening looking out for me and my son. Cole text me last night to let me know he had sent somebody. I know you must have had better things to do on your Friday night, I'm sorry to have interfered with that." I say, trying to detect any hint of irritation at the job he has been given but there is none, he only smiles and takes a sip of his coffee.

"Not at all, the pleasure is all mine, Lucille." he nods politely and I smile in return.

"How long have you worked for Cole?" I probe, circling a finger around the rim of my coffee mug.

"For too long," he laughs to himself. "The crazy bastard is more like family now than anything but I still appreciate him as my boss. I owe him my life in more ways than one. And you should know that whoever it is you're scared of, Cole will personally see to it that he never bothers you or your son again." The seriousness in his voice lets me know that he is telling the truth but also sends a shudder straight down my spine. I awkwardly suck at my teeth not knowing how to respond. I wonder how many of my secrets Cole has spilled to the rest of his men. I wonder if the man in front of me now knows that I ran away from my abusive husband and have hidden his child from him for the last 5 years. My eyes glaze over at the thought of a scared little boy, beaten and abused and I imagine that boy being my own. What would I do if somebody took my whole reason for living away from me and locked him in a cellar. A loud cough brings me back to focus.

"Hey, are you okay?" he asks, scanning my face.

"Yes, sorry I'm fine," I stumble. "I better get back inside, Teddy will probably be waking up soon." I say quickly turning towards the front door.

"It's Enzo," the man calls out after me.

I turn to face him and nod. "Thanks again Enzo, I'm glad you're watching out for us."

"And thank you again for the coffee, Lucille," he says with a kind smile.

I head back inside and lock the door behind me as I fight back the tears that are burning beneath my eyes. This is so fucked up. Twenty minutes of breathing myself through another panic attack and I've somehow managed to whip up some chocolate chip pancakes for Teddy and placed fresh fruit in the shape of a smiley face ready just in time for him to make his way into the kitchen.

"Hey sleepy head, I've made you some smiley fruit and pancakes," I say, leaning over to kiss his bedridden hair.

"Are you OK, Mommy?" he asks, placing his tiny little hand onto my cheek. I feel my breath hitch in my throat but I swallow it down.

"Of course baby boy, why wouldn't I be?"

"You look sad," he says, as if it's the most normal thing in the world and those three tiny words feel like a vice right around my heart.

I sigh deeply and shake my head, "No baby, I'm fine." I say. "Now eat up your breakfast because Mommy's taking you swimming today so you need lots of energy to ride those big waves," I smile. Teddy's face instantly lights up and he practically catapults himself onto a stool at the breakfast bar where he gobbles down his fruit and pancakes in record time.

After breakfast and a round of reading from the book Teddy bought home from kindergarten, we're ready to go. Teddy enters my bedroom, just as I pull on some sneakers, with his neon blue trunks and Action-Man snorkel set perched on top of his head. "Ready Mom," he sings, pretending to swim through the room.

"Come on then Mr, let's go catch some waves."

As we leave the house I notice that the coffee mug I gave to Enzo is waiting empty on the doormat. I internally thank him for not driving off with it and quickly place it on the table inside before Teddy spots it and asks why it was outside. I also notice that Enzo himself has gone and has been replaced with the guy I met outside of Silas' club.

I drive us to the best indoor pool around, fitted with a huge wave machine that fills the entire pool with waves like the sea, large slides that wind all around the room and a smaller section of childrens slides and fountains for the younger kids to play in. Teddy loves it here but we haven't been able to spend the day here for ages. We manage to grab a couple of lounge chairs right next to the children's area and place down our towels and bags then head straight into the pool. The water is warm and inviting and not overly busy for a Saturday afternoon.

"Are you ready for the waves baby?" I ask, noticing the large wave countdown is almost at one minute to go on the wall above the side seating area.

"Yes!" Teddy exclaims loudly and starts paddling a little further into the water but making sure to stay within my reach. "Waves, waves, waves," he squeals, watching the timer slowly tick away the last ten seconds.

"Here they come," I call to him, as eagerly excited as he is.

Five, four, three, two, one. The timer screen flashes blue and the intercom announces that the waves are now commencing, giving other swimmers a warning. At the furthest end of the pool the water begins to swell and within seconds a large wave covers the width of the pool and pushes towards us. We're not far enough in the water that they become overwhelming and so they carry us up when they build and push us down when they fall. Teddy wails in excitement and thrashes his arms into the water.

"WAVES, WAVES, WAVES," he sings loudly as another swell moves us. I can not help but laugh and join in when the next one hits.

"WAVES, WAVES, WAVES," we sing together as we float up and down in the water.

"I love this Mommy," he calls to me, paddling his way into my arms and wrapping his hands around my neck.

I smile instantly, "And I love you," I whisper, giving him a tight squeeze.

We stay this way while the rest of the waves continue and slowly begin to lessen.

"Shall we go and grab a drink?" I ask. "I think I saw the milkshake man as we came in."

Teddy's eyes light up at the mention of milkshakes and his mouth forms a simple O, "Ooooh, yes please!" he squeals, letting go of his hold around me and already making his way towards the edge of the pool. I thought that might be the answer. We order two large chocolate milkshakes topped with cream, chocolate chunks and smothered in chocolate sauce and Teddy is all but drooling as we walk back to our chairs and sit down to drink them. "This is amazing," he groans, wiping the excess cream from his face.

"Definitely a good choice, well done," I praise, taking a large finger of whipped cream from the top of my own and sucking it into my mouth. I'm definitely going to have to suggest to one of the guys that they let me lick cream off of them, or even better, that they lick it from me.

"Can I go back in the water now please?" Teddy asks, interrupting my fantasy and I look to see he's already polished off his entire milkshake.

"Well you sure weren't wasting any of that were you, you greedy monkey," I laugh. "Of course you can. I'm going to stay here and finish my drink for a little while though so make sure you stay where I can see you please." I add, making sure his armbands still have enough air in them.

"Okay, I will," he says, jumping up and heading straight for the water fountains at the shallow end of the pool. I rest myself back in my chair and sip slowly on my milkshake, scanning everybody around us. I notice a few familiar faces, mainly other parents with their kids from Teddy's kindergarten and a few of the other moms hold up their hands to say hello. I smile back politely but make no effort to go over and make a conversation, I'm really not in the mood for that today. Through all the laughs and smiles for my son, I can't get Cole's words out of my head and even now I'm aroused at the thought of what he called his playroom. I shudder at the thought of being trussed up against a wall with shackles around my ankles and wrists and have to clench my thighs together to subdue the ache. Jesus, surely this isn't normal. No wonder he warned me, but the mere thought is driving me insane, I need to tell him I want it, I want him. All of him and his fucked up kinky shit. I don't need any longer to think about it. I pull my phone out of my bag and fire out a quick text and send it.

I want you.

Hopefully that lets him know he hasn't scared me away. I think it's even made me want him more. My sweet troubled soul, I'll gladly be there to let him release his demons on me. A warmth spreads between my legs and I have to quickly slurp down the remains of my milkshake to try and distract myself. "Mommy come on the big slide with me," Teddy waves me over from the water. Oh what the hell, what would cool me off more than plunging into a swimming pool. I jump up and splash my way through the water towards him.

"Let's go kiddo, we're doing the monster slide today. The biggest one!" I announce as I lift him up into my arms and wade us both through the pool to the set of three large slides at the far end, heading for the biggest one. As we get to the top I give Teddy's hand a reassuring squeeze. "I'm going to be right there with you," I say. He's never been brave enough to go down this slide before but today I have every bit of confidence that he will. He looks up at me, his face beaming and his eyes full of excitement and determination. I pull him onto my lap as our turn comes up next and wrap my arms around his waist waiting for the green light at the top of the tube.

"I'm so ready for this Mom!" Teddy squirms in my lap.

The lights switch green and with a push we descend into the enclosed tunnel, twisting and turning on our way down. I'm not sure who screams louder as we plummet to the end of the tunnel but we both come up for air and end up in fits of giggles.

"That was AMAZING, can we go again?" Is the first thing Teddy says when he finally takes a breath. That's my boy!

I smile, "Okay, I'll race you to the top," I blurt as I rush over to the slide entrances again.

"Hey, no fair!" he calls from behind me trying to beat me to the ladders.

Well and truly exhausted after being dragged on multiple slides multiple times, I finally managed to persuade Teddy to leave the swimming pool with a promise to get burgers on the way home for an early dinner followed by a movie night on the couch with his choice on what to watch. I end up carrying him to bed halfway through his favorite Ice Age movie and in turn curl up into my own bed with a cup of chamomile tea and flick on the TV above my dresser.

I mindlessly flick through my Netflix suggestions until I find a good crime series to watch and getting myself comfy I press start. It's been a long but good day today and this right now, just snuggling in my own bed with a cup of tea is exactly what I need at the end of it. There's still a black SUV watching the house and just the knowledge that it is there makes me feel so much more settled than last night, knowing that if I need somebody, they're right outside. I haven't had a reply from Cole to my earlier revelation, but that's fine. I can accept that because I know what he wants to say, it will be with more than just words. I sigh wantonly but shake it off. All in good time and all that jazz. I finish my tea and fall asleep peacefully watching the horrors of other people's lives on TV, and feeling like my own might just be okay. For now.

Bright and early the next morning, I jump straight into the shower to wash the overwhelming chlorine smell from my hair. Once I'm clean and dry I pull on a pair of jeans, plain t-shirt and oversized hoodie. *Comfy clothes all the way today,* I mutter to myself as I scrape my wet hair up into a bun and apply a subtle covering of makeup. My need for coffee isn't as dire this morning as I had the deepest night sleep in a long while but still, like it's tuned into my body. I automatically turn on the coffee machine and make myself a steaming mug of black coffee as I lay out a cereal selection for Teddy when he wakes up. Right on queue a loud "ROAR!" startles me and the box of Cheerios scatters across the floor.

"Oh my God, Teddy!" I gasp, clutching onto the kitchen countertop.

"Did I scare you?" he asks playfully, jumping up and down on the spot.

"You really did. You crept like a little ninja," I say joking along with him.

"YES!" He squeals, clapping his hands in delight.

"You're up early kiddo, did you sleep alright?" I ask, grabbing the dustpan and broom from the cupboard and starting to clean up the spilled cereal.

"Yeah I was just so excited at being a ninja and wanted to make you jump," he cheers, pouring milk over his mix of Cheerios and Cookie Crisp. "Can we go to the park today Mom please?" he adds on with a mouthful of food and milk dribbling down his chin.

I laugh and push the kitchen towel towards him. "You mucky pup. You've got more of that on your chin than anywhere else. But yes OK, if that is what you want to do."

"Yes please, I can practice my ninja skills on the squirrels, and the birds," he says, flinging his arms around in ninja chop actions.

"Good luck with that baby," I smile, finishing off my coffee. "We can go whenever you're ready, just make sure you put something warm on because it looks a bit cold today, and maybe your boots," I say, taking a peek out of the kitchen window. "It looks like it might rain."

"Not my boots Mom, they're not for ninjas," Teddy groans into his breakfast bowl.

I turn to face him and raise my eyebrows. "Yes Mr, you will wear your boots or there will be no park," I instruct and he rolls his eyes as if I can't see him do it sitting right in front of me. "You cheeky monkey, don't roll your eyes at me, it's a fair negotiation."

He huffs loudly and takes another spoonful of cereal as he admits defeat, "Fine." That was easier than I thought it would be, I praise myself. Teddy finishes his breakfast at lightning speed, even with my warnings to slow down or he'll give himself a tummy ache, then he canters off to his bedroom to get dressed.

"Remember to put a jumper on," I shout down the hall then quietly slip out of the front door quickly skipping across to the SUV parked just off from the bottom of the driveway and tap on the window.

"Hey Lucille, is everything okay?" Enzo asks, frowning at me.

"Yes everything is fine, sorry it's just I'm taking Teddy to the park. I just wanted to run out and ask if you wouldn't mind sort of hiding a little bit. I'd rather he didn't see you or know the house was being watched if you know what I mean." I mumble, trying not to make it sound so awkward.

Enzo just smiles at me and nods. "Of course, I understand. Don't worry, he won't know I'm there."

"Thanks so much, Enzo. I best get back." I reply in a rushed whisper then half run half tiptoe my way back into the house and start putting the breakfast plates ready to be washed like I had been doing it the whole time.

"Ready to go," Teddy calls out as he runs into the kitchen living area then jumps and karate chops the air.

"Wow, okay big guy, you better take it easy on those squirrels," I laugh. "Go put your coat and boots on and then we'll go." I shrug on my own coat and slip my feet into my own boots and then we leave hand in hand, I look back over my shoulder as we walk off the driveway and notice Enzo parked much further down the block and give him a slight nod, then we continue on our way, skipping, jumping and karate kicking all the way to the park.

"Mommy shush, don't move," Teddy part whispers, part shouts, as we step onto the park grounds and he pulls on my arm sharply so I come to a sudden stop. The hairs and the back of my neck begin to prickle and I wonder if Teddy has spotted somebody lurking behind the bushes. I swing my head around quickly surveying the area but see nothing.

"What is it Teddy?" I whisper, squeezing his hand in mine. Teddy releases me and crouches low to the ground and points over to the left towards a group of trees and bushes "Look, over there at that squirrel," he says and the breath I hadn't known I was holding whistles its way between my lips. Bloody child nearly gave me a heart attack. If only he knew.

"Wow, yes I can see him. You better be quick if you think you can catch him," I say, crouching down beside him.

"Watch this," he says, holding his hands out in front of his face as he makes his way around to the side of the bushes, crouching low the whole time being sure not to make any sudden movements. I make my way over to the closest bench and watch as he narrows in behind the bush and just as I can see he is ready to jump, the squirrel hops off up the tree and back into his little hole between the branches. Teddy lunges himself from the undergrowth shouting "GOTCHA!" as he does, but when he notices his prey has already disappeared he wanders round in a circle trying to find which direction it went in and I laugh as I watch him get too dizzy then fall over.

"Lost him," he sighs, finally walking over to me.

"Oh don't worry baby, you still made me jump when you came out of those bushes," I say in an attempt to cheer him up. Teddy looks up at me and grins widely.

"Really?" he asks,

"Really, really," I reply. "Now go and play." Teddy whips around instantly and gallops off towards the climbing frame. I sit back against the bench and feel the buzz of my phone in my pocket.

"Hey babe," I say when I answer.

"Hey honey, how are you? I haven't heard from you all weekend since the incident at kindergarten so I thought I'd ring to check in," Kat says.

"I know. It's been a bit of a weird one, sorry to ghosted you. I just needed to spend some time, just me and Teddy. We went to the indoor pool yesterday and now he seems to think he's a ninja, throwing himself off the climbing frame at the park," I laugh as I watch Teddy dive roll across the floor.

"These kids like to keep us on our toes don't they?" Kat says politely. "I'm glad you're OK, I was really worried about you."

"You worry about me too much. I'm alright, we're both alright. Cole has had one of his guys watching the house all weekend anyway so that has eased a bit of tension anyway." The line goes silent for a minute.

"You mean he isn't staying with you himself?" Kat asks with slight hesitation in her voice.

"No," I sigh. "I haven't actually heard from him since he left on Friday either but I know he must be busy with work." I'm not sure who I'm trying to convince more when I say that.

"Babe, I'm sure if he could be with you he would be." Kat starts but my attention is suddenly diverted as I hear Teddy shout "Uncle Max!" across the park.

"Uh Kat I'm sorry, I've got to go," I say and without waiting for a response I end the call as I make my way towards Max who already has Teddy on his shoulders.

"Look Mommy, look who I found," Teddy squeals excitedly as Max pretends to drop him, catching him just before he hits the floor.

"Yes, I can see," I say, narrowing my eyes at my brother who pretends not to notice.

He crouches down and looks Teddy in the face, "Hey buddy, go show me how far you can get across the monkey bars and I'll join you in a minute. I need to talk to your Mom first," he says, tapping him gently on the back.

Teddy looks up to me and I smile, "Go on baby, we'll be there in a minute," I say, nodding towards the monkey bars.

"Okay but I will beat you," he taunts Max as he runs away.

Max chuckles to himself, "Feisty kid isn't he," he says then turns to me and holds up his hands in a mock surrender. "I'm sorry OK, I really am but I can't go on like this. You're my sister and I would be lying if I said I hadn't missed you and Teddy over the last week," he says, glancing back over to where Teddy is swinging himself from bar to bar and I can see by the look in his eyes that he means what he's said.

I sigh, "Yeah, well I've missed you like a hole in the head," I whine and he laughs gently pushing my shoulder

"Piss off, we've never gone this long without talking before. I know you've missed your annoying big brother," he laughs and I roll my eyes at his blatant big-headedness, though he isn't wrong. I have missed him and I know Teddy has missed him too.

"You've been so good to us Max, I just think you sometimes forget that I am an adult now and I can make my own decisions about who I see and what I do." Max opens his mouth to say something but I hold my hand up to stop him. "They've been nothing but nice to me Max. They treat Teddy so kindly and he even asks to see them again. You may know them one way, but I know them another.

And they've been there for me when you haven't." I sigh and notice Max frown as he registers what I've said.

"What do you mean? What's happened?" he asks.

"Vinny tried to get Teddy from kindergarten on Friday."

Max sucks his teeth loudly and fists his hands at his sides. "What the fuck Luce, why didn't you call me?" I shake my head, unsure of the real answer as to why my brother, the one who has looked out for Teddy since he was born, wasn't my first choice of contact when I found out his father, my abusive ex-husband had tried to take him. I stay quiet, unsure of what to say and just as I think he will shout at me for being so stupid when Max pulls me into his arms and squeezes me tightly.

"It'll be okay, I'm here now," he whispers, and I melt, forgetting our recent arguments and letting the familiar feelings of love and safety and family all cocoon me until I'm no longer holding onto any hatred or anger towards him.

"How did you know where we were anyway?" I ask as he finally releases me.

"I have my ways," he winks and I can't help but roll my eyes, he chuckles to himself slightly before saying, "I actually went to your apartment first and the guy parked outside in the SUV recognised me and let me know you were at the park with Teddy," he pauses slightly and runs his hand up through his hair. "Come to think of it, I probably should have fucking shot him for doing a shitty job on surveillance considering you're not even in the house right now."

I roll my eyes at his sudden outburst but shake it off. "You fucking mafia men are all the same," I laugh.

Max steps back and puts his hand over his heart like I've just stabbed him, "Woah now, I take great offense," he jokes and pretends to start choking.

"Well I'm not taking it back so suck it up buttercup," I smile and give him a playful shove.

"Hey, let me watch Teddy for the rest of the day for you, he can stay overnight too if you want. Give you a bit of a break." Max says and I have to bite back my knee-jerk reaction to say no. He must see me dwelling over it as he taps me on the shoulder. "Oh come on Luce. It's not like he's never stayed over with me before."

"I know, I know, but I just don't want him out of my sight at the moment," I admit shrugging my shoulders.

"And he would be no better protected than with me. You know that. I love him more than anything," he sighs, holding me by both shoulders now so I'm looking straight into his eyes. I chew my lip contemplating whether or not it's a good idea and decide to ask him himself.

"We'll ask Teddy, see what he wants to do," I say and Max grins widely at me.

"You know that's going to be a yes straight away," he laughs, and yes I do know that. There'll be no talking him out of it either.

We make our way to the monkey bars and it's like nothing has ever happened, no arguments, no hatred, no fallouts. It's the wholest I've felt in a very long time. "Hey bud, how are you getting on?" Max asks as Teddy drops from the bars.

"I can almost get across," he says, climbing up to the beginning again and jumping up to catch the bar.

"You can do it baby!" I cheer as he swings himself across.

"Come on Tedster," Max calls from the other side, holding his hands out to catch him in case he falls. Teddy makes his way to the last but two bars and kicks out his legs.

"I can't do it," he wails and Max holds him up around the waist.

"Yes, you can," he says.

"Come on, come on!" I chant as he pulls himself to the last bar and swings forwards to jump off.

326

"WAHOO!" We all cheer and Max hoists him above his head cheering as he runs around the outside of the climbing frame. Teddy is beaming with pride when they return and he thanks Max for helping him, giving him a tight hug.

"Thanks Uncle Max," he mutters softly.

"You're welcome buddy. Hey, how do you feel about having a sleepover at mine tonight?"
Max asks and Teddy looks like his face might explode with excitement.

His eyes go wide as he looks up at me. "Can I Mommy?" he asks, bouncing up and down on the spot.

"Yes of course you can. I will pick you up and take you to kindergarten in the morning though," I say, looking to Max to let him know this will not be negotiable.

"Yes!" he shouts loudly. "Can I show you my ninja skills when we get back to yours Uncle Max?" Teddy asks excitedly, demonstrating his karate moves as we start to make our way back home.

"You asked for it," I wink playfully at Max as Teddy jumps up and down in front of us.

"I'll tire him out" he says. "But please don't worry, he will be fine. I have everything he needs at mine anyway."

"I'll just need to grab his bag for kindergarten and Little B because he won't sleep without him. Are you sure you really don't mind having him over night? You don't have work or anything?"

Max grabs my hand and squeezes it slightly. "I wouldn't have asked if I didn't want to. I've missed having him around," he smiles at me and I smile back.

"Thank you."

When we get back to the apartment, I notice that Enzo has gone, probably because he knew I was in safe hands with Max after it was revealed at the fight night that he's my brother. We all go inside and I ask Teddy to get a couple of things ready to take with him to Max's and he runs off to do so as I grab his kindergarten bag from the coat pegs and hand it over to Max.

"It'll be easier if you take it now for me because I'll probably forget it in the morning. If you could just make him a packed lunch in the morning please and I'll come and pick him up."

"I can take him to save you rushing over first thing."

"No, honestly I would rather drop him off after what happened on Friday." Max sighs but agrees to let me pick him up and when Teddy lumbers himself back into the room with a bag over his back and Little B tucked up under his arm I feel a sudden urge to squeeze him tight and never let go. I kneel down and smother his face with kisses.

"You be good for your Uncle Max OK?" I say, ruffling my hand through his hair and kissing his head.

"I will Mom," he says before walking over to Max and handing him his bag. My heart swells at the sight, "I love you," I choke out and Max notices my emotional fight so turns to leave.

"Love you too Mom." Teddy calls as he waves goodbye.

I look at Max, "You call me, for anything OK?" I demand, narrowing my eyes at him. He knows what I mean but he only nods. "See you in the morning," I say, waving as they drive off. I stand in the doorway for a long minute and breathe in a deep fill of fresh air before walking back into the house and heading straight to the bedroom to change my clothes. I know what I need to do now.

Chapter 34

Cole

Staring down at the information Linc has gathered on Lucille's cunt of a husband, I'm lost in thought. It makes me sick to think she's married to this piece of shit. But it also makes me jealous, he walked her down the aisle and made her his. That obviously changed the moment he touched her with his fists. As soon as my brother gets hold of him, he'll regret even looking her way. However, Silas may beat him to an inch of his life but I want to be the one to drain his soul from his body, I want to watch his fear grow with every last second. Linc did a good job in finding everything about this guy but it's unclear where he has been the last week or so. His neighbors haven't seen him and the guy Linc sent to watch him said he disappeared one evening after he entered a drug house with some hookers. He's my prey now and I need to find him before he finds Teddy or Lucille. Silas thinks I'm being paranoid, but he is on alert after someone tried to access Teddy at kindergarten. He's been having one of his guys watch the school and I've had Enzo track Lucille. Lincs guys have been taking over inbetween too, she doesn't know the lengths we will go to to keep her and Teddy safe. I look through the information from the last time Vinny was seen, I notice in the pictures of him entering the whore house, one of the bouncers outside is watching him very closely. He doesn't seem to notice, too eager to get his fix I expect. Why are they watching him? I need to track them down and find out who and why they are concerned about him.

I pull out my phone and call Lincs investigator. "Mr Henderson, I want you to look into the bouncers outside the club that Vincent Holland was last spotted at. I need all the information on them. Especially the one with the dark hair, blue shirt, that is eyeing Mr Holland in the surveillance photos."

"Sure Mr. Salvatore, my usual fee, expect your information in two days' time." he replies, straight to the point.

"Sure, you'll receive payment once I've got my information." I hang up.

As I bring my hands to my head, I rake my fingers through my hair thinking how I haven't slept since I left Lucille's side two days ago. Usually after I've gutted someone I sleep like a baby, but that didn't work this morning. All I want to do is catch Vincent Holland and until I do, I have a feeling my insomnia is going to be persistent, that or I need a good fuck and the only person I want is Lucille. So deep in thought, I don't hear the door open but I do hear the voice that pierces through the room.

"Cole, I did knock but you didn't answer. I tell you what, I'm surprised your body guards outside let me in. They've been trying to call you for the last 20 minutes. Good job Enzo recognized me and let me up." I'm in shock, just staring at her she continues to ramble on. "I've been thinking we need to talk. The way you left Friday night, I just can't stop thinking about it. I mean we are the same, me and you." I raise my eyebrow but say nothing, "Okay okay, maybe not exactly the same but we both have broken pasts, we both have our demons and we know what it feels like to be helpless and we hate that about ourselves." She takes a deep breath, and I brace myself for what's next. This must be when she's going to say she can't be around me, it makes her see her broken parts and she's not ready for that. It's okay, I've been expecting it. I'm a creature of the shadows and if she needs it to stay that way I will, for her and Teddy. "Cole, I guess what I'm trying to say is I want the good. I want the bad…. And I want the damaged parts of you too. I hope you can accept those parts in me too." She's staring at me now, and slowly she brings her hands up and removes her long coat, exposing what little she has on underneath. She's wearing a short, thin silk dress, no bra and then she kneels to the floor in the perfect submissive pose, knees spread and hands resting on her thighs, head down, no panties either showing teasing glimpses of her perfect pussy. I gulp, speechless and I think a little in shock. This was not what I was expecting. When I haven't said anything for a few minutes I see her fear creeping in.

"Maybe I've read it wrong, maybe it's not what you wanted," she quickly says, not lifting her head to make eye contact.

Shaking myself out of this frozen state, I move towards her and tilt her head up by the chin. "Topolino, you have rendered me speechless. I never in my wildest dreams thought you'd say you want me, the broken me. I just need you to know I will never hurt you and I will protect you with my life. You're mine now and I'm never letting go" I wipe the tears away that cascade down her cheeks. "I'm assuming you have done some research into dominants and submissives over the last couple of days? Now while I do love the submissive role for my partner's and for mine to be the dominant, It's important that you know you have the power here. You want me to stop, you say the word and I stop. Also, I ask you for your complete honesty if I ask you a question, be truthful, even if it's not the answer you think I want. Do you understand Topolino?"

She breathes out steadily and answers me, "Yes Cole, I understand."

I nod, happy that she understands "In the playroom you will address me as Sir but outside we are just us, Tomcat and Topolino, Cole and Lucille. Okay?" She nods. "Topolino, do you want to see my playroom now?"

She sucks in a breath and looks me in the eye saying the words I've longed to hear since I met her. "More than anything, Sir."

Smiling down at my beautiful woman on her knees I feel a sense of pride, "Come my love, it's time to play."

I expect her to stand and follow me but instead she blows my mind and asks, "Would you like me to walk or crawl, Sir?"

Oh fuck, she's perfect. "Someone has been doing their research. You can walk topolino. I'd carry you but I fear if I touch you now, I won't be able to control myself." I tell her truthfully. She blushes and rises to her feet. I take the lead as she follows behind me. I'm itching to touch her as we make our way down the stairs to my playroom and my cock is throbbing for her. I open the iron enforced doors and hold it open, I turn to my beautiful little mouse, "After you." I say, my voice catching in my throat. Lucille looks at me, her eyes meet mine and she nods, taking her first tentative steps into the room that I hope she will become very well acquainted with.

The room itself is white throughout, even the bed sheets are white. What can I say, I like the way it shows everything, including my pets blood. The thought of her lying there, strapped to the bed with her blood trickling on the pure white sheets has me hard as a rock. I snap myself out of the fantasy and turn my attention to my Lucille. She's looking around the room, her eyes are wide and I can see a slight purse of her lips as she turns to me. She looks me in the eyes just before she kneels before me in the most tempting position possible. I slowly bring my hand to her cheek, and stroke her softly. "So, my little mouse, do you want to play?"

"Always, Sir," she responds immediately.

I smile, "Okay, my pet. I want to explain some rules before I begin. We will use a traffic light system for your limits and pleasure. Green is more, amber slows down and red stops. Do you understand?"

Lucille, kneeling at my feet, nods her head, "Yes, Sir."

"Remember, it's all about pleasure here my sweet little mouse. I will test your limits and you will test mine I'm sure, but as long as we are truthful to each other we will enjoy every part of it. Are there any hard limits for you before we begin?"

"I'm not sure, Sir. I've not really been tested this way before." she whispers. Her innocence is killing me.

I bring her chin up to look at me. "That's OK, Topolino, we will work out what you are comfortable with," I say.

Looking at her plump lips, I bend down and capture them in a rough and dominating kiss. And as I pull away she makes my cock twitch, gasping "Green, Sir."

I laugh, "Greedy little one, aren't you my mouse. Don't worry, you'll have plenty more of those if you are good for me." She nods but doesn't speak, accepting my words. "I want you to crawl up onto this bed Topolino. Once you are on the bed, lie flat with your arms above your head and legs straight. Can you do that for me?"

"Of course, Sir." She moves gracefully and places herself exactly as I requested.

"Good girl, I will reward you soon." I'm desperate to touch her but I control myself. I've waited this long, I can wait a little longer. I look down at her. She's squirming slightly but trying so hard to be still for me. I smile as I reach over and secure her wrists and ankles to the bed. "These restraints will keep you secure my pet but I warn you now try to be still for me, the ones on your legs will widen along the bar as you move." Lucille is silent but looks at me with a horrified sort of smile. "Are you still greedy for me? I feel you are wearing too much clothing. I need to see that body that I want to worship like a temple Topolino," I tell her.

Lucille's breathing quickens, "I need more Sir, Green." I smile, then remove my leather jacket and unbutton my shirt removing it, my torso is covered in tattoos and Lucille looks hungrily at me as I remove my shirt. I keep my jeans on but remove my boots and socks so that I am barefoot. I'm waiting for her to see a certain tattoo I had done not long ago, and as if by magic her eyes go wide. "Cole, I mean sir, when did you get that?" She's looking straight at my chest, above my heart, I had a little mouse lay down sleeping inked on my skin not long after we met.

"Topolino, if I can't have you with me always, then I need to have something to remind me of you. Now are you comfortable? Shall we continue?" I ask her, I'm so eager to touch her and make her scream. It's almost unbearable.

She looks tearful as she says, "Yes sir, I'm just overwhelmed."

"Don't worry baby, I will help ease you soon. First I need to remove this lovely dress. Are you fond of it?"

"I brought it to wear for you, I'm bare beneath it, Sir." That I can see I think to myself. Smirking, I remove the small knife I have in my pocket and move quickly, slicing down the middle. The material falls away from her body, revealing that she was indeed telling the truth and baring her beautiful naked body to me. Her tits are magnificent, her nipples are hard and begging me to suck on them. My eyes travel down her body, over every inch of her perfect skin, she is a goddess, her pussy is glistening and I'm aching to dive my tongue and cock into her but I must remain in control, I will get my reward as will she soon enough. My little mouse's breathing has picked up, but her eyes are on me always.

"Pain and pleasure are like light and darkness; they succeed each other, do you agree with me, little mouse?" I say, looking into her eyes as I ask.

"I'm not sure, I've never mixed the two, but I'm willing to try, Sir. Green," Lucille breathes out.

I nod, "Okay, repeat the words for me Topolino before we start," I ask and I watch her squirm on the bed.

"Green is more, amber is slow down and red is stop," she says, almost panting.

"Good girl, now you deserve a reward, do you want my mouth on those hard nipples? They are begging me to taste them." I see the fire in her eyes as I move forwards.

"Yes Sir, please," she begs.

Placing my hand on her side and moving towards her tits, I dart my tongue out and lick up to her nipple, while my hand cups her other breast, stroking my thumb over her hard pink buds. I engulf her nipple with my mouth as she moans and writhes beneath me. As she does, she moves, making her legs widen on the bar restraint.

Lifting my head I whisper into her ear, "Remember to stay still pet, I'm going to mix some pain with your pleasure next, can you handle that?" She nods as I continue palming her breasts with my right hand. She's trying so hard to stay still as I remove myself from her body.

"Eyes on me now Topolino," I say.

She snaps her eyes to me and I am about to give in to all of her desires as I position myself between her legs. I caress her thigh and slowly bring my hand to caress her bare pussy. Moving my fingers into her folds, I insert two of them, making her whimper.

"Now Topolino, I feel how slick you are and I've hardly touched you, do you like my fingers inside of you? Can you take another?" I ask, greedy to watch her slick cunt swallow my hand. She nods, holding in her moans and trying desperately to keep still as I push my fingers into her tight hole. I take the knife that I used to split her clothes in half. "Keep nice and still now baby while I use my tongue. You're going to come and bleed so nice for me"

I dive into her sweet pussy, burying my face into her, tasting her delicious wetness. She's moaning as I lick and suck her clit, feasting on her, devouring her, and as I feel the inside of her pussy begin to clench around my fingers I stroke her thigh with my blade, applying pressure as she comes on my tongue and a drop of blood drips between her legs. Moving back slightly, I look to see her magnificent body breathless and panting. I press my finger into the slice on her supple thigh, eliciting a sultry moan from her body "Do you like pain with your pleasure little mouse?"

She is breathing heavily still coming down from her orgasm but manages to reply, "Green, Sir."

I laugh because she is more perfect than I imagined. Bending down, I lick the trail of blood that has weeped out of her, her cum is still fresh on my tongue and now it's mixed with her blood making me so horny for her. As I stand, I unbuckle jeans, pulling them down.

"You don't wear boxer shorts Sir?" my little mouse notices.

I chuckle. "Too restricting, when you are on my mind, my dick likes more freedom than they can give."

She smiles, "Can I taste you, sir?" she asks shyly.

"Topolino, you can taste me but not now, I need to get my cock deep inside of you. Maybe if you're good later you can have that as a reward."

She grins and licks her lips, "I'll try to be very good then sir."

In seconds I am plunging my cock into her slick pussy and it feels like home. I thrust in to her bringing my knife up to her throat as a fuck her hard and fast "Would you like to bleed some more for me my pet?" I grunt with each thrust.

"Green sir, Green," she whimpers to me.

I push the blade into her throat making a thin superficial cut but the ruby liquid trickles down her neck and between the valley of her breasts. Fuck, I think I might blow at the sight alone. I throw the knife to the floor and suck at the mark, her blood seeping into my mouth. She's moaning louder now, she cries sound almost feral as I plow into her over and over. She's as close as I am, I can feel her pussy tightening around my cock but I'm not ready for it to be over yet. I pull out of her leaving her whimpering before I grab the spreader bar and flip her over. Her ass looks phenomenal spread before me, and next time I'll be finding out if that's virgin or not, but I'm too thirsty for her pussy to be gentle right now, I dive back into her core, thrusting deep and fast making her scream for me with each slap of my hips on her backside.

"Cole! Green sir!" I love hearing her screaming my name. I thrust harder and faster, ripping back a fistful of her hair to snap her head upright. Her groans are guttural and I can feel her clenching. I pump myself faster, sweat breaking out across my back and with a final roll of my hips I slam forwards as I come inside her and she comes around my throbbing cock with a cry. Her cunt feels like a fucking vise that I want to get trapped in it forever.

Leaning down, I kiss her below her ear whispering, "Did you enjoy that my little mouse?" She's nodding, unable to form any coherent words. I smile and pull out from her. Turning her over I see my masterpiece, blood, sweat and cum leaking from my beautiful goddess all mixing into one. Fuck she's beautiful. Bending down, I undo her restraints and then lift her body against my chest, her eyes flutter open and she looks at me confused. "Don't worry little mouse, I'm just taking us for a shower, it's time for me to clean you up."

Carrying her out of the play room and up to my bedroom where I have an ensuite and walk in shower, I place her down on the bench, before turning the shower on and checking the temperature before she steps in. The water glides down her body washing the sweat, blood and cum from her skin. She looks so hot. My dick is already hard again, stepping into the shower behind her, I grab a washcloth. "Turn around, let me clean you," I order. She does as I ask without question. I kneel and begin to gently wash her blood from her leg. Moving slowly, I cup her pussy with the cloth and massage her swollen lips. Her hand finds the wall to steady herself and the other on my wrist as she moans. "Lucille, are you too sore for my cock again?" I ask her.

"I want you Cole, I want all of you, always," she says, rolling her head back as I continue to play with her clit. "You're so wet for me Topolino," I say, standing and dropping the cloth. I grab her by the back of the head and dive my tongue into her mouth. Using my other hand I grab her thigh as she hooks both legs around me, giving me access to her. I don't waste any time and plough my dick into her core. "Ti senti così bene piccolo topo," I thrust my hips up into her as she screams.

"Cole, don't stop!" I continued to move my hips, feeling her slick all over my cock.

"Sei avido del mio cazzo," I whisper as I nibble her ear making her moan again.

"I love it when you talk dirty Italian, Cole," she pants

"Sei pronto per venire?" I ask.

"I don't know what you said Cole but I'm so close," she moans. I smile and bite down on her neck as I use my hands on her ass to spread her open further for me as I plunge into her with more force and speed, bringing myself to come as she explodes on my cock again. She screams my name as her whole body shivers and her cunt milks me empty. Slowly I remove myself from her dripping hole and gently lower her feet to the floor. Her eyes are on mine before she darts forward and captures my lips.

When she pulls away I say, "You're perfect Lucille Holland, now let's get cleaned up for real this time and get some sleep. I want to wake up with your mouth on my cock."

She smiles, looking a little drunk "Definitely, I think I might be too sore for a third round of your cock tonight," she giggles.

"Don't worry, I'll be gentle with my tongue for the third round, my love."

By the time we finally get into bed, Lucille doesn't take long to fall asleep in my arms. And just as I am about to doze off thinking what a perfect evening it has been, I hear I knock at my door. Kissing Lucille on the head, I slip out from under her to go see which brother is disturbing us. I pull the door open to find both of them looking at me with thunder in their eyes.

I tilt my head and push open the door "Come in, but be quiet, she's sleeping."

Silas looks confused, "Who's sleeping, Cole? You best not be in bed with a fucking whore when we agreed on keeping Lucille!" He whisper-shouts in my face. Always quick to anger but this time my patience is thin.

"I said be quiet, it's no whore that is in my bed!"

Linc then jumps in hissing at me. "Who is in your bed then, Cole? The boys said a woman came up here to see you earlier today. I can't believe you would do this!"

He's not shouting but it's still pissing me off. Just as I'm about to start throwing punches at these two shit heads, the woman in question steps out from behind the door.

"Hi guys, umm could you keep it down? I'm quite worn out and I'd like to get some sleep. Are you coming back to bed, Cole?" Lucille yawns. She's only wearing my shirt and looking sexy as sin. I grin like a love sick fool and slap her ass as she walks back into my room.

"Well brothers, I'm tired so you can let yourselves out, we'll catch up in the morning. You heard my little mouse, she wants me to return to her." They both look shocked as I usher them out the door before winking at them and closing the door behind me.

As I climb into bed, I wrap my arms around Lucille again, pulling her against me. "They aren't mad at me are they?"

"No Topolino, they thought I'd brought another girl to my bed, which I wouldn't ever do, I am yours. They were defending your honor and if anything, they are probably banging one out at the sight of you freshly fucked and in nothing but my shirt." She giggles quietly followed by slow breaths letting me know that she's fallen back to sleep. I smile at how perfect this feels before drifting into the best night's sleep I've had since I was a child.

Chapter 35

Silas

Checking my watch on the way down to the kitchen, it's a little after nine in the morning, I can hear my brother and our girl laughing in the kitchen. As I enter I take in the scene in front of me. My brother is at the cooker, sizzling bacon and eggs in the pan, with the biggest smile on his face. He looks younger than I've seen him in years, I'm taken back by how truly carefree he looks. My eyes lock onto the reason why. My Angel. She looks radiant, wearing one of my t-shirts which surprises me since she was in Cole's bed last night. Her beautiful smile is beaming at my brother as he serves her breakfast on her plate. As I step further into the room, their heads turn to me.

"Hey big guy," Lucille calls, batting her eyelashes at me. I smile knowing that I'm not intruding by just joining them. Moving closer to her, I take her chin in my hand and tilt it up so her face meets mine.

"Found a new wardrobe, Angel?" I whisper. She chews at her bottom lip as her cheeks redden at my words.

"Well, Cole said it was yours but you don't use it anymore. I figure you wouldn't mind?" She breathes out.

"You're right, and it definitely looks better on you than me, but tell me baby girl, is there anything underneath that shirt of mine?" I ask, dragging my finger slowly over the curve of her breast.

Lucille sucks syrup from her finger with a sultry pout before answering.

"Why don't you find out?" My girl is brave this morning. Maybe my brother has awoken a little minx by introducing her into his play room.

"Baby, I'd like nothing more," I all but moan, reaching for her hips and dragging her closer to me. My thumb strokes her bare skin as I pinch her nipple hard over my shirt eliciting a sharp gasp from Lucille's lips. She's panting already, desperate for more.

"Well brother, what do you think? Do you think our girl needs to be taken care of?" I ask Cole not breaking eye contact as Lucille shivers at my touch.

Cole has turned the cooker off and moved behind our girl, his hands have worked their way up her shirt to her breasts and I can see him teasing her nipples. She's breathing heavily and her eyes have closed. "Well why don't we find out. Do you want that, topolino?" He whispers into her ear. She nods, giving us all the consent we need. Cole grins at me, licking his lips, as our girl whimpers between us. I bring my lips to meet hers tracing my fingers beneath the hem of her shirt and gently grazing them against her already soaking pussy. My tongue dances with hers as I insert two of my fingers into her core, stretching her open, moving them in and out matching the rhythm of my tongue. She's moaning into my mouth as Cole continues his assault on her nipples, kissing and nibbling her neck. I pull away from her mouth and withdraw my hand, looking at her red bruising lips, swollen from my own. Her breathing is heavy as she looks at me with those fuck me eyes and my cock throbs at the sight.

"Are you sure you're not too sore baby?" I ask.

"No, definitely not. I need this" She turns to face Cole as she replies, his hands still gently kneading her tits "How will this work?" She asks all sexy and breathless.

My brother likes control, hence his kink for the playroom. But we have shared before and never had a problem. He's more of an observer and usually likes to direct, that's not to say he doesn't participate, he definitely

342

gets his dick wet just as much as mine, he just needs to be able to have control over all of the elements and that's completely fine with Linc and I.

"Topolino, don't worry about me. I've shared with my brother and Linc in the past. We all know the roles we like to play when it comes to this. Just remember not to be afraid to tell us to stop." He warns her and she nods.

I seize my opportunity and whisper into her ear. "La mia luce, he likes control, lives for it even and we can give him that. You just need to give yourself to us entirely, and we'll make you come so hard you'll see the stars"

She blushes a beautiful shade of red, "Well, that's an offer I can't refuse," she states with a grin on her face.

"Good girl, now remove the shirt baby girl, unless you want my brother to cut it from your body," I command.

Lucille lifts her arms above her head. "As much as I love that idea, I kinda like your shirt." She giggles and Cole removes her shirt, leaving her naked, her nipples are hard and she shivers when she notices the feral stares we're giving her. Meeting eyes with Cole I nod, letting him take control.

"OK Topolino, I'm going to sit you down on my lap, and play with these beautiful nipples while my brother has his breakfast. Let's see how many times he can make you come on his tongue," Cole teases, flicking her rosy peak. I'm more than happy to have my face between her creamy thighs as she comes on my tongue. I can't wait to taste her and hear her screams as she drenches me, drowns me. "You'll be coming on more than just my tongue baby.

Don't forget, this is just the warm up."

Cole removes his shirt so that his chest is bare and then positions himself on a bar stool before pulling Lucille onto his lap with her back against his chest. His legs hook over hers, keeping them spread for me, opening up her glistening cunt. With one hand holding her hip tight enough that I'm sure it will bruise and the other at her throat, he nods at me to begin.

Kneeling down before my queen, I wink at her before burying my head between her thighs. I have no reason to take my time, I've craved to taste her sweet nectar for too long. I use my tongue to fuck her relentlessly while using my fingers to tease her delicious hole until she is screaming and writhing through her first orgasm, leaving my face soaked from her juices. She tastes amazing, it's definitely a meal I won't be able to get enough of. "Brother, you better save some for the rest of us." A rough voice booms from behind me. I pull back grinning at Lincoln standing in the doorway with Lucille's cum dripping down my chin. I glance back at Lucille who's still riding the waves of ecstasy.
"Can we all enjoy your sweet body baby girl?" I purr swiping my finger against her clit causing her to squirm as she's still held in Cole's embrace. Cole's eyes are full of fire as he stares at her, waiting for the green light.
She lets out a deep throaty moan as I flick her swollen bud, and throws her head back into his shoulder.
"Oh dear god, YES. You have my permission to have me anyway you want." she whimpers.
Linc smiles a wide, toothy grin. "Let's take this party upstairs, I don't want anyone walking in and seeing what is only ours to behold"

In one swift swoop Cole has Lucille over his shoulder, her bare ass showing as he strides out of the kitchen and down to Lincs master bedroom. Lucille squeals as Cole spanks her ass and shouts over his shoulder to us, "First one to get upstairs gets to fuck this tight little ass." Linc and I are elbowing each other as we sprint behind the cheeky bastard but he legs it down the corridor, all I can hear is Linc cursing under his breath the whole time.

Tumbling into the room we find Lucille already on her knees, her mouth full of my brother's cock. I instantly harden on the spot then look over to Linc and nod, allowing him to make the first move. He slowly stalks forwards towards Lucille, and caresses her breasts from behind, teasing her beautifully reddened nipples. The thought of sucking those perky little buds whilst burying my cock deep in her pussy with Lincoln filling her ass has me practically salivating. Lucille's moans are stifled around Cole's cock as he thrusts his hips, plunging himself to the back of her throat and Linc tortures her clit with his forefinger. Her eyes are streaming as she fights back a gag and Cole fists his hand into her hair as he stiffens, shooting his load straight down her throat with a satisfied groan. I knew she'd take it but as she swallows him down like a good girl, I feel like I'm already about to explode. When Cole slips from her swollen lips her eyes are glossing over as she looks up to him with pure lust and fire burning through.

"Topolino, you look so fucking beautiful swallowing my cock. Now do you think my brothers can take your sweet needy holes at the same time?" He coo's as he swipes his thumb across her bruising lips. Lucille whines loudly in response as Linc pinches her nipples again and kisses her neck.

"OH GOD, YES! PLEASE YES"

It's fucking music to my ears.

Cole moves to sit down on the arm chair in the corner of the room with his cock still out and already fucking solid again "I would love nothing more than to watch that, so boys you best be ready to put on a good show," he grins salaciously.

I look to Linc, he's already moved to grab a tube of lube from his desk. I don't even want to know why he kept it there. I stalk towards Lucille pulling her to stand, she wobbles on her legs at first but grabs my arms to steady herself.

"My sweet sunshine, you are so beautiful. Are you ready?" I ask her kissing her forehead tenderly before gazing into her perfect face. She sucks on her bottom lip then nods and steps closer, molding herself to me, taking my mouth against hers and undoing my buttons to my shirt. Her tongue fights against mine as I reach down to tease her clit with my thumb before diving straight inside her with three fingers. She gasps immediately and pulls away from my kiss but I keep her in place. "You are such a good girl, so wet for your men." I praise her then slip my fingers out.

Removing the rest of my clothes so I'm as naked as she is, with my cock standing as hard as fucking steel, I sit myself down on the bed and instruct her, "Ride me, while Linc prepares your ass baby." She wastes no time and climbs onto my lap, looking me straight in the eyes as she lowers her tight cunt down on my cock.

"*Merde*. You're so fucking tight sunshine. So tight"

She rocks slowly for a minute, adjusting herself with my size, whimpering as she does. "Silas, oh god, you're so big."

"Are you ready for me Lucille?" Linc whispers as he begins stroking her ass. He's already naked and his cock is glistening with lube as he licks his lips,staring at her pussy enveloping my length. She stills around me as he inserts his finger slowly into her tight little hole. He's all the way in and inserting a second one as she cries out and I feel her pussy clench around my cock like a fucking vise before a warm gush of liquid rushes between us.

"Keep tightening around my cock like that, la mi luce and I won't last long." I grunt into her ear. She shivers at my words but rolls her hips quickly, challenging me.

"I'm going to fuck your ass now sweetheart," Linc says almost desperately. He stands behind her and eases his tip into her ass making her gasp as she braces herself against me. "You can take it sweetheart" he coos, spreading her cheeks further apart with his hands and spitting onto her asshole. I gaze at him over Lucille's shoulder as she bites into my chest stifling her cries. He looks feral as he pushes forwards burying himself to the hilt inside of her cunt before giving her a second to relax. I tilt my hips and she cries out, a pure fucking song to my soul. Linc pulls back slowly before thrusting himself back in and we begin steadily working her, in and out, in and out. Sliding against each other's heads through the wall that separates us. Its fucking agonising, fucking glorious and she's taking it so fucking good. Linc picks up his pace, holding Lucille firmly by the hips as he grunts, slamming into her backside. Her screams are wild, like nothing I've heard before, her nails are biting into my skin as she devours our brutal onslaught. I glance over to Cole, he has his dick in his hand, vigorously pumping at the sight of our girl impaled between us. Thrusting my hips up harder, I feel the delicious clench of her muscles as she explodes on my cock screaming profanities. Linc almost screams himself and I can only assume her ass feels as good as her pussy does when she comes. I'll need to test it out for myself soon. Suddenly Linc pulls out spraying Lucille's back with his cum, painting her and claiming her. And instantly, I'm coming myself, but because I'm a greedy bastard, I come into her weeping pussy, filling her up, implanting her with my seed. Without looking, I hear the tell tale grunts from Cole in the corner, knowing he's reached his climax too.

Lucille collapses down on top of me and whispers, "That was the best sex I've ever had." And as she closes her eyes, Linc bends down and kisses her head, whispering something that makes her smile before leaving the room to shower. I stroke her hair and she breathes softly on my chest, with my cock still inside her.

"Mi Luce, I need to move my cock otherwise I'll be ready for round two, and you need rest." She giggles quietly,

347

slowly removing herself from my lap. As she does, Cole reaches for her and she willingly glides towards him like the angel she is. He captures her mouth and then murmurs something to her and she nods as he strokes her cheek softly. Not a side I'm used to seeing from my brother, he's kind and soft with her.

"Silas, I need to go check on the restaurant then I need to meet Linc for some shipments, would you mind taking Topolino to collect Teddy from her brothers?" Cole asks, his eyes never leaving Lucille's.

"Of course brother, my timetable is clear until lunchtime, so maybe we can finish breakfast before going to get Teddy." Lucille nods as Cole leaves the room. "Come here my angel, we have time for a rest before eating and getting our boy." Realizing I said our boy, I'm waiting to see how she reacts. My heart is beating so hard in my chest I can hardly breathe. It's always on fire with me and her, so I'm hoping she doesn't take it wrong by claiming him as my own.

"Our boy?" she questions. Turning my head I look at her, her eyes are glistening with tears.

"He's ours now angel, we protect what is ours." She smiles and kisses me, catching me off guard, making me laugh into her mouth.

"You know, I think that's one of the first times I've heard you laugh, Silas." she tells me before removing herself from my arms. "Are you coming for a shower?" She asks betting her eyelashes at me.

"Only if I get to clean you with my tongue," I reply, smirking at her.

"Catch me if you can," she giggles, running off to the ensuite.

By the time we finished, after what turned into round two of sex and managed a quick breakfast we head out to pick up Teddy. The journey in the car we spent talking about her childhood and how she always wanted to be a nurse. She asks about my family too which I indulge her with, leaving out a few minor details she doesn't need to know. As we pull up to Max's house, I notice the lack of security surrounding the place which makes my stomach twitch. Before getting out of the car, Lucille turns to me and grabs onto my hand, "Silas, I know you and Max don't see eye to eye but he's my brother and has looked out for me and Teddy since I came knocking on his door, pregnant and scared. I owe him my life. He's a good man, please try not to fight with him or kill him."

I smirk, "For you I would do anything angel. If he's important to you I'll restrain myself, however you might need to speak to Cole and Linc too. I might be quick to temper but they hold grudges longer than me."

She shakes her head smiling. "Well if they want another performance like this morning, they'll take my request seriously," she states as she exits the car.

I round the car and follow Lucille to the front door. She stops just short of the step. I peer around her frozen body to see blood coating the door handle and the lock split in tow. She moves to rush in but instinctively I grab her by the waist. "No Lucille. Wait here. Let me check it out first." I command before moving forward and nudging the door open. I have my gun out as I take a look around the house. There's evidence of a struggle, blood on the carpet, a lot of it and the furniture is smashed to pieces, but the place is empty.

I return to Lucille, whos a deathly shade of pale and chewing on her thumbnail. "Place is empty, it looks like there has been a struggle. We will find them my love." She doesn't say anything as tears form in her eyes and she pushes past me to see the chaos left behind. I follow her like a shadow and she sobs, gripping a note in her hand. I pull her into my arms but she pushes back, handing me the note.

Give me what I want darling, I'll be waiting.

Chapter 36

Linc

What a fucking glorious way to wake up on a Monday morning. I sigh happily to myself as I drive over to the shipping yard to check on this week's scheduled deliveries. I can still feel my cock twitch against my zipper when I replay the last hour in my head. The sight of Lucille's tight hole taking the full length of my cock while she fucked Silas at the same time was the most beautiful thing I'd ever seen. I groan loudly and have to rearrange myself as the strain on my trousers is becoming unbearable. Christ, I wish I didn't have to fucking work today, I could spend all day fucking her in every hole, in every position and thoroughly enjoy watching my brothers do the same in turn.

Pulling up behind an old shipping container, I get out of the car and light up a cigarette, hoping the nicotine will subside the throbbing in my pants before I'm forced to stand in front of my men with a giant erection. It seems to work so I straighten my jacket and walk across the yard into the warehouse we use to store our drug and gun shipments in, nodding to Jonesy, the old guy we pay as our security detail down here on the way in. He tips his cap to me and nods his good morning. He doesn't talk much unless it's necessary, that's why we like to keep him on the books. I stroll over to the back office room where I find Dax lounging with his feet up on the desk not noticing that I'm here. I rap my knuckles against the glass window making him jump and reach for his gun but I've already drawn my own.

"Eye's up buttercup. You'd be fucking dead already if I wanted you to be," I state, slipping the gun back into my waistband.

"Shit! Sorry boss, didn't see you there," he stutters.

"Yes I noticed," I say, walking around the back of the desk to filter through the delivery papers. "Everything on track down here?" I ask, not looking up from the paperwork.

Dax is silent for a moment and I almost ask again before he stutters again. "Uh almost, Boss. We're still waiting for the delivery from Friday."

I snap my head up and catch him trying to look anywhere but at me. "What the fuck do you mean from Friday? That's three fucking days ago!" I shout running my hand up through my hair, "Who is it?" I demand. Silence again and he still isn't looking directly at me. "I won't ask again." I hiss through gritted teeth, clenching my hands and cracking the knuckles.

"T..T..Theo boss, it's Theo."

I slam my fists into the desk as he says my fathers name. "FUCK!" I roar, ripping my hands across the desk and throwing everything across the room.

"I.. I'm sorry boss." Dex mumbles from the corner, slightly cowering behind his arms. I bring my eyes to his and fight hard against every urge in my body that's telling me to put his head through the window but I don't move a muscle.

"Why have I not been notified about this?" I ask as calmly as I can.

"He.. he said that you were aware."

I close my eyes and take a deep breath before I say through gritted teeth, "Does it look like I was fucking aware Dax!?"

Dax shakes his head, "N..n..no boss."

I rub my hands over my face and laugh, a psychotic, menacing laugh and Dax watches me carefully like I might snap at any moment but I'm feeling strangely calm now the sudden burst of anger has passed and I sit down in the office chair.

"What was the shipment?" I ask and with fumbling hands Dax picks up a clipboard off the floor from the mess I've made and scrolls down it.

"A case of AK-47's and a dozen revolvers," he states calmly without a stutter.

I nod my head, this is the second time we've had a late shipment of his now, there must be something going on. I get up, knocking the chair over as I stand.

"Clean this shit up," I bark before storming out and getting back into my car. I'm already tapping Cole on speed dial before I'm out of the yard grounds.

"Where are you?" I snap before he even has a chance to even say hello.

"Mezzanotte, I just got back from the restaurant. What is it?" he asks, noting the tone of my voice.

"My fucking father," I seethe and hear him huff in response down the end of the phone. "I'll be there in ten." I hang up and slam my foot to the floor.

I skid across the car park pulling on the hand brake, sending gravel flying in all directions. I say nothing on my way in and I know from the look on my face the men know not to ask. I take the stairs three at a time to Silas's office to find Cole waiting with two glasses of scotch already poured on the desk. I stride over and throw back the drink and pour myself another and repeat the action. I hiss through my teeth as the alcohol burns a path down my throat.

"He's fucking us right under our noses," I say, turning to Cole. His face is vacant as I continue but I can see the anger flickering behind his eyes. "After his last fuck up, when he held off on a shipment and spouted that shit about it being better for the club. I gave him a warning, told him Silas wouldn't stand for it again. That even though he was blood, he would still be punished the same to set an example to the rest." I reach for another drink but hold back and light a cigarette instead, needing something to keep my hands busy. "I've just been to the yard, he's three days behind on a delivery. AK's and handguns." I take a deep pull on my cigarette letting it fill my lungs before exhaling slowly.

"Cunt," Cole spits, necking back his own drink and shaking his head as he paces the room. "He must be selling for his own profit," he half accuses, half questions.

"Nobody would be fucking stupid enough to double cross us," I laugh.

"What about the Irish?" He asks, snapping his head up.

I think about it for a minute then shake my head. "No, Costello wouldn't write his own death sentence. Not now he knows we're interested in his sister."

"But that's just it isn't it," Cole shouts throwing his hands in the air, "he fucking hates us and the fact we're in Lucille's life. This would be his perfect revenge, his way to infiltrate the club."

I shake my head while he tries to convince himself that that's true. "No, I don't think he has anything to do with it."

"THEN WHO?!" Cole bellows, fisting his hair.

Before I can say anything else, there's a quiet knock at the door. Cole looks at me and shrugs his shoulders having as little of an idea as to who is stupid enough to interrupt as me. I swipe my hand across my face and puff on my cigarette as I open the door. I'm caught off guard, slightly expecting to see either Felix or maybe Enzo, but instead a nervous looking Crystal is standing before me. I open the door wide enough so that Cole can see her too then give her a questioning glance.

"I'm really sorry to interrupt but I saw you come in and I think there's something you both should know," she says quietly, looking back and forth between us and picking at her nails, a nervous habit I've seen her do over and over before she performs.

"I'm shocked and intrigued at what it is you think would be important to us sweet Crystal," Cole purrs intimidatingly from over my shoulder.

I see her tremble slightly then she squares up her shoulders and raises her chin in an act of confidence. "It's about Silas," she says, looking me dead in the eyes.

"Come in," is all I say as I step to the side and point her towards the couch.

She hesitates slightly but sits down regardless then starts again, "Well it's about Roxi really," she says and Cole interjects with a loud tut.

"Oh cut the shit Crystal. If she has sent you in here to ask me to take her back again, I'm not fucking joking when I say I will bury the bitch if she doesn't leave me alone."

Crystal shakes her head quickly and starts picking at her nails again. "No, no, it's not that. She's been spying on Silas. On all of you actually, since you've shown interest in Lucille and not her."

I frown as I stub out my cigarette. "I'm sorry Crystal, but why is some silly little school girl jealousy something we need to know about?" I ask, already dismissing her silly claims as I make my way back to the office door.

"Because she's been sneaking around with your father," she blurts and I freeze.

"Oh fuck this day is just getting better and better." I hear Cole seethe.

I turn to face Crystal who stares straight at me. "You better not be fucking with me." I spit, taking a seat on the chair opposite her. "Tell me everything."

She visibly takes a deep breath in and composes herself. "I've seen them and I've overheard them talking about Lucille and you, not just you, all of you. About Silas

355

and how they think he isn't fit to be the boss and something about somebody named Vinny."

In a split second, Cole has crossed the room from his seat behind the desk and is holding Crystal up by her neck with his face mere millimeters from her own. "What did you just say?" He asks so calmly it's almost chilling.

Crystal squirms under his hold but keeps her chin held high. "I heard them both talking about somebody named Vinny, said they would get him to sort Lucille out then she would be out of the picture," she says and I have to swallow down the anger burning up my throat. "I overheard Roxi gloating about being able to have you all to herself once the bitch was gone when she was talking to the other girls after a show a couple of nights ago," she admits, looking guilty for not mentioning it sooner.

"That psychotic bitch!" Cole shouts, pushing Crystal back onto the couch, she turns to me with an almost pleading look in her eyes.

"Mr Rossi met with this man, told him everything about Lucille and her son. He is the reason he showed up at the kids' kindergarten."

I snap my eyes to Cole, there is absolutely no way that Crystal would know this information unless what she was saying were true and Cole knows this too. His temper is at boiling point and I'm not sure how I'm managing to hold myself together either but this is so fucked up I feel like I've been complete blindsided and by my own fucking father. My own flesh and blood.

"Thank you Crystal, you can leave," I say, offering a curt nod of my head towards the door. Crystal hesitates for a moment then makes her way out. "I trust you know this conversation is not to be repeated," I add before she exits the room.

"Of course, Sir," she nod, closing the door behind her.

There's a tense static energy pulsing through the room and I don't know what's louder, my own heart thumping in my ears or Cole's boots pacing back and forth across the hardwood floor. He pauses for a moment and looks towards me like he might say something but closes his mouth and begins pacing again. Nothing he could say could make me feel any better, and I know that's what he wants to do. It's my father who has fucked over the business, my father who has placed an innocent young boy in a vulnerable position, who has schemed behind all our backs and put the woman we love in danger. As the oppressive thoughts tick me over, I slam my fists into the glass coffee table, over and over until the crack of the shattering glass echoes through the room and my hands are covered with blood.

"We need to ring Silas," I say, wincing at the pain through my knuckles as I flex out my fingers.

"No. What we need to do is find that double crossing piece of shit you call dad and his little whore and slit their fucking throats," Cole spits, grabbing the bottle of Scotch from the bar and necking it straight from the bottle.

It doesn't bother me at all the way he speaks of murdering my father because I will gladly be the one to take his last breath but this is not all on him, we should have known. I should have known sooner. I knew something was off with him but this was un-fucking-precedented.

As I reach for my phone to call Silas, it begins to ring in my hand and with some weird twist of fate Silas's number blinks across the screen. I answer immediately but before I can speak Silas's deep voice penetrates my soul. "Are you with Cole?" he asks and instantly I know something is wrong.

"Yes."

"Put me on speaker," he demands.

I look over to Cole who is stood watching me as I lower the phone and put it on loudspeaker. "We're here, what is it?" I ask tentatively.

"Boys, we need to go hunting."

Cole huffs out a small laugh. "Are we not already hunting, brother?" he shouts across the room, still clutching the scotch bottle in his hand.

What happens next happens so slowly but seems so fast all at the same time. We hear a scuffle from the phone and Silas breaks it with a sharp whisper, "Vinny took Teddy from Costello's house. The place looks like a fucking bloodbath." The words pierce the room and the bottle that Cole was holding flies through the air, shattering as it collides with the wall and he leans forward holding his head in his hands. "He left a note for her," he continues and I lean forward myself, barely containing the pure red burning anger I feel inside when I hear Lucille's heavy sobs in the background. Fuck, this is all my fault.

"I'm taking her to the safe house boys. She's a mess. She shouldn't have seen this place the way it is."

Cole snaps up straight. "Where's the fucking Irish!?" he bellows.

"No sign of him here but there's enough blood to let me know it's not looking good," Silas says, lowering his voice at the end so I assume Lucille doesn't hear him.

"Brother, we know who's behind this." I say, catching eyes with Cole and he nods with a tight grimace on his face. "My father and Roxi have betrayed us. They contacted Lucille's husband and told him about her and the boy. Planned to get rid of her and you by the sounds of it."

"You know this for sure?" Silas asks and I hesitate for a split second remembering the look on Crystal's face when she told us both. She would have no reason to lie about it and she knew information nobody else does.

"Yes we're sure," I say.

"Then you know what to do," he says in a stern voice.

"Take care of our girl, brother," I say then hang up.

"Let's go," I say to Cole as I get up and leave the room.

"Where?" he asks, already hot on my heels.

"You heard Silas. We're going hunting." I snarl, heading down to the basement where we keep our back up weapons. We both strip out of our suits and change into black cargo pants, strap on a bullet proof vest and cover it in a black t-shirt and hoodie. We grab as much ammunition as we can manage and even then we fill a duffel bag with extras in case we need them. We're heading into the unknown here and though I highly doubt Roxi knows how to hold a gun, let alone shoot one I am no idiot to what my father can do. I holster my gun and strap another around my back then strap a knife around each thigh and slip one into my sock. I watch as Cole does the same, and sheaths his lucky knife into his belt and makes sure it's securely in place.

"You good?" I ask, slinging the duffel over my shoulder.

Cole laughs and shakes his head. "I'll be better when I've spilled some blood," he grins salaciously.

Cole persuaded me to let him drive, saying he knows the way to Roxi's house so he'll get us there quicker. If I'm honest, I think he just needs to keep his mind busy to save from the distraction, because as I sit in the passenger seat while he drifts us wildly around street corners, all I can think about is Lucille and Teddy. I hope to fucking god Teddy is OK, I'll never be able to forgive myself if he isn't and I swear I love this woman more than sense so to see her hurt would break my fucking heart that I've tried so hard to protect.

"Fuck, Cole, I'm sorry," I sigh, sagging my head forwards.

"Don't you dare fucking apologize," he shouts, slamming his hand onto the steering wheel.

"He's my father, my blood that's done this and betrayed us."

"He is not you," he says abruptly. "You have not made him do this. Don't you fucking apologize to me. Just wipe this son of a bitch off the face of the fucking earth," he growls as we skid to a stop outside what I can only assume is Roxi's house. A cheap looking building with dead plants in the pots outside and tacky animal print curtains you can see lining the windows from the outside.

I touch Cole's arm as we get ready for our entrance. "Remember, we need her to talk first," I say, reminding him not to go all headstrong and kill her on sight. He nods then shoulder barges his way through the front door. A loud shatter of glass from the kitchen draws our attention and we head straight for it. I strike my hand across my gun hidden at my side then nod to Cole as we jump forward. Roxi stands cowering with a smashed coffee mug at her feet, and her face changes with relief when she spots us to instant dread when she realizes why we're here.

Cole strides forwards and raises her from the ground by one hand securely around her throat then slams her body down against the breakfast bar. His teeth are bared when he leans to her face and asks her a simple question. "Why?"

Roxi squirms and grabs at Cole's hand around her neck, kicking her legs out to give herself some leverage but his hold is firm and unwavering. "Answer me or I'll snap your neck right fucking now!" Cole spits.

"I don't know what you're talking about," Roxi whimpers in reply, still trying to free her neck from his hand as he squeezes tighter, cutting off her air supply.

"Don't fucking lie to me you sick bitch we know everything!" he screams at her.

I step forward to remind him I'm still here and not to kill her just yet, his eyes flick to mine then he lessens his grip as she chokes bringing the oxygen back into her lungs. "I won't ask again," Cole warns and she eyes him but doesn't answer. Big mistake. In a fluid swoop she's off the breakfast bar and scrambling her legs to keep herself upright while Cole guides her by her throat to the dining table where he shoves her onto a chair.

"Don't fucking move," I instruct standing in front of her while Cole runs off into the bedroom and arrives back holding two pairs of handcuffs.

"I knew these would come in handy one day you slut," Cole spits, attaching both hands to the arms of the chair. "Now fucking answer me and I might make this easy on you," he says, now standing beside me.

Roxi eyes us both then drops her shoulders and begins to sob. "It was all Theo's idea, not mine. I had nothing to do with it, I swear Cole. I wouldn't do that to you," she whines. "Please, you have to believe me."

I can feel the disgust building in the back of my throat and want nothing more than to shut the bitch up but I don't, I know this one is on Cole.

"DON'T FUCKING LIE TO ME ROXANNE!" he bellows, slowly stalking behind her chair and flicking out his knife then slowly grazing it along her neck. Roxi shivers beneath the blade and her eyes go wide as a small bead of blood follows in its path.

"You won't kill me," she snickers.

Cole crouches low to her ear. "You want to fucking bet?" he sneers. "I will wipe your fucking life away without even a second thought. You were nothing more than a fuck to me and you will never be more than that no matter how hard you try. You're only good for one thing, and even that you were never any good at."

I physically see the words pierce her for a split second, then her pain morphs itself into bitterness. "You fucking cunt," she spits. "Both of you, you'll never win this. He is always one step ahead of you."

I lash out, shouting at her to shut up, bringing my hand down sharp across her face. When she turns back to look at me a trickle of blood sprouts from her lip but her face is transformed, her lips pulled back in an ugly grimace as she

361

cackles maniacally. "You will never be your father," she spits, blood spattering my boots.

I slap her hard again, snapping her head to the side. "That's not a bad thing. Do you think I'd want to be anything like that piece of shit," I state, leaning forward to grab a fistful of hair at the back of her head bringing her face to mine. "He must be fucking desperate if he's crawling between your legs. Now where is Teddy?"

She hisses as I tighten my hold then smiles and taunts me, baring her blood smeared teeth, "Long fucking gone."

I shove her back in the chair and nod at Cole who steps forward and in a swift fluid motion drags his knife across her throat eliciting a wet gargle as she chokes on her own blood. Cole watches as her body quivers and the blood begins to pool across the floor. I hear a low satisfying grunt escape his throat as the light fades from Roxi's eyes and he wipes his blade clean across her shoulder.

"Let's go," he insists, before shoving the knife back into his belt and walking out of the room. I glare at Roxi's now lifeless body one last time noting how her blood is already beginning to clot as it seeps across the tiled floor beneath her, then I leave without a second thought of remorse. It's time to face my father.

I join Cole back in the car, quickly texting Felix to order a clean up crew at Roxi's address before setting off in search of my father. Cole has now taken up position in the passenger seat as I slip behind the wheel and drive in the direction of his house thinking it will be the best place to start.

We travel in silence for a while, the tension so thick you could slice through it.

"You good brother?" I ask, keeping my eyes on the road ahead. I hear the sigh escape his lips and catch a movement in my peripheral vision as he swipes his hands across his face.

"I can't talk right now. I can't think right now," he starts, pushing the heels of his hands into his eyes. "Because when I do, all I see is a scared little boy with that fucking piece of shit husband and it takes me right back to. ." His voice trails off but he doesn't have to finish the sentence for me to understand. I know where it takes him and I know how hard he is fighting his demons right now and all I can do is let him because my own are pushing through just as hard.

My fists clench around the wheel until my knuckles turn white but I stay silent until I pull up around the corner from our destination. I let out a long breath before switching off the engine and turning to face Cole. "Whatever happens in there, I am the one who ends it. It needs to be me who ends him." I say, looking him square in the face to which he nods. "But first we find out why." I add, reaching back for the duffel bag that holds our collection of weapons.

"Time to execute the executioner," Cole snarls, cracking his knuckles and exiting the car.

We walk slowly with purpose towards the front door where I decide to play aloof to the whole situation and knock instead of barging my way inside. It takes a minute or so of scuffling behind the door until my father opens it wide and stares at us both dumbfoundedly on the other side.

"Son, what a surprise to see you here, and with Cole too." My brows raise slightly at the utter ignorance of this man but I brush it off and offer him my most sincere smile.

"Just thought we'd come over and offer you a new business opportunity we've happened to stumble across," I say, quirking my lip.

He stands back and holds out his arm to allow us inside. "Of course boys, come on in. I've had a few ideas myself recently that I think you would benefit from." Cole looks at me as we step inside and I silently motion to him to play along.

"So what is this business opportunity?" he asks, walking us through to the small office room at the back of the house. He has no protection here, a stupid move on his part but I guess he never thought he'd get caught.

"Oh it's something you wouldn't want to pass up. Trust us," Cole answers, pulling his lips back into a chilling smile. My father shuffles on his feet slightly, probably hoping that the move would go unnoticed and I can see the uncertainty start to creep its way in.

"Sit down, Dad." I insist, gesturing towards one of the leather arm chairs facing the roaring fireplace. The office itself is cold in feeling but the fresh burning logs on the fire let off a warmth that's almost comforting. I stare into the flames for a long minute until the clinking of glasses brings me back into the room and I see Cole pouring out three glasses of whiskey from the bar in the corner. I drop the duffle bag to the floor beside me and sit on the chair opposite the man I'm about to murder.

"So what is it? Guns, drugs, security?" he asks, squirming like an excited school boy as he takes the glass Cole has offered out to him.

"It's more like filtering," I say, sipping my drink casually. I watch as he frowns, not understanding my answer.

"What do you mean?" he asks.

"We have been made aware that there is a mole of sorts in the club and it has led to the disappearance of a young boy." As I finish the sentence, I watch his face closely for any hint of recognition, but his face does not change. He's experienced it portraying whatever he wants his enemies to see, his son would be no different.

"We need you to filter them out." Cole interjects, circling around the back of his chair.

I catch the quick bob of my fathers adam's apple as he swallows before answering.

"This mole, so you say, who told you about them? How do you know we can trust them? Maybe it is they who are the mole." He takes another sip of his drink, and then another emptying the glass.

"We can't you see. We don't know who to trust," I say, "that's why we need you."

He smiles at me. "So who was it then that told you?" he asks again.

Cole paces behind him, fingering the rim of his own whiskey glass with one hand and caressing his knife with the other. "One of the club girls said she overheard a few things and came to us with it," he mumbles nonchalantly, like he isn't really thinking of plunging that blade straight through his neck and draining the life right out of him.

"It was Roxi, wasn't it?" my father half states, half questions, causing Cole to stop dead in his tracks.

"What makes you say that?" I ask. "Do you know something we don't?"

"Um what? No, no, but you know how she is. Running her mouth all the time, it's hard to get her to shut up isn't it," he laughs nervously.

I watch as Cole stalks slowly towards the raging fire and quietly removes the poker from the stand holding the pointed end into the flames heating it until the end glows red. "We want you to tell us who the mole is." I state, staring back at my father who seems to be breathing just a little bit faster than before, with tiny beads of sweat forming track marks down his neck.

He nods and tightens his lips. "I won't let you down," he assures standing from his chair, but as he turns to face the door, Cole is already there, the red hot poker plunged forward deep into his flesh.

The loud wail that escapes him sends a chill through my body but I relish in the feeling. I stand and drag him by the scruff of his jacket back to face me and snarl, "I think it's a little fucking late for that, don't you?" His face pales at my words and creases as he gasps for breath, grabbing feebly at the gushing wound at his side. "Get him downstairs," I grunt, shoving him forward into Cole who hauls him, kicking and screaming, from the room leaving me to my own intrusive thoughts. He's my father, can I really do this? Can I take the life of the man who gave me life? I grab the whiskey bottle from the bar and drink until the burn is too unbearable to take then throw the bottle into the fire causing the flames to erupt out across the wall.

When I walk down into the cellar and see my father strapped to a chair, bleeding and helpless, I feel nothing. No sorrow, no anger, just nothing. My body is numb but it knows how this must end and what it must do to make this right.

"How much do you want to bet he pisses himself before we're through?" Cole jeers from behind him as he circles the chair like a vulture circling its prey. I step forward and throw the duffel bag I carried with me onto the floor.

"He'll do more than fucking piss himself when I'm finished with him." I say, crouching in front of the man I once had every respect for. "Why?" I demand, holding his chin between my thumb and forefinger.

Theo straightens his back, pulling himself from my grip, "Who the fuck do you think you are talking to!" He shouts, wincing at the wound Cole had already inflicted.

I shake my head. "I'm talking to a traitor," I say so matter of factly, "and we all know what happens to traitors, don't we Dad?"

"Traitors get their just reward," Cole answers for me, circling back round to stand beside me.

My father looks as if he might explode with anger, his cheeks reddening before my eyes matching the blood stains on his shirt.

"We just want to know why?" I ask again.

"BECAUSE I DESERVE TO BE THE BOSS!" He screams, saliva spitting across his lap. I throw my head back and laugh at his outburst.

"You had your fucking chance years ago old man."

He looks me dead in the eye. "I never had my chance, it was stolen right under my nose when your fucking father got sick and Silas stepped up in his place." His eyes are now on Cole who is clenching the blade of his knife so hard I can see a trickle of blood seeping between his fingers. "IT WAS SUPPOSED TO BE ME!" he roars, thrashing against his restraints.

"So what? You just cook up some petty revenge with one of the whores at the club?" I ask with the feeling that I'm missing something. This can't just be over the fact that he's been snubbed over a role he thinks he deserved.

His laugh rumbles deep from his chest. "You always were stupid boy, just like your mother," he spits.

I see Cole's flicker of movement out the corner of my eye but I'm faster with my response. I hold the knife I've reached from my thigh and press it hard against the finger still banded by his wedding ring.

"Don't you fucking speak of her," I hiss, pressing the blade hard enough to hear the crunch of bone beneath but adding more pressure regardless. My father wails behind me, his throat raspy and cracking as I slice through the tissue until the blood spurts from the knuckle and his finger falls with a small bounce to the floor.

"You fucking cunt!" he screams, sweat layering his sickly looking face.

"You never fucking deserved her!" I snap, ripping the ring from his stump and dropping it into my pocket. "This is the least you deserve for all the shit you put her through," I growl, slamming my fist into his face, cracking his nose with the impact. I turn my back to him but the throaty laugh that escapes his lips stops me in my tracks.

"You stupid son of a bitch," he cackles. "You have no idea who you're dealing with."

"We'll be dealing with a dead man soon enough." Cole slips out before I can respond.

"And you, you stupid little shit. You should have died years ago, alone in that cellar." Cole lunges forward stabbing his knife straight into his thigh and twisting it until the sound of his blade grinding on the bone can be heard between the piercing screams that follow.

"I did die down there, but I was also reborn," Cole grunts as he yanks his knife from Theo's thigh.

"Never did find out who was really behind it though, did you?" My father taunts. "Bet it's haunted you for all these years." His sly devil grin makes my stomach flip and I know Cole knows it too.

"You?" I utter in disbelief. "It was you?"

Theo throws his head back and howls with laughter. "Right under your fucking noses," he cackles.

"This is bullshit, I've had enough of this." Cole states, grabbing a long metal chain from a workbench behind us. He swiftly removes the restraints around Theo that bind him to the chair then secures the chain to his wrists, swings it over a ceiling rafter and hoists him so much that his feet barely touch the ground. I watch with trepidation and excitement coursing through me as Cole slices the clothes from Theo's torso and lets them fall to the floor. He moves with purpose grabbing a blowtorch from the duffel bag and walking behind Theo who now looks like he's about to throw up. "Where is Teddy?" Cole asks through gritted teeth, his face has grown dark and serious and his eyes look almost black.

"Gone."

Without another thought, Cole flicks on the torch and presses the red hot flame against his skin. The blood curdling scream that erupts is something I will never forget and the smell or burning flesh will be ingrained in my senses forever.

"Tell us!" I shout, stepping closer. Cole switches the torch off and the screams trail off with it. I watch as Theo's head slumps forwards and his breathing becomes ragged as he tries to compose himself through the massive amount of pain his body is already in.

"Did you really think you would get away with this?" I ask, holding my hand out for Cole to pass me the torch.

"I already have," he stutters.

"Where is he?" I ask again, but there's no reply. I switch on the flame and hold it to his bare torso as he hisses in pain, writhing against the chains. I take pleasure in watching the skin boil and sizzle under the hot fire and as it starts to turn black I switch it off. "You're a worthless piece of shit, you know that?" I accuse spitting in his face. "All of this for what?" I ask, throwing my arms out and shrugging my shoulders. "For a crown you were NEVER fit to wear. You disgust me!" I snarl. "And you deserve every ounce of pain I'm about to put you through."

I light the torch again and cover his chest until there is no pale unburnt skin left to see. His screams become more like strangled wet gargles until he loses consciousness and hangs limply from his wrists, blood oozing from his skin in various places and the smell of his burning flesh consuming the entire room.

I stand and stare at his ruined body for a moment, taking deep breaths to regain the burning anger I feel inside, holding onto the blowtorch so tight that my fingers are numb. Cole places his hand on my shoulder in a silent reassurance and it's all I can do to just nod to let him know I'm alright; but really it's me who should be asking him if he's alright. It was my father who was behind his kidnapping sixteen years ago and the revelation of that has just been thrown in his face. I lock my eyes on his but he shows no hint of a grudge or hatred towards me. How was I to know? Should I have known? Have I let my friend down? I shake my head as the anger begins to resurface and slap my father hard across the face. "We're not done with you yet." I yell and he groans loudly as he comes too then pukes, spitting bile onto the floor.

"You don't get off all the shit you put me through that lightly," Cole sneers, kicking the wound on his thigh leaving him swinging on his chain. Theo whimpers as he regains his footing, slipping on the blood and vomit that coats the floor. Cole looks at me and grins. "Mind if I teach your father a lesson?" he asks, picking a small curved blade from his boot strap.

"Be my guest," I allow, leaning back against the workbench watching the light flash through his eyes.

Cole turns slowly to face Theo who's watching him with a horrified look on his face. "You took something from me all those years ago that was not yours to take." Cole advances pacing back and forth in front of him while twisting the blade in his hands. I see how Theo's eyes grow wide and the bob of his throat as he swallows back his nervousness. "I didn't fucking touch you, I'm not a nonce," he stutters, trying to pull himself further away.

"It makes no difference, it was at your hands and now I will take something of yours in return," he declares and before he can object Cole shunts the tip of his blade into Theo's groin, angles it in an upright position and rips the blade across his hip, tearing through tendons and fibrous tissue. I can't help but grimace at the revolting sight of my fathers shriveled dick being ripped from his body and the blood curdling screams that have erupted. The sinewy mess that trails from his groin is enough to turn any man's stomach and I have to bite back at the bile that rises in my throat as Cole flicks the bloodied mass of spongy tissue making a wet slap as it hits the floor. Cole stands at his full height, back snapped straight and covered in blood, with the look of triumph glowing from his eyes, but also something else I can't decipher. He nods at me and steps back and I know that my father won't survive much longer anyway but I must be the one to end this, to draw a line at his betrayal to the club, my mother and to me.

I raise the gun from my holster and slam it into his temple. "Do you have anything left to say?" I spit, watching his face covered in snot, sick, blood and saliva. He opens his eyes and looks up at me then drops his head and whimpers, "I'm sorry," and I laugh as I squeeze the trigger.

"You're pathetic."

Chapter 37

Silas

My arms are wrapped around my angel, she has finally tired herself out from sobbing. I wait until the tell-tale signs of her soft breathing let me know she's asleep. Kissing her gently on her head, I shift to move from her hold but she whimpers to me. "Please get him back Silas, I can't cope without my boy. Vinny, he's not stable and I don't want to think about what he could do to him."

Fuck. I lean down, giving her another kiss to her head as I whisper, "We will find him and bring him back to you sunshine, rest now while I get together some of my men and make a plan." She nods and closes her eyes. "I'll be back with something for you to eat once I've got a handle on things. Don't worry Angel."

Leaving the room, I silently pray to every damn God there is that I can bring him back to her. I will pull that bastard's innards out of his body for daring to take from me. The rage inside of me is hard to contain but I must remain calm until Linc and Cole return. I head straight for my office where I had already asked my men to gather.

Once I step inside, Marcello, Dario and Quinton are already seated, waiting for my instructions. I called ahead and told them to close the club and pay the girls for tonight even though no work would be done. This takes priority now. Out of respect they all stand as I walk forward.

"Boss, the club's locked down for the night. What do you want us to do?" Marcello asks.

I nod to him as I rake a hand through my hair. "Please sit, we have much to discuss. I need every ear to the ground and every eye in the sky. I need to know what the Costellos are doing. I need eyes looking for a boy, Teddy, aged five blonde hair and blue eyes. Search every corner of this city for a boy of that description, even if you think it's not him, I want it double checked. Also spread the word that I want Max Costello found and brought to me alive." My men nod. "Quinton, I want you to stay and guard Lucille, anything happens to her and I'll personally hold you responsible."

"I'll keep her safe, Boss," he nods.

"You're all dismissed. I need to contact Lincoln and Cole. I expect updates every hour and I'll inform you of information as it comes in."

As they leave the room, Marcello is last to go. A look of assurance in his eyes. "We will find them Boss, the boy and Costello. We won't let you down." With that he leaves the room.

I lean back in my chair, looking at the ceiling, thinking where the fuck Vinny could have taken Teddy. He's mine as much as Lucille's now and I'll burn the fucking city to the ground to find him.

Interrupting my thoughts, Cole and Linc come barrelling into my office. Cole is covered in blood, Linc too but it looks as though he has at least attempted to wipe some of the remains from his face. I raise an eyebrow before saying, "I missed out on the fun I see, did you make him sing before pulling the trigger at least?"

"He sang like a baby black bird squawking for his mama to feed him," Cole says dryly.

"So where are Teddy and Costello? Are the Costellos in with Vinny?" I slam my fist on the table, regretting it as I do. This can't have been an easy thing for Linc to have gone through with, sentencing your own father to death is one thing but executing the final blow yourself is a hard task to do. Taking a deep breath, I apologize. "Sorry Linc, I know this must have been difficult for you. What information did you get?"

Linc looks to Cole before replying. "Putting a bullet through that fuckers head wasn't the difficult part of today my friend. Hearing that piece of shit confess that he was responsible for kidnapping our brother all those years ago, and now he's done it again with Teddy! That was the tough part. He got what he deserved. He all but admitted that he's given Teddy up to the Costellos. We find them and we will find our boy."

The words out of Linc's mouth flaw me. I'm shocked and angered by this revelation. I look at Cole, his eyes look dark and more void than usual, he's barely holding it together. Before I get a chance to reply, Quinton barges through the door "Boss, I'm sorry. I got to the room and knocked on the door. She didn't answer so I tried to open the door but it was locked. By the time I broke it down, I saw the window was open and she was long gone. I found this note." he babbles, holding it out to me with a shaking hand. Rage is bubbling inside me. It's not Quintons fault, she was probably gone before he had any chance to stop her. Looking down at the note it reads;

Silas, Vinny has Teddy, he said he'll release him if I go to him. I have to do this, please understand. I love all of you so much but I can't leave my boy in his hands. Lucille.

Clenching the note in my hands trembling from head to foot with anger, I watch Linc and Cole rush out the room. Quinton is still standing by the door, panic racing through his eyes with his breathing coming out heavy and fast. I swing my fist into his face, knocking him to the floor, leaving his blood coating my fist. "Clean yourself up Quinton then fucking find her. Next time you'll get more than a fucking bloody nose."

374

I run to where I left Lucille and find Cole leaning up on the wall staring vacantly at the empty space. Linc is looking for any clues as to where she might have gone, tossing furniture around like a mad man. "She's gone to sacrifice herself for Teddy, I can't say I blame her but I wish she'd have come to us first." I tell them.

Cole smirks. "Little mouse wants a chase, and a chase she will get." Linc stops searching the room, turning to look at Cole, and we both frown at him. Maybe hearing Theo's confession has sent him over the edge. He's got his phone out now, refusing to look either of us in the eye.

"Don't look at me like I'm deranged, brothers. I told our little mouse once upon a time, she could run but never hide from me."

Linc interrupts snapping at Cole. "For fucks sake Cole! What are you on about? She's run right in to that sick fucks hands. We don't have time for this bullshit!"

"Oh but Lincoln, it's not bullshit. I might have put a tracker on her, not that she has ever been aware of it. She wouldn't have been pleased with me, that's for sure." He turns his phone to show us, there is a little dot moving on the screen. It's her! I look at my brother and I'm smiling because this fucker has some serious issues but I've never been so glad of them until this moment. I could kiss him.

Linc is shaking his head, "Forgive me brother, I was panicking. When we get our love back, we'll make sure to tie her to the bed until she does as she's told." he smirks, the relief he feels is palpable.

Cole grunts. "I'll tie her to the bed even if she does what she's told. Now, shall we go and catch our little mouse?"

"Let's go, Linc you can drive." I bark, exiting the room.

By the time we're ready to leave, we have suited up with enough ammo and guns to start a war. We check Cole's phone and see that Lucille has arrived at Vinnie's last known location. It's a warehouse on the Costellos side of the city.

"Looks like we will be entering enemy territory." Linc grins. Cole smirks and I let out a laugh. This might be more fun than we anticipated. We always like a bit of a fight, we wouldn't be who we are without enjoying the violence.

As we arrive at the warehouse, Cole turns to us. "She's inside, but I think we should split up, in case the Costellos are here and Teddy isn't with Vinny. I'll go look around while you both go get our girl and Teddy back."

I agree with him. "Good idea brother, I'll bring you a souvenir back from Vinny." I wink.

Cole smiles psychotically. "You always bring me the best presents."

As we move, Cole disappears into the darkness and we head towards the warehouse where Lucille is. As we near the door, we hear a scream, not just any scream, Lucille's piercing scream. Without hesitation, both me and Linc are through the door. The sight we walk into has my blood boiling and I am unable to be the calm, well versed leader I usually am. I explode with rage, rushing for the cunt that has dared to touch what does not belong to him.

Lucille is on the floor, her clothes are ripped and her lip is oozing blood. He's was about to rape her. That thought alone has me murderous. As I move to tackle Vinny to the floor, wanting to drive my fists into his face until his body has stilled beneath my own, he notices our intrusion. Quickly, he brings a knife to her throat, making me stop in my tracks. I shake with rage. "Get your filthy fucking hands off her, you piece of shit," the venom thick in my voice.

He laughs, grabbing my angel by the hair and dragging her to stand. She whimpers and he spits. "I see Lucille has been opening her legs for common thugs now. I'll teach you my girl, you won't be making this mistake again. Not after Ronan and his son have dealt with them all," he gloats at me and then continues looking between me and Linc with a sick smug smile on his lips. Did he just say

Ronan? "I tell you what boys, I'll let you watch me fuck her raw. Then I'll let his men have a turn before they put a bullet through your heads. How does that sound?"

If this shit head didn't have a knife to my angels throat, I'd have killed the fucker already. "Let her go, fight us on your own Vincent. Don't you want your revenge after we have all had a taste of your pretty wife?" Linc smirks.

I see what he's doing, he's calm and collected, trying to make Vinny lose his cool and slip up so we can take advantage of this fucked up situation.

"Two on one, I don't think that's fair. I'll take my chances, you let us out of this room and you have a chance at getting away from Ronan."

"Well your wife likes those odds, well three on one to be exact," Linc taunts, trying to get a rise out of Vinny but at that moment we hear gunshots outside. My eyes are glued to Lucille, I'm hoping that it's Coles gun that has shot the fuckers dead. But Lucille thinks the worst and screams.

"Let me go! That could be my son! He's out there, please Vinny!" She screams as she tries to get free of him, elbowing him in the stomach. Vinny doesn't like that and back hands her, knocking her to the floor before pulling out his gun and pointing it at her head as she's face down on the ground.

The commotion gives me enough time to get closer to them. I tackle Vinny to the ground and land blow after blow to his face. He fights back, landing some punches of his own but I am bigger and have the upper hand as I straddle him. With each blow, thick blood splatters around me, I am covered in it. As soon as I feel his body become still beneath me, I look around to see Linc checking Lucille over, she's hysterically crying into his shoulder, as he inspects her bruising face. My anger is not yet at bay. I pull my gun out and shoot the dead fucker in the head.

"Silas, I think your fists had already done the job" Linc yells to me.

"Better to be safe than sorry." I grunt, my eyes not leaving Lucille's.

She all of a sudden snaps out of her daze and stands, her voice resolute and strong now that we're here with her. "Teddy, he ran out of here, we have to find him. I told him to run."

"Let's find him," Linc replies, stroking her hair.

I pick her up in my arms. "Are you okay my Angel?"

She nods, "I'm fine but we need to find our boy."

Moving to the exit we hear another gunshot. Lucille's face pales as she jumps out of my arms and rushes for the door of the warehouse. What we see next rips my heart out of my chest, nothing could prepare me for the scene we are about to stumble upon.

Chapter 38

Cole

The moment Linc and Silas leave in the direction of Lucille, I focus on my task. I need to find Teddy. I can't let his fate be like mine. The need to save him is overwhelming. Trying to keep a lid on my emotions, I fade into the shadows and listen. I hear the sounds of two men talking to each other.

"Boss has the bitch and the dip shit over in the other warehouse. He said to leave them be now that the boy is with him." They head towards a door into the warehouse. I'm guessing it leads to where the Costellos are hiding.

I sneak behind them, pulling my knives out and slitting their throats simultaneously. Blood splatters the door in front of them, making beautiful red patterns on the pale background. I smile at how perfect this art is, and how I'd love nothing more than it to be the blood of that scum that has my girl, but I must focus. Breathing in, I remind myself that my brothers will bring me a souvenir and protect her. I must find our boy. I cannot fail my little mouse.

Wiping the blood from my knives on to my shirt, I put them back into the sheaths. I bring my gun out and carefully open the door, the room is empty and quiet. Moving quietly but quickly, I spot a staircase leading up to another room. I can hear voices and footsteps coming my way down the stairs. I conceal myself behind one of the cabinets as they enter the room.

"Come on boy, you want to see your uncle Max, right? Let's go find him." I hear from my position. I know this voice. It belongs to Ronan Costello. Max Costello's father. We've had dealing with him before, he's a nasty fucker.

"But my mom, she needed my help. Uncle Max needs to help her!" Teddy bellows at Ronan.

"Now, now, that's why we need to go get him. But if you keep shouting like that I won't take you to him, boy."

"But where is he?" Teddy says calmly. He's so innocent. I must fucking protect him from these scumbags. Max must be in on this.

"I've told you, just follow me," the fucker orders.

Hearing the door open to the outside. They see my artwork left for them. I hear the Costello scum curse. "Clean this up, this will give the boy nightmares and I don't want to deal with that shit." He barks at the men that are with him. "Don't look at it boy, eyes closed," he says, dragging Teddy away by his elbow.

Moving from my hiding place, I follow them out of the building to see the two men moving the bodies I left behind.

"Ciao, stronzo's," I say, grinning at the two trying to heave the bodies away. They look up, wide eyed as I bring my two Desert Eagle handguns up to their faces.

"What the fuck!?" one of them shouts as I pull both triggers at the same time, blowing their brains across the floor. The juices squirt across the dirt, and chunks of flesh land at my feet. Crouching down, I smear the blood between my fingers. "Buonanotte, figli di puttana" I grunt as I stand and wipe the blood on my trousers. I see Ronan with a gun to Teddy's head not far from me, holding him tightly as he walks them both backwards locking his eyes to mine. I hear a car burning toward them, and I'm already moving as fast as I can. The car stops behind them. I've almost reached them when Ronan shouts. "I'd stop where you are Mr Salvatore, unless you want me to blow young

Teddy's brains out like you did to my men?" That stops me dead in my tracks.

Eyeing Costello, I see three men get out of the car, all loaded with guns. I know I'm out matched but I won't let them take Teddy. Over my dead body will they take him. I just hope I can draw this out long enough for Silas and Linc to come to my aid. Failure isn't an option.

"Let the boy go, Costello!" I shout. He laughs and pulls Teddy closer to him, pressing his gun against Teddy's temple. I suck in a breath, I've never felt fear like this, it feels as if it's eating my inside. I have to play this safe and try to gain an advantage.

Teddy snaps me out of my panic, he's whimpering, tears staining his cheeks as he cries to me. "Cole, who is this guy? I'm scared. He says he knows Uncle Max." My heart breaks, this boy is so brave.

"Don't worry little bear, he won't hurt you." Looking at Ronan, the fear and anger making me feel physically sick. "He's innocent, let him go now before I lose my temper."

He laughs again, "Lose your temper? What was slitting the throats of my men and blowing their brains out then? You say he's innocent. Like you were? They took that, didn't they? You weren't much older than Teddy, am I right?"

He is goading me. Rage bursting through my veins. I'm on edge. He's not going to lose his innocence like I did that's for sure. "Don't talk of things you know nothing about Ronan! The boy is mine. You'll give him to me before you end up like your men. Would you prefer to gargle in your own blood when I slit your throat or feel the pressure of your brain exploding as I pull the trigger?" Teddy is shaking and crying silently, I'm trying to keep myself calm for him.

Ronan scoffs, "You won't get close enough to try boy. Who says I don't know what I'm talking about. You were bound in a basement of my choosing, they took their turns on you didn't they? Did you enjoy it, I wonder? You were a weak little boy. Maybe Teddy's fate will be the same but all will depend on how you Salvatore scum play your cards."

Anger is getting the best of me as I hum eenie, meenie, minee, mo, under my breath. I clench my fists and reply cooly and calmly. "If that was the best you could do to me Ronan, then I find your attempts to ruin me lacking. The only thing your attempts did were to make me even more dangerous than I was growing up to be. Did you know what we did to those men? They never did find where we got rid of their bodies. I still have souvenirs from some of them. Maybe I'll keep one from you too." I turn my attention to Teddy now. "Little man, you're so brave. Remember to leave me crumbs and I'll find you. OK?" I tell him this as I'm not sure how long I can drag this out. I need to act fast. "This is the last time I'm going to say this Ronan, and then it'll be play time for me. LET TEDDY GO!" I demand.

Ronan shakes his head and smirks. "I've got some more secrets to tell you before you enter the pit of hell boy. Not only was I responsible for your kidnapping and rape, I took the pleasure of assisting in your dear old friends tragedy." Frowning, not following his words. Ronan licks his lips and continues. "It haunts him every day that he couldn't save her. His mother wept beautifully as she bled out. The only thing sweeter than that was hearing the screams as her flesh slapped against mine when I buried my cock inside her cunt. How she screamed and fought that night. Then I slit her throat for the boy to find her. Of course, I left my cum inside the bitch as a little present." He laughs now like the sick fuck he is. "I wonder if your sweet Lucille will be the same, she'll come eagerly for me I'll make sure of it," he taunts.

I see red. I lose my temper, unable to keep myself sane anymore. I move my gun and shoot the man to Ronan's left, hitting him between the eyes, blood splatters over

Ronan, making him shove Teddy to the floor as he tries protect himself. "Run Teddy!" I shout before I hear gunshots and am hit with a searing pain in my chest, I know without looking I've been shot but I continue my assault to save Teddy. Another ring of shots are fired. This time I fall to my knees. Blood is puddling around me fast and I know I'm losing time. Looking up, I see I've taken out all of Ronan's men but Ronan is dragging Teddy into the car by the scruff of his shirt. He's screaming at him, fighting his hardest to get away. Just as he bundles him into the car, he looks back at me and smiles. "Your reign will be over soon Salvatore. It's time for me and my blood to take over this city."

The car speeds off as I fall to the ground, my vision is tunneling, and it hurts to breathe. I've failed my little mouse. I failed Teddy. As my head hits the ground I hear a piercing scream from behind me before a soft hand cradles my cheek and as I close my eyes I quietly mumble, "Erano i Costello. Mi dispiace, Topolino."

I hear my love's soft voice call through to me "Don't you leave me Cole!" Before I pass out of consciousness.

Chapter 39

Lucille

When I received that text from Vinny I had no other choice but to go to him. To get my boy back. I only hoped my men would understand. Nothing will ever stop me from keeping my son safe. I locked the door to my room knowing Silas would send somebody in to check on me soon and hoping it would buy me just a sliver of time before they realized I was gone. I scribbled down a note and without looking back, I hauled myself out of the back window and ran straight to Silas's car, thanking God that he'd left his keys inside his jacket pocket that he'd placed around my shoulders after I couldn't stop my teeth from chattering together. I pulled quietly out of the club's car park then hit the gas and raced towards the demon from my nightmares.

I follow my GPS, running red lights, cutting corners and coming way too close to crashing the car. But as I pull into a deserted looking warehouse on the East side of the city and skid across the forecourt to a stop, kicking up the dirt under my wheels, the only thing on my mind is finding Teddy. My stomach lurches as I step outside of the car and head towards the largest building out of the three. Taking a deep breath, I reach for the metal sliding doors and push my way through. I have no doubt that Vinny will already know I'm here, the sound of the car ripping across the gravel would have tipped him off to my arrival so I don't bother trying to conceal myself as I step into the light of a large holding room.

"Mommy!!" is the first thing I hear. I snap my head around and my stomach twists at the sight of my boy running towards me, his arms outstretched as he pummels into my body. My knees buckle as I sink to the floor holding him tight to my chest and breathing in his smell.

"Oh baby, I've missed you so much!" I choke, pulling him back at arms length to check him over. "Are you okay? Are you hurt?" I ask, raking my eyes over him from head to toe.

"I'm OK, Mommy. But that man over there said that he's my daddy," he says, pointing behind me.

I whip myself around quicker than lightning in the direction that Teddy is pointing, reaching my hands back to keep him in place behind me, and there he is. The devil who reigns terror in my nightmares, the man I wanted to spend the rest of my life with, who tricked me with his manipulative ways and lured me into his bed of lies.

"Hello Locket," he sneers, his lips pulling back in a sickening grin as he steps forward into the light. The use of his old nickname for me has the bile rising in my throat in an instant but I can't speak, can't respond, I'm frozen in every meaning of the word. The chill rising through my bones has me physically shaking as I hold tightly onto my son, keeping him close to my back and out of sight. Vinny smirks at me, and I know he is relishing in the power he possesses as I stand silent before him. He begins to circle us, slowly, methodically, like a hungry wolf stalking its prey.

"As you can imagine, it was a great surprise to find out that my darling wife, who left me without even so much as a goodbye note. Had given birth to a baby, my son, and was living her happy little life, fucking all the men in Vegas to find him a new daddy." With every step he takes, I counter it with my own, making sure I am always shielding Teddy from him. "Nothing to say?" He goads, stalking slowly closer towards us.

"Don't you come near him," I bark, my voice with much more bravado than I feel as I shift on my feet.

Vinny stands still for a moment and laughs, a deep throaty laugh that sounds almost psychotic. "You've already taken five years from me you stupid bitch," he spits. "You have no say in this, not anymore. You can stay here and open your legs for whoever the fuck you want, but my son is leaving with me."

Vinny takes a step forward and I mirror it again with another step back making sure not to topple over Teddy as I guide him back with me. I can feel his hands tight against my legs as he cowers behind me, unsure of what is really going on. "Over my dead body," I declare.

I watch as Vinny's face pulls into an evil grimace and he chuckles loudly. "That can be arranged."

I turn to Teddy and grab onto his shoulders, pulling him from my legs. "Go Teddy, go and find help, RUN!" I snap but his face crumples as he begins to cry.

"No Mommy," he whines, shaking his head and reaching towards me.

I blink back my own tears and push him. "GO NOW!" I demand, standing up as I turn back to find Vinny lunging at my throat.

"Mommy!" I hear Teddy scream from behind me.

"RUN TEDDY. NOW!" I scream before Vinny crushes his thumbs into my windpipe, choking me.

"You fucking bitch," he growls, pulling my face so close to his I can taste the liquor on his breath. "You'll fucking pay for that, for all the lies you've told and all the secrets you've kept from me."

I whimper slightly, trying to free myself from his grip but it only tightens the more that I struggle. With one hand still firmly around my throat, Vinny yanks me round so my back is pressed hard against his chest and as I fight for breath beneath my crushed windpipe. My eyes catch the glint of the blade he's pulled out of his belt as he wields it before me, taunting me with its sharp point.

"Let's have a little fun first for old times sake, huh?" He whispers into my ear before gripping my chin and angling my face as he trails his tongue from my neck up along my jaw to earlobe. "I think you need to be put back in your place Mrs Holland." His bite on my ear almost has me screaming out in pain, but the blade pressed against my throat has me stifling the sounds before they have a chance to escape. I close my eyes, praying to every God out there that Teddy has made it clear of the warehouse grounds already and that he doesn't stop running until he reaches somebody to come and help. "Have you missed me, my beloved wife?" Vinny mocks into my ear as he drags the tip of the knife down the length of my body pressing harder as he drags it over my breasts, shredding straight through my T-shirt. He doesn't stop as he trails the blade further down pushing the pointed end into my crotch. I wince at the pain as it shoots through my core, pulling my hips backward as an instinct reaction straight into his crotch. I hear his satisfactory hum low in my ear and he groans. "Oh how I've missed the feel of this ass pushed against my cock."

"Don't touch me," I hiss through gritted teeth, trying to push him away as his hand releases my throat and begins its assault on my breasts, pulling and tugging roughly at my bra, scratching his nails across my flesh.

"I'll do whatever the fuck I want, you stupid whore. Do you think I will let my wife get fucked by three other men and not retake what is rightfully mine?" His words are filled with venom and unsaid promises of hurt. Filling every fiber of my being with anger, boiling the blood deep in my veins.

"You have no right!" I object, slamming my foot onto his. He jumps back in shock, swearing under his breath. I take advantage of his state of shock and twist my body, shoving him as hard as I can to break free from his grip. As I twist I feel the sharp edge of his blade slice through my shoulder causing me to cry out in pain.

"You stupid fucking bitch!" he roars behind me but I run, kicking up my heels as quick as I can. I make it halfway across the room but I'm no match, he is faster and stronger and has gained on me within seconds. His paw-like hands fasten around my waist, pulling me from my feet. I won't go down this easy though. I need to fight, not just for myself but for my boy too. He needs to know his mother is a fighter. I scream and wail, kicking my legs back to try and catch and hinder his attack but he only lifts me higher.

"The more you fight, the harder I'll make this for you," he grunts, throwing me to the floor. I smart as my knees connect with concrete, sinking my teeth into my lower lip knowing it'll only please him more to know how much that hurts. I snap my head back in his direction, he's no longer wielding the knife but his fists are tight at his sides, he's ready for my next strike, I know it.

"I will never let you take my son." I spit but the grin that pulls at his lips has my stomach in knots.

"You don't get it do you, you stupid slut?" His taunting laugh makes me want to throw up. "You have no say in this anymore Lucille, he is my son. He will grow up with no memory of you. You pathetic bitch. He's already being taken care of."

Just as his last words filter through, a spur of rage lights in my belly. "No!" I scream, scrambling to my feet. His fist connects with my face and I'm back on the floor before I even register what's happening. The searing pain across my face burns as I bring my hand up to assess the damage. Blood coats my fingers as I pull my hand away and I grimace at the sight.

"Not this time," he whispers, bending down to my face and gripping my chin between his fingers. "It's a shame to mark such a pretty face so I suggest you keep your fucking mouth shut."

"Fuck you," I hiss, my spit hitting him in the eye. I watch as his demeanor changes instantly, the blacks of his eyes bleed out to his irises and I really am staring at the devil. I try to pull away but his face hardens as does his hold on me.

"Don't you think you can fucking spit at me you dirty whore," he growls at me. He stands up to his full height and pins me to the floor with his boot.

"Get off me!" I scream. "Get the fuck off me!" Scrambling my hands around his size 12 boots with little success in budging it from my hip. I can't stop his movements as he unhooks his belt and unbuttons his pants. My blood runs cold. He's going to rape me again. The look in his eyes tells me everything and I scream, it doesn't even sound human anymore as I tear apart my vocal chords in the hope that somebody will hear me.

As if the gods above have answered me, I hear them. My knights in their all black, assassin-looking armor, ready to defend me to the death. I watch the look in their eyes as they take in the scene before them. Silas has his eyes on mine and he looks like he could kill. Suddenly I'm ripped up to standing by my hair and Vinny once again has his blade harsh against my throat. I know my whimpering only makes this all the more fun for him, I can feel his erection through his pants, pressing against my backside but in that very moment I'm transported back five years to when I lay broken and bleeding on our bedroom floor. I lock up, I freeze. My fight or flight response truly fucked and I zone out of whatever is being said around me between the man I used to love and the men who will be my salvation, only one is missing. Where is my Cole? Where is my son? God I only hope they are together and safe somewhere. My thoughts are quickly broken by loud gunshots outside. Teddy!

"Let me go, Teddy could've been shot. Let me go please Vinny!" I beg, my screams are completely inhuman now. I struggle between his arms and bring my elbow back into his stomach but this only pisses him off more, he slaps me hard across the face and the connection knocks me back to the floor. I blink back the tears that threaten to spill but the atmosphere around us has already shifted, loud grunts sound from behind me and I shift myself around to watch as Silas and Vinny go blow to blow on the warehouse floor. Linc has kneeled beside me and wrapped a jacket around my shoulders as he whispers comforting words into my ear while I watch Silas snuff the life out of the person I thought was my everything but turned into someone I thought I'd never be rid of. I cry hysterically, gasping breaths as I come to terms with what is happening but I can only allow myself this one moment, I must find my boy. I breathe in deeply, swallowing my emotions.

"Teddy, he ran out of here, we have to find him, I told him to run." Silas, now covered in blood, gently lifts me into his arms and I know he's doing his best not to hurt me, but another round of gunfire has his footsteps faltering. TEDDY! I leap from the safety of his arms and tear through the warehouse doors. The light from the outside burns straight through my corneas, but when I focus on the sight before me, my stomach bottoms out and I do everything in my power not to throw up. "Cole!" I scream, taking in his debilitated state. "COLE!" I've reached him now, the blood pooling around him like something out of a horror movie, there's no way he will survive this. I pull his head gently into my lap as fresh tears begin to fall, his eyes don't even register me as he tries to mumble garbled words that are barely more than a whisper.

"Costello's," he chokes before falling limp in my arms.

My breathing hitches and the panic sets in. What does he mean? Did he say the Costello's have taken my boy? I need to know and he is the only one who can give me the answers.

"Don't you leave me, Cole." I scream, stroking every inch of his hair and face that isn't already plastered in blood. "Please don't you leave me."

To be continued.......

About the Authors

S.L Wisdom

S.L Wisdom is an aspiring new author, who lives in England. Her favorite color is black, she loves true-crime documentaries and has a soft spot for the bad guys in the books she reads (somebody has to be rooting for them). She's a wife and mother and when she isn't working at the hospital her downtime is spent listening to true-crime podcasts, reading, writing, baking, drinking tea and pretending to be a 'mommy monster' while she chases her daughter around the house for the tenth time that day.

Without the constant support and words of encouragement from her husband, who has had to do the bedtime routine on more than one occasion so she could keep on writing until early hours in the morning, she knows she would never have got to the end of this book, or even had the confidence to start it, and for that she will forever be grateful to him.

S.J Noble

S.J Noble is an adventurer, reader, dreamer, writer, mother and Aries star sign. She is obsessed with all things Zodiac, Harry Potter and Starwars and her favorite time of year is autumn. She has a hard time picking a favorite color, it's always mood dependent but it would be between purple, red or black. S.J Noble lives in England and spends her days working in the local hospital, rounding up her two strong-willed sons and trying to catch up on the latest Netflix shows. When those activities are not occupying her time she can often be found reading any book with a shocking plot twist and an anti-hero as the main character. Yes, she's a slut for the morally grey, feel free to stalk her and S.L Wisdom on the pages below to find out more!

For more information about both S.J Noble and S.L Wisdom upcoming releases please visit the sites listed below:
Facebook readers group:
https://www.facebook.com/groups/760611272268230/
Instagram: S.JNoble and S.L_Wisdom
Tiktok: WisdomNoble69

Please check out our amazing editor Ria at Moon and Bloom Editing.
Facebook page:
http://www.facebook.com/moonandbloomediting
Instagram: Moonandbloomediting

Also, if you're on your own publishing journey and in need of a book cover be sure to check out Francessca at Wingfield Designs.
Facebook page:
https://www.facebook.com/groups/wingfielddesigns/
Website: Book Cover Design | Wingfield Designs

Acknowledgements

First and foremost we'd like to give a huge thank you to our friends and colleagues who have had our backs since the very beginning of this book when the idea first came to life over a lunchtime catch up on what books we were reading. Without your words of encouragement and support this would have been a much more difficult task. So thank you for asking, thank you for being involved, thank you for hyping us up on all the hard work we've put in and thanks for your pre-orders guys! We love you all immensely.

Of course a HUGE thank you to our amazing editor Ria. You have been an absolute Godsend through this whole process for us, we would still be crying over our first draft if it wasn't for you. You are an angel, a total badass and we're super super grateful to have you alongside us on our new book journey. We hope you're ready Ria cause we'll be keeping you busy.

Thank you to Francessca for designing such a beautiful front cover for our book, our promotional images and social media banners and always being so patient when we have no idea what we're doing.

And last but not least, thanks to the world's #1 leading manufacturer of high performance batteries; Duracell, we love ya! Ladies, IYKYK.

What's next?

So now that part one is over, we bet you're wondering what the hell happens next? So many unanswered questions. Will Cole survive? Will we find out where Max has gone? What has Max's father got to do with this? And most importantly; Will Lucille be reunited with Teddy and get her happily ever after? Well, hang on in there guys, all will be revealed. We promise not to keep you waiting too long.

We also have lots of new and exciting projects lined up, which we will be revealing over in our Facebook readers group soon so give us a like and a follow and keep your eyes peeled for what's coming next from Wisdom and Noble.

Printed in Great Britain
by Amazon

35062356R00223